USA Today

D0052414

PATRICIA POTTER

Beloved Warrior

"Stories from Patricia Potter are jewels to treasure—gather some for yourself!"—*The Best Reviews*

BERKLEY SENSATION

$7.99 U.S.
$10.99 CAN

Praise for

Beloved Stranger

"An absolutely stunning read, rich in historical details, fast-paced and riveting in suspense . . . An emotional tale that will leave you with a lump in your throat and a tear or two in your eyes. Potter brings together a cast of new and fascinating characters as well as old friends from the first book in this wonderful historically set series of the Maclean family." —*The Best Reviews*

"The action-packed story line moves forward at a fast pace, but it is the lead pairing that drives a fine return to the Maclean clan." —*Midwest Book Review*

Beloved Impostor

"Ms. Potter has given us another thrilling drama. Every page proves the reason for her award-winning success . . . *Beloved Impostor* travels at a fast pace with outstanding characters and an expertly developed plot." —*Rendezvous*

"A wonderful Scottish tale wrought with emotion, tender in its telling and heart-wrenching in its beauty. Ms. Potter captures our hearts and gifts us with another beautiful story." —*The Best Reviews*

"[A] superb romance . . . It's Potter's unique gift for creating unforgettable characters and delving into the deepest parts of their hearts that endears her to readers. This is another masterpiece from a writer who always delivers what romance readers want: a love story to always remember." —*Romantic Times*

continued . . .

"The story was riveting, the execution and the telling of it and the characters involved showed spirit, courage, chemistry and mostly they had a heart and held on to hope. It held my interest and kept it." —*Pink Heart Reviews*

"Ms. Potter is a very talented storyteller, taking a much-used theme—lovers from warring families—and manipulating it, adding plenty of new ideas and twists, until the end result is the original, highly satisfying *Beloved Impostor* . . . Ms. Potter very adeptly whetted this reader's appetite for more about these two Maclean brothers, but for now, there is *Beloved Impostor*, which I highly recommend."
—*Romance Reviews Today*

Dancing with a Rogue

"Once again, Potter . . . proves that she's adept at penning both enthralling historicals and captivating contemporary novels." —*Booklist* (starred review)

"Gabriel and Merry are a delightful pair . . . Patricia Potter has provided a character-driven story that her audience will enjoy." —*Midwest Book Review*

"An entirely engrossing novel by this talented and versatile author." —*Romance Reviews Today*

"Interesting and fresh." —*Affaire de Coeur*

The Diamond King

"The story line is loaded with action yet enables the audience to understand what drives both lead characters and several key secondary players . . . a robust romantic adventure . . . [a] powerful tale." —*BookBrowser*

The Heart Queen

"This is a book that is difficult to put down for any reason. Simply enjoy."
—*Rendezvous*

"Exciting . . . powerful . . . charming . . . [a] pleasant page-turner."
—*Midwest Book Review*

"Potter is a very talented author . . . If you are craving excitement, danger and a hero to die for, you won't want to miss this one."
—*All About Romance*

More praise for Patricia Potter and her bestselling novels

"A master storyteller."
—Mary Jo Putney

"Pat Potter proves herself a gifted writer as artisan, creating a rich fabric of strong characters whose wit and intellect will enthrall even as their adventures entertain."
—*BookPage*

"Patricia Potter has a special gift for giving an audience a first-class romantic story line."
—*Affaire de Coeur*

"When a historical romance [gets] the Potter treatment, the story line is pure action and excitement, and the characters are wonderful."
—*BookBrowser*

Titles by Patricia Potter

THE BLACK KNAVE
THE PERFECT FAMILY
THE HEART QUEEN
THE DIAMOND KING
BROKEN HONOR
TWISTED SHADOWS
DANCING WITH A ROGUE
COLD TARGET
BELOVED IMPOSTOR
TANGLE OF LIES
BELOVED STRANGER
TEMPTING THE DEVIL
BELOVED WARRIOR

Beloved Warrior

PATRICIA POTTER

BERKLEY SENSATION, NEW YORK

THE BERKLEY PUBLISHING GROUP
Published by the Penguin Group
Penguin Group (USA) Inc.
375 Hudson Street, New York, New York 10014, USA
Penguin Group (Canada), 90 Eglinton Avenue East, Suite 700, Toronto, Ontario M4P 2Y3, Canada
(a division of Pearson Penguin Canada Inc.)
Penguin Books Ltd., 80 Strand, London WC2R 0RL, England
Penguin Group Ireland, 25 St. Stephen's Green, Dublin 2, Ireland (a division of Penguin Books Ltd.)
Penguin Group (Australia), 250 Camberwell Road, Camberwell, Victoria 3124, Australia
(a division of Pearson Australia Group Pty. Ltd.)
Penguin Books India Pvt. Ltd., 11 Community Centre, Panchsheel Park, New Delhi—110 017, India
Penguin Group (NZ), 67 Apollo Drive, Mairangi Bay, Auckland 1311, New Zealand
(a division of Pearson New Zealand Ltd.)
Penguin Books (South Africa) (Pty.) Ltd., 24 Sturdee Avenue, Rosebank, Johannesburg 2196,
South Africa

Penguin Books Ltd., Registered Offices: 80 Strand, London WC2R 0RL, England

BELOVED WARRIOR

A Berkley Sensation Book / published by arrangement with the author

PRINTING HISTORY
Berkley Sensation mass-market edition / April 2007

Cover art by Gary Blythe.
Cover handlettering by Ron Zinn.
Cover design by George Long.
Interior text design by Julie Rogers.

For information, address: The Berkley Publishing Group,
a division of Penguin Group (USA) Inc.,
375 Hudson Street, New York, New York 10014.

ISBN: 978-0-425-21573-9

BERKLEY SENSATION®
Berkley Sensation Books are published by The Berkley Publishing Group,
a division of Penguin Group (USA) Inc.,
375 Hudson Street, New York, New York 10014.
BERKLEY SENSATION is a registered trademark of Penguin Group (USA) Inc.
The "B" design is a trademark belonging to Penguin Group (USA) Inc.

PRINTED IN THE UNITED STATES OF AMERICA

10 9 8 7 6 5 4 3 2 1

Acknowledgment

With many, many thanks to Vickie Mazzola for her tireless efforts, encouragement and friendship.

Spain, 1514

"Wed? To a man I do not know?"

Juliana Mendoza couldn't keep the horror from her voice as she faced her father.

"You have always said you wish to see England," her father reasoned.

"To visit. My home is in Spain."

She glanced at her mother, who stood beside her husband. Juliana had never seen her look so sad, so defeated. She had known for years her parents' marriage had not been a happy one, but this was different. She saw a new kind of fear in her mother's eyes.

"Madre?" Juliana pleaded. "No . . ."

Her mother looked away, avoiding her eyes.

"According to your uncle, he is young and well-favored," her father said. "It will be a good marriage for you. Far better than I expected. Like your mother, you are too fair for Spanish tastes. But the Earl of Chadwick sees political advantages in this union with his son, Viscount Kingsley, and it will be beneficial to our shipping trade."

She winced at the statement. It was not the first time that her father had disparaged her mother's blond hair and her own, which was more the shade of honey. After her mother failed to produce a male heir, he had become more and more brutal and insulting. She feared for her mother, which was one reason she did not want to leave Spain.

Nor did she wish to be trapped in a marriage like her mother's own arranged union. "Can he not come to Spain?" she said desperately. "He may not favor me."

"He has already agreed," her father said. "Our families have planned this alliance for years."

"But with his brother," her mother intervened in a soft voice.

She received an angry stare from her husband. "His brother is dead," he said. "Chadwick does not want to risk another son here in Spain. Juliana is to be delivered to their property in northern England for the betrothal announcement. The marriage will be in London several months later."

Juliana had known her father expected a match with the influential Earl of Chadwick's family. Not only was her mother a distant cousin of the earl, the two families had extensive financial and shipping relationships.

Juliana had hoped that the death of the earl's oldest heir would end the prospect of marriage with a man she didn't know in a country far from all she knew and loved. Foolish wish, indeed, but she had seen the horror of an arranged marriage. Her beautiful mother had faded into a timid shadow.

"Both King Henry and King Ferdinand favor the match," her father continued. "They want to strengthen ties between our countries. The French still plot with Scotland."

Juliana did not care what the kings wanted.

She did not want to leave her mother. She did wish to wed, but she desperately wanted someone of her own choice.

She adored children and wanted some of her own, but she wanted a happy place for them to grow. Not a place of fear.

Now she had no choice. Her only purpose in life, apparently, was to enrich her father . . . to tie Spain to England . . . to be a dutiful daughter and do as she was told.

"Can *Madre* go with me?" she pled.

"No," her father said sharply. "She stays here. Go now. You have much to do. You will sail in two weeks. I have sent for dressmakers. You must be presentable. I would not want you to shame this family."

She hesitated, wanting to protest again, but she saw her mother shake her head and she held her tongue. She met her father's gaze directly, then lifted her chin with as much dignity as she could summon and turned toward the door.

Juliana softly pulled the door closed behind her but did not shut it completely. She lingered, knowing her father would have further words with her mother.

"Do not do it," her mother said, and a chill went through Juliana. She knew the courage it took for her mother to oppose her father. "Garrett was a good match. A gentleman. But Harry . . . I knew him when he was a boy. He was vicious. A bully."

"Do you believe I care? You are talking about the next Earl of Chadwick, heir to a vast shipping fortune," Luis Mendoza said. "Juliana is a fortunate girl."

"His brother, Garrett, should have been earl. And Juliana's husband."

"Garrett is dead. The match has much to offer us. Chadwick has markets closed to us, and we are heavily indebted. We need those markets, and we need trade with England. If I snub Chadwick, we will lose that trade." He paused. "And we need Ferdinand's continued favor. He fears an alliance between France and England. He wants his sister, King Henry's wife, to have a friend at court."

"Please," her mother begged with a persistence that was rare. The chill Juliana felt spread throughout her. Her mother rarely disagreed with her husband, and when she did, the consequences were harsh.

She heard a familiar slap, and she stepped away from the door. Juliana knew from experience that interference would only infuriate her father more and bring more blows to her mother.

She heard steps and quickly moved away from the door. She felt sick. Juliana had been trained since childhood to please and obey her father. Any rebellion brought about harsh consequences for herself, but even worse ones for her mother. Her love for her mother was his weapon. A weapon he would use with no remorse.

Juliana turned to head toward her room. What would her mother do without her? She was her mother's only reason for living. And now . . .

Juliana fought back tears.

"Senorita?" Carmita said shyly. "Are you in need?"

Juliana shook her head silently. The young girl had just recently been promoted to maid and was still uncertain in her duties. Would she be allowed to take Carmita with her? Or would that be unfair to the girl?

"No," she said, trying to keep her voice steady.

"Do you wish me to help you dress for dinner?"

Juliana did not want to go to dinner. She did not want to see her father. She feared she could not hold her tongue and that would provoke him to more violence.

But she nodded and sighed in resignation. She would dress for the evening meal for her mother. Just as she would go to England for her mother.

"ONE last canter, *Madre*," Juliana urged. "Our time is short." Her mother nodded and they both led their horses along the golden sands of the beach.

The days had gone far too quickly. Juliana dreaded the passing of every hour.

She would sail in two days' time. Her father had left to inspect the cargo of the ship. He and his brother, Rodrigo, owned a fleet of such ships. *Tio* Rodrigo would captain the ship that delivered her to Chadwick's castle in the north of England.

Ahead of her, Juliana's mother reined her gelding to a halt. Juliana drew up Joya, her Andalusian, as well. The salty spray of the ocean and the crisp breeze did nothing to lighten either of their spirits. Her mother turned toward Juliana and handed her a small leather pouch.

"What is it?" Juliana asked, accepting the bag from her mother's gloved hand.

"Jewelry and some coins. Go, Juliana," she said with sudden intensity. "Take Joya to the next town and hire a coach to Portugal, then take passage to England. My sister will find somewhere safe for you to go."

"Is Viscount Kingsley so bad, then?"

"He was as a lad," she said, her eyes clouding. "I remember too much. He used to like . . . hurting animals."

"And you? What will happen to you? Father will know you helped me."

"If I know you are safe, I will be happy."

"But you will not be safe." Juliana had witnessed, or heard, too many blows delivered by her father to her mother. She had received some as well. Her mother had not produced a male heir, and she never stopped suffering because of it. Juliana knew the courage inherent in this single act. If her father discovered she'd helped her daughter spoil his plans . . .

It was a risk Juliana would not accept. She would not take her freedom at the expense of her mother's life.

"Not unless you come with me," she said, holding tight to her mother's hand.

"I cannot. In the eyes of God, I am his wife. She steadied her gelding as the horse pawed the ground, anxious to run again. "Your *padre* could not bear the shame of his wife running away. He would scour the earth searching for both of us."

Juliana knew it was true. Her father was a proud and vindictive man. Still, she tried to convince her mother. "Your family . . ."

"They arranged the marriage. Nothing to them is more important than the sanctity of marriage. My sister might be able to help you secretly, but for me, no."

"Then I cannot run away, either," Juliana said. She reached and brushed away a tear from her mother's cheek. "The cost is too great, *Madre*. I must marry the Viscount Kingsley."

HEAVE! *Lift!*

Heave! Lift!

Heave! Lift!

Sweat dripped down Patrick Maclean's face, mingling with that on his body.

He tightened his grip on the splintery oar and heaved his weight forward, then pulled it back toward his scarred chest. His body strained to lift the oar in concert with the other prisoners on the bench, then plow it through the water.

Heave! Lift!

Denny, the man next to him, faltered, and Patrick willed himself to take on the added weight. He couldn't let the guards realize Denny struggled. His back was already worse than Patrick's own. The man's inability to comprehend orders made him a constant target.

Save yourself, Patrick thought selfishly. *If Denny pays the price, then so be it.*

His conscience hammered at him. Denny was an innocent in mind, even if he was a *Sassenach*, a hated Englishman. Patrick rowed harder, every muscle crying and straining inside him. How many hours had it been?

Heave! Lift!

Heave! Lift!

Heave! Lift!

He heard the crack of the whip before the pain sliced through him. The guards had spotted Denny. Only the whip found both their backs. He'd learned to steel himself against it, even as pain ripped through him and blood dripped down his back.

Ignore the pain. Ignore the hammering of his heart.

Pray. Pray for wind.

Think of the green hills and lochs of home. He retreated into that image even as his body labored, each repetitive stroke of the oar adding to his resolve to return once again to the highlands. To Inverleith.

Inverleith. Did his father still live? His brothers? If so, why hadn't they ransomed him? The Spanish don who had held him prisoner for months had repeatedly sent ransom demands, but there had been no response. After twelve months in a damp dungeon, he'd been sold to Mendoza as a slave.

Had his father died and his brothers believed—mayhap hoped—he would never return to claim his place as laird? The thought haunted him, and anger grew with each stroke.

They had never been close. They were half brothers, and his father had pitted them against each other since they were born. His father was an angry and bitter man and both he and Rory, the middle son, had competed for their father's rare approval. The youngest, Lachlan, was a dreamer who had enraged his father and was more often found hiding in the hills than training.

Or could they all be dead? Victims of the Campbells? Of the bloody feud that had ensued for a hundred years? Or had they died at Flodden Field instead? The Spanish guards had taunted him about a great English victory on the Scottish border. Patrick had hoped it had been nothing but lies, until a newcomer who had been captured after the battle—and sold to the Spanish by an English borderer—confirmed the fact that the Scottish army had been decimated.

That oarsman was gone now. Dead of exhaustion and thrown over the side, as had so many others. Patrick wasn't sure how he, alone, had survived this long. He was now known to the guards as Number One, the longest living rower.

He wasn't going to give the bastards the satisfaction of his dying.

Heave! Lift!

Heave! Lift!

Lift the oar, push forward, lower to the water and heave with every ounce of strength he possessed. He did it without thinking, but every muscle strained, ached. His heart hammered. His lungs felt as if they would burst. His breath came in short, painful spurts. His throat was desperate for water. Groans around him told him he was not the only one reaching his physical limit.

He didn't know how many hours they'd rowed this time. It seemed like days.

He couldn't keep pace for both himself and Denny much longer. Patrick was the strokesman on his bench, already the man with the most vigorous work. Denny had the next most strenuous job, but he had been ill these past few days.

The Englishman slumped over the oar and Patrick pulled his weight as well as that of the oar.

"Denny!" he rasped out.

Denny jerked upward, groaned. His face was red with exertion, the scar alongside his hairline even more vivid.

Denny wasn't his true name. Nor was Patrick even sure he was English, since he hadn't said a word since being chained next to him months earlier. But something about him made Patrick think English. Perhaps his fair coloring.

Think of anything but the pain.

Patrick didn't like the bloody *Sassenachs* any better than the Spanish. They were, in truth, his sworn enemies. But when the new man had been chained next to him, he appeared bewildered and helpless, almost like a lad, though he must be around Patrick's own age. He did not speak and barely responded to anything but the whip. Patrick, for wont of anything better, dubbed him Denny and reluctantly looked after him. He made sure no other oarsmen took his food, and that he received his quota of water.

"Row," he whispered.

Denny gave a slight nod even as Patrick felt a difference in the movement of the ship. "Blow, wind, blow," he muttered, and as if the skies heard him, he felt the ship surge forward. He heard orders yelled in Spanish from the deck overhead to hoist more sail.

Setting his shoulders to bear the effort, he continued to row until the order came to lift the oars and they were secured out of the water. Patrick and the other oarsmen slumped over in complete exhaustion.

Manuel, the water boy, started down the aisle, doling out water for the tin cups that, along with a tin plate and a blanket, were the oarsmen's sole possessions. He paused at Patrick's bench, gave him an almost imperceptible nod as he filled the cups passed from the end of the bench to Patrick and back again.

A rare glimmer of hope grew inside him. Patrick sipped from his cup, forcing himself not to gulp the dirty water while trying to interpret the nod. Had Manuel found a way to steal the key to the chain that locked the oarsmen to the bench? He'd claimed he could do so three weeks ago. He'd whispered that he'd been the best thief in Madrid.

Theirs was a friendship of sorts. At least as much of one as anyone had on the benches where speech drew the whip. Manuel hadn't been aboard long when he'd tripped and spilled water, much to the anger of the guards. None of the oarsmen had had water that day. It was Patrick who had taken the blame for the fall, saving Manuel from a beating and incurring it himself. Patrick had tried to help the lad as he tried to help Denny. Remnants of humanity. The cursed Spaniards weren't going to take that away from him, too.

Manuel appeared grateful, and since then, Patrick had tried to whisper words of encouragement to the lad. He'd learned, partly from Manuel and partly from the guards, that the boy had been sent to the galleys for theft from a very important official. He'd been too small and slight to man the oars and was made an errand boy. Patrick put his age at no more than thirteen.

Manuel, like Patrick, was desperate. He was being used in degrading ways by several of the officers, including the ship surgeon, and he knew well what lay ahead of him. More of the same until his body grew. Then he too would be chained to the bench. With his slight build, he wouldn't last long there.

They'd mentally weighed one another for months before whispers started. Patrick's obsession to escape. Manuel's possible access to the key that anchored them to the benches. *Freedom!* A few words exchanged, a bargain made. Sealed in desperation.

Then nothing happened. Nothing until now.

Could the lad really do it?

The leg and wrist irons were bolted on, but the bench had its own chain that ran through a ring attached to the leg irons. The chain was fastened at the aisle seat, but they all opened with the same key.

They both knew the lad's fate if he were caught. He would be flogged to death or keelhauled. Either way, it would not be an easy demise.

Even if Manuel could obtain the key, their chances would be slim at best. Each man would still be manacled at the ankles and wrists. They were unarmed. Most were weakened by labor and lack of food.

But even the slightest chance was better than giving up to despair and dying like a chained dog.

He'd kept his plan to himself. Some of the oarsmen would do anything for an extra crust of bread or promise of freedom. Even betray the others.

Devil take it, he wished he could talk to Manuel, but a guard had accompanied the lad. Mayhap when he brought the evening bowl of beans and stale bread, they could exchange a word.

Patrick sipped his water, savoring the liquid as it trickled down his parched throat. He put a restraining hand on Denny's to slow his intake. "Slow," he whispered in English. "You will get sick."

Denny nodded.

Would Denny be able to do his part, to follow his lead? The others? Could they coordinate their movements enough to take their Spaniard guards before they raised an alert? Or had they been too brutalized to act on their own? If so, they were doomed. There would be no second chance. Only a painful death.

A lot of questions, but staying there was worse than death.

He sipped the last dregs of his water, knowing if he didn't, the man behind him might try to steal it, or it would overturn as the ship rolled with the sails. If Manuel's nod meant what he hoped it did, he would need all his strength and wits.

He bent over and escaped into exhausted sleep.

JULIANA resolutely blinked back the tears as she gazed at the sea. Spain was there beyond her vision. As far away as the sun.

They had sailed at noon yesterday, and at last the ship moved swiftly with a brisk wind. She said a brief prayer of thanksgiving for the oarsmen below.

Until a few hours ago, the ship moved through the labor of men. She'd heard the rhythmic sound of a drum, the moans as oarsmen struggled to keep pace with its demand.

But now that the wind blew briskly, the hammer was silenced. She looked back toward Spain. She was leaving all she knew—and loved—for a husband she didn't.

And on a slave ship.

She'd noticed the oars when she'd boarded and asked

her uncle about it. She knew, of course, her father owned ships, but he had never mentioned they were powered by oars as well as sails.

He'd dismissed her concern with a shrug. "The oarsmen are criminals, Juliana. Murderers. And heretics. Sentenced to death, all of them. Would you rather they die at the hands of the Inquisition?"

She'd had no answer for that. She had heard the horrors of the Inquisition, knew the fear the very name invoked in people.

Still, the sounds from below yesterday had resounded in her head all night. . . .

She tried to dismiss them now and consider her own situation. What if Viscount Kingsley was like her father?

She knew she was nothing but a pawn in her father's quest for power and money. He'd never loved her. She suspected he didn't love anyone.

Her mother had compensated for his disdain, for the fact that he'd wanted a son and received only her instead. Lady Marianne Hartford had been educated in London and she'd given her daughter a love of learning and books despite the opposition of her husband. An education was wasted on a woman, he said.

But Marianne had defied him in this one thing and he'd relented eventually. The English, her mother protested, educated their daughters, and if Luis Mendoza wished an English marriage for his daughter, he would be wise to provide her with an education equal to that of English misses.

Her mother had protected her for years. Now Juliana must do the same for her.

Even marry a stranger . . . one her mother feared.

Juliana gazed upward. Her hand shook on the railing as she considered the injustice of it. She had been sold. It was as simple as that.

Please God, don't let him be a monster.

"Juliana, *es muy bello, no?*"

Her uncle joined her at the railing. No matter how much

she tried to avoid him, he always seemed to appear at her side. She duly nodded. It *was* a lovely day except for the company. She'd never cared much for her uncle. He was too much like her father. Hungry for position and power. That he used slave labor did not raise him in her estimation. How could she not have known? Her home, her jewels, her clothing, all came from the misery of others.

"Si, Tio," she replied.

"Do not get too much sun," he said, his eyes roaming over her as if she were a prized animal. "It would not be well for the Earl of Chadwick and the Viscount Kingsley to see you when you are not at your best."

She saw no reason to answer and gazed out at the sea. With a good wind, her uncle had said, they would see England in five days. They would not stop at London but go up the coast to the Handdon Castle, the northern home of the Earl of Chadwick. Though she had an intense curiosity about her mother's country, she did not look forward to meeting her intended husband.

Maybe she should get sick. Very sick. Then Viscount Kingsley would not want her.

"You look pensive," her uncle said, breaking the long silence between them. "Looking forward to seeing England?"

"I wish I knew more about the man you want me to marry."

"The man you *will* marry," he corrected.

"And if I find him lacking?"

He shrugged as if that was of no matter. "This union will help your family and your country."

"And if Viscount Kingsley finds me lacking?"

"He has already seen a miniature of you. He is quite entranced, I'm told."

She had hoped otherwise. "Have you met him?"

"*Si.* He is a handsome lad."

Juliana heard the rattle of a chain through the grated latch that ran to the galley deck, and she shivered.

"You are cold," her uncle said, removing his uniform jacket.

She shook her head. "I can't help but think about those men below."

He shrugged as if they were of no consequence. "They are treated well if they do their work. You need not worry about them. Look ahead, instead. Look to England. Your home."

"My home is in Spain."

An impatient look flashed across his face and the charming uncle dissolved as his voice took on a harshness. "I must leave you now," he said. "You and I and my first officer will sup together tonight."

She didn't want to sup with the first officer, who looked at her with greedy eyes and never missed a chance to brush against her. He was coarse and loud and seemed to enjoy the misery below deck.

"I am tired," she said, "and if I am to be at my best I should retire early. Also my maid continues to suffer. Could you please send something to my cabin?"

"I will send something for her, *querida mia*." He fastened her with his dark eyes. "But you *will* join me for supper."

Her uncle left her and she remained where she was, enjoying the fresh sea breeze.

Then she heard the sound of a key turning in a lock and turned toward the grate leading down to the rowing deck. A young boy waited as the grate opened. His ankles were encased in metal bands linked by a chain and he carried a bucket that seemed too heavy for him. He had no shirt, and his arms were bruised. His eyes were lowered as he descended into the oarsmen's deck.

She instinctively glanced down after him.

Rows of nearly naked men lay over oars. She saw blood on the back of one. She knew she should look away and started to do so when one of the oarsmen looked up.

Several days' beard covered his cheeks, but his hair had been cropped short. His eyes met hers and his mouth turned up into a sardonic smile, even as he straightened to hold her gaze. His eyes were fierce, glowing with anger. And hate.

Then he looked away, arrogantly dismissing her as if she were less than a bothersome fly.

"Juliana?" Her uncle returned to her side. "I would stay away from the grate," he said, a frown on his face.

She would have no trouble following her uncle's order. The image of the oarsman was seared into her mind, especially the hate. She'd shuddered and her uncle apparently misunderstood it.

"They cannot harm you," he said. "They are well secured."

But it hadn't been fear she felt, rather pity and horror.

"The boy . . ."

"A thief from Madrid. He is lucky he is not at the oars," her uncle said indifferently. Then he changed the subject, as if bored with the current one. "We will be running close to France," he continued. "Do not light a lantern at night."

"We are not at war with France now."

"Some do not recognize that fact," he said.

She glanced at the two small cannons, one on each side of the ship. They would be of little help if they encountered a hostile war ship.

"We should be safe," he said. "But do not shine light when it is not necessary."

She retreated to her cabin and tended to her maid, who had not been able to keep a morsel down. But in her mind she still heard the pound of the drum and the lift of oars and the ocassional cry of pain. She still felt the fury of the oarsman. She knew the image would haunt her sleep.

PATRICK leaned his head on the oar's shaft and tried to rest. Every bone and muscle in his body screamed in agony.

Don't think about the pain. Think about survival.

If Manuel's nod meant he could steal the key, they had little time. Things had to happen, and happen quickly. There would be no time to second-guess or ponder the consequences. The problem was that after hours of rowing, none of his fellow oarsmen were in any shape to overtake their burly guards.

Mayhap the nod meant nothing at all. Just false hope. The other rowers were a mixture of Christians, Jews and Moors. They came from a variety of countries and spoke a dozen different languages. They were here as prisoners of war, heretics in the eyes of Spain, Spanish criminals. And as rowers, they were even less than that.

They had been so brutalized and starved, some of them

would sell their mothers for an extra piece of stale bread. Many couldn't communicate with each other except by grunts and shared pain. He was unsure of most of them but, hoping for a chance to escape, he'd tried to build some trust in those around him. Sometimes he gave a piece of his bread to someone who needed it more than he did, or a sip of his water when he believed another's throat was burning more than his.

But beyond these three benches, he wasn't sure how the others would react.

He prayed they wanted freedom as much as he did.

The light that slivered through the openings for the oars faded. The oil lamps on both ends of the deck were dimly lit. The grate overhead had been closed and neither air nor light filtered through.

For a moment, he recaptured the image of the woman staring down at him.

Ach, but it had been a long time since he'd seen a woman, particularly one as bonny as this one. Just one glimpse had captured her in his mind. Hair the color of dark gold and the most unusual eyes he had even seen. Gray, or were they blue? Edged by violet.

He tried to banish the image. The devil knew it would do him no good. Still, he ached at the sight of her. Six years now in the galleys, longer than any man here. The painful swelling under the loincloth, though, told him he hadn't entirely forgotten some things.

He felt a touch at his shoulder and he swung around. Manuel was two rows back with a bucket of beans and an armful of tin plates. Plates were always collected after the meal because the guards were fearful of them being used as weapons.

Patrick glanced around. The eyes of the oarsmen were fixed on the slow progress Manuel made down the aisle. Patrick studied the fixed gaze in the lad's eyes, the bruises on his arms.

His body tensed as Manuel drew nearer, moving slowly

and cautiously. There were a hundred oarsmen, and he had to be careful not to spill a drop, lest he incur a beating.

Finally Manuel reached him. Patrick took a plate while Manuel filled it and passed it down the bench. Then a second.

Manuel lowered his head as he cautiously filled Patrick's plate. "I have it," he whispered in Spanish. *"A la noche."*

Tonight!

He nodded slightly.

"Sleep," Manuel said in broken English. "Guards sleep." With his hand he gestured placing something into a cup. If Patrick understood correctly, Manuel had drugged the wine.

Even better. Apparently he'd been able to steal some opium from the surgeon. Manuel had told him the surgeon used the drug on occasion.

"Gracias," Patrick said, his eyes indicating the plate.

Manuel moved on, his back obviously tense. He also moved as if in pain.

Patrick swore to himself. Manuel was a handsome lad with black hair and lively dark eyes. At least they had been lively when he'd first come on board. The last six months had taken their toll on him.

He busied himself with the beans. To do anything else would invite unwanted attention. But he glanced at the guards who were drinking wine. Their heads were nodding, and they would not be relieved until shortly before dawn. God bless Manuel, but Patrick flinched knowing what the lad must have suffered to get the key and the opium.

After gulping the beans and handing his tin plate back to Manuel, he leaned against Denny, who leaned against the next man, who leaned against the side of ship for sleep, but Patrick's eyes never left the guards.

Eventually, he noticed the guards' eyes were closed. Manuel quietly approached the sleeping guards. One sprawled against a wall, his eyes shut. Two others rolled over. The fourth, obviously aware that something was amiss, tried to rouse his companions. He had just opened his mouth to speak when Manuel quickly slit his throat, then calmly slit the throats of the others.

Patrick felt no regret. Those particular guards had wielded their whips with pleasure and had tormented Manuel. But he found himself aching for a lad who committed the acts so coldly.

Then Manuel was next to him, unlocking the chain that anchored the men to the bench. Denny stared at him, puzzlement in his eyes. But the Moor next to him, Kilil, had seen what had happened and was instantly on his feet.

Patrick had learned Spanish in the past eight years. He'd had to in order to survive. He also spoke English, Gaelic and French. He'd learned a few Arabic words from Kilil.

He left the bench and went down the aisle with Manuel, unlocking each chain, whispering to each man on the aisle, asking for silence. As stunned as they were at their new circumstances, they complied. Mayhap part of it was stark terror. They all knew the price of mutiny.

Patrick went to the dead guards and checked for keys to the grate that covered the entrance to the hold. Their freedom depended on getting that grate open. But as he feared, there were no keys. He relieved them, though, of their daggers and a cutlass one wore. After a second's thought, he added the bloodied whip to his cache of weapons, along with the short sticks the guards had used to beat the prisoners.

Two men appeared at his side. He knew neither of them well, though he thought they had been oarsmen for at least two years. But they had been at opposite ends of the ship and talking was not permitted.

He recognized from their manner that they were natural leaders. Good or bad, he didn't know, but he wanted them on his side. Needed them. He handed each man one of the daggers he had taken. He kept the cutlass for himself.

"We have to wait until the guard changes," Patrick explained. "They will open the grate then."

"Nae if they dinna hear the ones they replace. And those seem well dead, the devil take their black souls."

Patrick recognized the thick brogue of Highlands from the taller man.

"I am Spanish," said the other in accented English. "I can mimic the guards. The devil knows I have heard them too many times."

"Good," Patrick said. "We will prop the dead guards up where they are barely visible, just enough to fool their replacements." In the dim light, he studied the man's face. "Try the answer now."

The Spaniard did, almost a perfect mimic of the captain of the night guard.

"You will do," Patrick said in English.

"Gracias," the Spaniard said in a voice laced with irony.

Patrick wasn't sure how much time they had before the relief guards descended. He helped the Scot and the Spaniard drag the bodies to the bottom of the stairs leading to the locked grate above; together they positioned the guards to make them look as if they were engaged in a game of chance.

The other oarsmen remained on their benches, either in fear or confusion. The hold was utterly silent, as if every oarsman recognized the stakes. Not even the sound of a chain link hitting the floor. Thank God for that.

The ship was moving rapidly, meaning a number of sailors were probably working the deck above, tending the sails. He prayed the movement above would mask their voices.

" 'Tis risky," whispered the Scot.

" 'Tis death if we do *not* try."

The Spaniard stood there, listening, then spoke in Spanish, "Better to die as a man than a dog." He bowed to Patrick in a gesture ludicrous at the moment. "What more can I do?"

"Tell the oarsmen to stay in their places. If anyone glances down . . ." He didn't have to finish. He saw understanding on their faces.

"*Dios*, but we need good fortune," the Spaniard said in his cultivated voice.

"We need a bloody miracle," the Scot corrected.

"Both would do, but right now we make our own luck. Can you two communicate with the oarsmen?" Patrick said.

"I speak Gaelic and bloody *Sassenach*," said the Scot.

"Spanish, French. Some Arabic," said the obvious aristocrat among them.

Patrick wondered fleetingly what misfortune had brought him among them. But that was for later. "Talk to as many as you can, but you"—he gestured to the Spaniard—"stay near the ladder. I will let you know if the guards approach. Tell the oarsmen to be silent and sit in their usual places. Find the warriors among them. A blacksmith if there is one."

He paused, then added, "If we . . . are taken or killed, tell them to run the chain back through their rings and lock it. Mayhap they will not be blamed."

The Spaniard with the fine manners but the same tattered loincloth and filthy skin that made them all one nodded. "I am Diego," he said. "No longer a number tonight."

"I'm Hugh MacDonald," said the other one. He clasped Patrick's hand. "I will die before returning to that bench. I wouldna' let them defeat me by dying. 'Twould be no defeat to die killing them."

A surge of hope ran through Patrick. He had always been good at sizing up men. He had not hoped to find two like these. He prayed there would be more, that the Spaniard's voice could imitate the dead guards, that surprise would help them overtake exhausted sailors. "I'm Patrick," he replied.

His glance went to the dead bodies. His throat constricted with hate. He remembered the number of bodies stacked in the aisle, waiting to be thrown overboard like so much refuse. The cries of pain, the daily struggle against thirst and hunger and exhaustion.

The guards should not have died so easily. He wished instead they could have taken their places on the benches.

He looked up to the grate. Occasionally he saw shadows from the men above. He wanted to climb the ladder and determine how many sailors were on deck, but that would have to wait. They had to organize below. He had to be sure no one would yell a warning in hopes of being pardoned.

He joined Diego, who was talking to a newcomer to the benches. He was recognizable as such because of his size. In a month he would be half the man he was now.

Tonight, though, his fists were huge. Patrick saw his naked back was crossed by new whip marks.

"He says he's a blacksmith," Diego said. "He's a Frenchman, a Huguenot," he added dismissively.

A Protestant. That explained his presence.

"Can you break our shackles with a dagger?" he asked, stretching out his hands.

"*Oui,* but it will take time. A hammer would be better."

Wrists or ankles? He could use the manacles on his wrists as weapons, whereby he needed the use of his legs to mount the ladder and pull up others.

"Are you with us?" he asked, watching the man's eyes.

"*Oui,*" he said. "But then where do we go?"

"Scotland," Patrick said in French. "I will help any man who joins us. I will kill any who betrays us."

Patrick and the blacksmith moved to where they would be out of sight of the grate. Patrick sat as the blacksmith looked about for more tools and chose the hammer—the one used to beat the drum that signaled the speed of the oar strokes—and a thick stick.

"The leg irons first," Patrick said. "We need to climb the ladder. Break as many leg irons as possible. We can use the wrist irons as weapons."

"There will be noise," the blacksmith warned.

"We will have to risk it," Patrick replied. The blacksmith examined the leg fetters for any weak link, then settled on the bolt and started pounding with the hammer.

Every stoke jarred Patrick's leg, but he scarcely felt it. The exhaustion of his body was eclipsed by newfound hope, even though he knew the odds were terrible. A few manacled, emaciated men against a crew of healthy sailors.

As Diego said, 'twas better to die a man than whipped to death as a dog.

Chapter 4

THE night seemed endless as the blacksmith pounded at the chains, using a rag to try to muffle the sounds. Patrick felt a drop of sweat as the man worked diligently to break the shackles.

The blacksmith did not mention his name, and Patrick did not need to know. It was enough that the man was uncanny at finding weak spots in the chains. It took him a short time to loose the bolts on Patrick's leg manacles.

Patrick chose the Scot—MacDonald—as the next one to be freed. He was fairly new to the ship and stronger than most. Then the blacksmith worked on the Spaniard's legs, then his own.

The other oarsmen were still and silent, but he knew from their bodies that they were watching every movement. He had feared one might cry out. Unfortunately, he was forced to silence one who did.

At that moment the other oarsmen were more afraid of Patrick and his small band than of the Spanish above. They watched as the leg irons were removed one by one.

Then Patrick and the Spaniard went from row to row whispering, sometimes in different languages or by sign language, that they must work together.

"Those who can fight will have their leg irons released first," Patrick or Diego explained. "Diego will answer when the relief guards come to the grate, and they should open it. We will kill them one by one as they come down. We will take what weapons they have and go on deck.

"Pray as you have never prayed before to whatever God you serve." he added. "Pray for fog. We have had it the past two nights. Pray for it tonight."

Heads nodded. Some left their benches to stand in line before the blacksmith. Others stayed seated, their eyes fearful. To Patrick's surprise, Denny was among the twenty who stood.

The number was greater than he'd hoped, and yet there were at least sixty sailors above, maybe even more. The element of surprise would be in the oarsmen's favor, although most of the prisoners would be hampered by wrist manacles and some by leg irons. He darted a glance to assess the blacksmith's progress.

Fog. Fog would make the impossible possible. The air had been moist in the past few hours. If fog enclosed the ship, mayhap they could go about their business without notice until it was too late.

He tried to judge the time. How long did they have before the fresh guards appeared at the grate? He moved over to where the blacksmith still worked steadily.

They had to have enough oarsmen able to mount the steps. Once several were on the deck, they could pull others up as sailors were taken above. MacDonald and the Spaniard were working through the benches of oarsmen, instilling the courage to fight.

Patrick wondered how many sailors were on duty before dawn. Not many, he hoped. The wind was strong and steady now. Hopefully the effort required in raising the sails would have exhausted the crew.

He went back to the blacksmith. "Time to stop. I think the change of guard will come shortly."

Patrick quenched one of the two oil lamps that gave dim light to the interior. Then they waited. The air felt moist as it drifted through the grate. The beginning of rain? Or fog? He barely allowed himself that hope.

Minutes went by, then more. It had never been as quiet on the rowing deck. No movement. No rattling of chains. No snores of exhausted men.

Then he heard the familiar question at the grate. "All well?"

He nodded to Diego, who called out in his native tongue, "*Si.* All is well."

Patrick's shoulders tensed in anticipation. He heard a key turn in the lock on the grate and the loud groan as it opened.

He should be nothing but a shadow. The blacksmith was just out of sight, behind the ladder. Diego stood next to the blacksmith. MacDonald was in the aisle seat on the last bench, which was adjacent to the ladder. His head was bowed as if he slept.

There should be four guards. Patrick, Diego, MacDonald and the blacksmith would each take one. And they would have to do it without making a sound.

The thud of heavy footsteps indicated the approach of the relief guards coming down the ladder. "Where's the lantern?" asked one of the guards as he reached the bottom of the ladder.

"Just went out," Diego replied softly as he grabbed the first guard around the neck, cutting off any outcry, and pulling him into the dark.

The next was handled by the blacksmith, who broke the guard's neck with a twist of his massive hands before he dragged him away from the ladder. The third guard came down, unaware of the fate of those who had gone before him. His loud grunt was unexpectedly covered by a loud makeshift coughing fit from an oarsman on the bench. The last was halfway down when he apparently realized something was wrong. He had started to call out when Patrick seized him and wrapped the chain binding his wrists around the guard's neck. A quick twist and the man was dead.

He felt nothing for the guards, and for the first time real hope stirred in him. Before he had nothing to lose. Now he had everything to gain.

In any event, there was no going back now. Not for any of them. In the dim light of the one lantern, the other oarsmen realized it, too. Those who had agreed to fight were already on their feet, but now others were standing as well, grabbing anything they could to defend themselves.

Patrick donned the cap of a Spanish guard and poked his head out of the grate. Elation filled him. Fog eclipsed most of the ship. A few oil lamps cast enough light to see forms moving, and he could hear the routine shouts of orders.

Maybe there was a God after all. He'd just been hiding these past eight years.

He could not see the helm from his position. Probably the first or second officer was at the wheel. Whoever it was should be weary now.

His leg irons had been struck but others had wrapped theirs with fabric ripped from the shirts of the slain guards and worn blankets, hoping—nay, praying—it would quiet the sound of iron clanking on the wood deck.

He gave a sign with his hand then moved out onto the deck. He waited in the shadows until the Scot and Spaniard were behind him, then each moved after their predetermined targets. Patrick would work his way forward. Diego would go to the right, and MacDonald to where he was needed.

Patrick had tied the cutlass from one of the dead guards to his waist with a piece of a worn blanket. He held a dagger and moved with the shadows toward a sailor who was working on a knot in the lines. Again he used the chain that linked his wrists to break the man's neck.

He heard the start of a cry to his left, but it was cut off, and he hoped the wind carried it back toward the sea rather than toward the helm. Then he heard a whistle from the Spaniard. Another sailor down.

Two other shapes materialized in the fog. One sailor had obviously heard something and turned toward Patrick, a dagger in his hand. He was ready to throw it when he was taken from behind. In another second, he died, stabbed by his own weapon. To Patrick's astonishment, Denny stood over him, a smile on his face.

Another movement. Peering through the fog, he saw a sailor blinking in surprise at the sight of what must have looked like a demon in front of him. MacDonald threw the sailor overboard.

Several more went down without more than a low moan. Patrick did a quick tally in his head. Fifteen of the crew dead and no alarm raised. Now to get their own motley crew organized.

Patrick, the MacDonald and the Spaniard would make their way forward, taking care of anyone they encountered as quietly as possible. Other prisoners, waiting for their chains to be struck, were assigned to watch the various hatches and kill anyone who came on deck. If and when there was an alarm, they were to join the battle.

They now had the daggers and cutlasses of fifteen Spaniards. Other oarsmen found makeshift weapons in addition to those taken from the guards. Ropes were cut to be used as lashes or garrotes. Oars from the long boat could be used, even with the manacles. A quick-thinking oarsman managed to break the end off a broom and then partly split the handle to make a spear. The odds, though heavily against the oarsmen, were fast getting better.

The first gray of dawn was visible through the fog, which would soon burn off. Patrick suspected the cook was awake and working. Sailors were probably rising. They had to hurry and take as many of the enemy as possible.

Patrick and Denny moved forward on the port side, and the MacDonald and Diego on the starboard side. Patrick heard more orders being given as they moved up toward the helm. He almost crashed into a figure ahead of him. He took advantage of the man's surprise to break his neck. He had no remorse, nor pity for any of them. They had chosen to sail on a hell ship, and now it was his life against theirs.

A grunt came out of the fog, then evaporated into the air. He knew one of his companions had killed another member of the crew. In truth, every man aboard had to be killed. There was no room for compassion even if he had wanted to bestow any. They were doomed men when they first entered this ship. Now they were mutineers as well—regarded as lower than animals by every civilized country in the world. There could be no witnesses to what they were doing. None. All the evidence must be forever lost at sea.

He had not mentioned it to the others, but most would be aware of the laws of the sea. And they shared Patrick's hatred for their tormenters.

A cry rang out. This one sharp and piercing before it was quickly silenced. Then there was the splash of a body overboard.

A number of shouts quickly followed. Then a bell rang. And rang. Patrick took a deep breath. The time for hell was at hand.

He moved forward to the wheel. They had to take the officers first. Once the leadership was gone . . .

Night had turned into dawn. The fog had thinned, and he could see three figures by the wheel. One stayed at the wheel while the other two took positions to protect him. One had a sword, the other a club.

He heard a whistle and knew MacDonald was approaching from the other side. Holding the cutlass he'd appropriated from the dead guard, Patrick attacked the man on the left, the one with a sword, as MacDonald appeared to attack the second.

Patrick easily avoided the first wild swing; he'd trained all his young life with a sword. As the sword completed its momentum and went back, he countered it with the heavier cutlass, knocking it from the officer's hand. The sword skittered across the deck and into the sea.

He took advantage of the brief second of shock and surprise to kill the startled officer, whose last thought, no doubt, was wonder at being bested by a galley slave. One still hampered by chains.

MacDonald was having a harder time. His opponent was a big man in far better health. Patrick took the dagger from his makeshift sash and thrust it into MacDonald's opponent, then turned on the man at the wheel.

"No," the helmsman cried in terror, and Patrick for one brief second remembered this was a merchant ship, not a warship.

He hesitated.

Diego did not. He emerged from the fog at that instant, wielding a sword in his hand. He drove it into the officer's heart without the slightest hesitation.

The battle was in full action now. Screams tore at the morning's silence, high-pitched shouts of alarm, death cries.

Patrick turned around. Denny was guarding his back. Crew members poured out of the hatches, engaging with the oarsmen in desperate battles. He went to the aid of one oarsman, using the cutlass. Another large sailor assaulted Patrick, thrusting a dagger at him. Patrick tried to block it and turned, but the edge of the blade caught his arm, leaving a deep red gash on his skin.

The crewman turned to attack again. Before he could reach Patrick, though, Denny hurled him overboard. He'd again saved Patrick's life, though he seemed to make no attempt to save his own. He stood there as two sailors rushed him.

Patrick swung the cutlass. One went down, and the other was grabbed from behind by an oarsman who used a belaying pin to crush his skull.

Patrick nodded his thanks for the assistance, then looked down to see blood running from the gash in his arm. He felt no pain, though, only the compelling need to be free. Desperation had turned into hope and now hope into possibility.

His oarsmen were armed well now, having taken weapons from those they'd killed. He felt their anger, their bloodlust, the need to avenge months and years of abject misery.

Thrust and cut. It became as natural as the refrain that drove his body hours earlier. *Heave! Lift!*

He had rowed to stay alive.

Thrust and cut.

Now he killed to live. To get home.

Gradually there was no one else to fight. A deadly silence fell over the ship except for the occasional groan or cry of pain. The deck was awash in bodies. The smell of blood mingled with the heavy moist air. It was not a stench easily forgotten.

The Spaniard, Diego, appeared at his side.

"How many of the crew live?" Patrick asked.

Diego shook his head. "We are still looking. Some might be in hiding."

Patrick knew he should feel some sorrow, but he did not. Every slain man was here by choice. Every one was part of his slavery.

"And the oarsmen?"

"Eight dead. Nine wounded."

He nodded. Far better than he'd dared hope.

He was alive!

And free!

Diego was covered in blood, his filthy loincloth a bright red. "And you."

Patrick shrugged. "Some slices. No more." He was silent for a moment.

"I do not believe it yet."

Neither did Patrick believe it.

"We have to search the ship, cabin by cabin," he said.

As if summoned, an oarsman came through the hatch. "There is a locked door. It is likely the captain's cabin."

"A coward as well as a villain," the Spaniard said. "I cannot wait for him to feel my sword."

"Nay," Patrick said. "I have been here the longest. He is mine. Have two men wait outside the locked cabin," he said. "Have others check the rest of the ship for anyone who may be hiding."

"Why wait?"

"I want these chains off before I meet the captain of this hell ship," Patrick explained.

The Spaniard hesitated. 'Twas obvious to Patrick that Diego wanted the captain as much as he did. It was a test now. Would the oarsmen follow him or dissolve into a mob that would make success a temporary thing?

"*Si,*" the man finally said. "I will be at your back."

Patrick nodded as relief filled him. They still had a nearly impossible task in front of them.

The Spaniard eyed him warily. "We have a slight problem. Who will sail the ship?"

"I know something about navigation and sails. The others can learn."

JULIANA had never known such stark terror before. The new silence was more frightening than the screams of minutes earlier.

She sat on the bed, clasping an equally terrified Carmita. Her hands trembled.

When the first sounds came, she'd opened her door and a sailor told her to shut it and keep it locked. Apparently there was some kind of mutiny. . . .

She tried to still the trembling of her hands. It would do no good.

But why hadn't her uncle come for her? Or a member of the crew? Even the face of the first mate would be welcome.

She looked around the cabin for something with which to defend herself. There was a small knife she had for cutting fruit and cheese that had been brought to her cabin.

She rose and went over to the small table where the blade still rested in a slab of cheese. The knife looked small and useless, but it was all she had.

She clutched it and went to the door, listening.

Then she heard her uncle's voice. "Open."

She threw the door open. He stood disheveled, the first time she had ever seen him that way.

"Come," he demanded, grabbing her arm.

"What is happening?"

"The galley slaves. They broke free. Come to my cabin. It has a sturdier door. My crew will defeat them. They are nothing but rabble."

"Carmita comes with me."

"Bring her if you must, but hurry. We have only a few seconds, if that."

She grabbed a trembling Carmita and followed her uncle down the corridor to his cabin. They were both thrust inside, then he slipped in with them before bolting the door.

"Should you not be out there with the crew?" she asked.

"My first duty is to you, my niece," he replied. "I swore to your father that I would bring you safely to England."

Voices grew stronger. Curse words in several languages. Some she knew but others she could easily guess from their vehemence. Accompanying their voices were doors slamming open and shut. Had the oarsmen somehow gained control of the ship? But how could that be? They were in chains. There were armed guards.

She shied when she heard a pounding at the door. Curses in a language she didn't understand came through the door. More pounding. Then nothing.

Were they really going away?

Perhaps her uncle's men had regained control. But then wouldn't they have told her uncle?

The questions pounded at her when she heard a scream that ripped through her. It was one of terrible pain.

She clutched the knife in her hand. She would use it on herself before letting herself be violated.

Or maybe she would use it on someone else.

Her heart pounded, and her throat was dry with terror. Should she use the knife now? Or wait until she wouldn't have a chance?

Madre!

Chapter 5

WITH a mighty stroke of the hammer, the blackmith once again broke the bolt that fastened the irons, this time on Patrick's wrists. When the blacksmith finished, Patrick stood. Free of fetters. He spread out his arms in victory. Not in joy. He didn't think he would ever be joyous. But the sheer pleasure of moving the way men were meant to move was intoxicating.

"You did it," the blacksmith said. "I never thought . . ."

"Nor did I think we would succeed," Patrick said.

His hands were free now to confront the captain unencumbered. The man who had made his life, and those of hundreds before him, a hellish inferno.

He took satisfaction from the fact that the captain, the man who had bought and sold human beings for profit, was apparently cowering inside his cabin, knowing that his life was nearing an end.

It did bother him that others may still be alive and trying

to surrender. He'd thought the honor had been drained from him these last years, but something in him clenched at killing a disarmed man. Mayhap a tiny wisp of humanity remained in him. He didn't know how much remained in the others who had shared the benches.

That was why he had asked for these few minutes, to let the bloodlust fade, for reason and conscience to return.

Patrick headed toward the captain's cabin, passing exuberant oarsmen. He heard thanks in different languages, some he knew and some he didn't, but the sentiment needed no translation. Even the sickest of them had been now pulled up on the main deck, and incredulity had been replaced by glee. Some had obviously attacked the food stores, others barrels of ale.

He took an offered mug of ale and tasted it, but nothing more. He had to be clearheaded for the day ahead, the days ahead. . . .

Patrick saw MacDonald, the only other Scot. "Weapons?"

"They be distributed among the oarsmen."

Patrick only nodded. They would have to be collected. But first he had to finish this. "Have you seen a sword?"

"Aye. There was a cupboard full of weapons. I prefer a dirk, but the Spaniard took a cutlass. There were several left."

"Take me there."

MacDonald's wrists were still bound by irons, but he smiled as he led the way to the weapons cache. The sound of laughter echoed along the corridors.

Patrick knew he would never forget it.

He found a sword, a rapier, among the clumsier cutlasses and balanced it with his hand. As a lad, he had trained mostly on the heavy Scottish Claidheamh Mor, the two-handed broadsword that relied on its mass to crush through the armor of an enemy. But during his years on the continent he had used the lighter rapier.

This one felt right in his hands.

Then he went with the MacDonald to the locked cabin.

* * *

"WHAT do you think has happened?" Juliana asked as she paced the large, elaborate cabin. The silence had grown ominous now.

Her uncle, obviously stunned, shook his head. "We should have heard something." He looked at her. "Your father entrusted your safety to me, and I have no way to protect you now." He hesitated, then handed her a dagger. "Do not let them take you alive."

She closed her fingers around the hilt. Better than the small knife she'd grabbed earlier.

"They have been without women for a long time," he said simply. "Go for your heart. I should kill you myself, but . . . I cannot. Perhaps I can bargain with them."

She saw fear in his eyes, in his face, and she wondered whether he had stayed in the cabin to protect her, or to let his crew fight the battle for him.

He must have seen the question in her eyes.

"It was too late, *querida*. I came back to . . . but I cannot do it. I cannot kill my own niece. The Church . . ."

His hand trembled, and she wondered whether it trembled for her or himself. But his words struck less terror in her than the expression on his face.

Cries of jubilation came from outside. Then a pounding at the door.

Her uncle ignored the sound, though his fingers tightened around the hilt of his sword. Her own gripped the dagger. She knew the men roaming the ship must hate her uncle and, therefore, her. She remembered the fury glowing from the one oarsman.

All of a sudden, the pounding stopped. She heard loud voices, then indistinct voices. Languages she did not understand.

"They might listen to you," she ventured finally, knowing they wouldn't, yet unwilling to stand like a sheep to slaughter. "If you offer to free them . . . take them somewhere safe."

He looked at her as if she had two heads, and she realized how incredibly foolish she must sound.

She had dreaded every moment of this journey to wed a man she did not know, but even that was preferable to what she knew must be coming.

Still, she tried again. "They cannot know how to sail a ship. They need you."

"I doubt they care about that," he said, stiffly, and she saw her father's pride in him. Pride and arrogance. Pride and arrogance that would kill them both. He buttoned up his coat and looked in a mirror. He carefully placed a captain's hat on his head.

"They are not breaking down the door," she ventured hopefully.

He lowered his voice, the pride dropping away. "They are in no hurry. There is no place for me to go."

The new silence was as frightening as the shouts outside the door.

He touched her face. It was the first sign of affection he'd ever shown. "Say your prayers," he said. "I intend to say mine." He lowered his sword to the floor, knelt and crossed himself.

It was the first time she had seen his arrogance slip from his face.

She knelt next to him. Carmita joined them, tears flowing down her face.

It seemed irreverent to pray with a dagger clutched in her fingers. Instead, she made a vow. She would use the dagger on someone else before herself.

As Patrick made his way along the corridor of the ship, the elation of being free from his fetters warred with his need for retribution. He felt nothing but contempt for a captain who had hidden while his crew was being slaughtered. Neither he nor any of the oarsmen had seen Mendoza during the fighting.

Patrick wanted to be the one to kill him.

Three oarsmen stood outside the cabin, their nearly naked bodies covered with blood, their hands holding clubs.

Ready—nay, desperately wanting—to do what he planned to do. It was a good sign that they had obeyed him in this one thing.

"He is mine," he said.

Manuel held a sword nearly as tall as he was, and stood, rocking on his feet. He flashed a quick, feral grin. "I thought we would die."

"We may still do that," Patrick said grimly. Unlike the others, he knew the dangers that lay ahead. He'd been thinking of them ever since Manuel had given him the nod that started it all.

Scotland. They had to go to Scotland. He had to go home. Once there, he could help the others return to their homes.

That meant sailing hundreds of miles with men who knew nothing about sailing a ship, and himself with hellishly little knowledge. Now he wished he had paid more attention when his father sent him with one of his ship's captains to learn about the sea. He had resisted every moment of it. He'd wanted to be a soldier, not a trader.

Now he was about to be the sailor he'd never wanted to be.

He pounded at the door and shouted through it. "Open or we will break down the door."

Silence.

Then he heard the sound of a bolt sliding from inside, and the door opened.

Mendoza appeared, arrayed in an elaborate uniform, defiance in his eyes, but fear was there as well. He moved out into the hall and closed the door behind him.

"Aha, the captain of murderers," he said.

Patrick almost admired his bravado. But he remembered the times Mendoza walked above them, seeing the welts and rips on men's skin, the bodies that were far too thin to drive his ship.

Familiar hatred welled in him.

Particularly when Mendoza glanced around with the same contempt he had shown the oarsmen before.

"My crew?"

"Muerto," Patrick said coldly.

"You will all hang," Mendoza said viciously.

"You will not be around to see."

Mendoza looked at the sword in Patrick's hand, then raised his own. If he'd been a coward earlier, he obviously intended to fight now that he had no choice. He knew he was going to die today, either by Patrick's hand or by that of the bloodstained and bloodthirsty men behind him.

Patrick stared at the man he hated above all others, then parried the man's first stroke of the sword. He had no shield. Nor did his opponent. It was metal against metal, skill against skill, and Patrick knew instantly from the way Mendoza moved and held his sword that the Spaniard had the advantage. Mendoza had not been in chains for six years, did not have the stiffness of movement. Patrick, though, had the will.

Patrick was aware of the gathering number of oarsmen watching him, daggers or clubs in their hand, ready to finish the job if Patrick couldn't. But Patrick also knew he had to win to keep the confidence of a crew made up of thieves and murderers as well as prisoners of war. He had to have that confidence to get home.

He tried an experimental thrust. Mendoza skillfully parried it and lunged at him. Patrick parried that stroke, moving backward until he felt the wall blocking farther motion in that direction. He moved to the side as he feinted and lunged. Sheer will fueled his weakened body.

Mendoza defended against the attack easily enough, but Patrick saw surprise on his face. It was obvious that Mendoza had expected a fast kill against a slave.

Patrick tried a riposte. He was weak but he felt a surge of strength as Mendoza was forced back. The retreat lasted only a second before the Spaniard lunged at him. Patrick sidestepped, but not quite quickly enough. Mendoza's blade caught his forearm just above the knife wound he suffered on deck. A fresh trickle of blood mingled with his sweat. It enraged him that the captain fought as if he were the man being wronged. This man, this captain, had wronged every man aboard this ship.

Their swords clashed, then disengaged, and Patrick's breath became labored. His steps slowed. Mendoza met his every move with skill, and Patrick couldn't find an opening. One small mistake would mean his life. He saw the desperation in Mendoza's eyes, the hate that equaled his own. Patrick knew anger would affect Mendoza's abilities. It would cause him to make a mistake. Survival, more than anger, was Patrick's goal.

An opening! He thrust once more, but Mendoza blocked it with his sword and with a sudden movement knocked Patrick's sword from his hand. Patrick dived after it, rolling on the ground to avoid Mendoza's blade as he grabbed the hilt and sprang to his feet.

Mendoza looked startled, giving Patrick time to balance on his feet. Patrick feinted, then sprang forward suddenly, only to find his rapier parried once more.

Mendoza was trying to wear him down, his fury directed at the man he obviously held responsible for taking his ship. Patrick was sustained by another kind of outrage, one built over months and years.

Mendoza, obviously tired of taunting his opponent, wielded the blade as if it were a part of him, driving in. Patrick danced away from the sword and saw that his opponent was angered enough to make a misjudgment. Patrick sprang forward suddenly, his sword driving toward Mendoza's heart. He felt it go into his enemy, and the man started to fall, a surprised look on his face.

Patrick pulled the blade out as Mendoza landed on the floor of the deck. There was a moan. The captain tried to say something, but blood bubbled from his mouth. Then he stilled.

Shouts came up from the men around him.

Several took Mendoza's body.

"Overboard," yelled one.

Four of them headed toward the steep stairs up to the

main deck, each carrying an arm or leg. The clanking of chains accompanied their every step.

Others started into the cabin, grabbing anything they could.

He wanted nothing more from Mendoza. He had everything he wanted. He started toward the hatch of the main deck, then turned back. There would be maps in the captain's cabin. Maps he had to have.

Just as reached the door, he heard a scream.

A woman's scream.

Chapter 6

HER heart pounding in fear, Juliana waited inside the cabin as her uncle stepped outside and closed the door behind him. She held Carmita's hand.

"All will be well," she tried to soothe the terrified girl, knowing her words were lies. Nothing would be well again. Although she tried to hide her own terror, she realized they had no hope. She also realized her uncle was probably going to his death, hoping he might divert the mutineers' interest to himself and that Juliana might in some way be overlooked. At least, she wanted to think that of him. If she could avoid detection, perhaps she could later steal down to the hold.

Illogical, *si*. Impossible, *si*. But she had seen in *Tio*'s face that there was nothing else. A thin hope, indeed, against rape and pain and death.

She'd never really cared for him, and she was certainly angry with him since she saw her uncle as the architect of this marriage, but sorrow mixed with terror as her uncle stepped out of the cabin and closed the door behind him. She left Carmita kneeling next to the bed and praying in quiet earnest. Leaning against the door, she listened, hoping that those on the other side could not hear her heart pounding.

She heard her uncle's angry words, the clash of swords, the grunts of men engaged in mortal battle.

Then she heard the shouts of elation and knew her uncle was dead. Elation for a man's death! She was sickened by it.

She moved away from the door. There was no good place to hide. No room under the bed. No cupboard. Only two chairs, a trunk and a table overflowing with charts. She and Carmita looked at each other, and she saw her own fear reflected in the young girl's eyes. She took Carmita in her arms, holding tight.

Fists pounded on the door, and she knew she had only seconds before it slammed open. She stiffened, the dagger her uncle had given her held tightly in her fingers. She may be cornered but she would not die like a rabbit.

She shoved Carmita down between the bed and the cabin wall. "Stay there," she said. At least she might divert them from Carmita, as her uncle had tried to divert the mutineers from her.

Her blood froze as the door crashed open and blood-smeared bodies crowded inside, grabbing at whatever they could find.

Then one reached out for her, a blood-stained finger touching her hair.

She couldn't stop a scream from rising in her throat and shattering the air. She clutched the knife, ready to thrust the blade into her heart. Then she hesitated.

I don't want to die!

Suddenly the man holding her was swept away, and another stood before her. A giant of a man, covered in blood, his eyes as cold and hard as any she had ever seen. Eyes she'd seen before. Eyes that had been filled with fury when he had looked up at her just a few days earlier. She remembered every feature of that face. It had haunted her.

She tried to hide the panic she felt. Though other oarsmen remained in the cabin, she could not take her eyes from him, nor from the blood dripping from two wounds in his arm.

From her uncle's sword?

He was so dominant she was only slightly aware of other naked forms devouring her with angry, hungry eyes.

God help her, he looked like *el diablo* himself.

She forced her glance away and toward the door. Then she raised her eyes back to the savage before her, trying desperately to keep upright when her legs wanted to fold beneath her.

Fissions of pure terror ran through her. This was the end of her life. The only question was how she would die. And how soon.

She tried to control the trembling in her legs. In her hands. *Do not drop the dagger. Not now.* Show him that she could die as well as her uncle had. With a weapon in her hand.

He stepped closer, hard, cold eyes running over her as if she were a prize cow.

Then to her surprise, he asked, "Senora Mendoza?" His voice was hoarse and she heard a slight burr in it.

She didn't answer. She didn't want him to hear the tremor that undoubtedly would be in her voice.

Should she claim to be her uncle's wife? Or daughter? Or just an innocent passenger? There were documents. She knew her uncle had the marriage contract with him. But would they find them? Read them?

She shook her head.

"Senorita?"

His eyes pinioned her against the wall. "Who are you?" he finally asked in Spanish. He spoke it well, but the burr in his voice was thick.

A Scot?

He took another step toward her, and instinctively her hand went up and she slashed out at him, striking his chest. Just as it did, his left hand caught her wrist, tightening around it, forcing her to drop the dagger.

Blood flowed from the gash on his chest.

He looked at it with surprise, his large hand holding her small one tightly.

She would die now.

Instead, he thrust her into the arms of another near-naked man. "Lock her in up in a mate's cabin. Make sure she has no weapons." There was a slight hint of wryness in his voice that startled her.

Another man shouted from behind him. "There is another one, Scot. Behind the bed." Then the speaker grabbed Carmita. The girl fought back as the brigand leaned over and tried to kiss her.

"Stop," said the Scot sharply, and to her surprise the man did.

Still another oarsman pushed to Juliana's side. "I will take her, Scot. Teach her a lesson," he said in bad Spanish.

"Nay," *el diablo* said. "I will tend to her myself in good time."

"We should share," another man said in Spanish. "She is nothing but Mendoza's whore."

Others agreed vocally. Voices rose. They moved forward, almost as a whole.

The man she had wounded turned around and faced them. Blood dripped from him, from the wound she had made and another. He disregarded both.

"There will be but one leader here," he said in Spanish and in a voice as cold as his eyes. "If you want to live to see your homes again, you will do as I say."

"You cannot tell us what to do. We 'uns had enough of that," said one man stepping forward. "We all fought. You have no right to take her for yourself."

"Can you sail a ship?" the giant asked. "Do you know navigation?"

She noticed the burr sounded even stronger, though his Spanish was good. There was an air of a natural leader about him.

Perhaps . . .

Angry muttering. Oaths.

"Take what clothes you can find," he told those still in the cabin. "Have those manacles struck," he continued in Spanish. "There's spirits aboard, but do not take too much or you will sicken."

The muttering faded, but one man objected. "We will take what we want."

Her captor stared him down. "We are in the sea lanes. I will have to turn you into sailors if we are not to be taken by the English or Spanish. Then you *will* have a rope about your neck if not worse."

She saw some turn to one another, obviously not understanding. There were simple translations dotted by crude words she recognized by tone if not by language. Still, they did not leave.

Juliana saw the tension in her captor's body. He was asserting leadership to a bloodthirsty rabble. She tried to shrink into the wall. She was helpless now without the knife. But she understood what would happen if the devil's apprentice did not convince them. She would be taken then and there by all of them.

A few hours. Perhaps we will encounter another ship.

One of the mutineers still held her wrist. Her hand shook slightly. She looked up at her captor's face. It had not the ice of the *el diablo*, but she did not like the speculation in it as he glanced at her and then at the man who appeared to be the rabble's leader.

Then a third man pushed through the door toward her. He still wore manacles on his wrists and ankles, though the chain linking them was broken.

His face was thin but aristocratic.

"And what is this?" he asked in perfect Castillian Spanish, his gaze roaming over her.

"A woman," said the apparent leader. "And a wee lass. A servant, I expect. Neither will speak, but the woman shook her head when I asked if she was Mendoza's wife." He shrugged. "Mistress, mayhap."

The Spaniard looked at the man's chest. "Another wound, Scot?"

"The lass."

The Spaniard roared with laughter. "You take a ship with this tattered crew, and a wisp of a senorita wounds you."

The Scot shot him a sharp look.

But the Spaniard didn't pursue it. Instead, he took his place next to the Scot in an obvious gesture of support.

Muttering, the others started to back off.

"Is there a cook here?" *el diablo* asked of the men crowding into the room, obviously trying to divert them.

One man advanced. Like the others, he was filthy. *"Si."*

"Go to the blacksmith. Tell him I said to strike your irons first. Then prepare some food. You," he said to another, "ration the spirits aboard. Give every man two cups. No more."

To another, he said, "Make sure all the bodies are overboard. I want every man here to be dressed and look as if they belong here as crew."

Charged with duties, the oarsmen backed off, some sullen, some responding to having something to do.

El diablo said something to the man holding her, but it was in a language she did not know.

Then he turned to the Spaniard. "Now take the two of them to a cabin," he said in English.

"Why am I so fortunate?" the Spaniard said.

"They do not appear to understand English," *el diablo* said.

Juliana intended it to remain that way. A small advantage for her.

"I want someone watching the cabin at all times," *el diablo* added. "And make it clear that anyone touching her—either of the women—will fight me." Then he turned and left.

Oddly enough, his leaving frightened her. He had prevented a mob from attacking her. His motives might be vile, but he had given her a few hours of grace.

A few hours of life. If that much. She had wounded him. What would he do to her in return? *I will tend to her myself in good time.*

The Spanish oarsman bowed in a gesture that was ironic at best. "Senorita, you and your servant will come with me."

She paused at the door.

The Spaniard looked at her curiously, then he took her elbow and guided both her and Carmita down the passageway. He reached a cabin door and opened it. Juliana knew it had been occupied by the first mate, the one with the leer on his face every time he'd looked at her.

She did not want to stay there.

"Not here," she said in Spanish, wondering where that bravery came from. Her heart pounded frantically even as she said the words. "My cabin is two doors down."

His hand still firmly around her wrist, he nodded and continued down the corridor to her cabin. He opened it and she went inside.

He followed her, his gaze searching the cabin for clues. "You are Mendoza's mistress?"

She stood there in shock at the thought. "He is my uncle. He was taking me to be wed in England." She hated the fear she heard in her voice.

The cool expression in his face did not change. She was only too aware of the noise made by the ends of the manacles he wore. She remembered how only hours ago she'd thought about these same men below and the sympathy she'd felt.

Now *she* was the prisoner.

She did not like it. The helplessness was terrifying.

She watched as he went through her clothing. Blind terror returned. Despite his civilized speech, he wore only a loincloth and his body was marked with scars, new and old.

"Sit," he said, "while I search for weapons." His gaze went to Carmita. "Both of you. I would not want to suffer what my companion did. You are fortunate he did not take revenge," he said, then added thoughtfully, "though he may not be finished." The words sent a new chill through her.

She eyed the door as he went through her trunk.

"Do not do it, senorita," he said, obviously reading her face. "I should hate to hurt you. But I will if you try to run or hurt me as you did the Scot."

He didn't sound as if he would hate it at all.

"I was frightened," she replied. "I only defended myself."

He frowned.

"Who is he?" she blurted out.

"The Scot?"

"Si!"

He shrugged. "I do not know, any more than he knows my name. The guards forbade any speech between us."

"But he leads you?" She had to know about the man who had her life in his hands. Perhaps she could turn the oarsmen against each other.

But what good would that do her? She would still be on this ship.

Time, she reminded herself. *Time.*

"No one leads us."

"But you obeyed him."

"Because it suited me."

"You are Spanish?"

"Si," he said roughly.

"Your name, senor?"

"It no longer matters," he said curtly.

He finished searching the cabin, then straightened. "I would suggest you bolt your door, senorita, but open it when you hear the Scot. From what I have observed, he does not brook opposition well."

"What . . . will he do?"

The Spaniard eyed her. "I do not know."

"You are Spanish. You would leave me to him?"

"I am nothing, senorita. Your uncle made me less than nothing. I have no loyalty to Spain. Or liking for anything or anyone that comes from Spain."

"Why do you obey him?" she cried out desperately.

"He can sail and navigate," the Spaniard said. "I need him."

His voice was as cold as the Scot's had been.

She had sensed the hatred in her uncle's cabin, but this was very personal.

She had to break through that hatred. Despite the fact that he, too, was covered with blood and still bound with broken chains, there was an aristocratic feel to him as well as to his speech. Surely he was—had been—a gentleman.

Beg.

She couldn't. Perhaps more of her father was in her than she thought. These men, despite how they had been treated, had killed her uncle and, as far as she knew, every other living soul on the ship.

She wasn't going to beg before them. She suspected even if she did, it would do little good.

She was alone on a ship full of men determined to obtain revenge and freedom.

Men who had been without women.

Men who could not afford to leave a living witness to mass murder.

Chapter 7

PATRICK blessed the weather as the *Sofia* sped across the sea, as if—like its passengers—it had been released from bonds. Winds filled the sails and swept away the early morning fog as the ship moved farther from land.

But the two women presented the devil's own choice.

He'd never expected to take the ship. He thought he would die in the attempt and therefore pushed aside that glimpse of the woman. Only her scream had reminded him of her presence and the danger she presented.

He had no compunction at killing those who had enslaved him and beaten him. Or profited from it. But women? A woman and a mere slip of a lassie?

Patrick stood at the helm, his feet hugging the deck and his body rolling with the rhythm of the ship. He reveled in the clean bite of the salt air, the fresh scent of freedom. He had grabbed a pair of ill-fitting breeches from a mate's cabin, then returned to the captain's cabin—and his vital charts—before joining the Spaniard at the helm.

Patrick would need someone to relieve him at the wheel, and the Spaniard seemed to hold the greatest promise. Though he admitted it to no one, Diego seemed to have more experience than anyone else on the ship.

The Scot also had potential. A man as tall as himself and larger despite the meager rations, the MacDonald had been charged with safekeeping the food stocks and spirits, as well as evaluating the motley crew upon which Patrick's life depended. Patrick wanted to know the skills of each man. Had any sailed before their captivity? Had any cooked? Did any have knowledge of medicine? Were there warriors among them?

Now that all the chains had been struck, he'd watched as each reacted to his freedom. Some were raiding everything they saw. Others were destroying what they could. Then others recognized they had not won their freedom yet and asked what they could do.

So far no one had really opposed his orders, but Patrick knew they'd had no time to fully realize their newfound freedom. Or the dangers that continued to lie ahead.

According to the charts, they had been traveling up the coast of Spain. They were probably near Brest and the English Channel. He had to change course to avoid England and reach the Hebrides Islands.

Most of all they had to avoid Spanish warships, the French and privateers. They might well be challenged, even flying the Spanish flag. The next two days would be crucial.

That led to the next problem. The two women.

What to do with them?

He did not trust the oarsmen. Too many were maddened by rage and deprivation. Many had not been near a woman for years, himself included. He could not deny his own reaction when he saw the two of them. One huddling in a corner, the other ready to kill him.

Because she feared him. He had seen the terror in her eyes despite her attack on him. She was beautiful, or mayhap he had been celibate too long. Her eyes were an unusual color—the blue-gray of a summer dawn ringed by violet—and her hair, pulled back in a long braid, was a dark gold, like the color of wheat. Her back had been rigid with defiance.

But she hadn't quite controlled the shaking.

What in the hell was he going to do with her?

He didn't know if he could control the oarsmen. God knew they had gone through enough hell to corrupt them all. And she was a danger to every one of them.

The women—if freed—could hang them all. There were few countries, including Scotland, that condoned mutinies and piracy, no matter the reason. Crews were often not treated well, and one mutiny might lead to others.

"Senor?" The Spaniard asked. "You are worried?"

"We should all be worried."

"The women?"

"They are a complication," he said.

"You are understating the matter," the Spaniard said, looking at the cloth that Patrick had tied around his wound.

"They are safe now?" Patrick added.

"For now. Two men are guarding the cabin. Manuel is there also. I threatened them with a fate worse than death if anyone went inside." Diego put his hand on the sheathed dagger at his side. "They believe me." He hesitated, then said. "What do you propose to do with them?"

Patrick shrugged. "God's blood if I know. I don't make war of women. I will not have rape, not even of a Mendoza. But there's a hundred angry men on board who have been without women for a long time. They also know those women represent a danger to all of us."

The Spaniard's eyes lit with amusement. "A problem I will enjoy watching you solve. Harder perhaps than taking this ship with chained, starved men."

Patrick did not care for his amusement. He took his gaze from the Spaniard and turned it toward the sea ahead.

"There is something else, *el capitán*," Diego said slyly.

"Aye?"

"I found some papers in Mendoza's cabin. The senorita is his niece and traveling to England to marry an English lord."

"Who?"

"The son and heir of the Earl of Chadwick."

Patrick groaned. Not only would the Spanish government be enraged, but now the English one as well. He fought rising apprehension and instead turned his attention to his companion.

"Is your only name Diego?" he asked.

The humor disappeared from the Spaniard's eyes. "Just so."

Patrick accepted the answer. Probably many of the oarsmen wanted their names forgotten.

"Take the wheel," he said.

The Spaniard looked at him questioningly.

"I want to see how you handle her."

Diego took the wheel.

"Feel it," Patrick told him. It had taken all of Patrick's strength to keep it on a steady course. The Spaniard was smaller than he was.

The Spaniard spread his feet, his linen shirt blowing against his back. Apparently the Spaniard had taken his garments from Mendoza's cabin.

Diego handled the wheel well, if not masterfully, and Patrick wondered if the man was testing him as much as he was testing the Spaniard.

Satisfied the Spaniard could manage the ship, Patrick passed among the crew, grateful they were too busy enjoying their freedom to ask where they were going. He hadn't had the heart to tell them they may have to take their places on the benches again if the wind died.

If the wind died . . .

So much to do, and the danger still so high.

* * *

THE more time passed, the more terror festered and grew.

Exhausted by weeping, Carmita slumped in a corner, her hands shaking and every word a wail.

Juliana had tried to comfort her, had held her in her arms for some time, then decided she was not going to surrender with a whimper.

She started to scour the cabin for a potential weapon. The Spaniard had done a very good job. She found little that could be used as a weapon.

There was no window toward the sea, even if she had been wont to throw herself out. But suicide under any circumstances was a sin. Would it be a sin to allow herself to be raped? She had few illusions that she would outlive this voyage unless the ship was engaged by either a Spanish or English warship. She was, in truth, surprised that she had not been immediately ravaged and killed.

Ravaged. She closed her eyes as fear renewed its hold on her. *I will tend to her myself,* the giant had said. A giant with a body covered with the blood of her uncle and countrymen. A man with a fearsome countenance and angry, contemptuous eyes that roamed over her as if she were a sow to be bought and butchered.

She shivered. Surely there was something she could do. She would hide behind the door and strike him with . . . something.

Only there didn't seem to be *something*.

The Spaniard had taken everything that could possibly be turned into a weapon. The silver. Glass. The steel mirror. Even the chair. He had gone through her trunk, searching even through personal garments to her great humiliation. He had been thorough.

She was left with a bed nailed down and several pieces of clothing remaining in her trunk. Surprisingly, he had left her small box of jewels. He had seemed not to care about them. At least not now.

She sat on the bed. The cabin had been a refuge during the first days of the voyage when the first mate had eyed her with such open lust. Now it was a prison for the condemned.

Juliana tried to block her memory of the mutineer. *His eyes.* If they truly revealed the soul, she could not expect mercy. She'd been mesmerized by them days ago, much as she'd heard a person could be by a cobra. Now that she saw them more clearly, nothing dampened that fear. It was difficult to describe them by color. Light brown mixed with gray and a moss green. But the shades were eclipsed by an intensity that sent shivers down her spine.

How had he taken the ship? She didn't doubt that he was responsible, that he was the leader. All had deferred to him despite the greed and lust in their faces. Even the Spaniard obeyed, and she doubted whether he bent to many men.

What crime had he committed to bring him to this ship?

She shuddered to guess. Her uncle had called them criminals, murderers and infidels. They had proved they were murderers. What else had they been? Or what had her uncle turned them into?

The last thought was truly chilling. She remembered the scarred backs, the thin, wiry bodies. They would have no pity for a Mendoza, not when no one had had any pity for them.

She knew only one thing. She would never see home again.

"*Madre,*" she whispered. Would her mother ever learn what had happened to her?

She paced, then sat, then paced again. *Think.* There had to be something she could do.

Drunken laughter came from outside the cabin. The sounds sent new waves of terror through her, and she saw Carmita cower, a whimper coming from her mouth. With all her heart, Juliana wished she had brought someone else with her. Someone older who had already lived long years, someone who had known love.

If only she still had the dagger.

That thought led back to her thrust hours ago. How badly had she wounded the leader?

Would he want his revenge?

Her comb. The pins for her hair.

Could she use those to defend herself? Or would it serve only to infuriate the mutineers more?

Yet it was not in her nature to wait meekly. Her mother had submitted meekly. She would not. She rummaged in her trunk for her box of hair ornaments. She had placed the pins there last night when she had braided her hair for the night. She couldn't remember the Spaniard taking them, but then she was comforting Carmita part of the time. She found the box and opened it. Jeweled combs lay on top of the pins.

She was puzzled that he had not taken the combs and the jewels, but perhaps that would come next.

It didn't matter now. All that mattered was that he'd left the pins, probably thinking them innocent enough. A woman's vanities. She took them out and laid them on her palm. Ten pins, half of them studded with tiny sapphires.

Long. Not very sharp. But better than nothing.

She looked down at her garments, aware again that she was still in the nightdress and robe she had donned when her uncle had fetched her a few hours ago.

A few hours?

More like a lifetime.

She undid her braid, and her hair fell around her face. She looked at Carmita. "I need your help."

Carmita sniffed and stood.

"Arrange my hair so I can take out the pins easily," she said.

Carmita's eyes widened. "You would not attack them again?"

"I will do what I have to do," she said.

Carmita's hands shook as she took a comb and ran it through Juliana's long hair, then started twisting it into a knot, using the pins to hold the heavy strands in place.

More than enough pins.

"Now help me dress," Juliana said, glancing up at her young maid. The girl's tears had dried.

"Which gown, senorita?" Carmita asked.

"The blue one."

"The best one?" Carmita asked in a shocked voice. It was to be the one Juliana was to wear when meeting Viscount Kingsley and his father, the English earl.

"*Si.* I will show them no fear."

"They will ravish us. Then kill us." The tears were back.

Juliana put her arms around her. "God will protect us," she whispered, hoping with all her heart she was right.

In case He didn't, she would have the pins.

"WHEN can we have the women?"

Patrick stopped pouring salt water over his body. He had washed off as much blood and filth as he could, but he thought with dark humor it would take weeks—mayhap years—to finish cleansing himself.

He straightened and turned toward the oarsman who'd just spoken. Four others flanked the man, giving their support.

Felix had sat in front of him on the bench. He was a thief, if the brand on his face held true.

"You won't," he replied curtly.

"Keeping them for yourself?"

"Nay," he said. "But the women will not be harmed."

"No orders anymore. No one tells us what to do now," Felix asserted. He was obviously spoiling for another fight.

"Nay? You prefer being back on the bench?"

"We voted. We want our turns with the women."

"Who voted?"

"Us," the oarsman standing behind Felix said in a rough voice.

"Ah, *us*. And where do you think *us* is going without someone who knows how to sail this ship?" Patrick said softly. "You want to go ashore in Spain with that mark on your face?"

Felix touched the scar. "We been gone from Spanish waters these few days."

"We are a few miles off the French coast," Patrick said softly. "You think they will welcome a branded Spaniard?"

"We do not take orders now. We are free."

"Believe that and ye are a fool," said the MacDonald from behind Patrick.

"*Si,*" added Diego, moving to Patrick's side. Denny, who had been his shadow since the takeover, joined them.

Fury crossed Felix's face.

"It is time for talk," Patrick said. "I want everyone on deck."

The men who had confronted him stood their ground, belligerent.

Diego seemed able to communicate best with most of the oarsmen. Patrick turned to him. "I want everyone but those guarding the women and the captain's cabin up here."

Diego hesitated, glancing at the rebellious oarsmen. Then he looked back to Patrick, his eyes measuring the Scot and Denny. Finally he nodded, but not before casting a warning look at the rebellious men.

"We should have a vote," grumbled one of them.

"*Si,*" said another.

"Do you want to captain this ship? Do you know navigation?" Patrick challenged them. "Do you know how to raise and lower a sail, or turn a ship? Know how to avoid rocks and shallows?"

"Looks easy enough," Felix said.

Patrick stepped back. "Take the wheel."

Felix stepped out and sauntered over to the wheel. The ship was already bearing to the right without a hand steadying it.

"You are going toward France at the moment," Patrick said. "In an hour you will see the hills. In another five, the ship will break up on the rocks. Turn the ship back into the wind."

Felix took the wheel. He couldn't move it. After struggling for several seconds, it started to turn. "What . . . where do I . . ."

"You decide. To the north are English warships. France is to the northeast. Both would hang mutineers. Or worse.

"Or," he continued, "you could just head out to open sea until the wind dies and supplies disappear. The ale will be gone as well. You will die of thirst. Or starvation. This ship is not provisioned for a long voyage."

The ship listed starboard. His companions, already unsteady from spirits, slid toward the rail and grabbed a rope to keep from going overboard.

Patrick took the wheel back and straightened the ship. "There is too much sail for the wind."

"What gives you the right to be master?" Felix tried to reestablish his standing among his comrades as more and more of the oarsmen came on deck and stood uneasily. Some staggered. Two were still in their loincloths.

"I have sailed before," Patrick said, refusing to take offense. None of them really knew each other despite being confined together for months, in some instances years. "Two years learning navigation and the sea. I have never captained a ship, though, and I would be willing to sail under any man here who has."

Diego joined him as the last of the oarsmen appeared on deck. He repeated the words in Spanish, and then in halting Arabic. Patrick repeated them in French.

No one stepped forward.

"We are mutineers in the eyes of the world. 'Tis no matter that we were slaves, many unjustly. All countries fear mutiny on their ships. No country will welcome us."

"Where do we go then?"

Now it came. "Scotland. I propose that we sail to the shores of Scotland. My family there owns ships. We will sell the cargo, then scuttle the *Sofia*. Our ships will take you wherever you want to go with enough gold to keep you in rum and women for years."

He waited as his words were translated. Some nods. Some frowns. Some expressions of agreement. Some of angry rebuttal.

"The women," one pointed out. "If they live, they can tell what happened."

The men were right. That was the dilemma that had plagued him since he found them in Mendoza's cabin.

"I swear they will not."

"How can you do that?" asked the man who had taken the wheel.

"My life is as much at risk as yours. I will not release them until I am absolutely sure. If not, then . . ."

He left the threat dangling in the wind, then quickly changed the subject. "How many have served aboard a ship as a sailor?"

Three men stepped forward. To his surprise, Felix was one of them, although it had been obvious he'd never handled the wheel before.

God help him. Only a total of three had any experience at all, other than rowing.

"Can anyone help the blacksmith?" he asked.

No one came forward.

"Cook?"

Two raised their hands.

"Fishermen."

One stepped forward.

"You've repaired nets?"

"Aye."

"Now you will repair sails."

One by one he discovered talents, or lack of them. Those who had none he asked to serve as apprentices to someone who had a skill.

"We haven't agreed on a captain," Felix complained. "Nor have we agreed on the women."

Diego stepped forward then. "The women can bring

money. And protection. Papers show the woman is meant to be the bride of a wealthy English lord," he said. "If anything goes wrong with the Scot's plan, we have her to bargain with. The English would pay for her freedom. But not if she has been spoiled."

Patrick was startled at Diego's intercession. He'd heard some of the crew talk about pirating. Mayhap the prospect of treasure could keep the oarsmen from raping the two women. Diego was proving to be a man of many talents.

"As for captain," Diego continued, "you would not be free if not for this man. Many of you saw him kill Mendoza. He is a warrior and he knows navigation. We need him. I suggest we name him captain and accept his offer."

"Aye," the MacDonald agreed.

"How do we know he has what he said in Scotland?" persisted Felix.

"Spaniards will not be welcome in Scotland," said another.

"You will have to take my word," Patrick said simply. "It is all I have."

More translation. More mumbling among the crew.

"We will have to work together," Patrick said. "You will have to learn to sail. You will learn skills. There could be places on our ships if you need work." He prayed silently that the Macleans still had ships. Or that the family, as he knew it, even still existed. He was making promises he might not be able to keep.

He would solve that problem when he returned home. *If* he returned home.

"I say we follow the man that freed us," someone said in French.

A translation, then a chorus of agreement.

Felix was silent but Patrick saw the displeased expression on his face.

"It will mean discipline," he said. "I expect orders to be obeyed."

Heads nodded.

"The first is to ration the food and wine. Some of you

who ate too much are probably feeling sick now. Eat small amounts until your stomachs are used to food again. You can eat all you want the rest of your life, but you must be careful now."

A few reluctant nods of agreement.

"You will often work as hard as you did on the benches. You may have to row again if we lose the wind."

He heard grumbling. "There is no other choice," he continued. "I promise you that you will not row as slaves. There will be no whip. You will not be chained or forced. And, if we make it . . . you will be free."

The grumbling subsided and Patrick saw grudging acceptance.

"Diego," he said, indicating the man next to him, "will be my first mate. He looked at Felix. "The MacDonald will be quartermaster. Felix will be second mate."

Felix's scowl gave way to a surprised grin.

"Does anyone here know about stores?"

A hand went up when the translation was made. It was a man of obviously Moorish descent. He was a man who had every reason to hate not only Mendoza, but every other man aboard the ship.

"Choose someone and ration the food."

Felix stepped forward. "What do I do as second mate?"

"Enlist those willing to work on the sails. We need men healthy enough to climb the rigging."

A few moments later, the men dispersed to perform various tasks. Diego glanced at Patrick. "Felix?"

"He's a leader. Better to have him on our side than his own."

Diego smiled. "This will be an interesting voyage, senor."

AFTER Patrick satisfied himself that Diego could keep the ship steady and on the course he'd plotted, he went below.

The women would be terrified. The older one was defiant

but she hadn't been able to hide her fear. The other, little more than a child, had obviously been struck speechless with fear.

He told Diego to ring the ship's bell if he was needed, then hurried down to the captain's cabin. He found a bottle of wine miraculously overlooked during those first moments when the oarsmen entered. Clutching it in one hand, he went to the cabin that housed the women. Manuel and two other men sat cross-legged, playing dice.

Manuel scrambled up.

"Sit back down, lad," Patrick said in Spanish.

He knocked, then turned the knob and entered without awaiting an invitation.

Mendoza's niece—Juliana, according to Diego—stood defiantly. She had changed from the nightclothes she'd worn earlier. The gown was an elaborate one, a royal blue that made the most of her eyes. Another act of bravado. Of defiance. He saw the battle in her eyes now, making the violet rings even more startling.

"Juliana Mendoza?" he asked the woman.

"Si," she said. "Carmita is only a child. I beg mercy for her."

He thought immediately that she had probably never begged before. "None for yourself?" he asked.

"Would it do any good?" she asked in Spanish.

"It might," he replied in the same language.

"You speak Spanish," she observed.

"Not by choice."

He saw by the way she flinched that she heard the bitterness in his voice.

He saw himself in her eyes. Though he had washed blood away with saltwater, he was naked from the waist up and his wet breeches clung to him. He knew his back was a mass of scar tissue, and he hadn't taken time to wash his beard or hair. He suspected she remembered the blood splattered over him several hours ago.

"You did not answer my question. Would you beg for

mercy?" It was a cruel question, but he was disturbed by his reaction to her, by the way heat had started to rise inside him. The snug trousers became even tighter.

"For Carmita, or myself?"

"Both."

Her face flamed. Her hand went up to her hair and he noticed the pins there.

He reached out and took them from her hair, causing it to fall in wavy ringlets nearly to her waist. "Nay, lady. You will not have another chance to wound me or my men."

"*Your* men?" she asked.

By all that was holy, she was lovely with her hair flowing down her back and her eyes sparking.

"Aye," he said coldly. "I have control of the ship." *Keep a distance.*

"What have you done with the crew?"

"Sent them to hell," he said grimly, "if there is any justice."

"All of them?" she said in a horrified voice. "No one lives?"

"After months of beatings and starvation, the men were not feeling merciful," he said.

Her hands trembled, the only sign she was terrified.

She followed his glance and buried her hands in the folds of her skirt. "What of Carmita?" she asked in a soft voice. "She is but a child."

"What, senorita, would you do to protect the girl? I assume she is your maid."

"She is my friend, and my responsibility, and I would do a great deal to protect her."

"Lie beneath me?" he taunted. He did not like the attraction he had for this spawn of the Mendozas. "It has been a long time since I have had a woman, much less a lady of rank."

Her face paled.

"Would you, lady?" he persisted. "It was easy enough to sink a knife in me. I seek repayment by sinking something of my own in you."

He was immediately shamed by the comment, but her coolness—even contempt—had spurred it.

He moved toward her. She didn't flinch. "Murderer." She spat.

"You are not helping your young friend's cause. And it is not murder when you are fighting for your life. 'Tis your uncle who murdered. Over and over and over again."

JULIANA forced herself to return his stare. She was determined not to show the terror she felt, but she feared the trembling of her hands might well do it, instead.

She would not give him the satisfaction of seeing more.

Her heart had almost stopped when he entered the room and she saw it was the tall prisoner who had killed her uncle. Her blood ran cold.

Despite the fact he no longer wore the loincloth that had revealed so much, his wet breeches revealed far more than she wanted to see. And though most of the blood was gone, she remembered it all too well.

El diablo! His eyes were as soulless as before.

He held a bottle of wine in his hands.

She struggled not to show fear even as he insulted her and mocked her and tried to frighten her.

Tried? Holy Mother, he succeeded.

She quickly raised her gaze to where a piece of cloth had been wrapped around the wound she'd inflicted. Other pieces of cloth were wrapped around his arm. Then her gaze went to the bottle in his hand.

"I should live," he said, acknowledging the gaze, "unless it festers. That would be most unfortunate for you since I am the only one standing between you and a hundred bitter and lustful men."

She did not answer. Instead she couldn't take her gaze from the heavy scarring around his wrists. The trousers were not long enough for him and she saw similar scarring around his ankles. Like before, his chest was uncovered, but now there was no blood to cover the scars.

"Can you sew?" he asked unexpectedly.

"Si."

"Then you will sew up the wound you inflicted.

She started at that. "There is a doctor onboard." Then her mouth tightened in grim line. "You killed him, too?"

"Not me, though I would have liked that honor. There's a lad outside. The doctor used him in not very pleasant ways," he said, watching as realization reached her eyes.

He stepped to the door, opened it and glanced out. "Manuel, fetch some water. Heat it."

"I have . . . never attended a wound," she said when he finished speaking.

"If you can sew, then you can do what is needed." He paused. "Remember what I said. Only I stand between you and the crew. And I will stand there only if you make yourself useful."

Her back straightened. "Useful?"

"I will find various ways, senorita. Can the girl cook?"

The woman shook her head. "She is a lady's maid."

"I . . . used to help in the kitchen," Carmita stuttered, obviously taking his words to heart.

His gaze turned to the girl and he softened his voice. "No harm will come to you," he said softly. "I swear it."

Then he turned back to Juliana. She was painfully aware he had not included her in that oath.

He untied the bloodied cloth from around his chest. She had to suppress a shudder when she saw it. Had she really done that?

"Manuel, the lad I mentioned, is bringing some hot water. You have sewing needles and thread?"

She turned to Carmita, who carried the small sewing box to fix any small rips. "Carmita?"

Carmita stood, wavered slightly. "The man who brought us here took it with him."

"There must be someone with more knowledge about wounds," Juliana protested once more, a note of panic in her voice.

"Nay," the devil said. "I wish *you* to do it." His cold eyes bored into her as if he could see her soul. "And I would recommend you doing your best."

His tone sent shivers through her.

A knock at the cabin door was a welcome respite. The Scot opened it and the slight lad she'd seen several days earlier entered, placing a bucket of water near the door. Like her captor, he had scars around his ankles, and his eyes were nearly as cold.

"Manuel, ask the Spaniard where he put the lady's sewing kit and fetch it for me."

"*Si,*" he said.

After the boy left, she gazed at the Scot. "You are the leader?"

He bowed slightly. "At the moment."

"You have the advantage. You know my name. How?"

"The Spaniard found the marriage papers in your uncle's cabin. Ah, to wed one of the most important families in England. I am doubly blessed to foil those plans."

"You have not told me your name."

"Nay, I have not," he agreed in English.

She responded before she thought. "Why? Had you blackened it before becoming a mutineer and pirate?"

He smiled and she realized she had made a mistake.

"So you do speak English."

"*Si,* some," she responded.

"Why pretend otherwise?"

She shrugged.

"Do not to lie to me again," he said harshly.

She said nothing.

"I would also advise you not to anger me at this particular moment," he added darkly.

He went to her trunk and selected a white chemise. He tore it into strips, then opened the bottle of wine. She tensed.

Instead of taking her, though, he poured the contents of the bottle on the wound.

He did not even flinch, though his face hardened to where it could have been a marble statue.

Juliana shivered. She saw a muscle jump in his throat,

and knew the pain was probably agonizing. He turned slightly and she saw his back, the deep scars. Some old. Some obviously recent. Very recent. She had not seen them before. He'd been too covered with blood. His own and that of others.

What had he done to deserve such punishment? Her uncle had said the galley slaves were criminals. Murderers.

Yet this man was no common murderer or thief. He spoke well and appeared a leader, one strong enough to keep a mob from ravishing Carmita and herself. Was he saving them for himself?

She guessed he was Scottish from the burr in his voice, though he also spoke Spanish. His face and eyes gave nothing away except for that brief, unguarded moment when he'd tried to comfort little Carmita.

He poured more wine into the wound, then took a couple deep sips of what was left in the bottle.

The lad slipped inside the door again, carrying the small box with Carmita's needles and threads.

"Should I stay?" the lad asked.

"Nay." A faint hint of softness in his voice again. "Get some food and clothes."

The boy looked up at him as if he were a saint. "I would rather stay, sir," he said in rough Spanish. "She might stab you again."

Juliana bit her lip against hysteria. This small lad protecting the devil?

The devil looked down at him and one side of his smile crooked into a half smile. "Aye, lad," he said. "Ye may stay."

Juliana took the box. She had worked on tapestries. It had been one of the womanly skills forced upon her. But human skin? A shudder ran through her body.

She looked at the lad. "Can you hold the skin together?"

The lad looked at the man she consideredel *el diablo.*

"Si," her captor said, and the boy pulled the skin together as Juliana pulled thread through the needle's eye.

She said a silent prayer, then stuck the needle through

his skin. He didn't move, didn't even flinch. She looked up and his eyes were fixed on something in the far distance.

In and out. In and out. She had to wipe away blood as she worked. Then she was done. He looked down at her workmanship. Nodded.

"The other two now," he said, motioning to his arm.

Again she sewed. Despite her fear of him, she felt his pain with each stitch and wondered how he bore it so stoically.

Then she was finished. He had her tie a strip of linen from her underdress around his chest, then his arm. He stood, and she followed.

She could not take her gaze from his face. Though covered with a red beard, it was lean and hard and merciless. All angles, she noted. He was probably suffering horribly, but neither his face nor his eyes reflected it.

What would happen now?

He surprised her by going to the door.

"I have a ship to sail," he said.

"To where . . . ?"

"That is not your concern," he said.

"It is," she protested.

"Be content to be alive," he said.

Then he left her to ponder that statement.

PATRICK thought he was used to pain.

It was humbling to find he wasn't. Or mayhap it was the loss of blood from the injuries on his arm and chest, but he stumbled as he returned to the captain's cabin and studied the charts.

The ship seemed to be sailing well enough, but if they encountered a storm . . .

He had many lessons to teach, though he certainly was not a master mariner himself. He could but hope for fair weather or they all might be doomed. Either way, it was a fate no worse than what they could have expected from the oars.

At his father's insistence, both he and Rory spent two years at sea. Trading had been the clan's livelihood for nearly a century. Patrick had not loved it as his younger brother had. Rory had a feel and love for the sea that Patrick did not. The sea had assuaged his brother's loneliness. It had deepened Patrick's.

Loneliness had left its mark on each of the three brothers Maclean. They all had different mothers, and each one had died within a few years of marrying their father. The old laird had been unable to find a fourth, all the eligible women and their families being all too aware of the Campbell curse that decreed no Maclean bride would live long.

Patrick, like his youngest brother, had vowed not to marry and perpetuate the curse, and had, instead, turned his energies toward war, where he sold his services. Only Rory had married, and within a year he had lost his wife in childbirth. His youngest brother planned to go into a monastery, but his father had prevented that. Instead, Lachlan had retreated into books, much to their father's anger.

Patrick had watched Inverleith sink into gloom and despair, and his father refused to give him any authority to combat it. In frustration, he left, the last meeting with his father explosive.

Do not think of the past. Nothing could change it. Only the future could be changed. Freedom lay only days ahead if he could remember enough of what he'd learned during those two years at sea.

Concentrate. Remember the lessons learned so many years ago. Remember the stars, the navigation tools. A hundred lives depended on those lessons.

Hours later, he felt the rhythm of the ship change. A surge in speed. He put the charts back down and went topside. The sun's last glow was diffused behind clouds of crimson and gold. A treacherous beauty, like the woman below. He'd hoped for stars, not clouds. He might be able to navigate by the former.

Diego was at the wheel, looking relaxed there. Patrick suspected that many things came easy to him. His speech, his knowledge of language, his quick understanding of what needed to be done, told Patrick that Diego was no ordinary oarsman.

"Senor," Diego said, "the wind seems to be quickening."

Patrick agreed. The sea seemed rougher as well. The last thing he needed now was to confront a storm with an inexperienced crew. As much as he wanted to sail as far away as possible from the Spanish coast, they had to trim sails and strike the topsails. The sailing lessons would begin now.

He sent a man after Felix. He might as well learn now how well his makeshift crew took orders.

To his surprise, Felix appeared almost immediately with a group of men behind him. He and one other man nodded when Patrick asked if they knew how to trim sails. Felix and the men followed Patrick's instructions as they practiced.

Not quickly, not even competently. But they got it done. Patrick gave the wheel to the Spaniard, who had appeared back on deck and climbed up in the rigging to secure the sheets, hoping those below were watching and learning.

When Patrick returned to the deck, he was met by Felix.

"We did well, me and my mates," Felix boasted, his pride at his status clear on his face.

Patrick nodded. "Aye," he said. "You did, but we will have to work faster. A storm is brewing. Teach as many as you can to handle the sails."

Felix paused, shifted from one foot to another. "I . . . well, should not have . . . questioned . . ."

"You had every right. You are a free man now."

"You really meant that we can go anywhere we want when we reach Scotland?"

"Aye," he said. "I will do my best to help."

Felix nodded, accepting the words. Again, Patrick hoped he could fulfill the promises he made. *Let there be a family left. A clan left. Ships.* The *Sofia* rolled to the leeward side, and he took the wheel. "Get some rest," he ordered Diego.

Diego gave him a hard stare. "What about you?"

"After you."

"We need you awake," Diego said.

"I want to get home," Patrick said simply.

"I heard about Flodden Field," the Spaniard said. "What if there is nothing there now? What about the promises?"

"My family has an uncanny way of surviving. The men, anyway," Patrick replied dryly. "I meant it when I said I would help every man who helps me." Then he went on the offensive. "You said you had not sailed before. You have."

"Have I?" Diego asked, raising one eyebrow.

"Aye, no one could take the wheel as you did without having done it before."

"A small smuggling bark," Diego said. "A coastal vessel. Nothing like this. And I wanted to see how good you were," he added without apology.

"You were a smuggler?"

"Among other things."

"Navigation?"

Diego shook his head. "We followed the coastline."

"Is that why you were sent here? Smuggling?"

Diego shrugged without answering.

Patrick was not going to pry. He had his own regrets. He asked only because he had to know what skills were available to him.

"Do you really believe we can make Scotland without detection?" Diego asked.

"Did you really think we could escape those chains?" Patrick asked in return.

"You are saying nothing is impossible."

"Aye, I have to believe it."

"How much sailing did you do?" Diego asked.

"Two years, and that was more than ten years ago."

"As a captain?"

"Nay. Not even a mate. I was there to learn. My father owned several ships. He thought all of us should learn about the ships and trading. I was a reluctant student."

"But you learn well, I think. I thought you made a mistake with Felix earlier, but he is surprising me."

"He's a troublemaker," Patrick said. "But he will now fight to keep his authority and to prove he should have had it earlier."

Diego shook his head. "I wouldn't have taken that chance." He paused, then said, "You said *us* earlier."

"Aye, I have two brothers."

"Will they agree to your grand plan to help a ship full of mutineers?"

"I am the heir. My father is laird, contrary as the devil, but he will honor the word of his son."

"When did you leave?"

"More than eight years ago. I spent one year fighting with the French before being taken by the Spanish."

"They say many Scots died a year ago on the border."

"My father would have been too old to go and in too poor of health. One of my brothers wanted to go into the church, and the other captained one of the ships. He hated Inverleith."

"Inverleith," repeated Diego. "It has a fine sound to it."

Patrick didn't reply. Inverleith was a fine place if not for the feud with the Campbells and the bloody curse that had haunted generation after generation.

He adjusted the wheel slightly to make the most of the wind. The Spaniard lingered, and Patrick understood. He wanted to be sure, or as sure as possible, that going to Scotland was a good choice.

Diego glanced down at the linen bandage around Patrick's waist. "Someone made a pretty bandage." There was a question in the statement, though not a direct one.

"The Spanish woman sewed the wound."

"And the cloth?"

He hesitated, then said, "Her chemise."

The question persisted in the Spaniard's eyes.

"She and her maid are unharmed."

"You are more courageous than I. I do not believe I would allow her around me with a needle."

"I was prepared this time."

Diego's eyes hardened. "If they live . . ."

"I know. Everyone on the ship will have a price on his head."

"The older one . . . she is *muy bella*."

"She is a Mendoza," Patrick replied.

"*Si,* but she looks more English than Spanish."

Now that Diego mentioned it, Patrick had to agree. The light hair, the blue eyes and pale skin—all spoke of England.

Even if she were part English, it would change nothing.

She was a danger to every man on this ship. So was the wisp of a lass with her.

He had lived with that every moment since he discovered them. What rotten, bloody luck. There shouldn't have been passengers. Not on a slave ship. What had been so bloody important about this marriage?

The Earl of Chadwick's son. The heir apparent.

He tried to remember if he'd heard the name mentioned before. Something tickled in the back of his mind. *Chadwick.*

"Have you eaten anything?" Diego asked.

Patrick welcomed the interruption. He didn't want to think of the fearful women in the cabin below. He didn't like the fact that he had probably deepened that fear even more.

"Nay."

"I will have someone bring something. There is bread, better than what we had, even some fruit."

"Fruit?" Holy Father, but how long it had been since he'd last had fruit. He had feared losing his teeth to scurvy.

Diego's lips turned into a tight smile, or as close to one as Patrick had seen. "Fruit," he repeated.

"Aye, bring me some." He paused, then added, "Have Manuel take some food to the women. He's the least threatening."

"*Si,*" Diego replied.

"Then get some sleep. Take the first mate's cabin. I will send someone for you when I tire."

Diego raised an eyebrow. "That should not be long."

"You haven't had any more rest than I have."

"I am not sure of that. I saw that exchange between you and Manuel. How long had you planned this?"

"He mentioned a few weeks ago he might be able to get the key from the blacksmith. Then he was able to steal a few drops of a sleeping potion from the physician."

"He paid a price for it," Diego said softly, and Patrick realized he, too, had been aware of Manuel's life.

Patrick only nodded. He suspected Manuel had to pretend, had to fool the doctor into believing him harmless.

Diego left, and Patrick concentrated on the wheel. Felix and the other two oarsmen who said they'd been sailors moved around him, showing others how to work the sails and tie knots. Others were washing blood from the decks.

He stood, his feet braced against the deck, once more relishing the feel of the wind. He hadn't felt it in too many years. Even the clouds gathering above couldn't dampen the pure exultation of being his own man again.

But something about the Spaniard nagged at him. He gave very little away, and Patrick realized he had extracted more information from Patrick than he had given.

Was he an ally or merely biding his time to see how events went?

Exactly how much seamanship did Diego really have?

Even worse, he really didn't get a sense of what the Spaniard wanted to do about the women.

But then he didn't know what to do with them, either.

The image of the two women deviled him again.

Later. He would worry about that later.

WHEN the door to her cabin opened again, Juliana's heart jumped. She and Carmita exchanged glances.

Hours had gone by, and Juliana decided to pass the time by teaching Carmita a few English words. Juliana feared that if something happened to her, Carmita would be helpless.

She despised the fear that bubbled inside her, the remembrance of the hard, cold eyes of the leader.

But instead of *el diablo*, the boy named Manuel entered, his hands carrying plates of food and a pitcher.

"*Capitán* Maclean said to bring this to you."

"*Capitán* Maclean?" She could not stifle the mockery.

The lad glared at her, put the tray of food down and turned to go.

"Wait," she said, knowing she'd made a mistake.

The boy hesitated.

"You were not an oarsman?" she exclaimed.

The boy ignored her.

"Do not go," she implored, hating the sound of begging in her voice, but she desperately needed information.

He turned, his eyes going to Carmita.

Juliana didn't like that expression, as if he knew something they should know, but didn't.

"Thank you for bringing the food and drink," she said softly.

He simply ducked his head in recognition.

"Please stay," she pleaded.

"I have other duties," he said stiffly.

"And I am a Mendoza," she said softly.

"*Si,* senorita."

"You were an oarsman?" she asked again.

"I am too small," he said. "I had other duties."

"I have not seen you much since I came aboard," she tried again. "Before the . . ." Her voice trailed off.

The boy gave her a joyless smile that tore at her heart. "You did not go below," he said. "You did not go into hell."

And he left.

Chapter 10

YOU did not go into hell.

The hopelessness of the words echoed in the small cabin as the boy closed the door.

She was a Mendoza. She was beginning to realize the complete misery on which her family had built its fortune, a fortune that now depended on a marriage that would never take place.

No wonder the oarsmen hated her and, because of her, innocent Carmita.

To think that once she believed the arranged marriage was the worst that could befall her!

Juliana looked at the food, her appetite gone.

"You do not wish to eat, senorita?" Carmita asked. "It has been more than a day since you last ate."

A day. In little less than twenty-four hours, her life had again changed dramatically.

Did the mutineers know how to sail the ship? Would it

shatter on rocks, or would they sail until all aboard died of thirst? Would she and Carmita die far sooner? Or would they suffer an even worse fate at the hands of desperate men?

Juliana sat down on the edge of the bed and tried to think. Carmita would not eat unless she did. Perhaps an ordinary activity like eating would calm the young girl.

"You sit as well," she instructed Carmita. "You must eat with me."

"I cannot, senorita," Carmita said in a horrified voice.

"We are here together," Juliana said. "We must both be strong if we are to survive." The boy had brought them a jug of wine as well as cheese, fruit and bread that had not yet acquired mold. It *had* acquired some bugs.

Juliana pushed aside the bread and took a piece of cheese. She nibbled on a small piece while thinking about what could be done. There was always a chance that when they did not arrive on schedule, the Earl of Chadwick would alert outgoing ships to look for the *Sofia.*

"What will they do to us?" the girl asked, as if reading her mind.

"If they meant harm they would already have done it," she tried to assure her young companion.

"The tall man frightens me," Carmita said.

"El diablo," Juliana whispered. He had frightened her, too, although he had protected her when the ship was first taken. He had killed her uncle without any regret.

"The Spaniard . . . he did not seem too . . . fierce," Carmita ventured hopefully.

Juliana wished she could agree. Despite his indifferent courtesy, she sensed the same barely restrained violence in him as she saw in the fearsome Scot. There was something about the Spaniard's control that frightened her even more than the Scot.

And could anyone really control the crew? There were many barrels of fine wine aboard as cargo, along with a cheap wine for the crew. She shuddered. She and Carmita were the only two living witnesses aboard a ship full of drunken mutineers.

* * *

THE wind increased through the late afternoon. By evening they were caught by a gale. The ship rose and fell as the untrained sailors tried to strike the topsails and raise the storm jib.

Controlling the ship was becoming more and more difficult. Diego returned to the helm and took over. "Do you know how to handle the sheets?"

"Aye, I used to," Patrick replied.

"I know this sea and its weather," he said. "I smuggled wine from France and lace from Spain." He paused, then added with a slight smile, "French wine is far better than that Spanish swill. Apparently, the English are just as uncivilized in their tastes if they are buying from Spain."

Just a bit more information than Diego had offered earlier. Patrick knew enough about trading to agree, but he was far more interested in the fact that Diego probably knew these waters better than he did.

A blast of wind hit the sails and the ship listed before Diego was able to right it.

Patrick looked upward. Bulbous clouds sped across the heavens, eclipsing the stars. A squall of rain struck several furlongs off the bow, and they were running toward it.

He felt the first drops of rain, then the water came down in torrents. One sail tore partly loose and flapped in the wind.

He had to tie it down before they lost it. That meant climbing the mast.

He'd hated climbing into the crow's nest when he served aboard one of his father's ships. It was the first time he'd been terrified. But he had to do it to prove to the rest of the crew that he was not just the owner's son.

It had been calm that day.

Now the ship tossed violently, lurching from one side to the other as the sails swung out of control. He could well be flung into the sea.

He started climbing, never looking down. He clung to

the rope, ducking once as the sail swung against the mast, nearly toppling him. He continued to climb.

Rain and wind whipped at him. The ship heeled to port. He hugged the mast with both arms to keep from falling.

He didn't know what time it was, but the sky was dark. The rain fell cold and hard, but he was far too used to deprivation to let it deter him.

He forced himself to climb again. He made the mistake of looking down. Felix was staring up at him. Diego was looking directly ahead, his body braced against the wind and his arms straining to keep the ship running before the wind.

He grabbed for one of the sheets that fluttered in the wind.

Missed.

Try again. One hand held the rope ladder. He reached out for the sheet with the other. He caught it, but it ripped away.

Another gust of wind sent the ship heeling to starboard, and the sail began to tear. That would doom them all. They needed every sail to get to Scotland.

Scotland.

He reached out again. This time he grabbed the sheet and started to pull it in. Every inch took more strength than he thought he had. Finally he'd pulled it to the mast and tied it down. Then he leaned against the mast.

Don't look down.

God's blood but he was tired.

And frozen. The rain mixed with the frothy sea whipped at him. His feet felt wooden.

Step by step he descended. His feet finally hit the deck. Even rolling as the ship was, the deck felt like a gift from the gods.

The relief did not last long. He worked with the others to complete the trimming of the sails as the ship seemed more like a wooden toy batted back and forth.

When they finished with the sails, Patrick told the crew to tie lifelines to everyone on the top deck. They had been at sea during storms before, but previously they'd been anchored by their chains. None had ever walked a sopping deck with towering waves washing over them.

Fear was evident in their faces.

The wind howled. Lightning pierced the water not far ahead, and thunder roared like volleys of cannon. Then lightning hit the foremast and seemed to trail fire to the deck. One of the crew went down. Patrick ran over to him. He was dead. He lifted the body and took it inside. Unlike the bloody Spaniards, he deserved a proper burial at sea.

A Frenchie, he recalled. On the ship for mayhap two months. Not long. Despair settled in the pit of his stomach. What if he had done as the others wanted and headed toward Morocco? Sell the cargo and buy more cannons? Take up pirating?

He had talked them out of it by making promises he might not be able to keep. Now they all might die because of it.

JULIANA held Carmita as the contents of the maid's stomach went into the pail that Manuel had left for them.

She could couldn't even see the pail. All the lights had been quenched when the storm started. The danger of fire was too high. In between Carmita's heaving, they held on to each other and the bed to keep from being thrown from one side of the cabin to the other.

Would it never end?

At least it kept the oarsmen's attention away from them. Which horror was worse? Being taken by the oarsmen or drowning in a freezing sea?

Her own stomach seemed stalwart. But then she had eaten only a bite or so. Carmita had eaten even less.

"Senorita . . . you should . . . not . . ." Carmita tried before she started to heave again.

"Nonsense."

The ship rolled again, so far to the left that she thought they must topple into the sea.

Carmita screamed and clutched at her.

Juliana wanted to comfort the young maid, but her terror was just as strong. Any words of comfort would be a lie.

The ship righted. The fury from outside came through the timbers. She heard the waves thunder against the hull. How could the *Sofia* continue to withstand such battering?

The ship rose again, then dropped suddenly.

Carmita started praying again. Loudly.

Juliana rolled against a wall. She prayed, too, then added a few Spanish curses she'd heard her father utter.

By the Holy Mother, she was not going to die like this. She simply would not.

THE storm subsided as dawn came.

Gray crept through the clouds. The winds lessened, though they still blew strong. Exhausted men dropped where they'd stood.

Several had been wounded by loose sheets and objects sliding along the deck. One of the ship's boats had torn loose and injured three men. One man was missing, probably lost at sea.

Patrick surveyed the moaning men lying on the floor in the surgeon's cabin. He knew a few rudimentary things to do, but there were too many needing help. Kilil, the Moor who had shared his bench, had taken over the surgery and was doing what he could in binding wounds.

Then he thought the women might help. Mayhap it would do two things. Add more hands to tend the wounded when the rest of the crew was near dead from exhaustion, and give the men a reason to respect them.

He was desperate for sleep, had reached the end of his endurance. Since the takeover, he hadn't slept at all. Diego had slept only for a very few hours.

All of them needed to keep their wits.

His side was bleeding again, reopened by the stretching and pulling of the past few hours, but his wound was minor compared to some of the others.

He went down the steps to the women's cabin. Manuel was dutifully still there, sitting outside. His head lolled from side to side. He was asleep.

Patrick knocked on the door, waited a moment, then went inside without waiting for a response. It was obvious one had been sick, and he soon realized it was the young girl. Her face had a greenish tinge, and her dark brown eyes looked bloodshot.

The other woman, the Mendoza, had her arms around the girl. A Mendoza with a soul.

Mayhap.

Or mayhap she was using the girl as a shield.

"The storm?" she asked uncertainly.

"Over. For the moment."

A shudder shook her body, but he did not see tears. He had yet to see them.

She stood. She still wore the dark blue gown, but her hair was pulled back in one long, thick braid. Her face looked wan and tired.

She was also coping far better than he believed any other woman of his acquaintance would do. She obviously feared for her virginity and her life, and that of her young companion, but her back was rigid and her chin set and her eyes determined. Admiration rushed through him.

She glanced down at the wet and newly bloodied bandage. "You have opened the wound."

"Does it matter that a slave bleeds?" he asked.

Her face reddened. "It matters if anyone bleeds," she said shortly.

"The oarsmen wish your uncle had felt the same way."

"He and the crew paid for it, though, did they not?" she said.

He had to grudgingly respect her defiance. She did not

cower despite the signs that she was very badly frightened. Instead those tired eyes sparked with outrage.

"They tried bloody hard to kill us," he defended himself.

"Some of the crew must have tried to surrender," she persisted.

He shrugged. There was no point in reminding her that the oarsmen had been starved and beaten for months and, in many cases, for years. They wouldn't recognize surrender.

"You did not want witnesses?"

He tensed. She was confronting the fact that had nagged him since he found the two women. She was right. He did not want witnesses. But he knew it was not in him to kill women.

Nor to see them killed.

He was one among one hundred. He was not sure how long he could keep the others from rape and more murder.

"You slaughtered them," she persisted.

"They would have slaughtered us. I suspect you would have preferred that," he added with bitterness.

"Nay," she said slowly. "I would not want any man to die."

"But given a choice?" he retorted.

"I had no choice."

"Your wealth, that dress you wear, are the fruits of the labor that killed countless men. They died of exhaustion, starvation, whippings. Then they were rolled off the ship for the sharks."

"I did not know."

"Or care."

"I do care," she cried out. "I know it was terrible, no matter what you did, but . . ."

"No matter what I did," he repeated softly. "What do you think I might have done, Senorita Mendoza?"

Her mouth trembled slightly as she sought an answer. To her credit, she did not dissolve into tears.

Then she finally spoke. "My uncle said you . . . they . . . were criminals, murderers, infidels."

"You would see men die in agony because they did not embrace the same religion as you?"

She shook her head.

"It was battle. Our lives against theirs," he said, wondering why he was trying to justify his actions. "I fought for the French and was taken prisoner by a Spanish nobleman. He sold me to your uncle when ransom was not paid."

Her unusual eyes searched his for the truth.

"Over half the oarsmen are prisoners of war sold for coin to your uncle," he continued. "Honorable men, many of them, but made into animals by your uncle. Expect little mercy from them."

Her face looked stricken.

"We need help with some injured men," he said. "You did well enough with me yesterday."

"Is that a request or an order?"

"I do not make requests."

"I will do it." Her fingers knotted into a fist. "*For them.* Not because you ordered it."

"Aye, you will," he said. "You owe every man here. You and your family. We were rowing because you were hurrying to a rich marriage," he mocked. "You and your fine clothing." He couldn't keep the bitterness from his voice as he remembered those last strokes of the whip. On both Denny and himself.

He had to maintain that anger. She was entirely too appealing, despite being Mendoza's niece. He did not want to admire her. He did not want his body to react in treacherous ways, nor to feel the hot stirrings he had suppressed these past years.

Too long without a woman's body.

She stepped back from him. He wasn't sure whether it had been his words or something in his eyes. "I had no choice in the matter. I did not wish to go to England. I was forced . . ."

He stared at her for a moment, looking for the truth, but then it really did not matter. The only thing that mattered at the moment was keeping her alive. Getting more of the crew on her side. "Manuel will take you to where the injured are."

"Carmita is coming with me? I . . . I do not want to leave her alone."

"She can go. Manuel will stay with you. If there is any trouble he will come for me."

Her eyes closed for a moment. *"Gracias."*

"Do not thank me," he said shortly. "You should not have been aboard this ship. You are a complication. Try not to make yourself more of one."

He had turned to go when she asked, "Who are you?"

He turned back to her. "On the ship? I was One. That means I lasted longer than anyone else. After me there is Two, Three . . . One Hundred arrived the same day you did. He might have lasted longer than the man he replaced, which was a little less than a month."

Shock filled her face, widened her eyes. He wondered whether she believed him or not.

It doesn't matter, he told himself.

"You are a Scot," she said.

"Aye."

"How . . . long to be . . . One?"

"Nearly six years to my count," he said. "Before that I rotted in a Spanish dungeon for a year."

"I cannot do anything about that," she said softly. "I wish I could. Words mean nothing, I know. I will try to help where I can."

Regret in the soft voice sent frissions of heat through him. He did not see a lie in her eyes. He wanted to touch her cheek. It looked soft. It had been so long since he had touched anything soft. . . .

He fisted his hands into a fist. *They* weren't soft. They were knotted with calluses.

Bloody hell, but he was going weak. The worst thing he could do was to touch her. He had forbidden her to the rest of the crew. He would lose any control if they thought . . .

He turned toward the door. "Manuel will be outside. We have a shortage of clean cloth to bind the injuries. Tear your chemises and bring them with you."

Her face flared red.

"And anything else we can use," he added. "I will be making sure that you do." He purposely made his voice harsh. Bloody hell, but he wanted her terrified of him. He wanted her to do exactly as she was told. It might be the only way to save her.

It astounded him how she stood up to him, asked so many questions. She was intelligent enough to want to know her enemy. Or was she just waiting for a chance to take his dagger, to try again to plunge it into him?

"How many are injured?" she asked.

"Ten."

"Does that include you?"

"Nay."

Her gaze went down to his shirt that had turned pink from blood and rain.

"Will you be there?"

He shrugged. "Mayhap."

He turned around and went out the door. He'd wanted to linger much too badly. To erase the memory of the stench of the rowing deck by smelling the rose scent of her. Even more, he wanted to ease his sore body into hers.

Manuel was waiting by the door.

"Take both of them to the surgery," he said. "They will help the injured."

"Si," the lad said. He looked as weary as Patrick felt, but he knew there would be precious little sleep for any of them in the next ten or twelve days.

"Stay with them. If there is any trouble, come for me."

"There will be trouble," the lad predicted.

Patrick knew he was right. There would be trouble, and he wasn't sure whether his plan to alleviate some of the hatred against Mendoza and his family would work. Was he wrong in thrusting the women among them, hoping that some of the crew would see them differently?

If not, he would soon have another rebellion on his hands. He didn't even know how far he could trust Diego and MacDonald.

His hold was tenuous at best. If the crew felt they could sail the ship, they might go with the Moors who were urging them to turn to piracy. If they didn't learn, then another storm might well kill them all.

This one nearly did.

Inverleith.

It seemed as far away as ever.

Chapter 11

JULIANA was able to breathe again as the door shut behind the Scotsman.

His presence filled the room. Even after he left.

The anger was all too obvious in his reply when she'd asked who he was.

Just "One."

But everything about him screamed he was far more than an ordinary Scot. From his speech and obvious natural leadership, he was probably a noble. And he'd said a ransom had been asked. That meant his family was known to have wealth.

Why hadn't they paid the ransom?

A shudder ripped through her as she relived the quiet rage and barely suppressed violence in his voice.

She'd expected the worst when he'd entered. Sweet Mary, she'd expected the worst from the moment the mutineers took over the ship. She thought she would die during the storm, knowing that the ship was in the hands of slaves.

Surprisingly, she and Carmita were still alive. Still untouched. She didn't know how long that would last, but she would grab every moment she could.

She also welcomed the idea of keeping occupied rather than waiting in this cabin for whatever fate awaited them. If she and Carmita proved their worth, then perhaps they would be set ashore somewhere.

A faint hope, but nonetheless a hope.

She wished she understood more of the tall Scot. She'd seen a flash of something like lust in his eyes, but he had not acted on it. Instead, it seemed to anger him.

"Carmita, help me sort what can be used as bandages," she said to the girl.

"Do we have to leave the cabin, senorita?"

"I think we will be safer if we do. If we help . . ."

It was obvious from the look on Carmita's face that she did not agree, but nonetheless she rose from the corner into which she'd tried to blend during the Scot's presence and knelt next to the trunk.

Her new dresses spilled out. How enraged her father would be if he knew what had happened to the dresses he so hastily and at great expense had provided for her wedding.

He wouldn't particularly care what happened to her, except for the loss of the union with the Earl of Chadwick's son. But her mother . . .

The first tear fell down her cheeks. She had tried to hold them back. They would not accomplish anything but to give satisfaction to the barbarians who had murdered the entire crew. She thought of her mother and the fact that the woman would have no more hope; it was more than Juliana could bear. Would her *madre* ever know what became of her?

Juliana wiped the tear away and willed no others to follow. She saw Carmita's quick glance and tried to explain.

"I was thinking of *Madre*," she said, trying to relieve Carmita's new apprehensions. "I miss her."

"*Si*. I, too." She bit her lip. "There is no one to mourn me."

"There will be no need to mourn," Juliana said with more conviction than she felt. "If they were going to do anything, they would have done it. We must now make ourselves valuable to them."

Carmita shuddered. "I do not know how."

Juliana reached out and clasped her hand. "I do not, either, but we will learn together."

Minutes later they had torn her five chemises and several underdresses into strips. She prayed it would be enough. Then she tried the door.

It was unlocked.

The boy, Manuel, stood straight against the opposite wall. Slight. Terribly young to have taken part in murder. But she knew he had. Just as all her captors had.

"The *capitán* said I was to take you to tend the injured," Manuel said.

She didn't try to argue that she knew little about tending wounds of any kind, much less challenge his description of the Scot as *capitán*.

She followed him, Carmita at her side.

The surgery was crowded. It was little more than a large cabin. About the size of her uncle's cabin. It had six cots, and now all were full, and several men were on the floor. A man splattered with blood seemed to be acting as a physician.

He was olive-skinned. A Moor, she knew instantly.

He regarded her with open curiosity.

"I . . . the Scot thought I could help," she said.

"Any are welcome," he said.

"Are you a physician?"

His smile was thin. "No. But I have experience with wounds." He spoke in heavily accented Spanish. He paused. "Do you?"

"No. I can stitch, though, and I learn fast."

"Then we begin."

"I am Juliana," she said. "This is Carmita."

"My name is Kilil," he said. His eyes were dark and unreadable. Neither friendly, nor hostile. Just . . . hard.

"What can we do?"

"A leg is smashed. I must cut it off and burn it. The upper leg should be tied off as I cut so he will not bleed to death." His gaze never left her face, and she knew he was testing her.

She nodded, not knowing whether she could bear the man's pain. But her life might well depend on it. As well as Carmita's.

He nodded to two men who were in the background. They lifted a man onto a table. The wounded man moaned with pain as Kilil examined the mangled leg.

She winced. The leg was ripped open and a bone was protruding from a large gaping wound. Her legs barely held her. It was not the lack of courage on her part, at least she hoped not. It was the man's agony.

Kilil gestured with his head toward a table. A box lay on its top as well as several bloody instruments. "Medicines."

She opened the chest. Most of the bottles contained herbs she recognized. She knew herbs. Her mother loved gardening and had her own herb garden. There were also two bottles that contained a powder she did not recognize. *Opium*, according to piece of paper tied around the container.

Opium.

She had read about the powder. It came from the east and was rare but very valuable in Europe. It lessened pain. It was also said to destroy people.

The Moor looked at her with that inscrutable stare that was unsettling.

"There is opium here," she said. "I have read about it. A very small amount can cut pain. And I can make a poultice for the wound."

Kilil looked down at the man writhing on the table and nodded. "Make the mixtures," he said.

Juliana found a jug of water and a tankard. She mixed

a small amount of opium with water, then helped the injured man drink it as Carmita held his head. He tried to spit it back up.

"No," she said softly. "It will help."

He grabbed her hand. "Do not let the infidel take my leg," he said.

She saw the Moor stiffen.

"He wishes to help you," she said.

"I would not be a man."

"Si," she said softly. "You will. Do you not have a family waiting for you? A wife? Children?"

The man quieted. Then she saw his eyes begin to close.

The Moor ran his fingers along a saw. The two men who had quietly watched now stepped up and grasped the injured man.

Then the Moor tied a piece of rope around the leg and showed her how to release and tighten the pressure.

Then he started to cut.

Despite the opium, the man bucked against the hold on him and screamed. Everything in her wanted to turn away and run. The sound of the saw on bone went straight through her, cutting a swath of pain as if she herself were feeling it. Every one of her nerves screamed with every crunch of bone.

"Loosen the rope," the Moor said.

She did as he asked, even as the body on the table shuddered, trying to escape the pain.

Then he collapsed and went still.

The Moor, still emotionless, finished. Then he gestured toward a piece of linen on the table. He cut several pieces and pressed it against the wound, then gave a larger piece to Juliana. "Sew a cap around the stump," he said.

He did not wait for an answer but went to the next man. Juliana fitted the linen around the pad and stump. To her surprise, Carmita was next to her, holding the cloth together as Juliana stitched.

The next few hours flew as she held the hand of a mutineer as Kilil tied a piece of wood to the man's arm to hold it steady. She stitched cuts and tied bandages around limbs. She held the head of one man as he died and sang a short Spanish lullaby to him. Then she looked up and saw the Scot in the doorway. He was watching her intently.

The loose shirt he wore was pink with rain and blood. He entered the surgery, and Kilil approached him. He took off the shirt, and the bandage around the dagger wound looked scarlet with fresh blood. Kilil cut it off.

"It must be burned," the Moor said, surveying the wound, which had been ripped open sometime during the storm.

The Scot didn't blink. Only nodded his assent. The man who'd lost a leg had been moved to the floor. The Moor pointed to the bloodstained table and the Scot sat.

She watched as the Moor heated a knife.

She put some opium in a cup and added water, then offered it to him.

"What is it?"

"Opium," she said. "It will help the pain."

"Nay. I want nothing that will dull my brain."

"That is foolish."

"Mayhap it is."

She looked for a piece of wood and found one. She offered it to him, and he took it. He didn't flinch as the Moor took the knife from the fire and approached him.

To her surprise, she thrust her hand into his and held it tight as the knife hit skin, sizzled. The Scot bit down hard on the wood and his hand tightened around hers so forcefully she feared he would break it.

The smell of burning flesh mixed with that of blood as the Moor drew the knife away.

The Scot's body shuddered, then stilled. The grip on her hand gave way and she lowered her arm to her side.

He started to move, then stopped, but she didn't hear a sound from him. The self-control amazed her.

One of the men helping the Moor stepped up and offered him a cup of what looked like wine. The Scot did take that and drained it.

His gaze caught hers again. His eyes were lined with

exhaustion and pain, and for the first time he appeared vulnerable. But that impression was fleeting. He stood, nodded to the Moor. He took a step, leaned against the wall for a second, then continued through the door.

Though he had uttered few words, the intensity of what had just happened still crackled in the air. She realized she'd barely breathed during those moments. Her heart pounded again.

Bringing breath back into her lungs.

Not because of any other reason.

She turned to the next patient.

HER touch had electrified him. He hadn't expected her to offer her hand. More than her hand. She had offered something else that had affected him as nothing had before.

She had offered part of herself to relieve his pain.

God, but she had looked appealing as she sang to a dying man. Patrick leaned against the door and was mesmerized with the softness, the sweetness, of her voice.

Her gown had been bloodstained and damp. Clumps of hair had escaped her long braid and hung limply alongside her face. Yet she'd appealed to him more than at any other time. When she turned toward him, there was a look of caring on her face. She wasn't there just because he'd ordered it.

That startled him. Astonished him, in truth. The last thing he wanted now was to admire her. He had enough complications. Holding the crew together long enough to reach Scotland, then to do what had to be done. He tried to remind himself she was the blood kin of a family who made their fortune from the blood of others. But her face in the flickering light had been anything but venal. There had been true compassion.

When their gazes met, he'd felt an entirely different heat than that which touched his body. A more dangerous heat, he knew. He had grown used to pain. He knew how much he could take. He also knew that he had neared the limit.

Which is why he had accepted her hand. And probably almost broke it.

He returned to the captain's cabin and lay down on the bed. He'd told Diego that he would take a few hours to rest. God knew he would not have to try hard.

THE wind blew hard and the ship fairly flew across the water, toward Scotland. Two days had passed without sight of another ship.

Patrick stood at the wheel. Diego was finally getting much-needed sleep. One Moor, a man named Gadi, stood by him. He had asked to learn. Patrick suspected he wanted to learn navigation for his own reasons, but Patrick needed all the help he could get, and refusing the request could further raise the suspicions of the Moors.

He knew they were angry. They, quite naturally, wanted to head to their own countries. He suspected that only the fact that there were more Spanish, Scottish and French prisoners on board than Moors prevented them from trying to take the ship themselves.

He understood why. Patrick was taking them to a Christian country, and why should they believe they would be treated any better there than in Spain? They had been fighting Christians most of their lives.

Only the fact that few of them had any sailing ability had stayed their hands. But for how long?

He gave the wheel to the Moor, watched his concentration as he held the *Sofia* steady. The wind blew clean and strong, filling all the sails. They would make the Hebrides in five or six days if the wind stayed true.

He looked at the sun. It was his guide at the moment, until the stars appeared and he could better judge their position.

But what if he was wrong? If he made a mistake? They could wander the seas until they ran out of food and water.

He glanced around the deck. The crew, this ragtag group of nationalities, were teaching each other what skills they knew, sometimes by sign rather than speech. Then his gaze caught a flutter of skirts.

His thin shoulders straight, Manuel stood at the railing with the Mendoza lass and her maid. They were his charge and he was doing his duty.

Patrick left the helm and walked over to them. The eyes of both women were wary.

"We came up for air," Juliana Mendoza said defensively. "Kilil said I might."

"He says you have been useful in the surgery."

"Little more than comfort, and I am not sure anyone wants comfort from me."

"They will take help from any who offers it. They are not so used to it."

"They needed a real surgeon," she said with a spark of anger in her eyes. "Perhaps you should not have been so quick in killing him."

"He never helped the likes of us," Manuel interjected bitterly, then stalked away to another part of the ship.

Her gaze followed the boy, then returned to Patrick. Her eyes were wide, surprised.

"The surgeon used him in ways you might disapprove," he said.

"No!" He had said it before but she hadn't believed him. "My uncle would not permit . . ."

Patrick shrugged. "Believe what you will. But the surgeon was not the only one." He paused, then said in a tightly controlled voice, "You should not be out here. There is still much anger."

"I needed some fresh air. Kilil . . ."

"Kilil is not the captain."

"And you are?" she challenged him.

"It appears so. At the moment."

"At the moment," she repeated softly.

He stiffened. "What have you heard?"

"Mumbling."

"You had better pray that it was no more," he said.

"Why? You are no better than the rest," she countered.

"Aye, I agree," he said. "But far better than the likes of your uncle."

She turned away from him, and to his surprise he saw her shoulders shaking. To his greater surprise he found himself reaching out to her. He put a hand on her shoulder.

A jolt of heat ran through him. She jerked and turned around, her eyes widening. They were glistering with unshed tears. Devil take it, but he wasn't prepared for the sudden hesitation of his heart. It just . . . paused for a few seconds, then started beating all too rapidly.

God help him, that had never happened before. For a moment he stopped thinking at all. His hand did not move from her shoulder. Instead, he wanted to take her into his arms and wipe the fear and uncertainty from her eyes.

He took a deep breath. He had been celibate far too long.

He took his hand away. "If you are not in the surgery," he said roughly, "you and your lass should stay in the cabin. 'Tis dangerous here."

But her gaze held his for another minute or so, and, mesmerized by the violet that ringed the silvery blue-gray of her eyes, he almost lost his ability to reason. What in the bloody hell was he doing?

Her back stiffened, and he saw from the flash in her eyes that she felt the bright flash of attraction—nay, more than that—that so violently assaulted him. She took a step back and her hand went up as to ward against a physical blow.

A princess. A Spanish princess. And he was so recently a slave and now a mutineer.

He muttered an oath and stepped away.

"Stay in your cabin," he ordered again as he tried desperately to feint the arching need in him.

This time he did not wait to see if she obeyed. He turned around and returned to the helm. He felt as if a hundred eyes were watching him.

And her.

God help him but it was going to be a far longer journey than he'd imagined.

JULIANA'S legs barely carried her to the hatchway and down the steps. She had to steady herself with a hand against the wall.

Carmita was behind her. Silent as usual. Manuel had taken up his post as their guard.

She was stunned by the magnetism of the Scot, by the pure need that had skittered along her nerve edges and settled in her stomach. An undefinable but powerful craving seemed to take control of her body. Her mother had told her about the ugliness and pain of coupling, but she had said nothing about these strange, turbulent feelings that ran amok inside.

Nor the way she'd longed, for a moment, to run her hand along his heavily muscled arm and settle it in the large, callused hand.

She reached the cabin and went inside, waited for Carmita to join her, then stood at the door and regarded her young guard. "I am tired," she said. "If I am needed, I will come, but . . ."

He nodded. "I will bring you something to eat." He turned to go.

"Manuel?" she stopped him.

"Si?" He turned to face her.

She looked at the slender lad. His dark eyes belonged to someone much older. There was altogether too much knowledge there. "Do you not get any rest?"

"I am free, senorita, and no one will touch me again. That is all the rest I need."

So the Scot had not lied.

She closed the door softly and leaned against it.

She could not undo what her uncle and father had done, but now she understood some of the hatred she saw in the eyes of the oarsmen.

She was not going to ask any more questions about what brought any man to this ship. She was already becoming leaden with guilt for her father's and uncle's sins.

Her father!

What would he do when he learned the ship—and his daughter—were missing? It might be months before he realized she had disappeared. Probably not until he and her mother arrived in London for the wedding.

Would he grieve? Try to find her? Would he take out his disappointment on her mother? That was her greatest fear.

The ocean was a vast place. The ship could have gone down anywhere. No one would know except for those now on the *Sofia*.

That reminded her more than ever of the jeopardy she was in. Ironically her fate seemed to be mostly in the hands of a man who hated her family, who had killed her uncle and probably many more.

A man who also stirred new and heated feelings inside her, feelings she'd never known existed.

Feelings that she suspected could lead her to far more dangerous places than she'd ever anticipated.

Chapter 12

PATRICK stood at the helm, gazing up at the moon and the thousands of stars that sprinkled the sky. It was after midnight on the sixth day since taking the ship.

It was easy now to chart a course by the stars. Home was a few days' sail. Reaching Inverleith had gone from impossible to possible to likely. It had been in doubt so many times, including during the last few days as the ship passed through the English Channel. Fog had been both a blessing and a hazard. The *Sofia* was invisible to hostile eyes, but the persistent fog had presented its own dangers. He couldn't see the stars, nor the shore, and they ran the risk of going on the rocks. He'd taken the ship farther out in the Atlantic until the fog dissipated, then he'd had to turn back against the wind. The crew was still clumsy with the sails and he almost lost the wind.

But earlier that day, at sunset, he had a glimpse of land.

He had not seen Juliana Mendoza in the past day. He

had made sure of that. She aroused feelings that were disastrous. If the crew thought he was taking something denied to them, he might not be able to control them. He still wasn't even sure what should be done with her when they reached land.

He did know he was having feelings he'd denied for years, even before his imprisonment. He'd known from boyhood he could not marry. Unlike Rory, he believed fully in the Maclean curse. There was no other explanation for the string of tragedies that plagued the Macleans.

Now, though, he concentrated on keeping the crew together. He was very aware of the tensions on the ship as the *Sofia* continued north. The Moors gathered in small groups and he heard them mumbling. He knew that they expected to take the ship once they arrived in Scotland.

No matter his promises, they made it clear they wanted no part of another Christian country. Nor did they believe an infidel. Not completely.

"Ye are a natural sailor." The MacDonald's voice interrupted his thoughts.

"Diego more than me."

The MacDonald frowned. "I do not trust him."

"Because he is Spanish?"

"Nay. There is too much he doesn't say."

"We need him," Patrick said. He changed the subject because he had the same reservations. "Have you checked the cargo?"

"Aye. Silks from the orient. Lace. The wine, of course. Small quantities of opium. And you know about that chest in Mendoza's cabin."

Patrick nodded. The blacksmith had broken the lock and opened it to find a small fortune of gold and jewels—obviously the dowry for Juliana. "The Mendozas clearly wanted this alliance badly." He paused, then asked, "Where are the gold and jewels now?"

"Locked securely in the hold," the Scot said. "No one knows of them other than the blacksmith, you and me."

"Except Juliana Mendoza."

The Scot nodded. "She may not know how much there is, though it was listed in the marriage contract."

"Destroy the contract," he said.

"Aye." The MacDonald left him alone again with thoughts that plagued him.

He didn't know who he could trust other than the MacDonald, who wanted to reach Scotland as badly as Patrick. MacDonald had been taken as a hostage after the Battle of Flodden and held for ransom. It was paid, but he was sent to the galley anyway.

The MacDonald had taken charge of the stores and weapons as well as teaching some of the hands how to fire the two small cannons on ship. Though they lost some cannonballs during the storm, there were about twenty shots still available. Not much, but something.

He did not have the same feeling of trust about Diego. The MacDonald wanted to go home. Patrick wasn't sure what Diego wanted.

And Felix. He seemed to have given Patrick loyalty, but Patrick had seen him whispering to the Moors as well.

The few times Patrick slept, the door to his cabin was locked and his dagger and a cutlass he'd appropriated were by his side.

As if the captain's very thoughts had summoned him, Diego slipped beside Patrick.

"My turn at the wheel," he said.

"Not yet."

"You need sleep. You will have to stay at the wheel when we reach the coastline. You know it. I do not."

Patrick hesitated, then asked, "You know there's talk about taking the ship."

"Si."

"And you?"

"I have no desire to be a pirate," Diego said, obviously reading Patrick's mind. "Too dangerous."

Patrick gave him a thin smile. "And this voyage is not?"

"This is self-preservation."

Patrick wondered how far self-preservation would go.

He'd worried from the first day of the revolt that Diego might side with those who wanted to take the ship to Morocco, that he might be biding his time.

"What do you plan to do when we reach Scotland?"

"Accept my share of the cargo and go somewhere far away from Spain. Mayhap to the New World."

Patrick was startled. "Spain is that dangerous for you?"

"There are those who wish my death. They thought to bury me on that ship." For the first time, Patrick heard rage in the Spaniard's voice.

Patrick was suddenly tired. Diego was right. He needed to be fully awake tomorrow as they ran along the Scottish coast.

"Are you sure you will be welcome at your Inverleith?" Diego said.

Patrick didn't answer. He bloody well wished he knew. Or even whether there was an Inverleith now.

"I am the heir," he said.

Diego's eyes met his. "We would not be free without you. I will stand at your side."

Patrick nodded and gave the wheel to him.

He walked to the hatch and went down the steps. He had approached his cabin when he heard a scream.

A woman's scream.

He ran toward their cabin. Manuel lay in front of the door, blood coming from a wound on his head.

Patrick swore under his breath. God help any man who had injured the boy.

The door was locked from the inside. He used all his strength to ram his body against wood, and the door splintered open.

One man held the young lass down while a second was mounting her. Another man was holding Juliana Mendoza, who was struggling to get away. The smell of ale and sweat was thick in the air.

All of them turned toward him as he stood in the doorway.

"Get the bloody hell out of here."

"You ain't our better," slurred one of the men.

"Leave now or I will kill you," Patrick said.

It was three to one, and none of them were in the best of condition. But men who forced women were cowards, and he was angry enough to kill.

His hand slipped to the dagger tucked in a sash around his trousers.

"We got as much right to her as you do," added the man holding Juliana.

"I will not repeat myself," Patrick said in Spanish. These three were not Moors, from which he expected opposition, but obviously true criminals from Spain.

The man holding the young lass let her go and took a knife from his trousers. "We want the women," he said as he lunged at Patrick.

But Patrick had not been drinking and the assailants obviously had.

He stepped aside and the attacker went straight out the broken door, curses rolling down the corridor.

Patrick heard other voices coming from outside the cabin. But his eyes were on the man holding Juliana. The other was trying to pull up his trousers.

He instinctively knew the first was the most dangerous. The assailant released Juliana, tossing her on the bed, and approached Patrick with a cutlass.

He swung it, and Patrick barely evaded the blade. Through the corner of his right eye he saw the second man maneuver around him.

To his shock, he saw the Mendoza lass pick up a metal pitcher and swing it at the attacker with the cutlass. Hard. He didn't have time to think about it, but instead thrust his dagger at the other man. The oarsman went down, the dagger embedded in his chest.

Patrick turned. The leader, the man who'd held Juliana, was trying to stand. Patrick grabbed the cutlass and pressed it against the man's throat. He badly wanted to end the man's life with a twist of his weapon. He needed no more malcontents.

He hesitated just long enough for the man to kick up and try to knock the weapon from his hand. Patrick plunged the weapon down in his chest and instantly it was over.

The MacDonald burst into the cabin, cutlass in hand.

"A wee bit late," Patrick said, breathing hard.

Two men held the man who had plunged through the door. He was babbling. Asking for mercy as his gaze darted between his two dead companions.

"We had . . . the right," he insisted again in a shaking voice.

Patrick turned away from him to the two women. The young lass was frantically trying to cover herself with a torn chemise. Tears poured from her eyes. Juliana Mendoza's face was pale. But there were no tears. Instead, she seemed frozen.

"Take him to the cage," he said, referring to a small enclosed area beneath the rowing deck that was capped with an iron grate. Prisoners were placed there when they were too sick to work.

"No," the survivor yelled. "I fought, too. He has no right," he said, turning to the newcomers for help.

The MacDonald grabbed the squirming prisoner. "I dinna do my job, Maclean."

"Just get him out of my sight," Patrick said. "As well as the bodies."

"Aye, I will do that. The lasses . . ."

"They will be all right," he said roughly, "but I think we need more than a lad to guard them."

The MacDonald directed one of the curious onlookers to take the drunken sailor below, and two others to drag the dead men away.

Manuel!

Patrick went out into the hall. The lad was holding his head in his hands.

"Senor, I . . . tried . . ."

Patrick put his hand on his shoulder. "I know. You will have help from now . . ."

"They *were* help."

Anger drew into rage. A blinding rage. He turned around and looked through the smashed door to inside the cabin. Senorita Mendoza had moved over to her maid and wrapped a shawl around her.

The small lass, Carmita, trembled. He walked over to her, saw the vivid bruises. He uttered an oath. "It will not happen again," he said.

He started to reach to her, and she shrank against the bulkhead as she desperately clasped the shawl. He dropped his hand. "Are you . . . did he . . . violate you?"

She shook her head, her gaze moving frantically between him, the men crowding in, and her mistress.

Juliana Mendoza placed herself between Carmita and him. "You said we would be safe," she accused him.

"Lo lamento."

"Your sorry is not enough. She is a child."

"Aye. You both will move into the captain's cabin. You can lock that from the inside. It has a strong door. Do not open it for anyone but me, the MacDonald or Manuel."

"And you? I should trust you?"

"As much as anyone on this ship."

"That is not much assurance. Murderers. Thieves. Despoilers." She stopped. "You have not told me where we are going."

She would know soon enough. "My home in Scotland. The Hebrides."

"But the others . . ."

"Will have enough gold to go where they wish."

Her back stiffened. "What do you plan for me? And Carmita?"

He was silent.

"I will not speak against you," she offered.

"And why would that be?" he said dryly. "I killed your uncle, stole your ship and all its goods, even kidnapped you. Do you think your intended husband will not believe the worst? And that once free you would not speak against me? And the others?"

"I swear," she said desperately.

"How would you explain your sudden appearance without a ship?"

Her face clouded.

"You are so eager then to go to your intended husband?" he persisted, trying to find something, anything, he could trust.

"Si," she said. But her eyes belied her words. She was stiff with tension, her face full of righteous wrath. There was a touch of fear there, too. More than a touch. It was like a knife slashing through her.

A confusing rush of emotions assaulted him. He wanted to protect her. He wanted to touch her. Devil take it, but he wanted more than that. He felt no better than the three who had intended to rape her.

He took a deep breath. At least he wore the loose seaman trousers that concealed his arousal. He was only too aware his body was reacting just as his mind was. "Take what you need when you move to your uncle's cabin," he said harshly.

He went out the door. The hall had cleared with the exception of Manuel. "Go to Kilil," he said, "and have him look at your head."

"The senorita can do it," the boy said. "Kilil says she is better than him."

There was almost worship in his voice. Patrick raised an eyebrow.

"She is kind," Manuel said, ducking his head.

Patrick didn't want to think in those terms. He turned to the MacDonald. "Tell Denny to join Manuel on watch. Pick one other man."

MacDonald shook his head. "Denny?"

"He killed a man who was threatening me. If he decides someone needs his protection, he will protect them."

"Aye."

"And ask the woman to look after Manuel."

MacDonald nodded. "I will ensure their safety." He hesitated, then said, "And after we arrive?"

Patrick wished to hell he knew.

He simply shrugged.

Problems were multiplying as they sailed closer to Scotland. Part of him thought they would never make it with the oarsmen as a crew. Too many languages. Too many age-old disputes between religions. Too little knowledge about ships. Too little armament if they met hostile ships.

But now that they were within range of Scotland, he had to consider what he was going to do with thirty or so Moors at Inverleith, not to mention the rest of the motley collection of prisoners of war, thieves and probably a few murderers mixed in.

What was he going to do with a Spanish galleon on the Sound of Mull? How was he going to keep a hundred people silent?

And what would his father think about kidnapping two Spanish women, one the intended bride of one of the most powerful families in England?

Simple battle had been far easier.

His stomach in knots, he left the corridor to clear out what few items he'd appropriated in the captain's cabin and move them in with those of Diego.

Then he would return to the helm. He doubted he would sleep today.

Or tomorrow.

BECAUSE of the broken door, Juliana heard part of the conversation. Her stomach had clenched when there was a silence after the other Scot had asked, "And after we arrive?"

She knew the subject was their future—hers and Carmita's.

She had considered taking Carmita and hiding somewhere in the hold. But then she'd heard something about scuttling the ship. She had no wish to go down with it.

Thank Sweet Mary that the Scot came before the oarsman raped Carmita. She was not quite sure why he was protecting them when he'd made it clear they were a danger to him. She still feared his protection was a temporary thing, a whim. That he was pondering some dreadful fate for them.

His eyes were usually so hard. She could read nothing in them.

Yet his anger had been very real when he had attacked the villains who had forced themselves in.

God help her, but he had been magnificent. Something had shifted inside her as he had started so gently to touch Carmita, only to draw back when he saw her fear. For the first time, she'd seen something in those eyes. Regret? No, something deeper.

Then the chill settled inside again.

He was her enemy and she his. Her testimony could condemn him.

And young Manuel as well.

She went over to the boy. Though he had the form of a child, his eyes were nearly as hard as the Scot's.

Her fingers brushed his hair back. The skin was broken and he'd bled profusely. She would need to stitch it and would need Carmita's help as well. The move to the other cabin would have to wait.

So would her fears.

Chapter 13

THE hills of coastal Scotland had never looked so welcoming.

Patrick looked over at the green hills and uttered a prayer of thanks. It was a prayer he hadn't made in more years than he could remember.

At daybreak he'd glimpsed the Firth of Clyde on the Scottish coast and hours later the Sound of Jura. Now Patrick glued his eyes to the coast, watching for the firth that led to Inverleith.

Kilil joined him at the helm. With his neatly trimmed beard, he was almost unrecognizable from the man on the bench.

"We are nearly there?" Kalil asked.

"Aye."

The Moor's dark eyes searched his face. "We have trusted you."

Patrick nodded.

"We want the ship," Kilil stated. "Not only the Moors, but many of the others as well. We would sail to Morocco."

"Think about it," Patrick urged Kilil. "Think what will happen if you take the *Sofia*. You can change her name, but there is no hiding the fact that she is a Spanish galleon. The seas are heavily patrolled approaching Morocco because of piracy, and you have but two small cannons. The crew would not be large enough to combat a storm like we saw days ago, much less an English or Spanish or French warship."

"I know all you say is true," Kilil acknowledged. "But then none of us believed we would reach your country. Freedom and hope are mighty swords."

Patrick knew that was true. And he could not deny to others what he had won for himself. "Do you know enough navigation?"

"We have been learning." He paused. "I hope to persuade the Spaniard to go with us."

Diego was called the Spaniard by nearly everyone. Despite the fact there were other Spaniards aboard, he had become *the* Spaniard.

"He is free to do as he wants," Patrick said. "But for the safety of all, we should unload the cargo and scuttle the ship. Then none of us should mention this again."

"My brothers . . . they want to return home. To our desert," Kilil persisted. "This is not our land. We will not be welcome, even if no one learns about the *Sofia*. We, more than others, may well end up as slaves again simply because we are different." Then he said with more forcefulness, "We are grateful, but we will take the ship. We have learned much these past weeks."

"Not enough," Patrick said softly. "You will never survive the voyage, and I doubt the Spaniard will go with you. He is a practical man."

"We can force him."

"Can you? We almost did not make it here, and I know these seas. He does not." He paused. "I can offer you a better way home."

"I do not understand."

"We are a seafaring family. My father will purchase the cargo and take those who wish to leave to Morocco or the coast of Spain. Each would have an equal share of the cost of the *Sofia*'s cargo."

"You give us your oath?"

"I have not been home for more than eight years. There has been a great battle between my country and England. But if there is a ship left, anything left, I swear you shall have it."

Kilil hesitated. "And if there is not?"

"If I cannot provide passage for you in one of our ships, I will myself navigate the *Sofia* for you," he said slowly. "I will sail you home." It was a painful offer. He would be returning to sea in a vessel he hated. But he could not take his freedom at the cost of freedom for those who had helped and trusted him.

"And the cargo?"

"The cargo should fetch a good price and I think it should be divided equally among you, either in Scotland or in Morocco. I hope the Macleans can purchase all or a portion of the cargo and distribute the funds equally between all the oarsmen. I suspect not all wish to go with you."

After a long moment, Kilil nodded. "You are not like other infidels."

"In truth, at one time I would have said there was nae a good Moor," Patrick shot back. "I have reconsidered."

"A lesson hard learned for both of us," Kilil said as he walked away.

Patrick spotted the entrance to the Firth of Lorn. He gave orders to turn the sail. He would pass Campbell land, although Dunstaffnage, the Campbell ancestral home, was farther down the firth on the Isle of Lorn. Word would travel that a Spanish galleon had sailed through.

He just hoped no one would believe it.

Campbells. Rage rose in him at the very thought of them. They had come close to destroying the Macleans. Were they still raiding Maclean lands?

Did the Macleans still hold Inverleith? Was his father alive still? His brothers?

His stomach churned, not from the sea this time, but from nerves. So much depended on the next few hours. The *Sofia* passed the rock on which one of his ancestors attempted to drown his Campbell wife, an act that had brought misfortune on the Macleans for the past century.

They sailed past Inverleith, the towering keep that overlooked the sound. Despite his lengthy absence, it looked much the same. Had he really expected it to be different? To his surprise, he felt a skip of his heart at the sight of the massive walls and two towers.

He ordered the anchor dropped in a natural harbor several furlongs from Inverleith. The Macleans would have seen them by now. They would be gathering, probably trying to decide how best to confront a Spanish enemy.

The longboat was lowered. Twenty men could crowd inside but he took only ten oarsmen, the Spaniard and himself. He left the MacDonald to keep peace aboard.

Once on land, he knew eyes watched him. The coast was always watched by Macleans. And he most certainly would be regarded with suspicion. He wore the clothing of a Spaniard sailor. He had not had time nor the inclination to shave in the past weeks. He doubted anyone would recognize him as Patrick Maclean. He doubted he would have recognized himself.

His thoughts turned to the women. He tried to think of them as one. Not as a wisp of a girl named Carmita and a slim, brave lass named Mendoza.

He had no more than dismissed the thought of them when he saw horsemen riding toward him. They all wore the Maclean-dyed plaids.

The sight stirred something strong and proud inside him. Mayhap the Scottish heart of Patrick Maclean did beat strong yet.

They stopped, and one of the small band approached on horseback. The air of authority proclaimed him the leader.

"You are on Maclean land. Your purpose here?"

Patrick barely remembered his younger brother. Lachlan had been a stripling lad then, a dreamer with his head in a book. He was no lad now. Nor a dreamer, from the hard set in his face. His brother looked lean and strong, and his blue eyes steady as he regarded the scene before him.

Had Lachlan really changed that much? Patrick wondered.

His brother's eyes narrowed as if trying to place him.

How many years since they had last seen one another? Eight? Nine?

"Do you nae recognize a brother?" Patrick asked softly.

The young man jerked in the saddle. His eyes widened. Then he dismounted with a bound.

"Patrick?" He stared at him for a long moment, incredulity in his eyes. "It cannot be."

"The devil protects his own."

"Nay, not a devil. Mayhap an angel," his brother, Lachlan Maclean, said as he approached, his lips stretching into a broad smile. There was a confidence about him that had never been there before.

"If so, it was Lucifer," Patrick said, not quite certain about the sincerity of the welcome.

Lachlan continued to inspect him for a moment, disbelief in his face. Then he placed a hand on Patrick's shoulder. "God's blood, but we thought you dead."

He looked past Patrick, his gaze lingering on the Moors who had rowed the ship's boat in, then to the Spanish galleon.

"Spanish?"

"Aye."

"A story that needs telling." Lachlan stepped back and studied him again. "But now I must get you to Inverleith." He paused, then added, "I cannot believe what my eyes are telling me. You have changed much, Patrick." His eyes rested on the scarred wrists.

"As have you," Patrick said, his own gaze studying his

brother. Now he saw a slight scar along the side his face. "When I left you were little more than a boy who hated training. I see you have some scars of your own now."

"Aye. At Flodden Field."

"I heard of it. And the others? My father? Rory."

Lachlan went still.

"Fa has been dead since two years after you left," Lachlan said.

"What happened?"

"He was killed in a raid."

"By a Campbell?"

"Aye, but because of me."

Patrick knew he should feel something. Had he been so numbed over the past few years that all his emotions were dead? He should feel sorrow at the death of his father. Instead he absorbed the news silently, almost without feeling.

Mayhap grief would come. Joy at being home again. Emotions seemed alien to him at this moment. He had turned them off for seven years. It had been necessary to survive. He'd swallowed pride, anger, grief. Buried them.

Forever? The thought clenched his stomach. Never to feel again?

His father had been dead all these years, and he hadn't known it. He should never have left. But what was done was done. "I had feared the Campbell slew them all. Or that all had fallen at Flodden Field. The Spanish taunted me with it." He paused. "Was it as bad as I heard?"

"Aye, it was. King James died along with the best of Scotland. We lost many fine Macleans."

"Then Fa was alive when the demand for ransom came?"

"Ransom?" Lachlan's brow furrowed. "There was no demand for ransom. Most certainly it would have been paid."

"It was not. I was wounded and taken prisoner at the Battle of the Garigliano near Naples. A ransom was demanded. My captor said he sent several written demands."

Lachlan looked puzzled. "We received none. Fa would have done anything to have you back. But there were no demands. By God, Patrick, you should know we would have paid it, even if it took every pound we had."

His gaze met Patrick's and Patrick saw no guile in it. No lies. But repeated demands had been made. How was it possible that none had reached Inverleith?

Had his brother become a liar as well as a warrior?

"And Rory? Where was he?"

"He was at sea when our father died. It took two years to reach him and fetch him home. He loathed doing so, but I was of no value to the clan. I was no warrior, and I had little trust. His return turned out well enough, because he found a bride and now has two bairns."

"And what of the curse?"

"That, too, my brother, is a long story and mayhap Rory should be the one to tell it." His gaze ran over Patrick's rough sailor's shirt and pants. "We need to get you back into a plaid," he said. Then his gaze caught the scars around his wrists. Lingered there.

" 'Tis nothing," Patrick said.

Lachlan nodded. Then grasped his arm. "We have prayed for this."

"We?"

"Rory and myself. Fa before he died."

Lachlan put his arm around his brother's shoulder. He was of a height with Patrick but did not have his larger frame. "Come," Lachlan said. "Meet your Macleans and come home with us. Rory is at Inverleith, and he will rejoice at seeing you." He paused, then added, "I have a wife now, a daughter, and a babe waiting birth."

"You always said you wanted to be a priest."

"I did not think I could marry. Or live up to father and you and Rory."

"What changed?"

"Many things. Come now. 'Tis time to get you into an honest plaid. You can ride Callum's horse." Lachlan paused. "The ship? The crew?"

"Are mine," Patrick said to relieve any apprehension. More explanations could come later.

Patrick went to the Macleans on horseback. Each one dismounted and greeted him. Some he remembered, some he did not. He took the proffered mount.

Then he turned back to the men waiting at the boat. "Take the longboat back," he told Diego. "My brothers live, and I will come aboard tonight with news."

"Do you wish me to return to the ship?"

"Aye."

He would have preferred to have the Spaniard at his side, but he was needed more on ship. Strange that he felt more comfortable with the Spaniard than with his own brother. But then Diego had shared hell with him.

Patrick watched as the oarsmen rowed back to the *Sofia*. Then he turned to his brother, who had appropriated a horse from the Maclean named Callum. He remembered a Callum. A towheaded lad then. "Is Jock your father?"

"Aye," Callum said, obviously pleased to be recognized.

"He is well?"

"Nay. I lost him at Flodden Field."

"Och. I remember him as a good soldier."

A slow smile filled Callum's face.

"Come," Patrick said. "Ride behind me."

"I can walk."

"Nay. The horse looks like a sturdy fellow." Patrick mounted and offered his hand to Callum, who swung up behind him.

It had been a long time since Patrick had been in the saddle. Far too long. He looked at the men who surrounded him. They had apparently come to confront whatever invaders had come to their shores. Now they were swinging their horses around him in a gesture of protection.

Too few, Patrick thought. What if he *had* been a Spanish raider with armed brigands?

What if they had been Campbells?

The clan had grown careless while he had been gone. He would remedy that soon enough.

Patrick set the pace, drinking in every familiar sight. He glanced toward the rock that had caused the Maclean so much grief. It was high tide now, and the rock was covered. But he saw it in his mind.

Then he dismissed everything from his mind but the fresh crisp breeze that smelled of heather and the hills dotted with cattle. Timeless hills of tragedy and pain and blood. And too-brief moments of happiness.

Around a curve, and then there was Inverleith.

He was unprepared for the impact. If moments ago he feared he was devoid of emotion, now it hit him. As he neared the stone wall and the towers rising behind it, memories flooded back. Good and bad. Mostly bad. Inverleith had a history of tragedy. He felt his soul bleeding.

He slowed his horse to a walk, all his senses drinking in the sight of the home he'd both loved and hated. The stark rock towers rose in isolated splendor. Despite his longing over the past years of captivity, Inverleith had never seemed home before. It had been a cold, loveless place. Why had he so wanted to return?

Today it did not look quite as lonely as they rode through open gates. Or as bleak. Mayhap because of three bairns playing on the ground with a large dog that looked more bear than canine. Laughter floated in the air. It had been a long time since he'd heard laughter there.

Before he could dismount, Lachlan was off his horse and running to the door. Patrick heard him shout, "Rory," several times before a tall, dark-haired man walked out. The children playing outside stood and stared at Patrick, the newcomer.

Lachlan stood back without saying anything as Rory glanced at his younger brother quizzically, then, following Lachlan's gaze, turned to the man on horseback.

Patrick dismounted and stood next to the horse as he watched Rory's face. The expression changed openly. Puzzlement at first, then stern lips relaxed and creased into a wide smile as he strode toward Patrick.

"Patrick?" His voice was disbelieving.

"Aye, it would appear so."

Rory stood there, emotion roiling in his eyes. "I . . . we . . . have all prayed for this day."

"I did not think you were strong on prayer, Rory."

"You remember that? I did not approve of a God who put curses above prayer."

Patrick did not take a step forward, unwilling yet to embrace a brother he barely knew. They had trained together as children, then as young men, and their father had fostered competition between them, ridiculing the one who lost. And then . . . he could not forget the unpaid ransom.

Rory apparently had no such reservations. He stepped closer, not with the exuberant welcome that Lachlan had offered but with a hand outstretched. "It is good to see you, Brother."

Patrick took it, then looked over the castle and the children. The gloom of years ago was gone. Men were milling around, talking excitedly.

Rory stooped and urged the children to come to him. "This is Audra," he said, introducing the older lass. "She belongs to Lachlan and Kimbra. These two are mine. Maggie is two, and . . . the lad is Patrick."

Stunned, Patrick could only stand there and stare at the boy. *Patrick?*

"Sir?" the boy who had no more than five years asked anxiously.

"This is your uncle, Patrick," Rory said. "You are named after him."

Patrick stooped to the lad's height. "I am happy to meet you."

"I, too, sir," the lad said.

Patrick stood. "He has far better manners than I had as a lad."

"Than either of us," Rory said with a proud grin. "But beware. 'Tis only a temporary pose."

Patrick hesitated, then started to ask the questions that had been plaguing him for years. "You are laird?" he asked.

"Only until you returned home. I always hoped . . ." He

stopped suddenly. "What happened to you? Where have you been?"

"I was taken prisoner by a Spaniard. A ransom was asked," he said, watching Rory's face. He knew what Lachlan had said. He wanted to hear Rory's words and watch his face.

"When?"

"Seven years ago. Mayhap a little less."

Rory looked puzzled. "I would have been at sea then, but I know Fa would have paid anything to have you back. He always talked about how you were the best of us."

"He said the same of you."

Rory gave him a quizzical look. "He always did take pleasure in playing us against each other. That is one reason I went to sea. But he would have paid anything to get either of us back. If for no other reason than the fact that the Campbell had only one son."

Patrick considered the words. His brother was right. His father would never give the Campbell the satisfaction of seeing him lose a son.

"Mayhap he did not receive the message," Rory said.

"Several were sent," Patrick said coldly. "Refusals were returned."

Rory must have seen the suspicion in his face. "Come," he said, "let us speak in private." He turned toward the door and Patrick followed him through the hall to the office Patrick's father had once occupied. The great hall had greatly improved since the day he'd left. Fresh rushes covered the floor and the windows fairly glowed where once they had been coated with dirt.

"Things have changed," Patrick noted.

"Aye, due to my wife."

They reached the room that had served as an office for Inverleith for decades.

Then they stood awkwardly. Patrick had years of bitterness behind him. "Douglas? Is he still here?"

"Aye, he is still steward. And Archibald. But Hector was

lost at Flodden Field." He looked directly into Patrick's eyes. "What happened when the ransom was not paid?"

"I was sold as a galley slave."

Rory paled. "How long?"

"Nearly six years to my count. Mayhap longer. I was the longest surviving oarsman." He paused, then added, "We took over the ship off the coast of Spain. Every last one of us could be charged with mutiny."

"The crew?"

"Dead," Patrick replied flatly.

It was a risk saying that much. A hint to the Scottish crown, to England, and there would be a price on his head. And Inverleith would be his brother's.

Rory nodded, his face inscrutable.

"I have a ship full of Moors and Spaniards and a few French. As well as a Scot. The ship should be scuttled. Do we still own a ship?"

"Three of them."

"Are any in port?" Patrick persisted.

"One is in Glasgow, being refitted."

"Is it ready to sail?"

"It can be," his brother conceded.

"I want it." It was a challenge thrown out. He should be laird, though he knew well enough that the title came by clan acceptance, not by inheritance. Rory had it now. Part of Patrick longed for the warmth he saw in his brothers' eyes, but he had known betrayal too many times in the past years.

"You have it," Rory said simply.

"You do not know why."

"It does not matter. They are more yours than mine."

A gradual warmth started to fill him. Mayhap he had been wrong about Rory. And his father. "I promised to take them where they want to go. Most wish to go to Morocco. I also told them we would buy the cargo to pay those who choose to go home on their own."

"Then it will be done."

"Once we destroy the ship, they must have a place to stay."

Rory raised his eyebrows them. "Moors at Inverleith?"

"Aye. I would not be alive without them."

"Then they are welcome."

"There is a rich cargo," Patrick said.

"What is it?"

"Fine silks and lace, mostly. And Spanish wine. There are some jewels intended as a dowry. Some gold coins. We can transfer the goods here, then load them on one of your ships."

"*Our* ships, Brother," Rory corrected.

But even with his assent, Rory frowned, and Patrick realized the idea of scuttling a ship was abhorrent to his brother. Rory loved the sea, and it was hell on earth to Patrick.

"We can all be hanged as mutineers if anyone learns what happened. Every man aboard knows that. They wanted to take the ship and turn to pirating, but the *Sofia* has only two small cannons, and only a few know much about sailing. We almost did not make it here."

Rory raised his eyebrow. "If I remember correctly, you hated every moment you spent on the ship."

"A premonition," Patrick said.

A smile tugged at his brother's lip. "Mayhap it was. As for the other, aye, we have funds to pay for the cargo. We have done well with trading."

"There is one thing more," Patrick said.

Rory raised an eyebrow. "As interesting as the others?"

"Two women. A Spanish lass and her maid. They should not have been aboard."

Something flickered in his half brother's eyes. Something like amusement. "Is she bonny?"

"If you like Spaniards," Patrick said cautiously. "She is the niece of the captain of the ship. A man who did not deserve to live."

"You intend to keep her here forever?"

"I donna know," he said, lapsing into the language he knew as a lad. "I just know we cannot let her return to tell what happened, nor do I wish to be responsible for her death."

"How do you know all the others will keep their silence?"

"Because they are as guilty as I for murder and mutiny," Patrick said, watching his brother. He lowered his voice. "No one will risk returning to the life we escaped."

"It will be difficult to keep such a large ship a secret. Someone else might have seen it come up the sound."

"We painted over the name. I hope someone will believe it a smuggler."

"You propose then to keep the lady and her maid prisoner."

"Aye. Until we can decide what to do."

"We have had some experience with that," Rory said, the side of his lips tugging upward. "I will have a chamber prepared. I do not know, though, what my wife will say about it."

"Say about what?" A woman charged through the door like a gust of wind, then stopped abruptly when she saw Patrick. Her gaze went to his beard, the stained clothes, then back to his face. "I heard there was a strange ship. . . ."

She was a slip of a lass with flaming red hair and dark blue eyes that sparkled with curiosity.

Rory pulled her close to him. "This is Felicia, my love and mother of two wild bairns. Felicia, this is Patrick."

Her eyes opened wide. Then she flung herself into Patrick's arms. Against his best intention, he put his hands on her shoulders. To create a wall, he told himself, but she would not allow that. She stood on tiptoes and kissed his cheek. "Rory and Lachlan will finally be content," she said in a voice filled with what sounded like bliss.

He stood totally bewildered. Surely she would not wish to give up her position. But he saw only welcome in her eyes.

She was enchanting. Not beautiful in the accepted manner but full of life and, from the look of her eyes, laughter. She filled the room with pure joy.

"Do not make me jealous, love," Rory said. He moved over to his wife and put an arm around her possessively. "He has two ladies he wishes us to keep captive."

To Patrick's astonishment, Felicia Maclean's laughter filled the halls of Inverleith.

Chapter 14

PATRICK could only back away and regard his sister-in-law with astonishment and mayhap a bit of horror.

Had his brother married a madwoman?

The lass must have deciphered his expression, because the laughter stopped, though the smile in her eyes remained.

"You must forgive me," she said, "but you see your brother held me prisoner here for some weeks."

"Why?"

"His men were looking for a bride for him," she explained. "They thought they were taking Janet Cameron. They took me, instead."

He remembered Janet Cameron as a young lass. He'd even thought about making her his wife until the death of Rory's first wife reminded him of the curse. No woman—none with reason—would wish marriage to a Maclean.

He searched Felicia's face for any resemblance to Janet Cameron's blond hair and delicate features, but there was none. "And who might you be?" he asked.

Rory's arms went protectively around his wife.

"A Campbell," she replied.

Patrick stiffened. A sudden suffocating darkness swept over him as he sought reason from the statement. Hadn't Lachlan just told him the Campbells killed his father? Hadn't they all experienced the devastation to Maclean soldiers and lands over the years? Hadn't they buried enough Macleans who died at Campbell hands? He'd sworn a blood oath against them. As had his father.

And in their absence, his brother had betrayed both of them by marrying one.

The feeling of betrayal seeped deep in his soul.

"A Campbell?" He knew his voice had hardened.

"Aye," Rory said steadily.

Patrick's gaze pierced his brother. "You would betray Fa? All of us?"

"Not betrayal, Patrick. It was time for the feud to end. Time to bury that bloody curse for all time. I did not know she was a Campbell when I fell in love with her, and then it did not matter. She has the bravest and most loving heart of any woman. She saved my life, and Lachlan's. King James himself blessed the union."

"I care not if a king blessed the union." He turned to look back at the lass. She was slender and small, and it was difficult to imagine her saving his brothers' lives. "I am grateful that she may have had a hand in aiding you in some way, but to wed . . ."

"I would have agreed with you years ago, Patrick. But Felicia has won the hearts of every Maclean."

The lass, Felicia, did not move. Did not flinch. The laughter left her eyes, though. "I would like to think your father would be pleased to have grandchildren. Happy ones," she said.

"Fa would not have permitted it."

"Fa did not permit very much," Rory said. "I remember

how and why you left. His hatred harmed this clan far more than the Campbells. Would you wish it to continue until we were all gone and dead?"

Patrick heard the reasoning, but he could not accept it. He had been taught to hate and despise the Campbells since he was old enough to crawl. Almost that long he'd been training to kill them. His family's history was laced with betrayals by the Campbells.

"Do ye remember the last time a Maclean married a Campbell?" he said, lapsing into his Scottish brogue.

"Aye, he disgraced our name."

Patrick felt as if the world had turned upside down. Being taken prisoner by the Spanish had been a known risk. He had been a soldier. He'd accepted the fact he could be killed, maimed or imprisoned.

But this . . .

This was something else. Unanticipated. Incomprehensible. Certainly unacceptable.

"Fa must be spinning in his grave," he said.

"Mayhap," Rory said. "But that is his problem and no longer mine."

"I am the eldest," Patrick said. "I am heir." He disliked the arrogance in his voice, but his mind was spinning from the news.

Rory frowned. "Aye, Brother, and I longed for your return since you left. But things have changed and you cannot turn back events."

Mayhap, Patrick thought. *Or not.* "Someone will be sent to Glasgow immediately for the ship?" he asked, changing the subject.

"Aye."

"And a safe chamber made ready for Senorita Mendoza and her maid?"

Felicia Campbell stepped forward then. "I know the exact one. I will have it readied."

Och, but it was difficult to dislike her. Energy and goodwill radiated from her, and he sensed it was not false. She was obviously eager for him to approve of her because, he thought, she wanted to please her husband. Because she loved him. *A Campbell, by God.*

Patrick merely nodded. She disappeared in a whirl of skirts.

"I will stay on the ship until the unloading is done." He wanted to keep the Moors content to wait for another ship. And, God help him, he did not want to stay under the same roof with a Campbell.

Rory's smile thinned as if he knew exactly what Patrick was thinking. "As you wish," he said. "Fa's room is unused. We will refresh it now, and you will have it whenever you wish." He walked over to Patrick. "We would all like to see more of you."

"You will," Patrick replied curtly.

"I will send word to Queen Margaret that you returned."

"Why would the queen care? James's loyalty was to the Campbells." He paused a moment, then asked, "Does Angus still live?"

"Nay. He died the past year. Jamie Campbell has taken his title."

"And Flodden Field? I heard some news on the galley, but the Spanish were celebrating, and I knew not what to believe."

"King James was killed along with nine thousand other Scots. The best of us," Rory said bitterly. "The king. Two abbots. Nine earls. James's natural son, Alexander, the Archbishop of Saint Andrews. Every loyal family lost their best."

"How? Why?"

"James was no general. The English had longer-range cannons. And James allowed himself to be surrounded because he had too much 'honor' to attack the enemy as they crossed a river. They had no such honor."

"You were there?"

Pain and guilt crossed Rory's face. "Nay. Felicia had just delivered a child, and Lachlan wished to go. He nearly died, and would have if not for an English widow. We lost Hector, as well, and fifty Macleans."

"And the Campbells?"

"They lost many more. They took a larger force."

"I should have been there," Patrick said. "I should not have left."

"Then you, too, would probably be dead, and Scotland needs all her warriors. The king is still but a bairn, and the queen is pulled two ways—by loyal Scots and also by others who believe we must form an alliance with England."

"How many soldiers do we have now?"

"About a hundred trained men. Mayhap two hundred who could fight if necessary."

The number shocked him. The Macleans were once among the largest clans in Scotland. Their number was now one-third of what it had been when he'd left.

He would rebuild the forces.

But now he had to see to the ship. He would get the others home. He would fulfill his promise. He relaxed slightly, even as he could not quite adapt to the information he'd just heard . . . the loss he had to absorb.

"Do you have a plaid I can wear?" Patrick asked. "I tire of wearing these Spanish garments. Then I will go to the ship."

"I would like to go with you and see this ship," Rory said.

"If you wish," Patrick said. "You can bring the women back then. I want them guarded well."

"Aye. Felicia will enjoy the company, as will Kimbra."

"Kimbra?"

"Lachlan's wife. She is an English borderer."

"A *Sass* . . ." His voice trailed off as he saw the warning in his brother's eyes.

Another blow. Surely the devil must have been at work here during his absence. Two Maclean wives: a Campbell and an English wench. Every piece of news was another stroke of the hammer on what he once thought was so predictable. Fight Campbells. Protect Macleans. Fight Campbells. Protect Macleans. Fight the English.

Now his king was dead at the hands of the English, and his brother had married one. *His brother who had intended to be a priest.*

He would leave those explanations for later, though. He knew he had to get back to the ship or face seeing it sail away.

"You can have one of Fa's plaids," Rory said. "They are still in the trunk in his room. I will send a shirt and some fresh water and linens. In the meantime, I will have horses saddled for the women."

Patrick nodded and started for the stone steps that led to the bedchambers above. His head was still deciphering the news he'd received.

"Lachlan lives here as well?" Patrick asked.

"Nay, he is usually in Edinburgh, or captaining a ship. He's here now because we were discussing the purchase of a new ship."

"You were the one that loved the sea."

"Aye, but for the wrong reasons. It was an escape from the bleakness here after Maggie's death. After you disappeared and Fa died, I was called home. Lachlan believed himself responsible for Fa's death and could not seem to stir himself to do anything but compose songs. Inverleith was dying. Campbells were constantly raiding. Our Macleans were leaving for clans that could protect them.

"God knows I didn't want to come back," Rory continued. "Too many ghosts. I do not think you or I had a moment's happiness here as children. Then Archibald and Hector decided to find me a bride despite the fact I had sworn never to wed again. They thought I needed a reason to bring Inverleith back to what it once was."

"By marrying a Campbell?" He couldn't resist the shot. He still could not quite accept what had happened.

"That was the last of their intentions. They thought they were stealing someone else." He stopped, then looked away at a tapestry that decorated the wall. "Remember when we all swore the same oath?"

"Aye," Patrick said. They had been but boys then, and

that was the last time he remembered the three of them joining together. He had been fourteen and far more interested in arms than in foolish lasses. Rory had been ten, and Lachlan only seven, though even then he'd been more curious about books than arms. Shortly after, Patrick had been fostered and trained by another Scottish family. When he returned, his father pitted him against Rory, punishing them brutally when one failed to do the expected.

"I didn't really believe in it then," Rory said. "It was only a legend, and my mother was like so many others who fell to the fever at the time it ran through Scotland. But then my Maggie died. I married again, after you left, a lass named Anne, whom you never met. It was more a marriage of convenience but I learned to care for her. She died of a fever some sailor carried from another port. I swore never to wed again. Two dead brides were enough, as well as our father's three dead ones. 'Twas then I meant the words we spoke so carelessly as children."

"But you did wed again."

"'Tis a long story, and I will tell you when you have more time. But know that Felicia has stolen every Maclean heart, including Lachlan's. She will yours, as well."

"I have no intention of allowing my heart to be stolen," Patrick said. "Not by anyone."

As he strode upstairs to the chamber that once was his father's, he knew he spoke the truth. He had hardened these past six years on the galley when survival was all that mattered. He'd felt an odd aching when he reached Maclean land, but little else. He was pleased his brothers lived, but felt little sadness at learning of his father's death. Or mayhap that would come later. Had his heart so hardened that he felt only emptiness rather than grief? But his father had never been an affectionate or particularly worthy man. He'd allowed his own misfortunes to cloud his responsibilities to the Macleans.

Was he any better? Patrick did not particularly like that nagging question. He'd locked his emotions in stronger chains than those that had physically imprisoned him.

A good thing, he assured himself. Unlike his father, he would be ruled by reason, by responsibility, not by self-pity nor, like his brothers, by his heart.

JULIANA shivered in the cold wind that swept along the sound. This was not her warm, sun-kissed land. Instead, the hills—no, mountains—looked barren and cold. Unwelcoming.

Despair clawed at her. Would she ever see Spain again? Her mother?

She shivered, and Manuel was there with her shawl. Ever since she'd nursed his injuries, he'd been her shadow and declared himself her protector. But could a boy defend her from the muscled oarsmen? That he would give his life to do so was touching. But she did not want his life on her hands.

She glanced down at him. Had any other woman ever shown him the slightest kindness? She doubted it, and her heart ached for him.

It also ached for herself.

Since the Scot left the ship, she had heard the whispers. Different groups of oarsmen huddled in corners. The Moors in theirs, the Europeans in another. Only the MacDonald and the Spaniard kept them from lifting anchor and sailing away.

She looked for Maclean. Villain though he might be, she considered him her only protection. 'Twas obvious he had no love for Spaniards, but he had also made it clear to the crew that they were not to touch either her or Carmita. The question was how long could he hold them back.

Would he take her ashore? She had heard stories about the wild Highlanders who fought their battles naked. She had seen the Scot's fierceness herself.

He had been gone hours now. Worry grew in her. Better the devil she knew than the one she did not.

Manuel went to the railing and stared toward land. "Riders approach."

His eyes were better than hers. She leaned forward and finally saw three figures on horseback, two leading saddled horses. Apprehension ran through her. His family. What would they do with her? They must know, as he did, that she was a danger alive.

She watched as the figures grew larger. The longboat was lowered and six men, one of them the Spaniard, rowed toward shore.

A tall man dismounted. It took her several seconds to see that it was the Scot. But now he was wearing a strange wool garment over a flowing white shirt. The material was gathered at the waist by a heavy leather belt, and even from here she saw the long dagger that hung from it. His legs were bare, but his feet were covered with soft leather boots. His dark hair now showed hints of red as the sun touched it. Her heart caught at the sight of him, at the rugged features now plain to see without any beard.

At his side was a man as tall as he was, but with hair that was as dark as midnight. The third man had lighter hair that carried strains of gold. Both wore the same strange garments.

Despite the difference in their coloring, she knew immediately they were brothers. It was in the way they held themselves, the way they moved. The grace and confidence of warriors.

The longboat beached. The Spaniard leapt from it and approached the Scot. A few words, and both he and the Scot returned to the boat. In a few moments, they were climbing the rope ladder up to the deck.

"Senorita," the Scot said as he easily vaulted over the railing to the deck. "A few words with you."

He smelled of soap and leather and horse, a remarkably heady scent. And while he'd always carried an aura of leadership, even in a slave's garments, it was magnified now. She had never seen a man in such a garment before, but she decided she definitely preferred it to the silk and lace worn by men in Spain.

He touched her shoulder with his hand, turning her toward the hatch. Even through her gown and shawl, his hand burned her. He jerked it away almost immediately. She focused on walking, not stumbling, because her legs did not seem to work properly. He was too close, his presence too strong.

Still, she managed to reach her cabin and open the door before he could. But she was not quite quick enough and his hand landed on hers. She whirled around, their gazes caught and held. Something in her shifted as an almost palpable tension leapt between them. For a second, she could not move. She felt consumed by the power of the storm raging between them, the heat that surged through her.

"Senorita Juliana?"

Carmita's soft, questioning voice broke the spell, and she whirled around to see her friend's clear astonishment, her lips pursed in a circle as her gaze took in the Scot.

Juliana took several steps backward and looked at the Scot again. Despite—or perhaps because of—his new garments, he looked much the barbarian. Something of the savage remained in his eyes, in the athletic grace of his walk, in his hard, determined expression.

He met her gaze, then turned to Carmita. "You both will ready yourselves to leave the ship. You will be staying at Inverleith."

"As prisoners?"

His cool gaze ran over her. "As guests."

"Who cannot leave."

"Aye," he admitted.

"For how long?"

"I donna know," he replied softly.

He looked around the cabin. "I will have all your belongings moved to the keep."

"My dowry?"

"It will be divided among those who labored so painfully for your uncle."

"It will be my mother who will pay," she said. She swallowed a lump in her throat, but perhaps she could make him understand. "My father blames my mother when . . . anything goes wrong."

"Why would he do that when she had nothing to do with it?"

"Why do dogs bite?"

His eyes narrowed, and he frowned. "Is that why you agreed to this marriage? To please your father?"

She looked away from him. His eyes were too compelling. They demanded answers that she did not want to give. "Is that not how many marriages are arranged?" she countered.

After a moment's silence, he continued, "Have you met the prospective bridegroom?"

"Nay, but my father and uncle assured me he is a fine man. And well favored," she added.

"I saw the contract," he said shortly. "Your father did you no favor, pledging you to a man you have not met."

She was humiliated by the comment. And angered. He who had killed so many had no moral status to judge others. Not only that, Scots and English were mortal enemies. Of course he would think the worst of them.

Remember what your mother said, a traitorous internal voice reminded her.

But then she could not bear to think of that last conversation. She did not want to believe or think well of the man in front of her. He was too dangerous. Too deadly. Too foreign to all she knew.

"Pack," he said, interrupting her thoughts. "I will return shortly, and you both will be rowed to shore."

"And you?"

"I will stay aboard until the ship is unloaded," he said.

A shiver ran through her. She knew not what to expect on land.

"My brothers will see to your protection," he said. "You will nae be harmed." He turned and left, leaving a void in the room, as if it had been drained of something vital.

"I do not want to go ashore," Carmita said.

"The ship is no safer," Juliana said. "At least there might be women at Inverleith. Someone who will help us."

Carmita remained standing. "I want to go home."

"We will," Juliana promised. "We will. But for now we have to pretend to accept his . . . hospitality. We will find a way to England. I swear it."

Carmita looked dubious but picked up the nightclothes Juliana had worn and started packing the trunk with her. A gown, the one still stained by blood despite Carmita's efforts, was next. Her brushes and combs. A shawl.

He would stay here on the ship, he said. She was befuddled by the fact that the thought was most unwelcome. She still felt warm from his touch as well as an odd tingling in the most intimate parts of herself. He frightened her and attracted her at the same time. He had from the first moment she had seen him on the bench. That spark of rebellion had struck a chord inside.

What was wrong with her? He was a savage. A murderer. A plunderer. No gentle manners had he.

Yet there was something that radiated between them. Something compelling and irresistible. Or was it only her imagination? He did not even like her. In truth, he despised her for what she was. Spanish . . . betrothed to an English lord.

And she despised *him.*

She kept telling herself that as she and Carmita finished packing and waited for him to return.

Chapter 15

MANUEL stood the moment Patrick left the Spanish lass's cabin.

Patrick paused. "You have done well in protecting them," he said. He had come to have a strong appreciation of young Manuel these past weeks.

But the sooner he got the lasses off the ship, the better. He'd been playing a dangerous game these past few days, trying to hold the crew together. He'd taken a risk leaving even for a few hours.

Now he had to do something that would test the oarsmen's mettle, and he wanted the women safely off the ship.

The image of Juliana's face had remained with him while he'd been at Inverleith despite all his attempts to distance himself from her. The uncertainty and even fear in her face drove directly into his gut. He was too familiar with slavery not to sympathize with her plight. She had gone from privileged lady to captive. He'd been trained to endure whatever came his way. She had not.

Och, but she was reaching somewhere in him he thought dead. He could not let that happen. Even if Rory and Lachlan no longer believed in the Campbell curse, he'd grown up with the certainty of it. He had seen his father's second and third wives die and knew he had been cause of his father's first loss—his own mother. He had lived with the guilt every day of his life.

Patrick was not going to risk a woman on his brothers' assumption. Not that Juliana Mendoza would be interested in a former slave, nor he in a Spanish wench. She would run like bloody hell away from him if she had the chance, even though there was some kind of perverse attraction between them.

It was something he did not wish to dwell upon. He had to keep his mind on the immediate problems. He located MacDonald and the Spaniard, and they went to the captain's cabin.

He quickly relayed the conversation he'd had with his brothers. A ship would be available to sail their companions to Morocco, which seemed to be the port of choice, even for the Europeans.

"They are getting impatient," the Spaniard said. "Scotland is an unfamiliar place to them and they worry you will steal the cargo and have them killed."

"Do you share that opinion?" Patrick asked.

"I am familiar with temptation," the Spaniard said in his usual enigmatic way. "Nothing would surprise me."

"And what would you do?" Patrick asked.

"Exactly what they are grumbling about."

"Then why have you not left with ship and cargo?"

The Spaniard raised an eyebrow, then grinned. "My friend, MacDonald, would never allow it."

"Bloody well right," MacDonald said with a glower.

"The Maclean ship should be here in a week or two. In the meantime, my family will purchase the contents of this ship and divide the funds among the crew," he said. "I will make sure it is a fair price, and I will take none of it."

The Spaniard stood. "I will want to know the amount," he said. "The total and the amount each man will get."

"I would suggest each receive the same amount, regardless of what they did during the . . . revolt. Mayhap it is not the fairest way, but it is the best way to keep the peace."

"It would not repay them for the price of the ship," Diego persisted.

"A ship without men who know how to sail it is of no value," Patrick replied. "It will be wrecked or sunk."

"I know how to sail."

"But you said you do not know navigation."

"We could find someone," Diego said, a smile playing around his lips.

He was baiting Patrick, who was having none of it. "Then do it," Patrick challenged. "I will not ask my family to pay for the ship as well as the contents."

"When will we unload?" MacDonald asked, ignoring the Spaniard. "I am riding home as soon as the ship is scuttled. I would like to be taking something wi' me. I donna know what I will find."

Patrick nodded. "Diego, you go with the women to Inverleith. They know you. You can do some of the bargaining if you wish. MacDonald and I will stay here until the ship is unloaded."

"Your family will welcome a Spaniard?"

"Aye," Patrick said.

"Then I will be delighted to accompany the senoritas," he said. "Despite Senorita Mendoza's unfortunate relatives, there is something about her . . ." His voice trailed off but the implication lingered.

Patrick shouldn't feel the surge of anger he felt, nor the jealousy. She was nothing to him, and if she admired the Spaniard, so be it. In truth, it might solve a problem.

Hell, no!

He still did not trust the Spaniard—Diego—despite his

assistance these past few days. There was something about him that did not inspire confidence, mayhap his refusal to answer any questions. But he was uncanny at getting things done.

In truth, he wanted the Spaniard gone. Hopefully to Morocco or some other faraway place. He had a feeling, though, that the Spaniard was not going away any time soon.

Which brought him back to Diego's last comment. Patrick wished there was someone else, but Diego and the Scot were the only two people the women really knew or halfway trusted. Except mayhap for Manuel.

"Manuel will go as well," he decreed.

"You do not trust me," Diego said.

"No more, I suspect, than you trust me," Patrick replied.

"Ah, but you have me wrong. I trust you very much."

"Which is why you wish to be present for any discussions about the ship's cargo?"

Diego shrugged. "I am merely looking out for everyone's interest."

"Aye," Patrick said, filling his voice with incredulity.

MacDonald interrupted. "I have a list of the contents of the cargo, including the dowry."

"I will call a meeting after the women leave and tell the crew what is happening. Several of our boats will start unloading the ship this afternoon. When all is unloaded, we should take the ship out to the middle of the sound and scuttle it."

"I wouldna be telling them tha'," the Scot said. "They still have hope to take the ship."

Patrick nodded. He did not like lying to the men, even by omission, but he did not need a mutiny at the moment. Any more than he wanted a reluctant—and appealing—prisoner at Inverleith.

But he had to get rid of the *Sofia* as soon as possible, or it would not matter what he wanted. A sighting by a Campbell, a ride to Edinburgh or London, and his future would be over. No matter that his brother's wife was a Campbell, he would never entrust his life to one.

"'Tis time to get the women into the boat," he said abruptly. "My brothers are waiting."

"Your brothers do not object to surrendering a fortune?" Diego probed again.

"They know it is not theirs," Patrick said shortly.

"That would not have deterred mine," Diego said softly. Though the words were low, a hard bite of bitterness accompanied them.

Another small piece of a puzzle that was the Spaniard. Something to be explored later. But not now.

He left and returned to the women's cabin. Manuel, as usual, was outside. "I want you to go with the senoritas to Inverleith," he said. "Diego will be going as well. You will watch out for them."

"*Si,*" Manuel said. "I watch very well."

"I know."

To his surprise, the lasses had packed everything and were ready when he returned. They were standing when he entered. Juliana had changed gowns to a dark blue one with a tight-fitting bodice and soft pleated skirt. The dark blue velvet turned the violet ring around her blue-gray eyes more distinctive. She wore an English hood and veil that drew her honey-colored hair back and allowed it to fall in ringlets down her back.

She was very much the lady, yet oddly vulnerable, and he realized she was using the clothes as a shield. She could not quite keep the apprehension from her expression.

"We are ready," she said, chin held high.

He turned toward Carmita, who stood resolutely beside her mistress. She, too, had obviously donned her best garment. A clean, plain gray gown.

But he could not keep his eyes off Juliana Mendoza as he tried to control a sudden hastening of his heartbeat.

He forced his gaze away and picked up Juliana's trunk and lifted it to his shoulder. Manuel took the remainder of her luggage. They went back on deck. Patrick used ropes to lower the trunk into the longboat, then waited as the lad scrambled down like a squirrel. Diego followed.

Then Patrick helped Juliana over the rail, her hand snug in his, as if it belonged there. Even as warmth spread through him, he could not help but notice the trim legs beneath her underdress. His hand continued to hold her arm as she clasped the rope ladder and swung for a moment, then pulled her hand away.

No timid miss here. She balanced on the ladder, then climbed down. Diego waited beneath, ready to catch her if she slipped, but she did not. The Spaniard's hands wrapped around her waist as she reached the boat and he seated her in the bow.

Jealousy boiled inside Patrick as she said something to the Spaniard, a smile on her lips.

There had been no smile for him.

He tried not to let his discomfort show as he assisted Carmita over the rail. The young lass, who had been tearful most of the voyage, scampered down as well. Manuel was there to help her.

Patrick watched as the boat reached the shore. His brothers helped the two women out of the boat and assisted them in mounting the horses.

He continued to watch as they disappeared over the hill. He finally turned away, wishing he didn't long to be with them.

JULIANA had tried not to show any weakness as she climbed down the moving rope ladder. Her skirts impeded her progress but she was not going to give the Scot the satisfaction of seeing her fear. Not again. Not ever.

Yet it had taken all her strength to release his hand. His touch burned through her, and his strength made her heart pound. She did not want to go without him, without the protection he had provided. She trusted him to a point, but she did not trust his clan.

She felt no more comfortable as the Spaniard caught her and lowered her to a seat. She had seen little of him since those first few days, and she had no sense of him. A Spaniard enslaved by his country. What had he done to warrant that?

The Scot had said he'd been a prisoner of war. But the Spaniard did not have that excuse. She did not trust him, though now washed, he was well favored in looks. His dark eyes laughed, mostly, she thought, at himself. His lips formed far too easily into sardonic smiles.

Once in the boat, she clasped Carmita's hand as they neared the shore.

She did not know what to expect. Certainly not the warm welcome she received from the two men in plaid. Neither looked like her captor, but both, like him, were startling in their features. One had dark hair and dark amused eyes. The other had sandy-colored hair, several shades darker than her own, and the most striking blue eyes she'd ever seen.

Blue eyes that were gentle, unlike her captor's cool ones.

The latter stepped up and lifted her from the boat so her skirts would not get wet. The Spaniard looked surprised, then did the same with Carmita.

"Senorita," the younger Scot said as he set her down. "My brothers and I offer the hospitality of Inverleith. Be assured you will be safe and comfortable."

"And a prisoner," she said dryly.

"A problem we hope to solve," he said with a quick smile that had none of the Spaniard's secrets.

On the surface, he was as unlike his brother as two men could be. His eyes were warm, his smile real. Now that she was closer, she saw a scar along the side of his cheek and saw that his arm was held at a slightly awkward angle, though it had been strong enough in lifting her.

A warrior as well.

Her eyes turned to the taller of the two, the dark-haired man who stood watching her with eyes that seemed to invade her every thought. He bowed slightly. "I am Rory Maclean. The gallant brother is Lachlan. But I echo his words. You will be safe and welcome at Inverleith."

"Even if I choose not to be there?"

"Aye. I am not sure of all the circumstances yet, but the Macleans do not harm women."

"At least not by intent," Lachlan corrected, the smile spreading as the two brothers seem to share a secret.

She did not care about that. Nor their welcome, though it came as a surprise. In the past days she had worried more and more about her mother. About what her father might do when he realized his plans had been thwarted. When her mother believed her only child to be at the bottom of the sea.

She could not stay here.

But she would pretend otherwise until their guard was lowered. Then she would make her escape. From a man who intrigued her far more than he should, and a situation that could end in disaster for the one person she loved above all.

She smiled and curtsied slightly. "Carmita"—she tossed a glance at her friend—"and I appreciate your welcome."

The Spaniard stood at her side. "I am Diego," he said. "My young friend here is Manuel. Maclean said we were to go with the senorita."

"You are welcome as well," Rory Maclean said. "We had several rooms made ready at Inverleith."

It was the older Maclean who helped her onto a saddle, and Lachlan Maclean who helped Carmita. Then he turned to Manuel. "You can ride with me. Diego can take the horse Patrick rode."

Then they were riding along the coast. Rory paced his horse beside hers.

They had brought a pretty gold mare for her, and despite all her concerns, Juliana found herself enjoying the ride. The gait was easy and the mare responded to her slightest touch. The cold edge of the wind had warmed with the midday sun and it cast trails of gold across the sea.

Now from land, the hills did not look as barren as they had from the sea. Small purple blooms covered the hills. Sheep and heavily coated cattle grazed contentedly. The dark-haired Maclean—Rory—rode with easy grace next to her.

She took these moments to memorize the terrain, the distance to the keep she'd seen as they sailed past. She saw several small fishing boats and some slightly larger boats, but nothing else. Then they reached the peak of a hill and she gazed at the high walls of Inverleith.

The keep stood on a point and overlooked the sea. Two towers rose up beyond the stone walls.

A shout came from inside the keep and the gates opened as they rode toward them.

The courtyard was full of activity. Men were training with arms. Sacks were being carried into a shelter that must be a barn. Women were drawing water from a well.

Several lads took the reins of the horses. Rory Maclean dismounted and came over to her, offering his hand, then caught her waist as she slid off.

The woman who had been looking on walked rapidly over to them. She wore a plain blue-gray gown and a lace cap. "Welcome to Inverleith," she said. "I am Kimbra, Lachlan's wife," she said with an accent far different than that of the three brothers.

Then another woman joined them. The newcomer had flaming red hair and dark blue eyes that sparkled with good humor. "And I am Felicia, Rory's wife. We will do all we can to make you comfortable."

Juliana doubted a prisoner had ever been greeted so effusively by her captors. If she had not been so worried about her mother, she might even have been amused by it. Now she considered it only an impediment, though her fear faded.

She nodded with no compulsion to do more, considering the fact that she was here against her will. Or perhaps she should befriend these Maclean wives, hoping to have sympathetic ears and perhaps even someone who would help her. At the very least, she had to get word to her mother that she had not been lost at sea.

But then her father would know the ship arrived safely somewhere, and she knew he would turn the earth upside down to find her. She also knew what that might mean to the Scot, to the Spaniard, to the others who had taken over the ship.

But her mother . . .

Her mother would have no one. Juliana could not even think of her pain when she heard . . .

She had to get word to her. Somehow she must.

Chapter 16

PATRICK threw all his energies into unloading the ship. He did not want to think about Juliana Mendoza and what he was going to do about her.

Much less what he *wanted* to do.

Rory had appropriated all the Maclean boats, most of them small fishing boats. Scores of Macleans—some Patrick recognized and others he did not—appeared to help with the unloading. They stared at the Moors, and the Moors stared back, then they all started working together.

Lachlan had decided to ride to Glasgow and captain the ship back to the sound. It would take at least a week as they would have to round the north of Scotland.

As the oarsmen loaded the boats waiting beneath, the Scots rowed the boats to shore, where others passed the items from one man to another until they reached a wagon drawn by two large horses.

Arriving in the first boat, Rory swung up the ladder and asked Patrick to show him through the ship. He lingered in the captain's cabin and went through the charts before folding them up and taking them with him. "These are better than any we have," he said.

Then Patrick took him down to the oarsmen's deck. It still smelled of sweat and blood, and chains lay in the aisles where they had been discarded. Red stains colored the wood planking.

Rory gazed around. "My God, Patrick. How long were you here?"

"Six years to my counting. One year in a Spanish dungeon."

"Och," Rory exclaimed. "How did you survive?"

"I was too angry to die."

He pointed to a bench in the middle, right beneath the grate that now stood open. "My position for the six years. The strongest always had the outside seat."

"When did you take over the ship?"

"Two days out of Spain."

"Who navigated?"

"The Spaniard and I."

"You hated the sea. I remember the arguments you had with Father."

"Aye, I wanted to be a warrior, not a merchant. During the past few weeks, I fervently wished I had paid more attention."

"Why are you are willing to stay aboard now? Ride home with me. Lachlan and my Macleans can see to the unloading."

"Nay. I made promises. I intend to keep them."

"Is that the only reason?" Rory's gaze seemed to see right through him.

"Aye," he lied. The truth was that he wanted the woman out of sight and hopefully out of mind. "I have lived simply these past few years," he continued. "A good bed might undo me."

"Are you sure it is not the woman?"

"She is Spanish," Patrick said roughly. "And she knows I killed her uncle. She believes me a barbarian."

"Then let her see otherwise."

"I am what I am," Patrick said. "One year of war, one year in a Spanish dungeon and six years on a galleon. Those years did not break me, but they took my soul."

"I do not believe she thinks so. Her gaze lingered on the ship."

"Because she feared leaving it."

"Mayhap," Rory said.

"In any event, she is promised."

"My wife was promised to someone else," Rory said. "Promises without love are meant to be broken."

"You forget the curse," Patrick said. "I cannot."

"I do not forget anything," Rory said. "I lost two wives. But I believe my marriage to Felicia broke the curse. We have had no more deaths of young wives in the past five years."

Enough! He could not fathom the changes. Nor did he want to. He had lived these past six years to exact revenge. That goal had kept him alive. And now he was being told that the world had turned upside down.

"Tell me about the Spaniard," Rory said.

Patrick shrugged. "He says much. And little. I know we could not have survived without him, but I don't like what he hides. I truly do not know whether he can be trusted."

"Your life depends on it. That he can be trusted and the others."

"Hopefully they will soon be at the other end of the world. I know I can trust MacDonald. And Denny. But I do not know what the Spaniard plans to do. Or where he'll go. I believe he did some smuggling along the Spanish coast. Beyond that . . ."

"You said he was a seaman. Mayhap we can use him on one of our ships."

"I would not trust him as a captain, and I do not think he would take a lesser position."

Rory met his gaze directly. "Do you really believe no one will discover what happened?"

"Aye, if not for the women. They are the complication."

"You were a prisoner of war. You had every right to escape."

"You know the law as well as I do," Patrick said. "There is a reason for it. Too many crews do not like their captains, particularly when the discipline is harsh. The only thing that keeps them in check are the mutiny laws."

"We will figure something," Rory said slowly, then smiled. "We just cannot let Felicia become involved. Her plots are far too complicated. They invariably lead to disaster."

Despite the words, there was so much love in his brother's eyes, an ache formed in Patrick's throat. He was thirty and seven years, yet he'd never known the kind of tenderness he saw in Rory's face, had never allowed himself to feel more than momentary lust.

"We had better get back on deck," he said. "I do not want to spill any of the goods into the sea."

Rory's eyes held his for a moment, then he nodded. "You won't go back with me, then?"

"Nay, not until the cargo is unloaded."

They climbed up the stairs from the benches. Once on deck, Rory took a deep breath of fresh air.

"It is a hell ship," Patrick said flatly.

"Aye," Rory said. "You are right. She should be burned."

"If the Campbells see . . ."

"Neither the Campbells or Camerons will say anything," Rory said. "Jamie Campbell is a friend and is now married to Janet Cameron. The three clans are united, especially since Flodden. We lost too many to a common enemy to lose more by fighting amongst ourselves."

" 'Tis hard to consider a Campbell naught but a foe."

"I had my problems with that as well," Rory said. "But he saved Lachlan's life after Flodden Field. He wouldn't give up looking for him."

"Trust does not come easily to me," Patrick warned. "Someone betrayed me to the Spanish. I suspect it was a Campbell. There were several fighting with the French."

"We will find the truth of it."

He hesitated, then clasped Patrick's arm. "It is a fine thing to have you back."

Patrick watched as Rory descended the ladder and jumped into the fishing boat with its small sail. His brother raised an arm to him in farewell.

Patrick turned away. He did not want or need emotion. They weakened a man. Locking away those feelings had enabled him to survive these past years. He needed to keep them in control now so he would make no mistakes. He had survived far too long to die at the end of a hangman's noose.

JULIANA felt a visitor in a very strange world.

If a prisoner she was, she was certainly a privileged one. It seemed that no one could do enough for Carmita and herself.

She had never met anyone like Felicia and Kimbra, nor had she ever been in a residence like Inverleith. Yet from the moment she walked into the great hall and saw the clean rushes, the tapestries lining the walls, the portraits on the walls, she felt not a prisoner but an honored guest in a place that seemed oddly familiar.

How could that be?

Her home in Spain was totally different, a place of space and light, not massive walls of rock. And yet . . .

Perhaps it was the chattering of her two companions who seemed as close as sisters, though their speech, temperaments and coloring were profoundly different. The one who said she was Rory's wife practically danced as she walked. Her smile was broad, and her eyes were full of laughter as if she cherished every moment of life. A child of two or three pranced behind her, an echo of her joy.

The other, Kimbra, had a broad English accent, more like Juliana's mother's, and serious eyes. Her smile was slower but just as welcoming. And her warmth seem to encompass someone she barely knew.

Juliana was determined not to let them disarm her. They

were obviously protecting their brother-in-law, and their goal was opposite to hers.

Felicia had led the way to a large chamber filled with fresh flowers and a bright blue covering on the bed. Pillows decorated two chairs, and a door led to an alcove for Carmita.

"Patrick said you were on your way to get married," Felicia said. "Are you in love with the man you are to marry?"

It was a personal question, and one Juliana did not feel required to answer.

Felicia's smile retreated a bit. " 'Tis a personal question, I know, and I have no right to ask it. But you see I was to be married when the Macleans abducted me. I believed Rory a monster. The Macleans and Campbells had been feuding for many, many years and I was told they were barbarians. Worse even than that. Women killers. So I know how you must feel. Afraid and angry and lost."

"You were taken captive?" Juliana could not keep the surprise—and interest—from her voice.

"Aye. Except when I was brought here, the keep was a place of sadness and tragedy and despair. I was terrified, but I could not show it. I kept trying to escape. I can warn you it is very difficult. But I want you to know we understand and would like to be your friends, and we will not let anything happen to you."

The words had run on and on, but the sentiment was there. So was that piece of knowledge: *I kept trying to escape. I can warn you it is very difficult.*

She said difficult but not impossible.

Felicia seemed to know what she was thinking. "Both Rory and Lachlan believed Patrick dead these past few years. It means everything to them that he is still alive. And now he will be laird. They will not go against Patrick, and I would do nothing that might bring harm to him."

Something hard lodged in Juliana's throat. Her only knowledge of marriage was that between her mother and father, and that certainly had nothing of the warmth she heard in Felicia's and Kimbra's voices, nor the loyalty inherent in

Felicia's words. There was no envy, or greed when they spoke of an older brother returning to take what had been theirs. Only gratitude.

"You speak English well," Kimbra noted.

"My mother is English."

"That explains your coloring then," Felicia exclaimed. "You look more Scot or English than Spanish."

Juliana did not reply. She did not want tears to show and they might well do that if she talked about her mother. Instead she determined to seek more information from Felicia. Exactly how had she tried to escape? And how did she become a Maclean bride? The more she knew about the Macleans, the more chance she had to escape them.

"Your husbands seem nothing like Patrick Maclean," she said. "They are . . . pleasant."

"My husband can be an ogre," Felicia said. "It runs in the Maclean family."

"It does not," Kimbra said heatedly. "Lachlan is the gentlest of souls."

"He does sing rather well," Felicia admitted with a grin on her face. "You must ask him," she said to Juliana. "He canna say no."

Juliana's head swam. She'd had few friendships with other girls, who always had *duenas* with them. Her father did not approve of most of them. Too bold, he'd said. But these two bantered like old friends.

"I think we should allow Juliana some rest," Kimbra said. "And some privacy."

Felicia flushed. "Kimbra's right. We do not often have visitors, particularly someone our age. I hope you will join us for supper tonight. I know you must be tired, but there are so few new faces, and I wish to hear all the news from Spain."

Juliana was torn. Part of her wanted the company that was offered, the warmth that was so very evident. But would it not be surrendering to the enemy, no matter how charming?

The more you learn the better chance you have to escape.

"*Si,*" she said.

Chapter 17

PATRICK Maclean had not been at supper, and the meal had been painful.

Juliana had been the focus of stares, both hostile and curious. Word of what had happened to Patrick Maclean had obviously traveled quickly, as well as her relationship to the man the Macleans held responsible. Her uncle had enslaved him, and that, she gathered, was the worst thing that could ever happen to a proud, free Scot.

But even without the stares, she felt uncomfortable. She was accustomed to supper with her mother and father and sometimes with a small circle of her father's friends and business associates. This . . . custom of dining at a table with some forty men dressed in various forms of plaid and baring naked legs was . . . unsettling. She continually saw in her mind Patrick Maclean in his plaid, recalled the pure masculinity and power—and magnetism—she felt coming from him.

Even the memory sent warm and tingly feelings through her. Feelings she not only did not want, but greatly resented.

Despite the courtesy and friendliness offered by Kimbra and Felicia, and even Rory, they were Scots holding her against her will, and their loyalty was to Patrick Maclean, not to her.

She retired early, but then Kimbra and Felicia knocked at the door.

"We . . . Felicia and I . . . want to see the ship," Kimbra said. "We thought we might go tomorrow before they finish unloading it. Would you like to go with us?"

The offer stunned her, but the suggestion of a ride—going outside the great walls of Inverleith—was heady.

"What about your husband? Will he agree?"

"Aye, if we take someone with us," Felicia said apologetically.

Juliana quickly accepted the offer and the two left to check on their children.

The invitation for a ride was welcome for several reasons. A diversion from thoughts of Patrick Maclean. A chance, perhaps, to escape, or at least learn something that would help her in the future.

Then what would she do? Where would she go? To London and her promised husband? Try in some way to return to Spain? How would she explain her survival without condemning the Maclean, Manuel, the Spaniard and others?

Sleep was restless that night, and she had little appetite for the meal to break fast. Still, she was ready and eager when Felicia and Kimbra appeared at her door. Both wore plain riding clothes. Like her, neither wore hats, and she felt a moment of kinship with them.

Felicia gave her a piece of apple. "For Duchess," she said, and the three of them went down the stone steps to the great door and then to the stables. Five horses had been saddled, including a great black stallion.

Juliana tried to hide the longing she felt as she watched him move restlessly. Kimbra went up to him and gave him a handful of apple, and he nickered for more.

"Greedy one," Kimbra whispered. Then a pretty child of perhaps eight years emerged from the barn with a big black dog following. "This is Audra," Kimbra said. "My daughter. The dog is Bear and this great fellow here is Magnus." Her hand ran along the head of the black stallion.

Audra curtsied nicely. "My mother said you are Spanish," she said. "I have never met anyone from Spain."

She was a lovely child, her eyes much like her mother's with their serious regard.

"And I had never met anyone from Scotland until a few weeks ago," Juliana said, kneeling so that her eyes met Audra's.

"I am not from Scotland," Audra corrected solemnly. "I am English."

"Then you will have to tell me about England. My mother is English, too, but I have never been there."

"I like Inverleith better," Audra said.

"Come, love," Kimbra said and lifted her daughter on a small white mare before turning back to Juliana. "The chestnut is Duchess. She's a royal lady, but slowing down and, despite her name, very amiable." Then Kimbra led the black horse to a mounting block and swung easily into the saddle. A stable lad appeared at Juliana's side, laced his fingers together and offered the locked hands to Juliana.

Juliana stepped into them and swung her leg over in a movement far more awkward than usual. She waited while Felicia mounted, then Rory Maclean joined them and mounted the last horse.

Her spirits fell. She had hoped there would be only the three women and she'd immediately eyed the black as the most swift of the mounts. Her mind had already been plotting ways to steal him.

She knotted her hands around the reins and purposely sat like a bag of potatoes. Felicia guided her horse to one side of Juliana, and Kimbra to the other. Protectively, Juliana thought, even as guilt crept into her thoughts.

Audra rode ahead with the Scot accompanying them while the dog named Bear remained at their heels.

All of Juliana's hopes of escape vanished.

She looked toward Kimbra. "Where is your husband?"

"Lachlan decided to ride to Glasgow, to make sure the ship arrives here as quickly as possible."

"How far?"

"The way Lachlan rides, two days," Felicia replied.

"Which way is it?"

The two wives exchanged glances.

"West."

"You are surrounded by water?"

Again an exchange of glances as if they weighed what to say.

But then Felicia pointed out at the water. The *Sofia* was just ahead.

Juliana saw a tall man in plaid jump from the fishing boat as it approached the shore and help pull it up. She felt a sudden warmth pooling inside.

Part of her wanted to kick her heels in the side of her mare and run. She knew it would be useless. Duchess had a fine gait, but Juliana knew it was nothing compared to the other horses with them. By purpose.

Instead, she waited for the Maclean's reaction to seeing her there.

IT neared late afternoon of the second day before the last barrel of wine was lowered to a fishing boat and rowed to shore. The crew grew surly, uncertain whether Patrick would indeed pay them for the cargo. He had resisted doing it until the entire contents had been unloaded for fear that once the gold was in hand, some might try to sail off.

But now it was time. He had left a few barrels of wine on board. Once the crew was paid, they would break out the barrels in celebration. Then when the oarsmen were happy, the Macleans would take them ashore and scuttle the ship. Rory had said the great hall had already been prepared with fresh rushes for the oarsmen until the Maclean ship arrived from Glasgow.

A very dangerous week.

He watched as the last barrel left the ship.

MacDonald appeared at his side. "We are done."

"I am in your debt," Patrick said. "I know you wanted to go home three days ago."

"Aye. I have a wife who does not know I still live. But I know not what I'll find there, and the gold may help."

"If you ever need anything, I hope you will turn to me."

"You say you are in my debt, but I would still be chained on that bench if ye did not start the revolt. So I make the same offer to ye. If ye ever need my assistance . . ."

Patrick nodded.

"I will stay until you return, then I would be grateful for a fast mount."

"You will have it. I would have you meet my brothers first, though, and have supper. You can leave at first light."

MacDonald hesitated, then nodded his assent. "How much will each man's share be?"

"I thought seventy pounds each. That would be a total of nearly seven thousand pounds. Rory says we have that sum on hand."

"It is generous. Most of these men have never held more than a pound in their hands."

"I worry about that. I do not want them gambling or killing each other."

"I will tell them what they will receive," MacDonald said, "but ye should wait to distribute it until your ship takes them to Morocco."

"I will give them several pounds immediately, with a promise of the rest," Patrick replied. He did not want any taking it into their minds to head toward Edinburgh. He needed them all out of Scotland.

"I will see this last load to Inverleith," Patrick said, "and bring back some funds."

He went over the railing and quickly climbed down the rope, dropping into the fishing boat.

Once the boat was ashore, he jumped out. Eight Macleans approached to unload the last of the cargo while one remained with the horses. Patrick lifted a barrel and carried it to the wagon, relishing an effort that would bring him closer to ending this ordeal.

He wiped sweat from his face and looked up. Five riders approached.

One was Rory. Another was young Audra. The other three were women, including—bloody hell!—the graceful figure that had haunted him far too frequently, the one he had tried to avoid these past three days by staying aboard.

And, God help him, she looked more enchanting than he remembered.

THE Scot looked startled when he saw her. That was one consolation. She suspected he wasn't usually surprised.

He came over to her, his gaze lingering on her face.

"You are being treated well?"

"*Si,* except that I cannot go where I wish to go."

He turned his cool stare toward his brother. "I did not say she could leave Inverleith."

"We have not left Inverleith," Felicia replied tartly.

He wanted to say something else. Juliana knew it from the look on his face, but he shrugged. "I will ride back with you."

Then he turned to Audra. His eyes seemed to soften. For a moment he looked almost paternal. "Audra," he acknowledged, then glanced up at Kimbra. "She has the look of you," Patrick said and bowed slightly. "Miss Audra, you ride very well."

"Thank you," Audra said solemnly as she looked from Rory to Patrick and back again. "I am pleased you returned," she said in that solemn voice that charmed Juliana.

Patrick actually smiled. "I am pleased as well, lass." Then he turned an admiring eye toward Kimbra's mount. "He is a fine horse. I saw him in the stables and asked to take him but was told he belonged to you."

Kimbra's cheeks flushed, and her eyes grew anxious.

"Do not worry," Patrick Maclean said softly. "I usually do not take what is not mine."

Then his eyes returned to Juliana, and she nearly melted under his gaze. She tried to compare this man who spoke so gently to a child and reassuringly to a woman he barely knew with the nearly naked man covered with blood. He was all warrior then. Now . . .

But when his eyes met hers, she saw the curtain drop over them once again. His gaze dropped to the awkward way she held the reins. "You do not ride often?"

"Nay," she said, but something warned her that he suspected her pretense.

He turned suddenly to his brother. "Where is the Spaniard?" he asked.

"Prowling through Lachlan's books."

"Does anyone watch him?"

"Aye. And the gates are locked. He will not be leaving without permission."

Patrick nodded. "We have some business to transact now that you have seen all the goods."

"There will be no problem selling them," Rory said. "Not in Morocco, but on the English border."

Patrick raised an eyebrow.

"We have reliable buyers there," Rory said.

"Scots?"

"And English," Rory replied.

"You have become more adventurous since I left."

"We needed the money. Fa stopped caring about anything but his wine, and our people were being raided weekly by Campbells. More and more were leaving. 'Twas the trading that saved us."

Patrick nodded. "I will require some money for the crew, then bring them back to Inverleith until the ship sails. I want some Macleans inside as well."

"You think there might be problems?"

"Nay, but many have not been home for years or do not have a home to go to. They've never had five pounds in their pockets, and they've gone through hell. I think sprinkling a few pieces of gold will assure their faith in me."

Rory nodded.

"I need a horse."

"Ride with Miss Mendoza," Rory said. "She is light enough that it won't overburden the mare."

Juliana saw the reluctance in Patrick's eyes. And why not? She was still the niece of the man who had caused him such misery. But before she could back away, Patrick Maclean nodded. "Move up in the saddle," he ordered.

That was the last thing she wanted to do. She already had far too strong a reaction to him. Before she could protest, he swung up behind her, settling in the saddle and taking the reins from her hands.

So much for trying to run away. She tried to think of escape as her body slid against his. She felt his warmth, the muscles carved into his body, the strong thighs touching hers.

She found herself leaning against him, her body heating at the abrasion of two bodies pressed against each other.

Her body also instinctively moved with the horse, and her fingers wrapped around the animal's mane as he urged the mare into a faster pace. Then they were racing along the crest of the cliff.

She thought she could hear the rapid beating of his heart. She felt his exhilaration in the movement of his arms and felt some of her own. She had raced her own horse on the beaches at home, but there was something about the cold, foaming sea below and the wind that whipped her hair. She heard laughter, only to realize it was her own.

For a moment, there were only the two of them and the mare, and they were racing against the wind and the demons—both her own and his.

The gates of Inverleith opened as they raced forward and he did not slow until they reached the courtyard. She found herself leaning back against him, relishing the strength she felt there.

Then he dismounted, and lifted her down.

"You are a good rider, senorita."

All the excitement suddenly faded.

He'd known she was a fraud. He had made her show it by riding with her. Without words, without accusation, he had exposed her ruse.

He hadn't felt the same sensations, the few moments of what had seemed perfect unity.

She was furious with him and furious with herself. More importantly she was tired of being a pawn, first of her father, now of Patrick Maclean.

Juliana took control the only way she could manage. She hit him as hard as she could.

Chapter 18

HE'D been struck many times in the past few years, and he'd sworn that no one would ever touch him again.

But then he'd never thought that person would be a woman.

It had been no womanly slap, but a full fledged blow to his chest, and so unexpected that it stunned him.

She looked as surprised as he felt.

He forced himself to look up at the other riders who'd reached them. His brother could scarcely control a smile. Felicia had a grin on her face. *An evil one,* he thought.

God's blood but he was still reeling from the unwise ride to Inverleith. For a moment, he had forgotten everything but the pleasure of a woman's body against his. He remembered how clumsy Juliana had looked when she'd approached the ship on horseback, but the moment the horse quickened his pace, he knew she was a natural rider and far more experienced than she wanted anyone to know.

He admired the spirit, the fact that she didn't surrender. He was also appalled at his own behavior, that he had given in to that momentary need to race the short distance from the natural harbor to the point Inverleith dominated. That he had reveled in the sensation of her body against his. The self-disgust had caused him to step back quickly. Physically. Mentally.

He was only too aware that everyone in the courtyard still looked on, each trying to guess his next action. It would, he knew, dictate the future, whether he could take his place as laird.

If he even wanted it.

"Well delivered, lass," he said. Then he added in a tone laced with humor, "There are a few better places if you wish to do damage."

The tense moment dissolved into laughter.

Her face flushed, but her voice was controlled as she replied readily, "*Gracias.* I will remember that."

"I fear that you might," he returned.

Obviously trying to keep her dignity intact, she walked to the doors of the keep, Kimbra following her. Kimbra glared at Patrick, then went after her.

Rory dismounted and the two men headed toward the small alcove that served as an office.

Once there, they sat. "You have seen the cargo now," Patrick said. "You agree then seventy pounds per man is fair?"

"Aye, but I am thinking you are missing the greatest treasure in that cargo," Rory said.

Patrick understood only too well. "Now I know there are reasons other than the bloody curse to avoid marriage."

"There are recompenses," Rory retorted, the gleam in his eyes making his meaning clear.

"We have business," Patrick replied shortly, cutting off any more talk of women and their frustrating ways.

Rory sighed. "The sum I suggested earlier is reasonable, and one we can afford. We have been hoarding gold to purchase another ship. We paid some as ransom for Lachlan but most has been replaced."

"And that new ship you planned to purchase?"

"Once we sell the cargo, we will have enough to purchase it. Just a delay for mayhap a year."

Patrick paced the office. He did not care for the fact that his brothers were not only risking money for him, but also their lives. He had not truly expected it. He had, in truth, thought to find resentment and obstacles. He still looked for both.

Betrayal could still happen. He'd had no say in Lachlan's journey to Glasgow. His brother had simply left, and Patrick had only Rory's word that he went to expedite the arrival of a ship. What if there had been another purpose?

"I want to take part of it and distribute it to the men before bringing them here. I want them to see it exists. They grow restless."

"I thought as much." Rory went to a closet built into the wall and unlocked it, then took out an iron box. He set it down on the table. A second key unlocked it, and Patrick saw piles of gold coins. Rory counted out a number and placed them in a leather pouch.

Then, unexpectedly, he handed the key to Patrick. "By rights, it should be yours."

Patrick felt as if he had been hit again. For years, he had simply dreamt of freedom and secondly, of leading his clan back to glory. Of paying back the Campbells in blood for years of pain. Of exacting a price from his brothers for not paying a ransom and sentencing him to what should have been death.

Now he was being offered everything he thought he wanted, and he was no longer sure it *was* what he wanted. Despite his brothers' welcome, 'twas obvious he had no place here. The crofts appeared prosperous, the families healthy and happy and the cattle and sheep fat. Apparently peace had finally come to Inverleith. He could barely accept the truce with the Campbells, at least not yet, and after what he'd heard about Flodden Field, how could he do otherwise?

He should never have returned. He would only bring disaster down upon the Macleans.

He had come too far now, though. The *Sofia* must disappear in the middle of the sound where it could never be found and he must fulfill his promise to the men who helped him escape. Then he could disappear.

But what of Juliana Mendoza? As long as she lived, his entire clan would be endangered, as would the lives of the oarsmen.

He damned himself for ever coming here.

"Patrick?"

His attention went back to his brother. "I should never have involved you in this," Patrick said.

"We involved ourselves," Rory said. "It was a decision Lachlan and I would have made even were you not heir."

"I am laird only if the clan approves," Patrick said. "I am risking all their lives."

"There is not a man who does not welcome you. They know the risks, but we have been a merchant clan a long time and often smugglers. The law means little to us. Bonny little Kimbra is a member of an English borderer family that robs as a way of life. Lachlan raided himself as he was healing from wounds." He paused. "They remember you well, Patrick. Archibald told them of the fights you had with father on their behalf. It was a sad day when you left. I have been a substitute. I prefer trading to the land, and so does Lachlan. You are more part of these men than we can ever be."

Patrick shook his head. "A good reason to leave. They would be giving loyalty to a shell."

"A shell does not organize a revolt, Patrick, and God knows Queen Margaret and her wee son need men who can fight and advise her. Too many are using her for their own purposes. One group of advisors want peace with England. Another wants to continue a war, even though most of our bravest died at Flodden Field."

"I do not like politics."

"Neither did I. But I am good at it. If you stay, you can take care of Inverleith while I tend to politics at court."

"And the lass."

Rory shrugged. "Marry her."

Patrick could only stare at him in disbelief.

"My wife tells me your Spanish lass was not happy about her forthcoming marriage. She is uncommonly bonny. Marry her."

"As you probably noticed, she is not fond of me, even if I were to ever wed. I am not convinced, as you are, that the curse is gone. It has been only a few years."

"The deaths always came within two years. Felicia and I have been together five."

"I will not marry, Rory, particularly now that you and Lachlan have children and can continue the bloodline. So if that is your plan, I might as well disappear again and save you trouble."

"I never believed you a coward," Rory said softly.

"She would not have me, even if I were willing. She heard me kill her uncle."

"Enough of this talk. Tonight we celebrate your return. Unfortunately, Lachlan will not be here to play his lute. In the morning we will bring your . . . crew to Inverleith until the *Felicia* arrives."

"I remember that lute. It infuriated father."

"It did until the day he died. He never understood nor appreciated Lachlan. To my shame, I did not, either. Not until I returned and discovered Lachlan probably had more courage than any of us. His were moral choices, not just a question of physical bravery. It took me a long time to understand that."

"It is too dangerous," Patrick said. "If anyone connects me with the *Sofia* . . ."

"Why would they?"

" 'Tis possible."

"You should make your case to Queen Margaret," Rory said. "She should know that Spain is enslaving Scots. It would be far better than if she learned of it later."

"I cannot risk that. You have already said she has those in court who wish better relations with England. My head would make a fine offering for the Chadwick family."

"I have come to know the queen. She has honor."

"But do those around her?"

"I will say naught of the ship, but she should know you are back," Rory said. "We will invent some tale for now." He paused, then added, "I think you should go with me."

Patrick hesitated, then said, "I will think about it."

"And the Spaniard?" Rory asked. "Is he leaving?"

Patrick shrugged. "I will not force him."

"He could be dangerous."

"He has as much to lose as any of us."

Rory nodded, but Patrick knew the subject was not finished, that Rory sensed something about Diego that worried him.

"It should be no longer than another five or six days before the ship arrives, but that depends on whether goods had already been loaded for the next voyage. If so, they had to be unloaded. I do not think either of us wants a valuable cargo aboard when the *Felicia* leaves with its new cargo of oarsmen."

"Most are honest men."

"Aye, but we have to consider the others who may not be."

Patrick knew he was right. He had just taken most of the clan's wealth to help the oarsmen. The Macleans would probably recover some or all when the cargo was sold. But in the meantime Rory was risking much.

"Do not forget the feast tonight," Rory warned him. "Our people have been planning this since you first arrived."

"I will," he promised, wishing he could avoid it. He had done nothing heroic. And now he was planning to leave again. He would do as Rory asked and visit the queen, because it was the only thing he could now do for Inverleith. After that? He did not know where he would go. What he would do. But he was the stranger here. He created danger just by being here.

THE moment her hand struck the Scot, Juliana had been horrified at what she'd just done.

Not just because it hadn't been a very wise thing to do in her position, but because a lady just did not do that type of thing. Not even when provoked. Her mother would have been mortified.

How many times had her mother stood there and taken blows without a sound? Then later explained it was part of marriage?

Just as humbling was the reason she'd so instinctively hit the Maclean in the chest. The fact that she felt betrayed by his test, that she thought he had felt something, then he'd shown everyone he obviously had not.

Foolish. Beyond foolish. Yet those moments on the horse had been magical. Enchanting. Or she'd imagined so.

Once in her chamber, she plopped down on the big feather mattress and fought back tears of humiliation. She remembered his retort, the laughter among his clan members.

Unfortunately, she also remembered, all too vividly, the way his body fit hers so perfectly as they rode, the heat that still puddled inside. Not just heat, but electricity. Painful. Exhilarating.

She moved to the window and looked out. The horses were being led to the stable, and small groups of plaid-clad men talked. Even with Carmita tending her, she felt alone.

Would there be a repercussion for her rash action in striking the Maclean? Especially in front of his clan? Yet at the moment it had felt very good. All the fear and past humiliation and uncertainty had been packed in that blow. And then his comment . . . and the laughter.

A knock echoed through the room, and Carmita opened the door.

He stood there. "You may go," he told Carmita.

Her little maid stood up as tall as she could and did not move. To watch little Carmita try to protect her humbled Juliana even more.

"It is all right, Carmita," she said gently. "You can go down to the kitchen and get something to eat."

Carmita did not move, but stood stubbornly ready to defend her mistress.

"I swear not to slay her," Patrick Maclean said with just a trace of dry humor.

With a dubious look, Carmita left.

"You have a brave champion," he said walking toward her.

"Si," Juliana said cautiously. Was he going to do now what he had not down in the courtyard?

But there had been no anger in his voice. And now she saw the smallest hint of a smile on his lips.

It was remarkable what it did to his face. A small but distinct dimple appeared in his cheek.

"I should not have struck you," she said. "It was not the act of a lady."

The hint of a smile turned into a full one. But then it disappeared as quickly as it had come. His gaze rested on her. She wished she could read his expression, but she had discovered that few could hide their feelings as well as this disturbing Scot. She wanted to turn from his steady gaze, yet she could not.

The beat of her heart quickened, and, Holy Mother, her legs were turning to melted wax. Their gazes caught, and the storm she'd felt earlier was nothing compared to the explosive energy radiating between them now. Heat flooded her. Expectation hung in the air. Frightening.

Compelling. Irresistible.

He skimmed his fingers over her skin, lingering on her cheek. Each touch sent new tides of warmth and sensation through her.

What men do to women is an ugly thing.

Her mother's words rang in her head. That last conversation about a woman's duty. But what she felt now wasn't ugly. Instead her body was reacting in exciting, expectant ways.

She swallowed hard.

"I am sorry for whatever offended you," he said in a voice that was intimate now. Not cold and harsh but melodic with the soft Scottish burr. "I did not want to hurt you. I never wanted to hurt you." He paused. "I should not have said what I did."

There was regret and something else in his voice, a sadness that transcended any lingering anger.

She put her finger to his mouth, quieting any more words.

He started to back away, one short step before he stopped. "Lass, I . . ."

His voice trailed off.

Lass. The word spread like warm honey through her consciousness.

She tried desperately to hold on to her dignity, to who she was. Who her mother hoped she would be. She was promised. It did not matter that the man had not been her choice. The papers were signed. The arrangements made. Her mother would be safe. Or as safe as she could be in her husband's home.

Yet when she looked up into the Scot's eyes, they were blazing with an emotion so strong it wrapped around her. She had never been kissed and now she desperately wanted his lips to touch hers. She wanted to run her fingers across his face as he had touched hers. She wanted to hold out her arms and erase all the pain-wracked days and nights he'd endured.

He leaned down and their breath became intermingled, the sound of their heartbeats melding as they pounded in quickened rhythm. Her fingers moved to his face, to the lines so deep for one his age, and her fingertips sought to ease the pain engraved there.

His lips brushed hers. Softly at first, then swiftly. Savagely. Hungrily. She felt his hunger and wondered at her own. How could she want something she'd never had? Her hands went around his neck, entwining her fingers in his thick, auburn hair.

A tremor ran through his body, and she felt it as if she were part of him. He stiffened against her, and that strange yet compelling want intensified. She knew she should move away. She was promised. And he was . . .

He was many things. Murderer. Pirate. Warrior.

Protector.

Emotions clashed inside her. Everything she thought she believed, knew, understood had changed. Her breath was gone, caught someplace between her heart and her throat.

His lips left hers. He touched his fingers to her chin and lifted her head until her gaze met his. His eyes were more amber now, and piercing, and there was a bright glitter in them. They weren't cold and empty, but raging with confusion and want and need, emotions she knew must be mirrored in her face. She swallowed hard. They had started a blaze together, and she didn't want to quench it.

He did, though. She heard a moan. It came from deep inside his throat like an animal in pain.

"Juliana," he whispered, and her name on his lips was like a song sung low. "Bloody hell, but I did not mean this to happen. I just wanted . . ."

He stopped suddenly, and she wondered whether she would ever know what he "just wanted."

His callused fingers touched her throat with lightness—and something like tenderness. He lowered his head and his mouth went to her throat, running his tongue over nerve endings. Then she knew why he'd moaned. She heard herself whimper with the burning inside.

Part of it was fear. She wasn't so much afraid of him as much as she was afraid of caring for him. There was an inherent violence in him. A tension that never relaxed. Whether it had been there before he had been taken to the galley, she did not know. She only knew it was now a part of him and she feared it would tear him apart, and everyone around him.

He moved closer.

Step back.

She couldn't. Instead she stood on tiptoe until his mouth was an inch away. His lips met hers, and her world exploded. All caution left with it.

Chapter 19

THE power of their kiss rocked through him. Need curled inside his loins, but even more compelling was the warmth in the upper region of his body, in the area of his heart.

That warmth, the odd sense of belonging somewhere, was more seductive even than the physical need of his body. The sensations more perfect. The need far deeper.

And more deadly.

Madness. It was madness!

He forced himself to step back, to release her lips, and as he did so, he saw she was as stunned as he was.

Surely the devil must have a hand in this. Patrick had had no intention of doing anything but uttering an apology for what he'd said in the courtyard, for the necessity of holding her prisoner.

His comment in the courtyard had helped his standing in the clan. But he'd seen the swift flush in her cheeks and he'd instantly regretted it. It had been ribald and biting.

It had been a very long time since he'd been with a woman, and longer still since he had courted one.

Not, he told himself, that he was courting one now. He'd lost the skill of courtly manners. They were buried deep on the *Sofia.*

And yet he longed to reach out and touch her again.

As if she read his mind, she touched his hair, and that gesture both inflamed and healed at the same time. His body—nay, it seemed his heart—longed for her with a compelling fierceness he could not control.

He stepped nearer again, knowing full well he was moving toward the fire and helpless to do anything else. Her warm breath tickled the skin of his cheek. Her scent intrigued him. Woman and flowers. A heady mixture. Her eyes—the soft blue-gray ringed by violet—were dazzling in their clarity and intent.

He touched her face, traced her lips, delighted in the softness of her skin and regretted the coarseness of his callused fingers. But she didn't draw back and her cheeks took on a soft, becoming blush from the passion streaking between them.

End this now! For his sake, for hers, he knew he should stop.

But no one had ever looked at him like that, no one had ever touched him like that.

He bent his head and kissed her slowly with a longing he couldn't control. He moved his hands over her gown, paused at her still-covered breasts, then moved on, exploring, feeling the shudders of her body as she reacted. His kiss deepened, his tongue sliding over her lips. She parted them, and his tongue entered, seducing, exploring . . .

Despite her welcome, though, he was experienced enough to realize she was not. He knew it from the small gasp as his tongue entered her mouth, the sudden tightening of her body as if she knew not what to expect. Then participation. Full and unqualified.

He pulled his mouth from hers and searched her face again, fascinated by the emotions running across it. Wonder. Anticipation. A touch of anxiety. He caressed her temple with his lips, then her cheeks. His mouth moved down her neck, his tongue fondling and stroking until he felt her body quiver and her hands go to his neck.

His mind commanded but his body refused to obey. There was no stopping, particularly when she raised her lips to his, and her arms went fully around his neck, burning their own brand on him.

He wanted her. He wanted her more than he thought possible. If it were only physical, he could control it. But he knew now that it was not just physical. Far more vexing was the tenderness he felt for her. He closed his eyes against the feelings assaulting him. How could he have come to care for her in such a short time? A *Sassenach,* for all that was Holy. *Sassenach and* Spanish.

But even if that had not been true, there was no hope for a union. Even discounting the curse, he had no future and he would not make a woman, any woman, pay a price for his bad decisions.

Rory had mentioned a possible marriage. Even if she agreed, how would he explain a Spanish wife? Someone would see her, ask questions and fit the puzzle pieces together. He knew now his presence alone might be a danger to his clan. Hers would dramatically increase it.

Still, as she gazed up at him with what he thought must be the loveliest eyes he'd ever seen, all those concerns faded away. They held so many emotions: passion, yearning and a touch of uncertainty.

"Ah, lass," he said. "I should not be here. I have taken everything from you and can offer you nothing."

"I know," she whispered, but certainty was missing. Instead, she seemed to be searching for something in him.

Something he feared had left him long ago.

Or had it?

God's blood, but he wanted her, and he suspected at this

moment he could have her. Her eyes told him, her tense body told him. The thought was torment.

That damnable attraction had been between them from nearly the first time they'd met. He'd felt it when she made the stitches with those gentle hands and eyes full of concern, even as she tried so valiantly to be defiant. And every time he'd touched her, by accident or purpose, she had warmed the cold parts of him.

But until this minute, he had not realized the full extent of that attraction, nor its power.

Now they were both caught in a whirlwind of something he didn't understand; nor, he suspected, did she. Swirling, compelling currents battered all reason, pulling down all obstacles but the irresistible attraction between them.

He felt the touch of her hand against his neck, the fingers almost reverent against his skin, and the sensation was warm and tender beyond anything he'd ever experienced. He was lost. . . .

A sharp rap came at the door.

They stilled.

Another rap.

She took a step backward, her face still flushed.

He moved to the door and opened it.

Carmita stood there with a tray of food. Manuel was behind her with a bowl of water. Both wore worried expressions as if they'd expected he had ravished her.

Carmita had obviously sought reinforcements. Patrick would have been amused if his groin didn't ache as much as it did, if his heart didn't hurt as well. . . .

A small maid and a young thief were ready to do battle if necessary.

Manuel had evidently switched his allegiance from Patrick to Juliana.

Stymied by two who were little more than children. Or saved?

He moved toward the door. "My brother is planning a

feast tonight with our clansmen," he said, but his gaze did not leave Juliana. "You will attend, senorita?"

She nodded her assent.

He turned toward Manuel and Carmita. "You both are welcome to attend as well."

Manuel's gaze had gone from Juliana's face to his. Thank God the plaid hid the swelling beneath.

He turned to Juliana. "I will come for you."

He left without another word, stepped outside and leaned for a moment against the cold stone wall. He needed that chill. Bloody hell, he needed a swim in the cold water outside.

What had he almost done?

AFTER Manuel left the room as well, Juliana stared at Carmita with confusion. Her body was still experiencing physical sensations. She knew her face was probably rose-colored, or even bright red.

But she couldn't scold Carmita, who so obviously was trying to be brave on her behalf.

"I am unharmed," Juliana said. "I *can* take care of myself."

But she was not quite so certain. Her insides felt as if they were on fire, and she tried to hide the tremors that still raked her body. Her eyes were probably glazed over.

"He is a devil, that one," Carmita said.

Maybe so. How else to explain her reaction to him? Her mother had never told her about these kinds of reactions. That she would grow warm and tingly all over. That she would be filled with a great want.

You must suffer what your husband asks.

Then why all the anticipation in her body? It was a puzzle that plagued her.

"You must help me dress," she told Carmita to avoid any more questioning looks.

"The food, senorita?"

"I am not hungry, and there is the feast." No matter how

hard she tried, she could not keep the anticipation from her voice. She knew she should. She knew he had been fighting that attraction between them. That he disliked Spaniards and her family. He had reason. She also realized the danger he was in, and that she was part of it.

She knew all that, but still she could not help the excitement, the anticipation already stirring in her at the thought of seeing him again.

This might last only a minute of her life, but for now, she was willing to grab this moment of freedom, of a passion she'd never thought she would experience outside of books. She closed her eyes, recapturing that second when his lips pressed against her, the odd sense of *rightness* about it.

What would have happened if Carmita had not knocked?

She wanted to know. She wanted to experience it all before . . .

Before what?

Slowly sense and sensibility returned. The brightness in the room dulled as if a candle flame flickered out.

I will take today. I will take tonight. I will worry about tomorrow, well, tomorrow.

"Now," she told Carmita, "I want to look my best."

But before Carmita could start, another knock came at her door and Felicia and Kimbra entered, flowers in their arms.

"We are going to make you even bonnier than you already are," Felicia announced as she brushed aside Carmita and started pulling away the pins that held Juliana's hair in place.

THE great hall filled with voices and laughter and drunken toasts.

It seemed every Maclean within riding distance had appeared. Platters and platters of food—beef and mutton and fresh fish from the sound—appeared in endless procession.

Two Macleans played their fiddles, and another played bagpipes.

Patrick felt a fraud as he accepted greetings and toasts and good-natured teasing. They all seemed genuinely happy to see him, and he might well be bringing death and destruction down on their heads. He had been foolish, and arrogant, to believe he could be their savior, that he could lead them to defeat the Campbells, only to find his brother had brought peace through other means.

A Maclean stood, held up a tankard and sloshed drink on the table as he said drunkenly, "To Patrick, the new laird. May he be as wise as Rory and as brave as Lachlan."

There was a question in the toast, obvious to all. He knew that as firstborn he inherited the properties, but the honorary title of laird was a distinction won only by consent of the clan.

Rory started to stand, but Patrick put a restraining hand on him. "They are right to question," he said. "It is their lives and those of their families."

Patrick toasted the clan, aware of all the eyes on him and the questions behind them.

He was also only too aware of Juliana's presence, of the electricity that darted between them like lightning. She'd been seated next to him. Rory's doing, no doubt. His brother seemed oblivious to the problems ahead and quite determined to bring about a union. Even as he silently cursed Rory for doing so, he could not deny the pleasure that ran through him when he saw her tonight.

She wore a blue velvet gown that emphasized that entrancing shadow of violet that ringed her irises. A necklace of sapphires circled the lovely neck he had so recently kissed. He recognized it as one that once belonged to his mother.

Felicia had been standing next to her, an innocent smile on her lips. Too innocent.

"Another toast," one man yelled from down the table. "To the Maclean, and thanks be to God who brought him home."

The table erupted into drunken shouts.

"And brought a bonny lass as well," shouted another.

Patrick turned and saw the flush on Juliana's face. She appeared fascinated with the noisy scene. The ribald comments seemed not to bother her, and her eyes sparkled like stars on a clear night. She'd taken only a few sips of her wine, one far better than the Spanish wine aboard the *Sofia*.

He, too, was careful. He did not know how he'd lost control today. He did not intend for it to happen again, and that meant he had to stay away from her. She was a fever in his blood.

There was one last toast. Then the guests stumbled out. Patrick stood, more clearheaded than he really wanted to be. Juliana stood as well.

He should escort her back to her room. But he was only too aware of what might happen. Instead, he bowed. "Thank you for supping with us," he said, keeping his voice as emotionless as possible.

God in heaven, but she was beautiful. Juliana searched his eyes.

"I have to return to the ship," he said, glad for an excuse. What would he use for an excuse once the ship was at the bottom of the sea and his fellow oarsmen scattered? "Diego will accompany you to your room."

"Diego?" she repeated.

"Aye, unless you do not trust him."

"I trust him more than anyone here," she struck out, disappointment and even anger obvious in her eyes. "I will be delighted with his escort."

He found he cared little for her response. In truth, it was a body blow. He simply nodded and left, strolling quickly toward the stable.

There was a half moon, light enough to ride without harming his mount. He remembered every inch of the road that ran from the keep to the deep natural harbor.

He would ride like the devil tonight, then row himself to the *Sofia*. Perhaps that would exorcize some of his demons.

"HE cannot keep his eyes off you, you know," Diego said as he faced her at the door. The Maclean who had become his shadow was not far behind him.

"You are mistaken," she said. "He always leaves me as soon as he can."

Diego threw back his head and laughed.

"He cannot tolerate me."

His brows raised. "Then you have no eyes, senorita. He wants you, and that terrifies him."

"Nothing terrifies Patrick." It was the first time she'd used his given name. It had come so naturally to her lips. She wanted to say it again.

Diego just grinned at her. "Good night, senorita. I do not believe Patrick Maclean will have one tonight." He opened the door and stood aside as she stepped in. She heard him whistling as he walked away.

She closed the door and leaned against it. Carmita had not yet returned. She surmised that she might be helping in the kitchen now that Patrick Maclean had left the keep and her mistress was safe.

Safe.

It had meant a great deal to her several days ago. A week ago. But now her world had changed. Certainly her view of it. Two weeks ago she might have been horrified to be seated at the front table within direct sight of nearly one hundred people, some drunk and many half-naked.

Yet there had been a warmth and companionship that filled her heart. She tried to compare it to the coldly formal meals she'd shared with her mother and father. No, not shared. Her father had dominated the discussion or sat in disapproving silence. All the servants feared him, where here servants were part of the family, and the soldiers were free even to question the laird. The music, too, was new. The pipes were haunting, but the fiddles joyous and free.

She felt free. It was odd indeed that as a prisoner she felt a freedom of spirit she'd never known before.

If only Patrick Maclean felt that same freedom.

NEITHER the ride nor the rowing did anything to cool the heat Patrick felt.

A stable lad had ridden with him to return his mount, but he hadn't been able to keep up with the reckless ride along the road. Not exactly reckless, Patrick assured himself. He would do naught to harm his mount, but he needed that cold wind and sense of freedom.

And he knew the road well. He'd ridden it enough at night when raiding Campbells. In his mind, as he had rowed those past six years, he'd traveled every foot of that land, recounted each raid and how he would lead the Macleans in the future.

There were to be no raids on Campbell lands now.

He was a warrior without battles to be fought.

He joined a startled MacDonald, who had returned earlier, then shared cups with him and the men as they passed their last night on the *Sofia.*

Several of the crew were engaged in games of chance with the coin he'd brought earlier. Felix, the man he'd made second mate, joined them, a cup in hand. "I did not believe you," he said haltingly. "I did not believe you would make good your words."

"I still have not," Patrick said. "Only part of them."

"But now I have faith."

"You, Felix? Faith?"

"*Si,* senor. You were right about the ship. It must go. I wish to go back to Spain someday. I could not have done so if we were taken in this ship."

"Why go back?" Patrick asked.

"I have a wife there. Two sons I have not seen in many years."

"Do others feel as you do?"

"Some," he said. He shuffled his feet. "Uh . . . did you mean what you said about needing sailors?"

"Aye, but you will have a fine purse."

"It . . . I want to send it to my wife . . . if you can find a way."

Patrick nodded. "I can find a way. Where is she?"

"Barcelona."

"It will be done. And I am sure my brothers can use you. They plan on buying a third ship, and you are a good sailor."

Felix shuffled again. "Even if I am Spanish?"

"You are a good sailor, Felix, and a natural leader when you wish. *I* would want you."

Felix stood a little straighter. "Will you . . . captain . . ."

"Nay," he said. "I have had enough of the sea for now."

"Will you stay here?"

Patrick shook his head. "Only until I am sure that all believe the *Sofia* was lost at sea."

"They will." Felix moved away.

He drank much of the rest of the night. Denny appeared and stayed by his side. He refused anything to drink.

Denny, Patrick knew, was another problem. Though Patrick saw growing comprehension in his eyes and thought Denny was far more aware of events than many thought, he still had not spoken, and Patrick did not know where he belonged. If, indeed, he belonged anywhere. Patrick knew he could not abandon him.

Denny. Manuel. Diego. What was he going to do with all of them?

And especially Juliana. Even the name was lovely. Soft. Lyrical. Beckoning.

He drank another tankard of wine, regretting that it was Spanish rather than the French wine at Inverleith. Then he had a third. Surely that would block the scent and sight and feel of Juliana from his mind.

Unfortunately it had the opposite effect. Early in the morning, the noise of celebrating oarsmen faded.

"Go to bed," the MacDonald said. "I must go to bed. I have a long ride ahead in a few hours."

Lulled by wine, Patrick made his way to the captain's cabin and fell on the bed. He needed sleep. He needed his wits about him. Tomorrow—nay, a few hours hence—would prove a challenging day. Still, his body ached with need, and his thoughts remained dominated by the lass with the unusual eyes, soft voice and mighty fist.

THE moving of men to shore went quickly the next morning.

Rory arrived with the fishing boats before dawn. It wasn't long before every oarsman was on shore and walking toward Inverleith.

Archibald and Douglas guided them, and other Macleans made sure none wandered off the road. Rory and Patrick, the MacDonald and Denny stayed aboard and readied the ship for the short sail to the middle of the sound, where the water was at its deepest.

Patrick welcomed the hard work of raising the sail. He hated the bloody ship and had no regrets at its loss. When the flap of the sheet caught, he climbed the mast to unleash it. Then he looked out over the hills of Inverleith. From where he perched, he saw the keep in the distance and beyond that the Island of Mull, where another branch of Macleans lived.

He stayed there for several moments as Rory steered the ship toward the site they'd chosen. Then Patrick climbed down. Rory tied the wheel steady. MacDonald was on deck with several axes and they started chopping down the masts.

The four of them—Patrick, MacDonald, Denny and Rory—climbed down to the hold. Rats scattered as MacDonald held the lantern high before lowering it to the floor. They made several small holes so they would have time to set a blaze, then leave in the longboat.

"Number One," MacDonald said, "you strike the first blow."

Number One. He closed his eyes. He heard the sound of the hammer beating out the strokes, the whistle of the whip just before it struck skin. He even heard the groans and cries of dead men.

He lifted the ax and struck with as much might as he had in his body. It pierced the decking but did not break through. Then Denny struck and then MacDonald.

Each stroke was liberating. Six. Nine. Twelve. Then a hole appeared and water seeped in. MacDonald grabbed the lantern and they climbed up to the main deck.

Patrick gathered gunpowder from the cannons and spread it about the ship, then cut portions of the sheets to feed the flames. He ordered the MacDonald and Denny into the boat. "You go, too, Rory," he said.

Rory hesitated.

"Go," Patrick commanded.

Rory reluctantly went to the side of the ship and climbed down.

Patrick took one last look and then threw the lantern down and watched the flames follow the gunpowder to the sheet. There was a whoosh of flame, and he climbed down the rope ladder and onto the boat. The four of them rowed away as the fire took hold. The entire ship became a fiery inferno, then the bow slipped into the water and the *Sofia* disappeared.

* * *

"RIDER coming."

Rory hurried out the door of Inverleith and quickly mounted the stairs to the top of the great stone wall. He signaled to those below him to move Patrick's oarsmen into the great hall.

Although all had worn mismatched britches and shirts on their arrival from the ship, the Macleans had tried to clothe the oarsmen in something more similar to Highland garments. Even then they looked different from the Macleans. And the Moors . . . there was no disguising their difference.

Rory looked out toward the rider. He was still some distance away, but Rory immediately recognized the white horse. He winced. Of all times for Jamie Campbell to make a visit. He was not sure Patrick was ready for that.

Thank God his older brother was out riding off his demons again. How long before he would return?

Patrick had surprised him. Rory remembered his older brother as a loner who had been focused, as he had been, on training and arms. He had been gone several years, fostered by a Highland family known for their skill in battle, and when he'd returned he had far surpassed Rory in swordsmanship and archery.

It was as if Patrick feared friendship would soften him, yet he had fought their father's poor leadership. Their father's lack of trust in his oldest son had driven Patrick away.

Since his return a week ago, he'd seen a different Patrick. There was still a sense of isolation, of aloneness, about him, and yet Rory noticed the bond he had with the oarsmen, an understanding that excluded Patrick's brothers and others. He saw the gentleness with which he introduced the man called Denny, the exasperated tolerance he offered Diego and the almost paternal concern for Manuel.

He even had a way with the mostly silent and sullen Moors.

But Rory wasn't sure that new tolerance would extend to a Campbell.

Patrick had been growling today, and Rory was pretty sure he knew why. After they scuttled the ship, his brother had gone for long rides and spent most of his time with the oarsmen. He had taken meals with them, spurning the upper table.

Only rarely did his brother allow his eyes to turn to the bonny senorita, who also tried to avoid looking at him. He knew exactly what both were feeling, because he had experienced the same madness only five years earlier.

He and Felicia had even plotted to bring them together, but thus far every effort had been foiled. His brother seemed to know exactly what he was doing, though he had said naught.

Rory knew his brother worried about both his own and Juliana Mendoza's presence at the keep, that it might endanger the Macleans. Certainly the Scots had been weakened since Flodden and could not afford another war with either the English or French. How far would Margaret go to protect her subjects, or how far would she go to appease the English?

If anyone learned what had really happened to the *Sofia*.

The best way to avoid that was a marriage between Patrick and Juliana Mendoza. Senorita Mendoza would disappear within marriage and become a Maclean. They could create a story for her accent. She could pass as Scottish with her fair coloring and gray eyes.

He never would have suggested it if he had not seen the smoldering attraction between the two of them. It was obvious to anyone with eyes. And Rory rather fancied having still another nationality for a third Maclean bride.

After seeing the blow she had inflicted on his brother, Rory knew Juliana would fit quite well with Felicia and Kimbra. There was also a kindness about her that he admired. Juliana and Kimbra were spending time with Denny. Reading to him. Trying to get reactions from him. Trying to discover whether he had a family.

And Manuel, who more than once tried to steal some silver, obviously cared deeply for her.

The rider reached the gate.

He thought about walking down and speaking to him outside the gate, but Jamie had saved his life and Lachlan's. Once a hated Campbell, he was now Rory's closest friend. Rory would certainly trust him with his life or that of any of his family.

They might well need him.

He waved at the Campbell, then quickly descended the steps and waited as the massive gate opened. Jamie dismounted and grabbed him by his shoulders, his fingers tightening in a gesture of friendship. "Since when have you started to lock your gates again?" he asked, his gaze wandering about the courtyard.

"Brigands," Rory said. It wasn't exactly a lie.

"Did they do any damage?"

"Nay. We chased them off but they could return."

"One of my Campbells was courting a Maclean. He saw a ship burning."

"Must have been fog."

Jamie's brows blew up. "Are you nae going to invite me in for a drink after my long ride?"

That was the last thing Rory wanted to do, but he feared Jamie would not take it well if he were denied hospitality. But the hall was filled with an assortment of villains, and his brother had no fondness for Campbells.

Mayhap Jamie could help them. He'd always had the queen's ear. Margaret was still a young woman, and Jamie, even well married, was a fine-looking lord who now was laird of the most important and influential clan in Scotland.

But that decision would have to be his brother's.

Jamie's gaze seemed to see right through him. "Something is odd, Rory. I am not going to leave until I find out what. If you have trouble . . . if you need more men, you can have some Campbells."

"You came alone, though you thought we may have been invaded?"

Jamie hunched his shoulders together. "I have more Campbells not far away."

"God in heaven," Rory said. "That's all I need."

Jamie looked offended.

"Let us have that drink," Rory said. "But avert your eyes when you go in." He had no choice. He knew Jamie. Knew how he spent months on the English border, looking for Lachlan after Flodden Field. He did not give up.

"Avert them from what?" Jamie asked suspiciously.

"Moors. Many Moors."

"God's blood. You've been invaded by Moorish pirates?" Jamie's hand went to the hilt of his dagger.

The only thing that could be worse was if Patrick returned to Inverleith at this moment.

Chapter 21

PATRICK approached the great gate with both anticipation and reluctance. He'd never before thought the two could go together.

The ride had become a morning ritual. His time to think. And slowly come to life again. After being locked in the dark, crowded oarsmen's deck for six years and a dungeon before that, he relished every breath of the cool air scented by heather. He had forgotten how heady it was.

The rides became longer as they all waited for the *Felicia* to arrive. Since his . . . encounter with Juliana several nights earlier, he'd made it his practice to explore the Maclean land and meet the crofters. He also went for a morning swim in a nearby loch. It was deep and freezing, and its color as blue as the evening sky.

It was the freezing he needed.

Unfortunately, the swim did not cool the lust that continued to roar through him every time he saw Juliana. And it seemed that the more he tried to avoid her, the more he saw her. She was everywhere.

She was even in Lachlan's library reading a book to Denny last eve.

She'd looked startled when she saw him, then ducked her head as color suffused her cheeks.

God's blood but she seemed to grow more beautiful every day.

How could that be?

He was grateful to Kimbra, who had taken swiftly to Denny. He had learned from Rory that his sister-in-law was a healer of sorts, that she had nursed Lachlan back to health. Denny had taken to her immediately, and he often saw Denny, Kimbra and Juliana huddled together in the library.

When he saw Juliana tending to Denny, he wanted her all the more.

He suspected he was not fooling Rory when he said he wanted to ride over Maclean lands and meet the families who worked it. It was Rory who suggested swims in the loch. "I know something about that," his brother had said with amusement in his eyes.

Patrick was just now piecing together the tales of his brothers' romantic mishaps. He could—would—be stronger than they. He could rein in his feelings.

Thus the solitary rides.

But as he rode through the gate of Inverleith, his hair still damp, he saw his brother talking to a tall stranger, one who matched his own height. The man wore a plaid that differed slightly from those worn by Macleans.

But he recognized the dyes in the plaid and the face. His stomach clenched.

The newcomer's eyes opened wider as recognition dawned in his face. *Campbells are no longer my enemy.* His brain told him that but his instincts said something else. Instincts honed by his father for many years.

"Patrick? Patrick Maclean?"

"Aye," he said coldly. The Campbell might be Rory's friend and Lachlan's. He was not his.

"Where in the devil have you been?"

Anger rose in him. Who was the Campbell to question him in his own courtyard? And what was he doing here?

"Your business?" he said sharply.

"I thought there could be danger. One of my people saw a strange ship . . ."

"There is no ship," Rory interrupted.

"I noticed that," the Campbell replied. "I will put my worries to rest."

Jamie turned to Rory. "Will you not offer me a drink after a long ride?"

Patrick thought of the Moors. The others as well. Even with Scot clothing, they stood out from the others.

His gaze met Rory's, who raised an eyebrow.

"The hall is currently crowded," Patrick said stiffly. "I brought some men back from France to sail the ship Rory wishes to purchase." 'Twas a weak explanation but all he could devise so quickly. The devil take it, but he had depended on Inverleith's isolation. When he was a lad, there were few, if any, visitors.

The Campbell's gaze did not leave Patrick's face. "I did not realize you and Rory had been in contact with each other. I was under the impression you were missing. Believed dead."

"A captain of a Maclean ship was in Paris," Patrick lied. "I had just arrived from a trip to the far east. There were pirates and . . ." He stopped and shrugged. "I am sure you do not have time for this."

"Oh, but I do," Jamie said. "I would like to hear every detail of such an adventure."

"Later," Patrick said curtly. "I have a horse to groom."

"I have time," Jamie said easily. "I want to see Cousin Felicia and the bairns."

There was something about the way he made that announcement that riled Patrick. He suspected the Campbell was enjoying his discomfort. Patrick remembered the last time they had met during games held in Edinburgh. They were an afternoon match, and it had continued a very long time. They fought to a draw, to a point neither could rise again. It had been the first time Patrick had not won. It was said it was the first time Jamie Campbell had not won.

"Your hair is wet," Rory observed with that damned amusement of his. "You apparently took my advice." It was obvious he was trying to break the tension.

Blasted brother. Patrick did not reply as he turned and walked his mount toward the stable. Devil take it, but this was the last thing he needed at the moment. A Campbell.

JULIANA sat in the small drawing room carved out of the massive stone wall with Denny and Kimbra. The room was designated as Lachlan's because he kept his books there.

Kimbra had taken her there shortly after her arrival. "It is Lachlan's room," she said proudly. "He purchases a book whenever he can find one he does not already possess."

Juliana had haunted the sanctuary since her arrival, though there was always a Maclean at guard.

Then two days ago, Kimbra found her there and asked if she would like to help her with Denny. Patrick had explained, she said, that Denny had not said a word since he had first been brought to the *Sofia*, and they knew not where he belonged, or whether he had a family. Kimbra had helped heal Lachlan. Mayhap she could do the same with Denny.

Of the two sisters-in-law, Juliana had warmed to Kimbra first. Felicia was often busy with her children and although she was always gracious and full of life, there was something especially kind and thoughtful about Kimbra. Juliana remembered Denny from the aftermath of the revolt. He was often the silent shadow of Patrick Maclean.

"Patrick says he has not spoken, though he appears to understand English," Kimbra said. "Patrick seems to think that I might be able to talk to him in some way, find out where he belongs. Lachlan told him I am a healer, but I am not. I just know herbs, and I do not think herbs will help Denny."

"What can I do?" Juliana asked.

"I have been reading to him, but I am not . . . good." She lowered her head. "I'm still learning . . ."

The words trailed away as if she were uncertain whether Juliana would agree to help Denny.

But she did, eagerly. After that magical hour with Patrick Maclean, he had avoided her, often leaving the keep early in the morning and not returning until late. On the few occasions their eyes had met, she'd felt his gaze consume her. The heat puddled in her stomach, and she felt a yearning so compelling she thought she would die from it.

She welcomed the distraction of Denny. Not only did she need to keep herself occupied but it was a way to appease her own guilt. She still shivered when she remembered the sounds and smells from the rowing deck, the scars she had seen on so many of the oarsmen, and Manuel as well.

"I think Denny might have lost his memory, and speech, because of a blow. There's a scar on the side of his head. Lachlan lost his memory when he was wounded on the head," Kimbra said.

"For how long?"

"Weeks."

"How long has Denny been like this?"

"Patrick said a year, mayhap more. Ever since he was brought to the galley."

Juliana's stomach clenched. No one seemed to blame her for the horrors of her uncle's ship, but she did. She felt tainted by it. How could anyone not blame her? Her family was responsible for Patrick's suffering. For the suffering of so many more.

"Is it the same as Lachlan then?" she asked.

"Lachlan was always able to speak. He just could not remember. I know nothing about wounds to the head. But Denny's eyes take in everything. I am sure he understands our conversations. Patrick said he fought well when they overtook the ship and had undoubtedly been trained. If only we could get him to speak."

"And if he doesn't?"

"He can stay here. Patrick has made that clear, but even if he hadn't, neither Rory or Lachlan would turn him away."

"You love Lachlan?"

"Aye. With all my heart. He is gentle yet brave. He loves my Audra as much as if she were his. I hope to give him another child soon."

"You are not afraid?"

"The curse, you mean?"

"*Si.*"

"I do not believe in curses," Kimbra said. "Even if I did, I would still take every day I could with Lachlan."

Juliana swallowed a lump in her throat. Until coming to Inverleith, she had not known that love really existed between a man and woman. It certainly had not between her mother and father, nor had she seen it elsewhere. She had never expected any in her life, certainly not with Viscount Kingsley. The best she'd expected was that he would not be like her father.

"Patrick cares for you," Kimbra said unexpectedly.

"No. He just does not know what to do with me," she replied.

"He looks at you as Lachlan looked at me when . . ." Kimbra blushed then, and Juliana thought how pretty she was. And kind.

It was the kindness that prompted the statement. Patrick Maclean had ignored her these last few days. Ever since the kiss that turned her world upside down.

Even the thought of it sent heat coursing through her and took her breath away.

She tried to thrust it aside by reading to Denny. In the small drawing room, she would read something from the Bible, then hand it to Denny. She saw Denny's eyes scan the words, even mouth them, but nothing came from his lips. He had never frightened her on the ship as the others had. Despite his scars and the fact he had been as bloody as the others immediately after the revolt, she'd not seen the hate and fury in his eyes that had been in the others'.

"I wish you could tell me where you are from," she told Denny.

Kimbra rose suddenly. "Rory has maps. If we spread one in front of him and pointed out places, perhaps he could point to where he is from."

Kimbra's enthusiasm spurred her own. At last. Something to do. Something worthwhile.

"I will find him," Kimbra offered.

"No, you stay with Denny," Juliana said. Denny responded to Kimbra more than anyone. Juliana suspected it was because Kimbra had no connection with the ship.

She left the room and passed the great hall, then stopped suddenly.

A stranger stood with Rory. He was as tall as Patrick, and he was glorious. His hair shone like spun gold and his eyes were as blue as the Spanish sea. His bearing made it clear he was a person of authority, of rank.

His gaze focused on her, and his eyes widened in surprise as he studied her, open curiosity on his face.

Patrick emerged from the stable. His steps hastened as he saw her and he joined the two men. His back was stiff, his expression wary if not hostile. It was obvious he did not consider the man standing with his brother a friend. More like an enemy.

The newcomer said something to Rory, but she was too far away to hear. She knew, though, that it concerned her.

Patrick replied, again beyond her hearing.

This might be her chance. Her opportunity. She could fall on his mercy, tell him she had been kidnapped.

And the stranger might die.

Even if not, she knew she could not do it. Too many lives were involved. Would Rory fight for his brother? Would the newcomer die? Would the oarsmen, including Manuel and Denny and the Spaniard, pay with their lives?

Then the golden-haired man walked toward her. Patrick moved to step in front of him but he adroitly sidestepped him. He bowed and gave her a smile that was blinding. "Jamie Campbell at your service," he said.

Then waited for an introduction.

And waited.

Rory finally said, "This is Anna, a friend of Kimbra's, who is staying with us for a while."

"Anna? A bonny name." He looked at Patrick, who had been standing silent, a deepening scowl on his face. "She returned with you?"

"Nay," he said shortly without explaining further.

The Campbell's gaze returned to her. "You will have to visit my wife, Janet, and me at Dunstaffnage."

"I do not believe she will have time," Patrick said.

"Mayhap the lady should make that decision."

"I have vowed to keep her safe," Patrick replied, the insult not very subtle.

Jamie Campbell raised an eyebrow but let it go. "Believe it or not, it is good to have you back, Patrick," he said mildly. "Your brothers have missed you, and I want nothing but peace with you."

"They said you . . . saved their lives. I am in your debt." Patrick's voice told Juliana how difficult it was for him to make that admission.

"Nay, because they'd have done the same. Things have changed, Patrick, and both our clans are better for it."

Juliana felt the tension in the air. She had heard the tale of Felicia's and Rory's romance, about the bitterness and hatred that plagued the two clans for a hundred years.

Rory broke in. "Tell us about Court. How is Queen Margaret, and who is her favorite now?"

"Not I, I fear," the Campbell said. "She is getting too close to England. She will lose the support of most of the Highland clans. Or what is left of them."

"And Spain?" Rory said. "Do you hear aught of their troublemaking?"

"They are seeking stronger ties with England. Advisors to Henry VIII are disappointed that Catherine of Aragon has not produced a male heir, and, since England's treaty with France, he seems to be moving closer to King Louis.

There are even rumors that he may marry his sister to the French king."

"God's blood," Patrick blurted out. "That would leave Scotland standing alone."

"Aye, and the queen knows it," the Campbell replied. "The clans know it as well. I cannot stomach Margaret's new overtures to England myself."

Juliana listened with growing apprehension. Her father seldom talked of politics in front of her. It was, he always said, the business of men.

"Spain is worried as well," Jamie continued. "There is talk of more marriages, the need to bring more Spanish blood to the English court."

Now she understood why her father and uncle wanted the marriage so badly. It was not only their business interests, but there was also a need to bind two nations closer together. Her father was a very distant cousin of the Spanish king, but he was a relation. He had royal blood, and therefore so did she, even diluted as it may be. Her father had only a minor claim to a title.

But it was an important connection if the Spanish king made it so. She froze. Was the marriage more important than she'd thought? If so, the danger to Patrick was far greater than either of them believed.

She should not care. She should care only about her mother. About those she had left in Spain. She should care about her uncle's brutal death.

"We are boring the lass," Jamie said, obviously mistaking her expression for tedium. She thanked the Holy Mother such was so.

She turned to Rory and tried to explain why she had intruded. "I . . . Kimbra and I are looking for a map to help . . ." She stopped suddenly.

"Help who?" Jamie Campbell asked, curiosity very plain in his face.

"Her daughter," she quickly said. "We are teaching her about the world."

"Young Audra?" Jamie said. "She is a wee charmer."

"Aye," Juliana said. It had been an easy word to adopt. "But the map . . ."

"I will find you one," Patrick interrupted.

He nodded briefly to his brother, ignored Jamie and turned toward the great door of the keep, obviously expecting her to follow.

She did. Questions and emotions were bubbling inside her.

He led her up to her bedchamber. Carmita was gone, probably to the kitchen to help.

He closed the door behind him. "Your marriage?" he said. "It was part of a larger scheme?"

She did not pretend that she did not know what he meant. She had been as startled—and alarmed—by the conversation as he apparently was. Until the Campbell had mentioned Spain's apparent interest, she had not considered her marriage any more than a business arrangement. "My father said nothing about the marriage other than the fact that he wanted stronger financial ties with the Earl of Chadwick. There was already a connection between our families. My mother was a distant cousin." She hesitated, then added, "My father did say King Ferdinand approved of the match."

"Why would he need to approve?" His question was harsh.

"I do not know, except . . ."

"Except?" he urged her.

"My father . . . is . . . he has blood ties to Ferdinand."

A muscle leapt along his tightened jaw.

"But I cannot believe it was that important. We rarely saw him. It was a very distant connection."

"Your father did not say your marriage was arranged at Ferdinand's request?" His voice was tight.

"I thought it was my father bragging. He always talked about his connection with the crown, but we saw little benefit from it."

"You did not tell me."

"You did not ask. And I did not understand until . . . now."

He turned away from her and went to the window and looked down. She followed him.

Rory and his friend were gone. Inside somewhere?

She felt Patrick's tension beside her.

"What does it mean?" she asked.

"That I have brought far more trouble to my clan than I thought," he said. "Mayhap to Scotland itself."

His voice was heavy with guilt, even anguish. He turned to her, and she saw glittering intensity in those usually curtained eyes. A knot of apprehension twisted in her stomach.

"No one will learn . . ." she started.

"More than a hundred people know what happened," he said.

"They will be gone in a few days," Juliana replied. "And their lives are at risk as well."

"Some also like their drink," he said. " 'Tis easy to let something slip then. And others have seen the *Sofia* as well. Our Macleans. A Campbell said he saw a strange ship. And you, lass, cannot stay hidden here forever."

She reached out and touched him. No matter he had tried to avoid her these last few days. No matter that she had known a terrible loneliness during that time. No matter that he had killed her uncle or foiled her father's plotting.

Nothing mattered but his pain.

"You had no choice," she whispered. "You would have died. As would the others."

"And others should die now in my place? Scotland is nae so ready for another war."

She already knew his sense of responsibility. He tried to deny it, but she had watched him with Manuel, the sweetness with which he tried to help Denny, the insistence that the oarsmen receive what had been promised. She knew not any other man who would have cared.

She could only share his pain now, not try to alleviate it, for she knew the latter would be hopeless.

"I can disappear. I can be Anna," she said, trying to give

him a smile, small as it may be. "I think my English is good enough to pass as an Englishwoman. And not many people have seen me. We were not active at court. My father was . . . said he was shamed by an English wife."

She decided not to mention that her uncle had sent a miniature of her to the Viscount Kingsley.

"Why would you do that?" he said. "I killed your uncle. We stole your dowry."

"A dowry I did not want, and an uncle I did not admire," she said softly.

"And your mother?"

The question was like a knife stab into her heart. She could deny all, but that. The thought of letting her mother believe her dead caused her soul to bleed.

Her mother's grief against the lives of so many?

He closed his eyes and his arms went around her, and they clung together in mutual desperation and anguish.

DESPITE his vows to keep away from Juliana, Patrick knew it was useless when he saw misery in Juliana's eyes as he'd asked about her mother.

Instead of backing away, he pulled her into his arms.

To comfort her.

Who in the devil did he think he was kidding?

He needed her as much as she might need his comfort.

He did not deserve it. When had he thought about her? He had made sure she stayed alive. And physically unhurt. But he hadn't fully considered the ravages to her life. He had taken everything from her, including her freedom.

And he had no answers for her. No solutions. No schemes. No strategies. No hope.

Now that the Campbell had found his way here, the danger to him, to his clan, to his fellow oarsmen, had grown. Jamie Campbell had seen her. He'd probably seen some of the Moors by now. Not only that, his clansmen had reported seeing a galleon. The English and Scots did not have ships powered by oars.

He leaned down and rested his cheek on her hair. It was newly washed and smelled fresh and sweet. For a moment, all the pain and loneliness of the past years eased. She was soft. So soft.

Waves of tenderness cascaded through his body, something he'd never felt with a woman before. Those feelings had been building over the past few days, from the moment, he now realized, he'd first seen her. Her gallantry, her readiness to do battle on behalf of her servant and herself despite her terror, had resounded deep inside him.

Touching her again was probably the most foolish thing he had ever done, and he did not care. From the moment he'd touched her lips days ago, he knew it had not been enough. God knew he had tried to stay away, but compulsion kept him coming back.

He pulled her even closer to him. He felt her every breath, her every heartbeat. Her body melted into his as if it belonged there. And then she lifted her face, her expression full of both wonder and question.

God's blood, but she was appealing. Her eyes were incredibly wide, the violet ring deeper, the blue-gray ever so clear. He leaned down and his lips touched hers. He meant it to be brief, but his lips hesitated and then responded to the yielding of her mouth.

Her hand went around his neck as he bent his head to kiss her. Her fingers ran through his hair, playing enticing games with the sensitive skin of his neck. Nothing had prepared him for the overwhelming hunger, the excruciating hunger that hardened his body. Her smallest touch was like a torch to him, her slightest movements against him firing new blazes until the ache inside became unbearable.

His blood turned to currents of liquid fire, searing every bone, every muscle. Despite the raging desire in him, he moved slowly, his hands gentle as he stroked the back of her neck.

•

She was a virgin. He knew that from the uncertainty of her reactions. And she was another man's betrothed. If he deflowered her, he might forever ruin her life. Devil take it, he probably already had.

"Patrick," she said in a voice that was part moan.

Not here. Carmita wandered in and out, and so did his sisters-in-law. As did the young lass Audra and Manuel and . . .

He sighed, pulled back slightly and delighted in watching her. Her eyes were glazed with passion, her lips swollen from his kisses. He watched as the edge of her tongue licked them, moistening them. Her cheeks were flushed, and a curl had come loose from the pins and tumbled down the side of her face.

She was a bedeviling combination of innocent and seductress, and, quite simply, the most desirable woman he had ever seen.

How could he let her go?

For her sake.

A groan started in the back of his throat.

"Do not go," she whispered.

"Juliana," he rasped in a hoarse whisper. The want, the raw, ragged desire that was pure exquisite pain burgeoned into something close to agony. "Unwise," he murmured helplessly. "So unwise."

JULIANA'S breath caught in her throat as he hesitated.

She did not want him to hesitate.

She found herself leaning toward him, her body seeking his warmth, the promise of relief from the aching need inside her. But the tenseness was still in his body, and she knew he was fighting against the attraction that was so powerful between them.

"Do not go this time," she said in a voice that did not sound like hers.

"I have done enough damage to you," he replied, his fingers touching her cheek with a sweetness and tenderness she hadn't expected. But instead of quelling the need inside, it served only to inflame her more.

"You will do more if you leave," she said shamelessly. She was not thoroughly aware of what she wanted. She only knew the craving inside was too strong, too deep, too compelling to be left unsatisfied. Her insides burned for him, the pressure growing until she thought she would shatter into a million pieces.

"The devil take it," he said in a low, barely intelligible mutter, and she knew she had won.

He released her and went to the door, turning the bolt.

She watched, reveling in his presence, the way he so filled the room just by being there. Then he returned and touched her again. She could not prevent a whimper as his fingers untied the back of her gown, and it fell to the floor, leaving only her underdress and chemise covering her.

His fingers played with a strand of hair, and he rubbed it against her neck, his hand moving along her pulse and dipping toward her breast in a slow, seductive movement that inflamed every part of her body.

She leaned against him, feeling an odd sense of belonging that contradicted all the pulsating sensations building in her. She felt the thump of his heart, the heat of his body, and she looked up and knew the pleasure of simply gazing at him. Nothing else mattered now as her lips lifted to meet his. She no longer had a will of her own. It was mixed with his, surrendered to the stronger need of their bodies.

He muttered something she could not hear as his lips reached for hers, then burned their imprint on her consciousness. The kiss was hungry. Ravenous.

Any reservations Juliana might have had disappeared as the kiss deepened and the yearning between them exploded. His tongue entered her mouth and she welcomed it with her own, instinctively exploring and seeking and delighting in the discoveries. The warm rush she'd felt earlier was nothing compared to the heat now flooding her. An uncontrollable tingling started in the core of her being and swelled to encompass all of her.

Her gaze darted upward and she was consumed by eyes that now burned with fire. Her heart raced as new sensations ran through her. Soft, longing ones. Fiery, demanding ones.

Again her mother's words came to her. But she no longer believed them. Nothing bad could come of these glorious feelings. She savored every taste, feeling, touch. She wanted to hold them all to her heart forever.

The kiss was enough for a few moments, and then a new wanting gnawed at her. Her body moved closer, so close she felt his heart beat against hers. She felt his hunger and wondered at her own. How could she so want something she'd never had?

She wanted to utter love words, endearments. But she was afraid. He had never mentioned love, or sweet words. Everything in the past few days told her he was fighting the attraction they had for one another. She did not want him to run again.

But it was so hard. She wanted to say so much. To ask so much. To know why she was feeling as she was, and where it led. She wanted words of love, of tenderness, but she knew in his eyes they were still opponents of sorts. He did not surrender easily.

This may not last beyond these hours, but she wanted whatever she could take. She wanted to hold these feelings and sensations in her mind and heart. She wanted to remember moments of joy and tenderness and passion.

His kiss deepened, became almost savage, and she returned it with as much fervor.

Then she was aware he was removing his thick belt and it fell away with a clunk, then his plaid fell as well. He stood there in a long linen shirt that outlined the muscled beauty of his body. Her fingers went to the opening at his neck and touched the warm skin. She felt a tremor run through his body.

He groaned and yet his hands were gentle as they ran

along her body. Her legs almost gave way as his mouth went down to her neck and he kissed her throat.

His head lifted from where he had been nuzzling her throat, and his eyes met hers as his hands moved to her underdress. There was a question in them now. And emotion. She could finally see it clearly. There was no curtain hiding his feelings. Instead there was a fierce, hungry light in them.

She swallowed hard. They had started a blaze together, and there was no stopping it. His hands untied her underdress and it fell to the ground, leaving only her chemise. Then that, too, was gone.

An unbearable tension was building inside. He paused, and she saw the hesitation in his eyes, even reluctance. Yet she continued to feel the tremors in his body. He wanted her.

"Please," she said, simply because she did not know what else to say. She did not know what to do next. She only knew she had to have it.

He muttered something before his mouth ground into hers. His tongue entered her mouth, deliciously voracious as it tantalized, then his lips moved to her neck, nuzzling, murmuring her name.

Before she could quite assess all the new feelings those movements provoked, she felt his lips on her breast, felt the incredible sensations as her nipple hardened and ached with his touch. She shivered as his mouth played with it, his tongue teasing until she could no longer stand the sweet pain of it.

She found her own fingers pulling off his shirt, touching the wiry reddish hair that sprung from his chest, which was now both warm and moist. She moved her head so it rested on his heart, and she heard its beat, steady and strong.

He picked her up and carried her to the bed. He laid her down gently, then he was kissing her again, his mouth moving down her body, making her glow. Her body sizzled with every touch, aching for more, yet still savoring every second of what was happening.

When she thought she could bear no more, he touched

and caressed the triangle of hair between her legs. His fingers entered the most private part of her, and she felt a wetness, then waves of the strangest pleasure. He lifted himself above her and the male part of him moved seductively until, in agony, she reached around him and pulled him toward her.

He entered slowly and she was shocked at the fullness of him. A sudden, sharp pain caused her to cry out, and he stopped, his body stiffening. The surprise had caused her cry, but after a few seconds, the pain receded, eclipsed now by her need for him.

The pain eased as did the strangeness of his body becoming part of her own. Yet he had not moved. Her hands urged him down again as her body arched up, seeking to bring him deeper inside her, to reestablish that communion they had. "Do not go," she whispered.

He stilled, then began to move again, slowly, tenderly, until their hunger matched again, and she caught his rhythm and responded with movements of her own. She throbbed with wonderful feelings, with the instinctive responses that brought him deeper and deeper into the core of her. He thrust faster and they were both racing, racing toward something Juliana knew was waiting for her. Then it came, a glorious explosion of sensation. Torrents of pleasure flooded through her.

He lay quietly for several moments. They both did, letting the aftermath of passion ripple through them.

She touched his face. "I never knew," she whispered. "*Madre* . . ." She stopped, not sure how to go on.

His gaze, lazy with lovemaking and warmer than she'd ever seen it, rested on her. "Your *madre* . . . ?" he prompted.

"She . . . she was wrong." She felt tears gather behind her eyes. A sorrow that her mother had never known what she had just experienced. No matter what happened now, she would know the glory of sweetness and fire.

His finger touched the edge of her eye, wiping the tear away. "I am sorry," he said. "I did not intend to hurt you."

"Oh, no," she said, horrified that he misunderstood. "I

have no regret. Never. It . . . is glorious. It is just that she never knew it. She warned me that a wifely duty was to be . . . endured."

"I think sometimes she might be right," he said, running his finger along her cheek.

"Have you . . . ever felt this way before? I mean," she added hurriedly, "does a man feel . . . ?" She stopped. She did not know how to continue, how to explain all the sensations she was still feeling.

"Nay, Juliana. I think it is something rare." He leaned down and kissed her nose with a bemused smile on his face. "Now I understand my brothers better."

"Umm," she murmured with satisfaction at his answer. She took his hand and pressed it to her mouth.

She wanted to utter words of love, but there was still too much between them. She did not want to ruin these moments of belonging by asking for something she could not have.

Instead her fingers went to his back and touched the scars there. She felt the ridges and she wept inside for the pain he'd endured. He stiffened at first, then relaxed slightly as she tried to heal those scars with tenderness.

"Ah, lass. Do they not repel you?"

"No. They cover me with shame. For you, they should be a badge of courage. You were strong enough, brave enough to survive, to fight back."

A flicker of emotion crossed his face, and she realized that he had truly believed the scars would brand him. He did not see what she saw. That he had a sense of honor about him that was far more appealing than any physcial perfection. He did not have to look after the oarsmen in the ship, but he had. He had not needed to protect her and Carmita from a maddened crew. He had not needed to look after Manuel or Denny.

She had never known such a man, or known they existed.

She would not use that honor against him now.

But she would take these moments of peace, of warm,

lovely sensations, of caring so deeply that she wanted to put him before herself.

She reached over and kissed him again, starting with his neck and working her way up.

"Ah, lass, you bring a magic with you."

"No less than you. I feel wrapped in a spell." She hesitated, then added, "I wish it to last forever."

His hand caught hers, and he brought it to his mouth. For a moment, he said nothing, then in a voice little more than a whisper, "All spells end, Juliana. And reality rushes back." His voice broke slightly. "This should never have happened. I have wronged you yet again, and there is no going forward. Nae with me."

"Why?" She hated the plea in her voice.

"I canna make promises," he said, and the Scottish brogue was stronger than ever. "I . . . want . . . but I canna. I might well be tried for piracy or worse. I would not have you involved in that."

"I am involved."

"Nay, you were a captive. You canna be blamed, but if . . ."

He stopped abruptly and she wondered whether she would ever know what the "if" meant.

Not if the stubborn set of his jaw was any indication.

"I must go," he said, touching her face with a gentleness she never would have expected days ago when she first saw him. "There will be rumors if I tarry longer."

"I do not care."

"I do, Juliana. I have not done well by you, and I will regret it all my years."

"I will not," she said. "No matter what happens, I will always remember the magic here. And be grateful for it." She cared not whether she sounded young or foolish. She had to give voice to all the emotions she felt, to the surge of . . . love that washed through her as she watched the pain in his face as he struggled between conscience and need.

She didn't care about conscience. Not anymore. There

could be nothing wrong with what she felt. What he had just given her.

Patrick untangled himself from her arms and stood. He looked down at her for a long moment. Though his eyes were shuttered again, the length of that moment told her he did not want to go.

As if burned, he turned swiftly and left.

She swallowed the rock that seemed to have lodged in her throat. Holy Mary, but she loved him. And God had played a very mischievous trick on both of them.

"NOW tell me what is really happening," Jamie said, as he followed Rory past the crowded great hall. He glanced curiously inside and started as he saw the dark complexioned Moors.

"Those," he observed, "are no ordinary seamen."

"I swear they are sailors," Rory said. And they certainly had been, though involuntary ones.

"Odd sailors," Jamie muttered.

"You get sailors where you find them."

They went into his father's office. Jamie plopped into a chair and took a draw of Rory's fine wine.

"I need the truth, Rory," Jamie persisted.

Rory merely threw him a quizzical glance.

"You are not a good liar, not with me," Jamie said with a frown. "What is Patrick involved in? Do not forget my cousin lives here."

"She is my wife," Rory said grumpily. "I would not let harm come to Felicia." He paused for a moment. "Patrick has been here only a few days. He was held for a ransom that was never paid. He is not yet sure who he can trust, and I canna fault that. Fa did nothing to promote brotherly feelings."

"Ransom?" Jamie said. "Demands were sent to you?"

"Aye, thrice, he said. Each time it was said the message was delivered."

"When would that have been?"

"Seven years ago." Rory did not like the look in his friend's eyes. "You would not be knowing anything about it?"

"Nay. But I will be making inquiries."

Rory merely nodded, not liking that flash of comprehension in Jamie's eyes.

"And the woman?" Jamie asked. "How did she come to be here, and who is she?"

"I thought we told you. A friend of Kimbra's."

"That is no English accent I recognize."

"I did not know you had met every person in England."

Jamie blinked a moment, then grinned. "No more questions then, but she is a beauty."

"Aye," Rory agreed cautiously.

"Your brother looks at her as if she is a particularly fine morsel."

"He is fighting it," Rory said, "but like Lachlan and myself he is probably doomed to failure."

"He is in love then?"

"He does not realize it yet, but, aye, I think so."

"That should soften him."

"I do not think much will soften him at the moment."

"Is there aught I can do?"

"Aye, there is. I need your ear in Edinburgh. The queen still holds you in high regard."

"Not so much now. I tried to tell her the truth about some of her favorites."

"But you are still received?"

"Aye. I believe so." Jamie hesitated, then said, "I am not sure what I can do without knowing more."

"I cannot say more at the moment."

"It is trouble. I smell it."

"It may be over in a few days. I can only ask on behalf of myself and Lachlan, forget about a ship. Forget about what you've seen here."

"So it is dangerous?"

"You do not have to help. Patrick is not your concern."

"Since when has that stopped me?" Jamie said with his old cockiness. It had diminished slightly after Flodden Field. Rory was amused to see it back.

"And what about Patrick?" Jamie continued. "I do not think he will relish any help from me."

"I didn't relish your help either," Rory admitted with a grin. "It was a difficult lesson."

Jamie chuckled. "How long do you need me at court?"

"I am not sure yet."

"And what am I looking for?"

"Any news of a missing ship. One I hope everyone believes lies on the bottom of the Atlantic Ocean." He paused. "I'm also trying to convince him to go to court to be recognized as laird and head of the clan."

Jamie raised his eyebrows. "He is opposed to this?"

"He might be."

"If his reaction to me is any indication, he will not welcome my help. I do not think he likes me."

"I didn't like you either," Rory admitted again with a grin.

"I remember," Jamie said ruefully. He had spent several days in the Maclean dungeon. "It takes Macleans a while to get used to me."

Rory decided it was a good time to change the subject. Jamie was intrigued enough to go to Edinburgh. "And how is Janet and the bairn?"

"Very well." He grinned. "She is with child again. That is another reason I came here. To give you the news."

"That *is* good news," Rory replied, but he could not keep concern from his voice. Janet had had a difficult time during the birth of her first child.

"I will ensure she takes better care of herself this time," Jamie said. "No more riding for a while." He hesitated, then added, "She would enjoy a visit from Felicia and Kimbra. That's another reason for the visit."

"Not a very good time for you to be away," Rory said, guilt weighing on him.

"I will bargain with you. If Felicia can stay with Janet, then I will remain at court, though I wish to know more about why."

"You will," Rory promised. "Now about that wine . . ."

Chapter 23

PATRICK felt he was in a daze as he sat at the head of the table. God help him, but his body still ached from bedding Juliana. It desperately wanted to repeat the experience.

He glanced toward her. She was inches away, but it seemed as far as winter from summer where Patrick was concerned. He could not help but notice that she looked different, and he feared everyone in the room had probably noticed it as well. Although they had parted two hours earlier, her cheeks were still the color of roses, and her eyes were luminous. If she had any regrets, they did not show.

He, on the other hand, had many, many regrets.

He knew, however, that given a choice he would still do it all over again. The simple fact was he could not stay away from her, could not keep his hands off of her, no matter how hard he tried.

Only distance would do that. Unfortunately he did not have distance. He only had his self-control, and it was desperately lacking.

"Jamie is going to Edinburgh to keep us abreast of news there," Rory said, breaking the tension. "We think you should consider going with him. It would be what the heir would do. Too many Macleans already know you are here, and it will be suspicious if you do not go."

It was obvious that Rory meant for him to stay at Inverleith permanently, whereas he had no intentions of now doing so, not when his very presence could mean danger to the Macleans. Nor did he want to be in debt to a Campbell. How much had his brother told him, this old enemy of the Macleans?

"Felicia is going to stay with my wife while I am gone," Jamie broke in. "She will be leaving with the children tomorrow. Archibald and some of your Macleans will escort them," Jamie said. "I will stay another day or two and see Lachlan, then we can ride to Edinburgh."

It was the last thing Patrick wanted. He had no interest in charming a queen, especially an indecisive one. He most definitely did not wish to go with Jamie Campbell.

On the other hand, it would take him away from Juliana.

She glanced at him then, and he looked away. He feared his face would say far too much, especially as closely as Rory and the Campbell were watching.

"I hope you will be comfortable here at Inverleith," Felicia said to Juliana. "Kimbra will see that you have everything you need."

"Thank you. You have been very kind," Juliana replied.

"I hope Patrick will bring you to Dunstaffnage. You will like Janet, and she will like you."

"I do not know how long I will be here," Juliana said.

"I hope it is a long time." Felicia glanced at Patrick, then back at Juliana, a slight smile on her face.

Juliana did not answer but turned back to her food. Patrick saw her glance several times at Jamie.

Did she hope that Jamie might help her escape? He had seen her study the keep. But he knew well that no one could get in or out of Inverleith without going through the large gates, and he had instructed every Maclean to check each living thing that went through.

The thought that she might consider the idea was excruciating. Yet, why not? He had given her few choices.

She had come to him willingly. Not only willingly but with eagerness. But that did not mean she did not want to return to Spain or continue on to England.

He took another sip of the wine, though he had to be careful. He had to keep his wits about him.

He looked down the table again. The Spaniard was laughing with several Macleans. He had a talent for fitting in wherever he went. Denny sat quietly next to the Spaniard, but his gaze wandered around as if searching for something.

The others were seated. Most were drinking heartily; some of the oarsmen were beginning to gain some weight, and their voices were loud as they bragged about what they would to with their freedom and gold.

But what of Juliana? What kind of position had he placed her in? What would be the best thing for her? But then he had to think of the clan as well. What if they conflicted?

"You are frowning, Brother," Rory said from his seat to the left of Patrick.

"Aye, I am wondering when Lachlan will arrive," he lied. "Every day is dangerous."

"He will soon be here."

"He has changed much since I left."

"He might be the strongest of us all," Rory said. "It takes more courage to fight if you have fear and a loathing for killing."

"And you, Rory, do you have fear?"

"Since my bairns were born, I have much fear. I want them to grow with love, not as we did."

"You have been happy here."

"Aye. I have learned to love Inverleith, but I also like Edinburgh. With Felicia and the wee ones, I cannot sail as I once did, but I can expand our trading interests. Believe me, Patrick, it is something I have longed to do."

"And Lachlan?"

"He has turned into a fine merchant. He has an eye for goods. Your staying here as laird can allow Lachlan and I to do what we do best."

Patrick searched for guile in the words but found none. There was only an invitation to belong. A real desire for him to take his place.

What had happened to those demands for ransom?

He no longer thought his brother was involved. His mind went back to his capture. He thought then it had been planned in some way. Two other Scots had been with him that day as they fought with the French. One had been a MacHugh, the other a McFarland. All he remembered about the day he had been taken was a blow, then darkness. When he woke, *his* hands were bound. He never saw his fellow Scots again. The MacHughs were known allies of the Campbells.

He had thought about it the year he had wasted in a Spanish dungeon.

Was Jamie Campbell truly a friend to the Macleans? He planned to find out.

PATRICK escorted Juliana to her chamber after the meal was over. They brushed against each other, and that brief contact brought back all those hot sensations in a rush.

Juliana wanted to reach out and touch him. She wanted more than a momentary brush, more than polite conversation in the great hall. She wanted what she'd had hours earlier.

They reached her chamber. She opened the door and stood inside.

"I will send Carmita to tend to you," he said.

She nodded, though her heart thudded madly. She did not want Carmita's anxious presence. Her maid had known immediately what had happened when she'd appeared to help her dress. She'd said nothing, but Juliana had seen the knowledge in her face.

She feared everyone had.

She wanted to hold out her hand to him. To invite him inside her chamber.

But there was no invitation in his eyes. They were shuttered again. Closed to her.

"Sleep well, Juliana," he said, almost tonelessly. But just as she turned, he touched her cheek. So lightly she barely felt it. It was more like a whisper of a breeze.

Then he turned and disappeared down the stone steps.

HE hadn't wanted to leave her that way, but he had matters to discuss with Jamie Campbell, and he wanted his senses intact. Juliana had a way of distracting them.

He went through the great hall. The Moors were gathered in one corner, the Spaniards in another. All were listening to a Maclean playing the lute. Denny was nowhere to be seen.

Then he reached the office in the back of the hall. Rory and the Campbell were sitting there, a small cask of wine on a table. They were both drinking from silver cups, a legacy from former Macleans. Patrick remembered them. His father used them only for special occasions.

"There is a third cup there," Rory said. "Join us."

"Let us go up to up to my chamber," he said. "We will have more privacy there.

Rory nodded and he and the Campbell rose. Rory carried the cask of wine.

Once in his chamber, silence settled in the room. Patrick glanced at the Campbell, who looked the portrait of an indolent lord.

"How did you come to help my brothers?" he asked.

"My cousin," Jamie Campbell replied. "Like your Juliana, Felicia was to be wed to a man I did not trust nor like.

It was decreed by the king, who wanted an alliance between the two clans. She tried to escape but my cousin does nothing the easy way. She was kidnapped by the Macleans as a wife for Rory and, well, she refused to return home. The only way to save Felicia was to prove her prospective husband a rogue and traitor. Rory had information, and I had ways to reach the king. We had a common objective."

Patrick waited for him to continue.

"We learned to tolerate each other," Jamie said with a grin. "It became something of a tangle, particularly since Felicia did not stop interfering."

"Without Jamie," Rory took over, "Felicia would have wed a traitor, and probably Lachlan and I would be dead. When, three years later, the king called for troops to go into England, both Lachlan and Jamie went. Lachlan disappeared, and Jamie would not leave England without him."

"I was bored," Jamie said, obviously ill at ease with the recount.

But Patrick would have been blind and deaf not to see the affection between the two men. For a moment, he felt a pang of loss, even of jealousy, for never having had that kind of bond with his brothers. Or with anyone else, for that matter.

He looked at Rory.

His brother nodded.

"You may be at risk," Patrick warned. "Your Campbells as well."

"I will not endanger them," Jamie said, "but neither will I ever reveal anything I hear tonight."

It was still difficult to accept this change in the world Patrick had lived with all these years. A truce between Campbells and Macleans was something beyond his ken. Yet he was beginning to trust his brother, and his brother trusted the Campbell, and there was no doubt Patrick needed help. Not only for himself but for the others involved.

He also had little choice. He needed to ensure the Campbell's silence. Jamie Campbell had seen too much. Patrick took a swallow of wine. Then he told the entire tale.

At the end, silence filled the room. Even Rory was still.

Jamie Campbell stood and walked around the room. "I will do what I can," he said. "I will make sure every Campbell who saw the ship is convinced it is one of yours. The mist fogged their vision; or drink, which is more likely." He flashed that quick smile Patrick had seen when they met in the courtyard.

Patrick did not smile back.

"I agree with Rory," Jamie said. "You should go to court with all the pride of a Maclean and make your claim. Anything else will prompt questions."

Patrick conceded and nodded. It was too late now to disappear immediately.

"What about your lovely captive?"

"That is none of your concern."

"That means you do not know what to do," Jamie said. "You Macleans have interesting ways of finding brides. I do not know why the Maclean brothers cannot model themselves after me."

"She is not my bride," Patrick said stiffly.

"I was watching her at the table. She is in love with you, Patrick. It seems you can solve that particular problem by marriage."

"At the moment, my future is in question," Patrick said. "Even if she wished it, which I question, I would not wed if I thought I could be charged with piracy or worse." He regarded his cup sorrowfully. It was nearly empty. "And if I did wed, questions would be asked about my new bride."

"Felicia is very good at making up stories," Jamie said helpfully.

Rory grimaced. "So is Kimbra, although she has more scruples about it than my wife."

Patrick frowned at him. He did not understand how they could be so casual.

To his surprise, it was Jamie who understood. "Only a fool would not see how you two look at each other, even when you try to avoid each other."

Patrick shrugged. "I would be doing her no favors. I

killed her uncle as well as several other men in front of her. She could never forget that." He paused, then added, "She has family in Spain. A mother she fears for. If we wed, she could never go back. She would have to forget who she is."

He stopped. It was madness to discuss it. To even consider it.

Jamie raised an eyebrow, and Patrick realized he *was* considering it, God help him.

"What about the other oarsmen?" Jamie asked. "What do you plan to do with them?"

Rory broke in. "We are taking them to Morocco, or if they prefer, to the coast of Spain, with enough money for them to start anew. They all know their necks are at risk as well as mine."

"That often does not matter when a man has had a drink or two," Jamie said.

"That is exactly why I cannot wed."

Rory interrupted. "How would Queen Margaret react if she learned of it?"

"It depends on the reaction of the English," Jamie said.

"The lady is promised to an English lord," Patrick informed him.

"Who?" Jamie asked.

"Viscount Kingsley, the son of the Earl of Chadwick."

Jamie stilled. "You just complicated matters. Kingsley is one of England's emissaries to Margaret."

PATRICK'S chest moved on a quickly withdrawn breath.

"The son of the Earl of Chadwick is Viscount Kingsley? He is at Edinburgh?" Rory asked.

"Aye. For the past month. An unpleasant fellow," Jamie replied.

"You have met him?"

"Aye. He is said to be a friend of the Earl of Angus, who currently has Queen Margaret's ear."

"Angus?" Patrick said with a snort of contempt.

"You might be thinking of the old Angus," Jamie said. "He died last year. The new earl is my cousin, but nae a friend. Margaret is guardian of James V, and Angus believes the way to become regent is to marry her."

"I see intrigue continues," Patrick said wryly.

"Aye. A battle wages between Angus, who leans toward England, and the Earl of Arran, who leans toward France."

Patrick considered what Jamie Campbell had said. When he'd left Inverleith years ago, James IV had been in control of Scotland, at least as much as Scotland could ever be ruled. He'd been a good king for Scotland. Fair, although he'd had his confrontations with the Highland chiefs as well as those in the Isles. He'd held many parliaments and had brought a rare unity to Scotland.

Now apparently it could be ripped apart again, especially with a child king who had as a guardian a young woman who was sister to the English king.

Jamie continued, "The opposition to Angus and his ambitions is led by the Earl of Arran, who wants to name John, Duke of Albany, as regent."

Rory interrupted then. "Arran has spent his life in France but he is cousin to the young king and would preserve the 'aulde alliance' with France."

Patrick thought how much he had missed in the past eight years. Even before that, though, he'd not been at court. Politics had not interested him, and Jamie's father had been an advisor to James IV. That meant the Macleans had not been welcome there, and he'd had no interest in the intrigues.

Now he had to learn as much about the court—and Kingsley—as possible.

"Tell me more about the viscount," Patrick asked.

"I can just tell you the rumors. His father had been an advisor to Henry VII but retired to the country when Henry VIII was crowned. The son is trying to regain the privileged position and volunteered to act as emissary to the Scottish court. Apparently he was the younger son until his brother, the heir, died. Now he is more than making up for his change in fortune. He is as arrogant a man as I've seen." Jamie's face suddenly changed, and his mouth creased into a frown. "He was boasting about a marriage that would put him at the side of the king, just as his father had been."

A chill ran through Patrick.

Jamie's gaze caught his and held. "He is a bully, Patrick. Mayhap worse than that. I saw him beat a horse nearly to death because he lost a race. He will not be happy to see his plans foiled, especially foiled by a Scot. 'Tis obvious he has contempt for us."

The chill deepened. What if he had not taken over the ship? He would never have known about Juliana and she would be readying herself for marriage with Kingsley.

"I want to know everything there is to know about him," Patrick said. "About his reputation in London, his relationship with the Mendozas."

"Lachlan can find that out," Rory said. "Lachlan can mimic any accent, impersonate anyone. And he has friends among the English borderers, the biggest assortment of thieves and murderers in either country."

"I cannot ask him to do that. It would be dangerous, especially since he was at Flodden," Patrick said.

"He will want to do it," Rory said quietly.

"Why?"

"We are brothers," Rory said simply. "I would do it, except Lachlan would be far more effective."

"Are you accustomed to volunteering him?"

Rory's face paled. A muscle throbbed in his cheek.

Puzzled, Patrick could only stare at him. He had not meant anything by the remark. 'Twas only an attempt at lightness.

Jamie's expression was fixed. No sign of the amusement usually there.

"I did not mean to . . . imply . . ."

"Nay," Rory said softly. "You did not know. Lachlan offered to take my place when King James marched south. I agreed because Felicia had just had another child and Lachlan had such guilt about father that he felt compelled to go. I feared he was dead for a long time, and I faulted myself." A ghost of a smile returned. "I was afraid I'd lost two brothers."

"You would risk him again?"

"Lachlan is uncommonly inventive. I do not know what you've heard about his capture, but a chess game with his English captor saved him. More than several times." He grinned. "He is far more adept at ferreting out secrets than I am."

"If Kingsley is close to Margaret, then you are risking your lives if she believes you are protecting me. I cannot let you do that."

"I still have some influence," Jamie said, "as does Rory. He and Felicia were married at court with the late king and Margaret as witnesses. I think Margaret has always had a soft place in her heart for him."

"Mayhap I should go with the *Felicia.* I will have been lost at sea with the others." The thought was like a sword in his gut. He had found a family, he was sure of it now. They were all willing to sacrifice for him. The loneliness of all those years was gradually dissolving.

"It's no good now. Too many Macleans know you are here," Rory replied.

"What about Kimbra?" Patrick asked. "How will she feel about sending her husband into danger again?"

"I think Kimbra will understand," his brother said.

"But I do not," Patrick said. "I cannot let you two risk everything. Not for me," Patrick said through a lump in his throat. He was not accustomed to the emotion flowing through him, nor did he know how to direct it. Anger had been there, and he'd learned to harness that, but this . . .

"It is not only for you," Rory said. "It angers me that Spain believes it can enslave our people without consequences. It is also for Juliana. I would not like her in the hands of Viscount Kingsley."

"We would be risking the entire clan," Patrick replied. "Possibly two clans if Jamie's part is known. The Earl of Angus would be only too eager to take us both down."

A noise came from outside the chamber door.

The three looked at each other, then Rory strode over to it, opened it and looked around. He shook his head. "No one."

Patrick stood. "We should have locked the door."

"No one comes up here but a few servants, and they are totally loyal," Rory said.

Patrick nodded, but he did not have the surety that his brother did.

"It is time to retire," he said. "We can discuss it more tomorrow," he said.

"THE map!" Juliana exclaimed.

In the aftermath of Patrick's lovemaking, Juliana had forgotten all about the map she'd been trying to find. The map that she hoped would spark some response in Denny.

"The map, Senorita Juliana?" Carmita asked as she paused in brushing her mistress's hair. She had already helped Juliana undress after the evening meal.

"I had meant to get a map of England from Rory Maclean to show to Denny. Perhaps he would recognize something. I was . . . distracted."

Carmita did not reply for a moment. Of course she knew what had happened there. The bedclothing was stained. It was all Juliana could do to keep her gaze from staring at the bed and to keep her cheeks from blushing.

"They say the ship is coming any day now," Carmita said, looking away. "Manuel says it might be here tomorrow."

What would happen then?

"What will happen to us, senorita?" Juliana's thoughts were echoed by Carmita's words in Spanish.

"I do not know."

"Will they take us away?"

Juliana could only repeat her previous answer.

"Manuel said he wishes to go where we go."

Juliana looked sharply at Carmita. There was a smile on her maid's face.

"Has he said anything about his life?" she asked, truly curious.

"He believes he has fourteen years, but he does not know. He had no mother or father. He grew up in the streets of Madrid."

Manuel was small in size, but Juliana knew he was much

older in other ways. Carmita was sixteen. The two had been nearly inseparable since they arrived, except when their duties required them elsewhere.

"I like it here," Carmita continued, a thoughtful look on her face. "They are kind, and the Maclean has promised Manuel he would teach him English. Manuel will teach me. And I am learning to cook in the kitchen. The servants are not like those in Spain who feared someone may take their place."

"I truly do not know what the Maclean has planned," Juliana said. "I know he will try to see us safe."

"And your marriage . . . ?"

Her marriage. Her blood turned icy when she thought of it. She was no longer the virgin that was promised. After the last few weeks, neither would she be the meek maiden. She had fought for her life, and she would continue to do so.

She would also fight for the Maclean.

The latter thought startled her but she knew it was truth. She would do battle on his behalf. She thought of her uncle lying dead in the passageway, but she truly could not summon regret. After seeing the rowing deck, she had only contempt for him. And her father.

But her mother . . .

"Senorita?"

Juliana brought herself back from her thoughts of Patrick. "I do not know what the future holds, but I will make sure you are safe," she said. Patrick Maclean had to grant her that boon at least.

Carmita finished brushing her hair, and Juliana stood in the night shift she wore.

The map, Juliana reminded herself. Or perhaps it was just something to focus on, so she could avoid all the feelings roiling around inside.

"Help me dress again," she told Carmita. "The gray gown."

Carmita's eyes worried. "It is late, senorita. He will probably be abed."

But Juliana was restless, and mayhap Patrick was with

his brother. She was not sure whether he planned to sail with the remaining crew members to wherever they would go. She did not know where she belonged in his mind, in his heart. She had to know.

"Carmita," she said with unusual sternness.

"Si," Carmita said. "I will go with you."

"No. I will not be long."

Carmita did not look pleased, but she found the gray gown in the trunk. "Your hair?" she said. "It is down."

And so it was. But now that she had an objective in mind, she did not want to wait. She did not worry about someone outside watching her. She had the run of Inverleith as long as she stayed inside the walls, and she doubted she could get outside if she wanted. Every man or woman coming to or leaving the keep was stopped.

In a matter of minutes, she was ready to go. Unwilling to spend the long time necessary to pin her hair, she merely put a cap on the top of her head and allowed the curls to tumble down.

"I will not need you again tonight," she said. "I can undo the ties on my gown." She paused, then said, "You do not have to work here in the kitchen."

"But I wish to, senorita. I am learning to cook."

"You do not like being my maid?"

Carmita flushed. "Oh *si*, senorita, but if they do not like me where we go . . ."

"It does not matter what someone else likes or does not like. As long as you wish, you will be with me." She truly hoped she could fulfill that promise.

Juliana left the room. The corridor was empty. Patrick's chamber, she knew, was to the left, just past the stone stairs. Rory's was beyond his brother's.

She tucked a curl behind her ear, tried to affect an air of indifference for everything except the map and walked to Rory's door. She knocked on the heavy wood.

No answer.

Perhaps he was with his brother. She returned to Patrick's room. She thought about knocking, but mayhap he had gone asleep and she did not want to wake him. *An excuse.* She recognized it, but nonetheless she could not help herself. She turned the handle and it opened slightly. Then she heard the voices.

She should close it again, or announce her presence, but the words seared themselves in her mind.

"Tell me more about the viscount," she heard Patrick ask. Her heart began to thud as she continued to listen through the crack. Then finally, Patrick's voice: "We would be risking the entire clan."

He was willing to risk that for her. That and his brothers' lives.

She was not.

She closed the door softly and turned, dashing toward the nearby steps and skipping down them. She was not ready to face Carmita again tonight.

Figures slept on the floor of the great hall. The torches cast shadows over their forms. Several snored. She heard one groan. Someone remembering the horror of the galley?

She opened the main door of the keep and slipped outside. The moon was full, and bright, though it ducked in and out of clouds. In a few days it would be but a thin slice and the night would be dark. She paused and looked around. Several fires were lit in the courtyard, and Macleans walked the outer wall. The great gate was closed.

How could she leave? She had been allowed to go anywhere within the walls, but it had been made very clear she was not permitted outside the gate. She was trapped inside as surely as she had been locked in a prison cell. How had Felicia escaped when she was held prisoner?

Juliana planned to find out on the morrow.

She went inside the stable. One lantern was lit inside, and a sleepy-eyed Fergus blinked when she entered.

"Miss," he said. "I did not expect anyone this late."

"I could not sleep, Fergus, and decided to visit the horses."

He nodded, but his eyes were watchful. Obviously he had been told to be courteous but cautious.

She went to the mare she'd been riding. Duchess. The mare nickered lightly and nuzzled her for a treat. She wished she had one, but instead promised she would bring one tomorrow.

Another mare raised her head and nickered lightly as a foal nursed.

"She is beautiful."

"Aye," Fergus replied. He was staying at her side. Patrick's orders?

"They all are."

"The laird takes great pride in his horses, he does," Fergus said. "All Macleans do. They say even the auld laird took care of his horses proper."

"Do Felicia and Kimbra ride much?"

"Felicia not so often now with the bairns. Kimbra rides nearly every day on the big black gelding. She is a foine rider."

The informality between the laird, his family and his servants constantly amazed her. It was similar to that between Patrick and the oarsmen. There seemed no resentment, or superiority, on either side, only a commonality her father would despise.

She turned her attention back to Fergus, who was still extolling Kimbra's riding skills. "She brought the stallion from the border. Few others can ride the beast."

Her mind was running ahead of itself. Would Felicia tell her how to escape? Would Kimbra help her? Probably not.

She had a thought that had been nagging at her for several days. There had to be a way to leave Inverleith and prevent any more damage to Patrick and the Maclean family. She owed him that. Her family had taken years from him, and unjustly. She could not live with herself if she were responsible for more grief.

The foal finished nursing. The mare came over and Juliana stroked the soft muzzle. The horse nipped, but Juliana knew horses well enough to understand it was a gesture of companionship rather than hostility.

She leaned over the gate and couldn't stop the tears welling behind her eyes. She missed her own horse, Joya, terribly. Still, she wanted to stay here. She wanted to be part of this family where husbands loved their wives, where children played and warmth filled the stone walls.

None of it was possible. She would only bring destruction down on Inverleith.

Juliana knew it would be far harder to accept the marriage with a man her mother feared, and the Campbell despised, now that she knew life could be different. That there was love and respect and warmth between people, not just cold, cynical bargaining with lives.

Still, she knew what she had to do. She had to save Patrick from his own folly in protecting her.

She wiped away the tears with her hand and vowed there would be no more of them.

Chapter 25

PATRICK rose later than usual. Sleep had eluded him most of the night and when it did come, it was troubled. He couldn't stop thinking of Juliana, the way she felt and looked and tasted yesterday. He still burned with want. Och, but he had been tempted time and time again to take the few steps to her chamber.

She was close; too close.

But the conversation last night had convinced him he had to keep his wits about him, and he could not do that with her. Nor could he leave her with child, not knowing her future. He despised himself for the lack of discipline, something on which he'd always prided himself.

After the meeting last night, Patrick returned to his own chamber, then looked out his window down in the courtyard. He saw Juliana leave the stable, her slight, graceful figure unmistakable. Her head was bowed against the night wind.

Her head was never bowed, not for anyone. How he'd wanted to go to her chamber, to warm her body with his. Then she entered the doors to the great hall. He imagined he heard her steps pause, then pass his door.

He now knew the true meaning of temptation.

Patrick knew he had to control it. He looked down over the sound below the walls.

When would Lachlan return?

Even if it was on the morn, which he fervently hoped, he still had not found a solution to Juliana. He blinked as he saw distant sails on the sound. He continued to watch as they neared. He heard the shout from the walls, a collective cheer from those fellow oarsmen who had preferred the courtyard to the great hall to sleep.

Patrick understood their immediate reaction. They wanted to go home. The Moors, he knew, were not used to the cold Scottish nights and frequent mists. The Spaniards were worried about being discovered here, and the others merely wanted to return to their own countries and disappear.

Relief surged through him as well. It had been dangerous having them here. A visitor would have been disastrous. After the Campbell's unexpected arrival, he and Rory had decided to meet any other visitor with the information that there was fever inside.

But by tonight, he hoped all would be aboard and sailing east. The only danger then would be an interception on the seas, but Rory had assured him that the ship—the *Felicia*—had a fine captain.

Mixed with relief, though, was the realization he would miss some of the oarsmen. They had suffered together, fought together, triumphed together, then shared the harrowing voyage to Inverleith. He would not easily forget many of them.

Would the Spaniard go with them? He had made himself at home at Inverleith. Despite his nationality, Patrick saw that the clansmen had taken to him. Diego had, in fact, instructed several in the art of swordsmanship. Manuel had already indicated he wished to stay with Juliana and Carmita, and Patrick trusted Manuel. He already had, with his life. He was still not as sure about Diego. Still, he would not force him to leave. And then there was Denny, who had no place to go.

Much to do today, and decisions must be made. He ran his fingers through his hair, splashed some water on his face and left his room.

He went past the stone steps and stopped at Juliana's chamber. He rapped on the door, but there was no answer. He entered to find it empty. A lingering smell of roses remained, though.

Reluctantly, he left and went to the great hall, where platters of food were arranged on the table, but he had no hunger. His stomach had become used to very little.

Though the table was filled with his fellow oarsmen, Juliana was not there. Then he saw Carmita, who frowned darkly at him.

"Where is Juliana?" he asked.

"She is in Lachlan's room," Carmita said with obvious reluctance. Accusation was in her eyes.

"My thanks," he said softly.

"I do not need your thanks," Carmita said sharply. "My senorita and I are your prisoners."

Her words startled him. She had always seemed meek. She was a bonny little thing with the dark hair and eyes of Spain, but she was young and had been obviously frightened. More than frightened. Terrified.

Now, however, she was evidently ready to do battle on behalf of her mistress. Juliana would need that kind of friend.

"DENNY, this is London. It is one of the largest cities in the world," Juliana said.

She and Kimbra and Denny sat at a table with the map she'd obtained from Rory spread across the table's surface. This morning she had gone to Rory, explaining exactly why she needed it.

"Tell me if something looks familiar," she said. "Just nod your head."

His eyes told her he understood. How much, she was not sure, but at times she thought he was far more aware of events than anyone knew.

He seemed to have an almost fanatical devotion to Patrick. He obviously worried when Patrick was away from the keep. It appeared that Patrick was the only one Denny trusted.

Almost as if summoned by her thoughts, Patrick appeared in the doorway.

Her heart leapt, but his eyes were cool, and his gaze rested on her only briefly before settling on the map. But he could not hide a sudden tightening of his mouth. Regret?

"A map?" he asked.

"*Si.* Rory gave it to us, Kimbra and myself," she hurried on. "Kimbra thought it might help bring back Denny's memory."

"It is kind of you," he said, but she heard an ironic note in his voice. For a moment, the air became thick with tension. She was aware of Kimbra's thoughtful glance, even Denny's suddenly interested one. She could not move, but her heart beat faster. Her chest ached almost unbearably as she remembered his hands touching her yesterday, awakening sensations.

Would it always be thus? Did *he* feel anything?

"The ship has arrived," he said.

The announcement was like a splash of icy water. She looked down at her right hand on the table. It had balled into a tight fist.

He turned his attention to Denny.

"A ship is here," he said. "Most of the . . . oarsmen are going to Spain or Morocco."

Juliana watched Denny carefully. Panic flashed in his eyes.

He shook his head.

He'd understood completely.

Patrick obviously saw it, too. He reached out and

placed a hand on Denny's shoulder. "You do not have to leave, but I thought you should have the choice." He hesitated, then added, "It could be dangerous for you here. If we are discovered . . ."

Denny shook his head, his eyes pleading with words he could not say.

"Would you like to stay?" Patrick questioned.

Denny nodded his head, gratitude filling his eyes.

"Then stay you will. You have a home here," Patrick said. "My brother agrees."

There was a gentleness in Patrick when he spoke to Denny despite the fact he thought Denny English. Juliana was very aware that the Macleans did not care much for the English, and to Patrick her half-English blood was not much preferable to her Spanish. Yet it was that gentleness with Denny, the patience he had with someone he once thought an enemy, that melted her heart. He did not hurry Denny, merely waited until he understood exactly what was being asked of him.

Patrick's eyes fell on her.

"Do I have a choice as well?" she asked.

"Nay," he said. "Not at the moment."

"If I swear not to say what happened?"

"You want to leave, lass?"

No! She hoped he did not see the denial in her face. "Aye," she lied. "I dislike being a prisoner."

"Even an honored one?" His gaze penetrated hers.

"A bird wishes to escape even the most exquisite cage," she retorted, angry at the coolness in his eyes when *she* felt anything but cool.

He continued to study her for a moment, then left without another word. She turned back to the map and tried to hide her disappointment. "This is Northumberland," she said in a voice that nearly broke. "And here is London . . ."

Kimbra broke in. "The sea, Denny. Do you remember the sea? Cliffs. Rocks. Or a city? A village."

"What about family?" Juliana said, regaining her composure. "Mother? Father? Brother?"

A second of emotion swept across his eyes, and then it was gone. But she would have sworn it was pain. Pain so deep that it silenced her.

PATRICK left her, guilt weighing on him like the chains he'd so recently worn. He went to the stable. Rory was already saddling a horse. The young stable lad was saddling several more.

"By God, I thought I would have to send someone to rouse you, Patrick. The *Felicia* has arrived and should now be anchored. A horse is being saddled for you and another to bring Lachlan back here."

"Aye, I saw it through the window. She's a bonny ship."

"More than bonny. She has twelve guns. She can defend herself well. She was built in Glasgow to my plans. She usually sails from Edinburgh, but was in Glasgow for some repairs."

"And the captain?"

"Amos MacDowell. A good, steady man. You can trust him."

"What will the crew be told?"

"That these men were shipwrecked not far from us. We will also spread word among the isles that a ship foundered near Inverleith, since there is no way to completely stop rumors about strangers here."

"An unlikely tale, but possible," Patrick said as he prepared to mount.

"Felicia's idea," Rory explained. "She can be very inventive."

"It's probably just as well your wife is leaving," Patrick said wryly. "I think Juliana has some of those same qualities."

Rory paused before mounting. "Juliana came to me this morning and asked for a map of England. She said Kimbra thought it might bring some reaction from that silent *Sassenach* of yours."

"I believe you might want it back," Patrick replied.

"You think she might try to leave?"

"Would you, were you held against your will?"

"I am not convinced it is against her will," Rory said.

Patrick did not reply. Instead he mounted the horse, taking the reins of the extra horse, and led the way out of the gate, turning to watch as it closed behind him. In a few hours, if all went well, his guests would be gone, sailing away to new lives. By now he knew which would probably make good use of the funds they would have and which would probably die at the end of a hangman's rope, or worse. He had hopes for Felix and the men he'd recruited to help him trim the sails and work the sheets. He had less for others who, on their release from chains, thought first of opening the barrels of wine. As for the Moors, they had kept to themselves, but several had thanked him for their release.

He increased the pace. The ship would have anchored in the natural harbor. He wanted to be there when Lachlan and the captain arrived on land. The sooner his collection of nationalities was gone, the safer Inverleith and his Macleans would be. The problem of Juliana and her maid would remain, however. He could not send them with the *Felicia.* Yet neither could he keep them here indefinitely. The sight of Juliana sitting with Denny this morning remained with him, especially the flash of anger—and hurt—in her eyes.

Had she really wanted the maps for Denny or for herself? He still could not exclude the possibility that she would try to leave and return home. Yet he would wager much that there was no pretense in her effort to help Denny. The image of the two bent over the map was branded in his mind.

They reached the harbor and Lachlan and a man Patrick had never seen were waiting on the beach. He was struck again by Lachlan's confidence.

Lachlan stood as they approached. "What kept you?" he asked with a roguish smile.

"Patrick slept late," Rory replied. "I am not sure he wants our guests to leave."

Patrick tensed, then relaxed. It would take time to get used to brotherly rivalry again, even that of an obviously affectionate nature. *Affectionate.* A lump formed in his throat as he remembered his bitter thoughts in the galley. God's blood, but he had been wrong.

And yet it had been part of what kept him alive.

The man with Lachlan approached and held out his hand. "MacDowell," he said, introducing himself. "Lachlan said you wanted us to leave immediately and you had nearly a hundred passengers."

"Aye."

"We are provisioned and can take on your passengers now." He paused. "He said some would be dropped off on the Spanish coast and the others off the Moorish coast."

Rory nodded. "Do you have any other cargo?"

"Nay, not this time, but I can stop in France on the return. Pick up some cargo there."

Lachlan looked at Patrick. "It would be wise to have a purpose for this voyage."

It was a question, and Patrick understood the courtesy being extended. He had nothing to do with the trading part of the Maclean business, but Lachlan was making it clear to MacDowell that Patrick was now laird and head of the family. The decisions would be his.

He nodded, again wondering at the open acceptance and generosity of his brothers. Even the Campbell, who was putting himself at risk. It astounded him. Befuddled him. Devil's pitchfork, but it humbled him far more than the chains ever had.

"We will start to load, then," MacDowell said.

"Your crew?" Patrick asked. "Some of the passengers may become a wee greedy."

"Lachlan explained that. I brought extra crew. I do not think it will be a problem."

"There are also several who might make good additions."

MacDowell nodded. "We can always use good hands."

"My thanks," Patrick said. "We will start bringing them here as soon as we return. Expect the first arrivals in an hour."

"We will be ready."

AFTER Patrick left them, Denny rose as well and went into the courtyard. He always looked lost when Patrick was gone.

Juliana's heart ached for him, but she turned and smiled as Kimbra's daughter, Audra, appeared with Bear. Bear always made her smile. The dog was huge with a big tongue that lolled around his mouth, but was delicately careful with Audra.

"You do not want to be around Bear when someone threatens her," Kimbra said. "He almost died attacking a pack of wolves that threatened Audra."

Juliana leaned over and scratched the dog's ear, and Bear rumbled with pleasure.

"He likes you," Audra said in the serious manner she had. "He doesn't like many people."

"Like Magnus, your mother's horse?"

"Aye," she said with grin.

Juliana returned the smile. She enjoyed those moments with Audra, and she was reluctant to take her leave. But she had things to discuss with the other sister-in-law. With Felicia, who had once been in the same position that she was. Who might be able to tell her how to escape and travel to England.

PATRICK wanted to avoid a long line of oddly misplaced men, just in the remote event that a stranger happened to ride by. Felicia's explanation might work if not too closely examined, but the mixture of Moors among

Europeans would, no doubt, raise more questions than he wanted to answer.

So when he returned to Inverleith, he separated the oarsmen into groups. They boarded wagons while trusted Maclean sentries watched the road. As soon as one group was delivered, the wagon started back for another. Several others who said they could ride were given horses.

Before each group left Inverleith, Patrick talked to them, stressing the importance of silence. That all their lives were at stake, every last man jack of them. They all swore to silence, but he knew too many cups of spirits might end that. He could only hope that no one would believe them then.

He had thought about when to give them their portion of the money. Before or after they sailed? But he feared they may not believe it would be forthcoming and might revolt once more. So he had pouches of gold for each of them.

Their eyes told him they had hoped for, but not really expected, the money. Too many disappointments in their lives already. One kissed him to the laughter of others, while several others made the sign of the cross and the Moors bowed to him.

Juliana appeared at his side as he watched the last oarsman mount the wagon. He would ride with them. He wanted to be there when they left. He had never thought himself a sentimental man. His father had called sentiment a weakness. But he'd shared too much with those men not to feel a catch in his throat.

"May I ride with you?" she asked.

He started to refuse, then saw the plea in her eyes. He had stolen her life. It was little enough to allow her to say good-bye. She had come to know some of the oarsmen well.

"Aye."

Diego also wanted to go. There was no request from Denny or Carmita or Manuel. He suspected they all wanted to end the horrors they'd undergone.

He helped her mount. A mistake. He knew it the moment he touched her. Mayhap he'd known it beforehand but could not resist. Or wanted to know whether he could.

But as she put her foot in his locked hands and he lifted her into the saddle, something cracked inside him and he knew he had failed the test he'd created for himself. She should despise him for what he'd cost her. He'd seen the disappointment in them earlier, but now her eyes sparkled with anticipation for an outing. As she took the reins from his fingers, their hands touched and burned as if lightning had struck them both.

"*Gracias,*" she said in the voice that was pure music.

He simply nodded and decided to mount his horse while his legs had enough strength to do so.

The Spaniard spurred his horse to walk on the other side of Juliana, chattering in Spanish about beautiful days and even more beautiful women and said something Patrick didn't hear but which made her laugh.

When last had he made her laugh? Or had he ever?

Patrick would have happily challenged Diego to combat that moment, but that would create even more notice.

Instead, he spurred his horse and raced ahead, wondering exactly when he'd lost the last of his senses.

Chapter 26

JULIANA watched the ship set sail with mixed feelings. It had been her one way to return to Spain. She did not move until the *Felicia* was no longer in sight.

"Do you wish you were on it?" Diego asked, moving to her side as they started back to Inverleith.

She looked around. Patrick was riding with Rory and their conversation was low and intense.

She did not answer Diego because truly she did not know. She still feared for her mother, but as for herself she knew her father would merely send her to England on another ship. And truth be told she did not want to leave Inverleith. And Patrick.

At the same time she wearied of being a pawn, being moved first by her father and uncle, and now by the Macleans. As she had told Patrick earlier, a prisoner in a gilded cage is still a prisoner.

No one had considered *her*. She supposed Patrick

believed he was protecting her, but it was by his standards and what he thought best for her, not considering for a moment what she wanted, or needed, for herself.

She *wanted* him. Unfortunately she seemed more a problem to be solved than someone with needs and feelings.

A seed of anger had sprouted inside since he'd walked out of the room after those magical moments. She suspected he felt guilt about bedding her. She knew now how worried he was about his clan.

But no longer would she be treated as a possession—or a toy—rather than the person she was. She had seen the respect given Felicia and Kimbra. It was new to her, and she wanted at least a small portion for herself. She wanted to make decisions as they made decisions. Most of all, she wanted to be valued. She did not feel valued by Patrick; instead she felt an inconvenience that he very reluctantly desired.

She did not intend a senseless rebellion, however.

Juliana would do nothing to hurt the Macleans. She would not be party to more injustice to Patrick, but neither could she leave her mother victim to her father's rage.

She had one possibility. She had to go to Handdon Castle, the family seat of the Earl of Chadwick and his son, Viscount Kingsley, in Northern England, and she had to do it in a way that no blame would come to Patrick or the Macleans.

She realized the idea was full of peril. When she arrived in England, if she made it to England, would Kingsley realize she was no longer a virgin? Would he want her if he did? If not, what would be her future? A convent, no doubt. Her father would demand no less.

But others would be safe.

She had to hurry. Felicia was to leave in a few hours. How could she discuss Felicia's escape from Inverleith years earlier without giving her own plan away?

She wished she could spur her horse and ride away now, but that, of course, was impossible. Her mount was an elderly and placid mare and Patrick's swift mount could easily overtake her.

No, she would have to be sly. Unfortunately, she had little experience with being sly.

"You are plotting something," Diego said with sly amusement.

"What could I be plotting?" she asked.

"I am not sure, but something. You have an expressive face, senorita, and now it is a study in concentration."

"Or are you just used to plotting yourself?" she said sharply. "I am not sure why you are staying."

"I like the Macleans," he said simply. "There is nothing left in Spain for me, and after months on the bench, I have no wish now to go back to sea."

His reply surprised her, especially by the fact that there was no amusement in his voice, no sardonic undertone.

"No family?" He had always puzzled her. From his speech and the way he carried himself, he was obviously well born and well educated. Yet she had watched him with the other oarsmen and with the Maclean soldiers. He became one of them. If anything, he was a chameleon.

"No," he said in a voice that discouraged further comment.

Could she use him in some way? Prevail upon him to help her? She would have sworn he'd been a gentleman. He had at times protected her, just as Patrick had. How much allegiance did he have to Patrick and the Macleans?

She was, in truth, startled that the Macleans had allowed him to stay. He could be dangerous to them, and yet he seemed to fit into the clan. His hair was the same dark color as Rory's and his English carried only the slightest accent.

But what did he want? And how much could he be trusted? By the Macleans? By her?

"And so you are not plotting?" he asked with that ironic amusement that distinguished him.

"Why should I?"

He shrugged. "Why? I do not know. There is . . . a certain fire between you and the Maclean. And I understand you were not overwhelmed with desire to see your prospective husband."

"You are imagining things," she retorted. "The Maclean has little interest in me other than the fact that I present a problem."

He chuckled. "You could not be more wrong, senorita."

Juliana did not answer, though she wanted to know more. Diego was a puzzle and she did like to solve puzzles. He could also be of assistance to her.

He was watched. She knew that. Just as she was. He, too, had been given a horse that appeared slower and older than the others. Despite his apparent freedom, he, too, was imprisoned within the walls of Inverleith by the locked gates. She had also noticed a Maclean was usually by Diego's side or nearby.

He knew. He had to know, but he did not seem to take offense. But would he want to escape this comfortable prison as he had so wanted to escape the galley? Despite his words about the Macleans, he had a restless quality about him, like a wild animal who could not be easily confined.

She would continue to test him. She might be able to convince him to help her, if she failed with Felicia.

PATRICK could not take his eyes from Juliana as she conversed with the Spaniard. Not for the first time, he questioned his decision to allow Diego to stay.

An ugly jealousy hardened inside him, just as it had with Jamie's quick glances toward her. Unreasonable. Unsettling. He wanted to ride up to them and order Diego away. He wanted Juliana's eyes to light with pleasure at seeing him and the appealing blush to spread across her cheeks. He wanted to hear her soft, melodic voice and touch her warm skin.

It had taken every ounce of will he had to stay away.

And now he was convinced that the only way to do that was to follow Rory's advice. *"You should go to court with Jamie. Announce you have returned home and will take your place as laird of the Macleans."*

Lachlan had agreed this morning. "*Word undoubtedly has spread that you have returned. You should publicly assert your rights, and your loyalty to the young king. Proudly. With nothing to hide.*"

Still, he'd hesitated.

"You can meet this . . . Kingsley for yourself," Rory had said, tempting him. "Lachlan is right. You have to present yourself as leader of the Macleans. You fought with the French, you were imprisoned, then fell ill. No one will question that."

Patrick thought he was probably right. He had been sold as a body, not an individual. He doubted his name was recorded by the Mendozas. Since the moment he'd been taken aboard, he had been a number.

If anything went wrong and he was discovered as an oarsman on the ship, he could claim he lied to his family. And he would put distance between himself and a temptation that was becoming stronger every moment.

He would be leaving Juliana here. Alone. With the Spaniard.

Kimbra would be here as well. In the past few days, he had learned a healthy respect for his quiet sister-in-law. There was no hiding the love she felt for Lachlan, nor the pure joy in her eyes when she was with her daughter, as well as with Rory's children. There were depths to her that appealed to Patrick.

The trip to Edinburgh would be best for all, he assured himself. Juliana would be well protected here. She would have Kimbra for company while he learned more about Kingsley. According to Jamie, there were unsavory rumors about him. If he could be discredited in some way, mayhap there would be no search for, of interest in, his missing bride.

A slight hope, he knew, but it was the only one he had for solving the problem of Juliana, allowing her to make the choice of returning to Spain or staying here at Inverleith.

For the first time, he admitted to himself how much he wanted the latter. Wanted her to stay.

He'd thought never to marry because of the curse. It was so deeply embedded in the Macleans that he'd never considered the possibility, especially after the death of Rory's first wife. He still remembered Maggie's joyful laughter and the cries the night she and her bairn died. They had racked his soul for years.

But mayhap Rory was right. Mayhap the curse had ended with his marriage to a Campbell. Mayhap there had never really been one. Just tragic coincidences.

FELICIA was placing clothes into a trunk when Juliana appeared at her door. "Juliana," she exclaimed with delight. "Come in."

Little Patrick was tottering around, dragging a wooden horse on a rope. Maggie was asleep on the bed, her red hair curling around an angelic face.

Juliana nearly tripped over the wooden horse, then could not resist a smile at Patrick's grin.

"They both are beautiful," she said.

"Aye, if a bit wild."

"And you are leaving?"

"Aye, Janet needs me now."

"You have welcomed me. I wanted to thank you before you left."

Felicia's glance sharpened. "Come sit with me," Felicia said, sitting on the huge bed that dominated the room.

Juliana complied, dodging young Patrick as she did.

"You are not happy here," Felicia said, her gaze searching Juliana's.

"Were you, when you were a prisoner here?"

"Nay. At first I was terrified of the wild Macleans. I was told they were the devil incarnate."

"And then?"

"You know parts of the story. I was kidnapped because his Macleans thought I was Janet Cameron and would make a good bride for Rory. He wanted none of it. He'd lost two wives already because of the curse. At least he halfway believed that." She looked quickly at Juliana. "You have heard of the curse?"

"Si," Juliana said.

"I feared that if I told him I was a Campbell, he would kill me and even deepen the feud between the families. Then I came to know him and fell in love. But I knew if he discovered I was a Campbell, he would be . . . repelled. So I ran away."

"How did you do that?"

Felicia's eyes sharpened. Studied her for a few moments. Then she sighed. "I asked Douglas to take me for a ride. I pretended to fall. When he dismounted to see whether I was injured, I grabbed his horse—and mine—and galloped off." She paused, then said slowly, "I do not think it will work again."

Juliana bit her lower lip, wondering how much she should say. It was obvious that she had not been sly at all.

Felicia gave her a sympathetic smile. "Do you love him?"

"I . . . he is a stubborn donkey."

Felicia laughed. "Aye, just like Rory. They both think they know best for everyone. Stubborn. Prideful. Rory has improved . . . a little. Now Lachlan, he is different."

"It is not only myself," Juliana said. "My mother is in Spain. She is half English and my father has always despised her for it, though he has used her family to increase his wealth. If this marriage fails to happen, he will have no reason to keep her alive. He could marry again, a Spanish woman, with a good dowry."

The laughter left Felicia's eyes. She took Juliana's hand with hers. "I had no one," she said. "No one but Jamie. My mother and da died when I was but a baby, and Angus Campbell took me in. But there was no affection, not then."

"Help me," Juliana pled.

"I might be convicting Patrick," Felicia said. "Rory would never forgive me."

"I would say the ship wrecked along the English coast. I was the only survivor."

Felicia stared at her with bemusement. "You would have

a very long and dangerous journey, then you would have to be very believable. I do not wish to insult you, but you are not a good liar."

Juliana had to smile at the statement. And Felicia had not said no. Had not run down to tell Rory or Patrick. Not yet. A glimmer of bittersweet possibility opened.

"I can be," she said. "*If* I can leave these walls."

"What about Patrick? He is in love with you." She said it with such certainty that Juliana nearly believed it.

"He wants nothing to do with me."

"Nay, he fears, as Rory did, to love. That thought tears down everything they believed. 'Tis a hard thing for a proud man to admit."

"Even if it were true, I am a danger to him here. And my disappearance might mean death to my mother."

"Such terrible choices."

Juliana realized from the tone in her voice that Felicia had probably made terrible choices herself. She waited.

Patrick had left the wooden horse and played wooden spoons against the table.

Juliana wondered what it would be like to be as content as Felicia appeared to be. She doubted she would ever know.

"Be sure you know what you are risking," Felicia said softly. "It is a long way to England, and then your tale would have to be convincing. If you fail, many could die."

"They may, if I do not."

"I tried to save people, too, and it never quite worked the way I planned," Felicia said. "I almost lost Rory in the doing, as well as Jamie and Lachlan. Plans that look noble and easy are usually neither."

"I do not know what else to do."

Felicia gave her a quick hug. "Think very carefully. You have a good heart, Juliana, and I think Patrick is in need of one."

Felicia's gaze met hers. Her eyes were warm. Sympathetic. How sympathetic?

Juliana took a deep breath. "Will you help me?" she asked.

"Nay," Felicia said softly. "I cannot betray Patrick as soon as he returned. Neither he nor Rory would ever forgive me. Even if I were willing to risk that, I do not think it can work."

Juliana stood. "You will not tell them . . ."

"Nay, I will not do that, either."

"Thank you," she said.

Felicia hesitated, then said, "You know he is leaving tomorrow for Edinburgh?"

Juliana felt sick inside. She shook her head.

"Men can be such fools," Felicia said. "Don't let that make you one."

Juliana nodded. Then she left before she said more. She was on her own.

PATRICK managed to stay away from Juliana most of the day. He rode escort with Felicia until she was well away from Maclean land. He remembered the old trails where once they raided Campbell cattle. The paths were overgrown now.

He arrived just as the evening meal was ending. Juliana was nowhere to be seen, and a servant told him she was taking her meal in her room.

Was she ill?

He found himself running up the steps.

He knocked, then opened the door without waiting. He wasn't accustomed to such panic.

But then she hadn't left his thoughts since he'd left her earlier. He'd been curt, even rude, as he tried to control his jealousy and the maddening impulse to grab her and claim her as his own.

She was in a night robe, her glorious hair falling down around her shoulders. Dishes that looked nearly untouched sat on the table.

"You may go," he told Carmita.

Carmita looked at her mistress, who nodded, then scurried out the door.

"You did not go down to supper."

"No," she agreed.

"Are you ill?"

"No."

"Did Diego offend you in some way?"

"No," she said with a smile that made him bleed inside.

He shifted from one foot to another. "If you are well, then . . ."

"I am."

He felt like a great oaf. He wanted to reach out and clasp her to him. God's teeth, but she looked magnificent. She was angry, he knew that, and he suspected he was the cause of that anger.

"Lass . . ."

"I understand you plan to leave tomorrow with Jamie Campbell."

"Aye."

"Were you going to tell me?"

"Aye . . ." Nay, he had been planning to sneak away like a thief because he knew exactly what would happen if he tried to say farewell.

"You wish me to stay and wait for you to return. You do not care that I would worry. About my mother. About Carmita. You."

He took a step forward. Her eyes were spitting fury now.

"Juliana . . ."

"You keep me captive, you bed me, you ignore me, you leave without a word."

Through the fury, he saw the deep wound he'd inflicted. He had thought to protect her by staying away. An error. One among many.

He reached out but she backed away.

"No," she said.

"I did not want to hurt you more, lass," he said. "There could be a child. And I could be hanged. I . . ."

"Will not give me choices. Go," she said. "Go to Edinburgh and play your dangerous games."

A tear ran down her face and she wiped it away angrily.

He touched her cheek with his thumb and caressed it. She went rigid.

"I have to do this, lass. When I come back . . ."

He saw something in her eyes he did not like. A secrecy that had not been there before.

Bloody hell how he wanted to kiss her. He ached all over with wanting her.

He leaned down and kissed her lightly. "I never meant . . ."

Then her arms were around his neck and the kiss turned into something wild and desperate and hungry and yearning all at the same time. He felt every bone in his body turn molten.

But despite her response, he knew this was not the time. Not for him. Not for her. He had left her once after lying with her. He could not do that to her again.

His kiss turned gentle, then he let go. Her eyes were dazed. His throat constricted.

He turned and left as if the devil were after him.

DENNY appeared in Patrick's room that night.

He stood awkwardly, obviously wanting something.

Patrick offered him a cup of wine.

Denny shook his head and waited, his eyes anxious.

"Do you wish to leave Inverleith?" Patrick asked.

Denny shook his head.

"Stay?"

Again a negative shake of his head.

"You want to go with us tomorrow?"

Denny nodded this time.

Patrick hesitated, too surprised to say anything. Kimbra had told him that she thought Denny understood everything that was going on, that he listened and absorbed, but then tried to melt into the shadows.

Patrick wondered if one reason for his silence had been

the rules on the ship. Silence had been enforced. The oarsmen knew that talk meant punishment. Some simply lost the habit. And then mayhap Denny had no past upon which to rely.

He studied Denny. While on the bench, his eyes had been dull, his actions slow, but now Patrick wondered how much of that had been an act while he was trying to comprehend what had happened to him. Now, with his beard shaved and his hair cut cleanly, he had the look of an aristocrat. His movements, though, were still slow and cautious, as if he were always trying desperately to find something familiar.

At least Patrick knew who he was, and he had brothers who, to his continuing amazement, had gathered around him in a protective wall.

What did Denny have?

Mayhap Edinburgh and new faces would prod memories. He could come along as Patrick's or Jamie's servant.

Jamie. It suddenly struck him that he thought of the Campbell as Jamie. And the skies hadn't fallen in.

Mayhap a similar miracle would strike Denny.

JULIANA watched the four—Jamie, Patrick, Denny and Lachlan—leave on horseback. She ached to go with them.

Kimbra stood next to her. Felicia had left earlier with an escort.

"I have done that many times," Kimbra said. "Watch my heart ride away."

How much had she given away? Did everyone know she . . . had bedded Patrick Maclean? "Why are they taking Denny?" she asked to change the subject.

"He asked Patrick to go. In gestures, if not words."

Juliana's gaze continued to follow Patrick until he passed through the gate, then she tried to concentrate on what Kimbra had just said. She should not have been surprised. He showed an uncommon devotion to Patrick even while she'd witnessed that glimmer of intelligence in his eyes, his intense need to remember.

Everyone was leaving. Patrick. Felicia. Denny. All but Rory, who meant to keep her prisoner.

"I think his memories may be coming back," Kimbra said. "Not many. It was like that with Lachlan's head injury."

"But it has been much longer with Denny," Juliana said. "Did not Lachlan regain his memory in a matter of weeks?"

"Not all of it. That took months. And he had reason to want to remember. I think Denny had none. He woke up to slavery and beatings."

"I will feel guilt for that all my days."

"You should not. It was not of your doing." Then she smiled shyly. "But I understand. When I heard my family was ordered to kill every Scot, wounded or not, I felt the same. A shame for being a part of it, even if I had no power."

She held out her hand, and Juliana grasped it. For the first time she did not feel alone. She knew the feeling could not, would not, last, but still the gesture touched her. Something else to remember.

"I have not seen much of Lachlan," Juliana said regretfully.

"Everyone likes Lachlan. Yet he had his demons, just like his brothers had. I think at times he still has them." She grinned suddenly. "You should hear him play the lute."

"I have heard your daughter. She is very good."

"Lachlan taught her. They are much alike, those two, even if he is not her natural father.

Pain tore at Juliana's heart. There was so much love in her expression, in the soft sound of her voice. This is what she wanted. She wanted it with all her heart and soul.

She stepped away from the window. The riders were gone now, and the gates closed again.

"I think I will go down to see the horses," Juliana said.

"Audra has been begging me to take her to the loch for a picnic," Kimbra said unexpectedly. "Perhaps you can go with us."

"When?" Juliana said eagerly.

"I will have to get Rory's permission," Kimbra said. "I will approach him later today."

"Thank you," Juliana said gratefully. Whether or not she could use the opportunity to escape she did not know, but she wanted to go outside the walls and see more of the land.

She left the chamber and walked out into the courtyard. She stopped when she saw Diego in the training area, fighting with a Maclean. They were using broadswords and though she had heard of his skill, she was startled at how good he was against a much burlier man. He never stayed still while his opponent advanced predictably. Diego neatly parried a strong blow, his shield taking only the edge of his opponent's sword, then he sidestepped and brought his sword down on his opponent's. The Maclean's sword went skittering away.

He turned his back, and the Maclean dove at him, bringing him down.

She watched as fury crossed Diego's face. He was wearing britches from the ship—her uncle's if she was not mistaken—and a full, white shirt that contrasted with his olive skin and black hair. He was all grace and anger as he sprung up from the ground and turned. His fist hit the Maclean with such impact she could hear it where she was standing some distance away. The Maclean rose to his feet and took out a dagger. Fury crossed Diego's face, an unforgiving anger that sent chills through her.

He took the knife away with one blow to the wrist. The movement was so fast, she nearly missed seeing it herself. Then he used his fist to pummel the man to the ground before two other Macleans pulled him off.

He stood, shook them off and strode away. She walked quickly to catch him. Blood spotted the shirt, and his dark hair fell onto his forehead.

He turned suddenly as if sensing danger, then that sardonic grin filled his face. "Has no one told you not sneak up behind someone?"

"I was not sneaking," she said with as much dignity as

she could summon. "I was watching you and thought I could help . . . with those wounds."

He looked down at his bloodied shirt and blinked. "It is a Maclean shirt. As for the wounds, I have had many worse ones."

"I know," she said. "I am sorry for them."

"Do not be, senorita. None of it was your doing. In truth, you probably saved us all."

She considered that for a moment. "How?"

"We were conveniently headed toward England, and you were a distraction to the crew."

They reached the stable. "They allow you to ride?" she asked.

"Not alone."

"I still do not understand why you did not leave. You could have been free, had you gone with the ship."

"At the moment, being aboard a ship is not my idea of freedom, Juliana. I like earth beneath my feet."

It was the first time he had used her given name. Her obvious surprise brought a smile to his lips again. But it was not a pleasant smile.

"I can call you senorita if you disapprove," he said with a bite in his voice.

"I prefer Juliana."

"Done, then."

He continued to the barn and she followed, not knowing why exactly.

No, she did know. He had always puzzled her. Nothing quite fit. His speech was that of a gentleman, but there was a raw, wild streak in him. He spoke both Spanish and English and yet she had just seen him fight like a ruffian.

They reached the stable and she watched him as he ignored her and murmured to the animals. They moved forward in their stalls, attentive. He seemed to have a way with them as he did with swords.

Then to her surprise, he went to the back, where a bitch was nursing her puppies. He looked at them with a curious expression. "It amazes me," he said, "how well she takes care of her puppies, even the runt."

"I think they are born knowing how."

"Si," he said. "A talent some humans do not have." He leaned down and picked up one of the puppies and rubbed its stomach. There was a gentleness about the gesture that so contrasted with the violence of a few moments earlier.

Yet the words had an unemotional flatness. Unemotional. Unpitying. Full of implication. Yet now was not the time to pursue the subject. But maybe another.

She turned from English to Spanish. "You did not really answer my question earlier. Why did you not leave with the others?"

"I thought I did answer," he replied in Spanish, though his expression indicated surprise. Then he looked around, saw a stable lad, and shrugged.

"You did not wish to get on a ship again and you said you like the Macleans."

He did not answer, just eyed her cautiously.

"I do not believe those are the real reasons. It would not have been that long a voyage."

"And the Macleans?" he asked.

"You do not seem a sentimental person."

"Ah, I do not?"

She wanted to stamp her feet. Getting a direct answer from him was impossible.

"Will you help me?" she asked suddenly, tired of the fencing.

He raised an eyebrow. "How?"

"I want to leave Inverleith."

The eyebrow arched higher. "So you *are* plotting. You said not."

"It is important that I leave. I endanger everyone here," she said. "You as well," she added, appealing to his self-interest.

"And so you wish to sacrifice yourself?" That irritating humor was thick in his voice.

"It would be no sacrifice. I would go to a wealthy family and a marriage arranged by my father."

"And why should I assist you?"

"I have some jewels. You can have them."

His eyes went cold. "And you believe I will take your thirty pieces of silver?"

She knew she had made a mistake.

"In truth, I do not know you well, at all," she said. "But if you do not care about money, then you must care about the Macleans. And you must realize that you and I are both a danger to them. A Spaniard here at Inverleith—especially two of us—will be more than a little curious. Word will eventually travel. Any query could lead to Patrick's death."

"This marriage . . . it is what you want?"

She had not told him the circumstances of her betrothal. She hesitated, then said, "*Si.*"

"I have no more freedom than you," he said. "How do you suppose I can help?"

"I think you are clever enough to find a way."

"And how would you explain your miraculous survival when your uncle, the crew and your dowry are gone?"

"The ship went down in a storm. I survived because you assisted me. No one else did. My father would reward you greatly."

"I am a convicted criminal."

"Patrick said the . . . oarsmen were only known as numbers. You could take the name of one of the crew members."

"You have thought this out. Were you so sure I would help you?"

"Nay. If you did not agree, I would go alone."

"I have not agreed, senorita," he said.

She waited.

"You have not told me how you expect me to help you leave Inverleith."

"Kimbra has suggested a picnic. If you can manage a ride yourself at the same time . . ."

"I will consider it," he said.

His face told her she would get nothing more now.

"Gracias," she said.

"Do not thank me," he said. "It is a wild scheme, and you are asking me to betray someone. . . ."

His words trailed off.

"I will tend those wounds," she said.

"No. I will do it myself," he said. The look he gave her was anything but friendly. He was angry and she was not sure what she had said to make him so.

She shivered. Would he tell anyone her plans? And why was he so angry?

Even more important, why did she think she could trust him? Both in helping her escape and, just as importantly, getting her to London safely.

She did not know whether he saw the questions in her face. She only heard his muttered curse in Spanish and then he left the stable without another word.

Chapter 28

LACHLAN rode both day and night after leaving Inverleith.

He led a second horse behind him, and he switched mounts along the way. The extra mount would serve a second purpose: a gift for the irascible Charlton, one of the fiercest of the English border reivers and at one time Lachlan's captor.

He would need the Charlton's help.

Theirs was a strange friendship. Thomas Charlton had little use for Scots but a great love for chess. Lachlan had found he had a talent for the game.

His mount now was a hobbler, a horse from the borders and a gift from the Charlton. Small and rough-looking, the animal was an extremely hardy animal that could travel over rough terrain for far longer than horses from the Highlands. In turn, his gift to Charlton was a Maclean-bred animal.

Thomas Charlton, he knew, coveted them to crossbreed with his own.

The journey had been bloody uncomfortable. It had started raining the day he left, and had not stopped during the past two days. He was wet and cold and tired when he arrived at the Charlton Tower.

He heard the alarm being given. He rode close to the gate before the sentry recognized him and opened up.

By the time he dismounted, Charltons had gathered around him asking about Kimbra. Then he strode toward the door. The tower had none of Inverleith's grace or comfort. Unlike Inverleith, with its huge stone walls, the tower was a far less sophisticated dwelling. It depended on the great door for defense and the fact that defenders above could hurl hot oil and rocks at any potential raiders.

Then the great door opened and Thomas Charlton limped out and held out his arms. Lachlan endured a rough embrace. "How is my Kimbra?" the Charlton asked.

"Well, as is Audra," Lachlan said with what he knew must be a foolish grin on his face. The thought of Kimbra always made him smile.

But already the Charlton's gaze had gone to the horse he led. "An extra mount?" he said, his eyes greedy.

"Aye. A gift."

The Charlton went over to the animal and ran his hands along its flank. "A fine gift." Then his eyes sharpened. "I imagine ye would like something in return."

Lachlan grinned. "Information."

"That is what I like about ye, Maclean. Ye speak bluntly. Come in. One of the lads will take the horses."

He followed the Charlton inside. The man was a bloodthirsty thief and bandit, but true to his own code. He would do anything for an ally or friend. But God help you if you were an enemy.

Charlton led him to up the steps to his chamber. It was obvious that his host's gout was no better than it had been before. But then he did not have Kimbra to mix the tea and poultices for it.

As if reading his mind, the Charlton collapsed into the chair. "I should never have permitted the marriage," he complained. "I need a healer."

"It just happens that Kimbra sent some leaves for a brew," Lachlan said with a grin.

"Need them all the time," the Charlton grumbled. "Should have brought her with you." He rearranged himself again. "Now what do ye want? Ye look as if you have been riding hard."

"I need information about the Earl of Chadwick and his son. He has property not far from here. You seem to know something about everyone."

"Why?" the Charlton asked.

"I cannot give you the reason. I can only say it is important to me."

The Charlton speared him with his gaze. "I know ye dislike asking for help. It must be important."

"Aye."

"His lordship is in the north often now," the Charlton said. "I hear he is ill."

"And his son?"

"Ah, the viscount. A bad one, to all accounts. Took his brother's place when Garrett was killed."

"How?"

The Charlton shrugged. " 'Tis said somewhere in Spain." He paused. "A pity. He was well-liked on the border. Participated in our games. He was a good swordsman and was said to have honor. As for the new viscount, we hear rumors. Nothing to his credit."

"And his father?"

"Like most lords," the Charlton said with contempt. "Ambitious. Ruthless. One must be if one is to sit next to a king."

"Have you heard anything about their business affairs?"

The Charlton shook his head. "They have ships but do no smuggling here, at least not with us. Not like ye," he said ironically, referring to Lachlan's occasional visits to the border on one of the Maclean ships. It had turned into a lucrative venture for both families with the added bonus that Kimbra could see her family.

"They have a Spanish partner," Lachlan said.

"I am not surprised. It gives them entrance to ports the English might not have."

"Some of the ships are galleys powered by slaves."

The Charlton raised his eyebrows. "And ye do not approve?"

"There are rumors that some may be Englishmen guilty only of being in the wrong place."

"I cannot believe that true of Chadwick. He regards his reputation too highly, and the crown would not look kindly on the practice. But his son . . . it is possible."

Lachlan shrugged. "That is what I wish to know."

Thomas Charlton raised his gout-swollen leg to a stool. "Ye wish to get rid of this Kingsley?"

Charlton, despite his rough exterior and reputation as a reiver and bandit, had never been a fool, although he often liked strangers to believe the opposite. He had become head of the family through ruthlessness and kept his position because of loyalty.

"I wish to know more about him, enough to destroy him . . . if he is guilty."

"I think ye are not that concerned with his guilt," Charlton said.

"If he is what you say he is, nay, I am not."

"God save me but I don't want to be an enemy of the Macleans."

Lachlan winced internally. He *had* changed from the idealistic young man who'd wanted to be a priest, more than he'd thought. But he despised cruelty, and to think of sending Juliana to a marriage to a man like that made his stomach curdle. "We feel the same about the Charltons."

"Come and sup with us. We will plot together, ye and I." The Charlton looked pleased at the prospect.

"It is urgent," Lachlan said. "I hoped you might have an ear somewhere in London."

"Ye wish to go?"

"Aye."

"I will have horses and a guide at dawn tomorrow. I know exactly the person."

"Honest?"

"Nay, the best thief in London but he knows everyone's business."

"I knew you could help."

"Always at yer service," the Charlton said with a grin that would do the devil proud.

RAIN. Rain. Rain.

Juliana had taken one of the puppies from the stable upstairs to Audra's room.

Bear nudged the puppy, which had just opened its eyes, and licked it with his great tongue.

It had been raining for days, and Juliana was about to go mad with waiting. There had been no word from Edinburgh, but the city was several days' ride away.

Diego avoided her and gave no indication whether she could expect any assistance from him.

Even in the rain, he trained as if he had a battle to win. She watched him from her window, wondering what drove him. What was important to him? She knew no more today than she had the day she had met him.

She did not know whether he would help her. Or whether he had reported the conversation to Rory Maclean. She doubted it, because her hosts said nothing, nor did they assign her a guard.

The Macleans went far to make her feel at home. Rory was charming, telling her she made him miss Felicia a wee bit less. She did not believe him. She'd seen the way he looked at Felicia. There had been so much love in his gaze that she ached. What must it be like to be so loved?

Audra laughed as the puppy rolled over. *The Spaniard has taught the puppy that,* Juliana thought.

If she stayed in this room any longer, she would never leave Inverleith. The true seduction was that she really felt they would like her to stay.

"Does it always rain like this?" she asked Kimbra, who watched her daughter like a tigress protecting her cub.

"Aye. Too often. Does it not in Spain?"

"There is more sun," she tried diplomatically. In truth there was a great deal more sun.

"I have not forgotten that picnic," Kimbra said. "I see you are becoming restless."

"I am used to riding daily," she replied.

Kimbra nodded. "I miss it as well."

Juliana disliked using a common interest for her own benefit, but at the moment she would take any opportunity to leave. As quickly as possible. Every moment she stayed was like sinking farther and farther into quicksand, except this quicksand carried a different kind of danger. The longer she stayed at Inverleith, the more she wanted to linger. Forever.

Juliana nodded. She replaced the puppy with its anxious mother in the stable and returned to the keep. She tried to find something to read in Lachlan's room, but she was too restless. She just could not stay here while others were off deciding her destiny.

Back to the window. The skies were still thick with bulbous clouds and a gray rain continued to fall.

What was happening in Edinburgh? In London? In Spain?

And when could she control her own destiny?

PATRICK rode next to Jamie into Edinburgh. Denny, dressed in servant's clothes, rode slightly behind him in the role designed for him.

Every step of his mount took him farther from Juliana. He could not block the memory of the look on her face when he'd left her the last time. A mixture of anger, of hurt and, most fearful of all, determination. He remembered her courage when she'd first faced him. And the recklessness of some of her words.

Would she try to do something rash?

Surely not. He'd told Rory to be careful, even though she seemed content enough to his brother.

He tried to turn his attention to the city. It had been nearly a decade and a half since Patrick had last been there, and that had been for games in which he competed against the man now riding next to him. He'd never thought to be riding beside him as a companion. Part of him still could not believe it.

The two of them had discussed what to do with Denny. They did not know who he was, but someone at court may, especially since there were English envoys there. Some of his mannerisms and skills indicated that he was of a privileged class.

Patrick glanced at Denny, who was also looking at the dwellings darkened with peat smoke. While Patrick knew it was a gamble that could prove troublesome if not catastrophic, Denny might remember someone, or something, that would help bring his memory back. That had become more important to Patrick as he himself had found his own place. Could he let Denny wander alone in darkness as he'd learned Lachlan had for weeks?

Except, for Denny, it had been years. He owed the Englishman that much.

They had done what they could to mask him. He was dressed in a servant's saffron shirt, an old plaid and a cap. No one looked at a servant. Kimbra had used a dye to darken his hair and Felicia had suggested putting wads of paper in his cheeks. Denny had been told that if he recognized anyone, he was to slip away and meet Patrick back at the inn.

As Denny trailed behind, Jamie caught Patrick's glance and moved closer to him. "You are worried about your friend?" he asked in a low voice.

"Aye. Kimbra said that Lachlan had started to remember bits of the past when the Maclean crest brought it all back," he said.

"We do not know whether Denny suffered the same kind of injury."

"Nay, but he sees and understands more than I thought. Mayhap he will see something in Edinburgh that will bring back memories."

The entire scheme was full of risks. But Patrick knew that since the forced signing of the Magna Carta, the English detested slavery. He could not believe King Henry would condone it. If Denny did belong to an important English family, then he might have allies, even against the powerful Viscount Kingsley. Those allies might be of use to the Macleans as well.

Jamie planned to stay in the chambers allotted to the Campbells in Edinburgh Castle. Jamie's father had been a close advisor to the last two kings, and as a reward the Campbells had been given chambers for their use.

Jamie had been informed the Earl of Angus was trying to change that arrangement. He wanted the rooms for his own friends, those who leaned toward an English alliance.

At the moment, though, they were still Jamie's, and Jamie planned to keep them that way. He would stay in them, but Rory and Denny would take lodgings in a nearby inn.

Patrick watched Jamie ride into the gates of the great castle. Jamie planned to ask for a private audience with the queen and announce the miraculous return of Patrick Maclean.

Chapter 29

THE sun finally emerged from behind clouds after nine days.

Panic had steadily grown in Juliana. There had been no word from Patrick or the others. What if Patrick had been taken? What if Lachlan had been discovered in England? What if word had somehow leaked about the missing ship?

Determined to leave today, she went down to the small room off the great hall to break fast. To her relief, she learned that Rory Maclean had left to settle a dispute over cattle some fifteen miles away. The sun would be close to setting by the time he returned.

She was too worried to eat the morning meal so she moved outside and sought out the Spaniard. He was saddling his horse. Stable lads were saddling other mounts nearby.

"You are leaving?" she asked softly.

"Nay, I am going hunting."

Her eyes questioned him.

"I was given a slow horse," he added.

"But weapons?"

"One must have weapons to hunt."

"I will ask Kimbra for that picnic today."

"Audra will be with her?" the Spaniard asked.

"Aye. I believe so." She waited.

He finally nodded. "Where is the picnic?"

"She mentioned a nearby loch. To the east."

He nodded again. "I have seen it." Then his lips thinned. "Patrick Maclean will come after us."

"He is not here."

"He will come."

"No," she said. "He will do nothing to hurt his clan. This is better for all of us." And it was. Patrick was drawn to her, as she was to him. But he had said no words of love and certainly none of marriage. He had left as if she was of no concern. They both had other responsibilities, he to his clan and she to her mother. And she could lay to rest forever any suspicions as to the fate of the *Sofia* if she convinced the Earl of Chadwick and her father that the ship sank in a storm.

"Do you have gold? Jewels?"

"You should know," she said tartly. "You took it all."

"I left a piece or so. I thought you may have something else hidden."

"No."

He shrugged as if it was really of no concern. "And you trust me?"

She hesitated long enough for the amusement to return.

"Do you not fear riding with a convict for company?" he pressed.

"No," she said and knew it was true. Despite the constant amusement in his eyes as if life were a bad jest, he had in an odd way been protective of both Carmita and herself. She had seen his spurts of anger when they surfaced, but they usually faded as quickly as they came.

He was an interesting man, but she'd never felt the pull that Patrick had for her. And he spoke English without the accent she knew she had. How he came about it, she did not know, but it would be invaluable.

"I am not sure I can do what you want," he said.

She stiffened.

"I am not yet trusted," he added, "obviously for good reason."

"I think you can find a way," she said dryly.

"Bring your jewelry."

She merely nodded.

"We will be stealing their horses. The Macleans will not take that well."

"You have gold from the cargo. You can leave some for them," she said. "You will be rewarded by the Earl of Chadwick. I swear it."

"I do not think you are in a position to swear anything," he said.

"We can use my jewelry."

"The Macleans fancy their horses more than coin and jewelry."

"We can send them back."

His gaze bore into her. "And if I do not appear?"

"I will find another way."

"I feared that," he said. "You have no judgment in men, senorita. Your trust in me shows that well enough." He paused, then said, "You had best go. You would not wish to raise suspicions."

He was right. Yet she had a reluctance to leave him and face Carmita, and her own doubts. Was she really doing the right thing?

Now for Carmita. Carmita could not come with her. For one thing, she was an even worse liar. Secondly, Juliana would never put her maid in danger again. She was convinced that Carmita would be safe here and well protected. It would be difficult to say good-bye, but that she must do.

She left Diego and found Kimbra. "May we go on the picnic this afternoon?" she asked.

"Aye. I have asked Rory and he agrees, though we will have an escort. The cook is preparing a feast."

"How long?"

"An hour or so."

"I will be ready."

She had to hurry. She needed paper and a quill pen. And ink.

She knew where to find it. She went to the small room where Duncan, the steward, kept the accounts for Inverleith. She said a prayer of thanks when she had the supplies in her hands and wrote two letters—one to Patrick and Rory, the other to Felicia—and tucked them both in her dress.

Seconds later she faced Carmita in her chamber. Carmita was cleaning one of Juliana's gowns.

Juliana put out her hand to her. "Come sit with me for a moment."

Carmita's eyes filled with apprehension. "Is something wrong, senorita?"

"*Si.* You know my father. I fear for my mother if I disappear," she said in Spanish. "And I fear for the Macleans if anyone learns I am here." Carmita nodded, but her hand clutched tighter to Juliana's.

"I must go," she said softly. "I alone can make sure no blame comes here."

"But how?"

"If I reach the Handdon, I can convince the Earl of Chadwick that the ship sank during a storm off the coast of England. A crew member saved my life but we were the only two to survive."

"I will go, too," Carmita said resolutely.

Juliana shook her head. "Two of us survived and none other. I want you to stay here with Manuel. He is happy here. You are happy here with him. Felicia and Kimbra are both kind. They will look after you."

"You plan to go alone?" Carmita said in horror.

"Diego will go with me." She silently prayed she was right.

Carmita's eyes narrowed. "You should have a *duena.*"

"It was a shipwreck," she reminded Carmita gently.

"I do not trust that man."

"I do," Juliana said. "You must trust me." She paused, then added, "You love my mother, too. You know what my father will do if foiled. He will no longer have need of her. But if I wed Viscount Kingsley . . . I can bring her to England."

"But you love . . ." She stopped suddenly, clapping her hand over her mouth.

"I am not free to love anyone but the man chosen by my father," Juliana said.

"You cannot go," Carmita cried out. "I will tell . . ."

"And perhaps condemn us all," Juliana said gently. "If my father ever learns the truth he will stop at nothing to regain my dowry and take vengeance for the death of my uncle and loss of the *Sofia*. He can do nothing about a storm, an act of God."

Tears started down Carmita's face. "I do not trust Senor Diego. He has ruthless eyes."

"He has done nothing to harm us," she said.

"I will be alone."

"You will have Manuel. I wish I could leave you something . . ." Her voice trailed off as she looked down at the ring on her finger. It had been a gift from her mother years earlier, and she thought the value was small. But it was certainly worth something.

The necklace and bracelet she'd been able to keep would go toward their journey and the reward for Diego. "Here," she said, placing the ring in Carmita's hand.

"I cannot take this."

"You can and will," Juliana said. "I want you to have it."

Carmita clutched it to her chest. "What if the Macleans do not want me here?"

"I have learned something about the Macleans," Juliana said, hurting inside. "They will find a place for you. You will be far better here than in my father's house." Or, from what she had heard, the Earl of Chadwick's castle.

Tears were coming faster from Carmita's eyes. They

broke Juliana's heart. "I will see you again," she said, pressing her fingers around Carmita's. "I swear on the Holy Mother. I will find ways of getting letters and funds to you."

She gave Carmita a hug. "Will you get my gray gown out?"

Carmita stood, hesitating, then slowly went to the wardrobe. Juliana quickly tucked the letters she had written into the bedclothes. She wanted Carmita to find them later, not hold them. The girl was already torn by loyalties.

Juliana dressed quickly into the serviceable gown, then waited as Carmita brushed her hair and pinned it into a knot at the back of her head before putting on a white cap.

"I will be back," Carmita said suddenly, then ran out before Juliana could say anything. She sat, wondering whether Carmita was going to the Macleans. If so, she would not get beyond the gates.

How long had it been?

She went to the window and saw that two horses and a pony had been saddled. A Maclean, dressed in the plaid, had already mounted and was waiting patiently. Bear was waiting with the horses.

She shivered. She was giving up everything she'd ever dreamed of for something she suspected would be a horror. Then Carmita was back, a pouch in her hand. "From Manuel," she said.

Juliana took it. Opened it.

It contained a stack of gold coins.

"I cannot take this." Her hands trembled slightly.

"You can send it back to him. He said he has more and wants you to have it." Her face flushed with pride. "He likes the horses. The Maclean said he would teach him to ride. He wants to be a soldier. He understands you want to help the Macleans."

What if the Macleans did not understand? What if they turned Carmita and Manuel out? Or worse? But they would not, she reassured herself. It was to their advantage to keep them here.

"Here," Carmita said. "I will sew the pouch into your cloak."

"My jewels, as well," Juliana said, grateful now that the Highland chill usually required a cloak.

In minutes, Carmita finished the task. Just as she finished, a knock came at the door.

Juliana hugged Carmita. "I will never forget you. If you ever need me, contact me."

"Aye," Carmita said, attempting a smile at her adoption of the Scottish word.

Juliana tried to smile as she went to the door. *Think of good things.*

"We are ready," Kimbra said.

Juliana nodded. "I am looking forward to it." *Lie.*

THE queen was as lovely as Patrick had heard. And Viscount Kingsley as unpleasant.

All had gone as planned. He had his audience with Queen Margaret, alone with James, three days after his arrival. During those three days he had paid a visit to the family's shipping office and reacquainted himself with Edinburgh. He also joined Jamie and Kingsley in a game of chance the evening before his audience with Margaret, the Queen Dowager.

Kingsley was a cheat. He used leaded dice. Patrick had seen enough of it during his days with the French army.

He did not call him on it. It suited Patrick to allow Kingsley to believe he was a bufflehead, a fool. He recalled the conversation. . . .

"A Maclean, heh. Heard you and the Campbells hated each other."

"We did," Patrick said.

Kingsley raised an eyebrow.

"Like England and Scotland, we declared a truce."

"And as temporary, heh," Kingsley said, sneering. It did not take more than a moment or so to know that Kingsley felt himself far superior to Scots.

Patrick tamped down on the bile that rose up in him. This man was to be Juliana's husband. The thought curdled his blood.

He thought of her back at Inverleith. The way she smelled of roses, the way her skin felt like fine silk, the way she smiled up at him as if . . .

But first he had to deal with Kingsley.

"I understand your family is involved in trade."

"Trade?" Kingsley looked offended. "A gentleman? No. My family has investments."

"I am interested in investments as well," Patrick said as he threw the dice and swore lustily as a five and three appeared. "God's blood but you have all the luck," he said while watching Kingsley.

The fool reveled in the words. Patrick surveyed him yet again. He was a handsome man, or would have been had it not been for the eyes that constantly darted around and the rounding body. His chin looked weak as well, or so Patrick thought.

He drank the ale in his glass, a poor offering, but then he'd had worse, thanks partly to the man across the table from him. The night wore on endlessly.

Finally, Patrick left early in the morning, had several hours of sleep, then left with Denny for Edinburgh Castle. He had purchased a cap for Denny, one that came down to his eyes, and Patrick wore the same leather bands around his wrists as he had last night to cover the scars on his wrists. He also wore the plaid, a linen shirt and soft leather boots that were higher than most.

Denny lurked in the shadows, his eyes always watchful, as Patrick bowed before the queen and said, "Your servant, Your Highness."

"You are as well favored as your brother."

"And you are as bonny as the poems and books written about you."

Margaret smiled. "As much a charmer as your brother," she said. "What has kept you away, now that you have finally ended that feud with the Campbells? My husband was much pleased about the wedding of your brother and the Campbell lass." Her face clouded suddenly, and the smile left Patrick's face as well. He noticed then the rings around her eyes that powder could not conceal. She was still young, having been wed at thirteen, and it was clear she still missed her husband.

"Many things. I fought with the French for several years. Then I was ill for a long time."

"You favor an alliance with France then?"

"I have no opinion on that," Patrick said. "I have been gone too long to judge whether England or France is the better ally, but I would always be wary of our neighbor to the south. He is close and greedy."

"He is my brother."

"That does not mean he is not greedy."

He heard the sharp inhale of the man next to him, then a movement behind him. He turned around.

Kingsley, dressed in popinjay purple, was striding toward them. "You call my king 'greedy'?" he said angrily, unwisely ignoring Margaret.

"Being your king does not make him immune to greed," Patrick replied mildly.

"The Maclean is right," Margaret said, a twinkle in her eyes. "I know my brother. He is exceedingly greedy."

Patrick thought Kingsley would burst of apoplexy, then quite abruptly he remembered where he was and bowed deeply. "I did not intend to interrupt you, madam, but I have been called home. I have come to tell you I will leave on the morrow."

"An illness?" she asked, concern clouding her eyes. There was real feeling in her face. So Kingsley had been making progress with the queen.

"Nay, but it is time to leave. The ship carrying my bride should have arrived by now, and I have already lingered too long."

"Aye, the Spanish connection," Margaret said with irritation. "My brother seems determined to ally himself with every major country through marriage."

"And isolate Scotland," Patrick said, apparently idly.

Margaret held up her hand. "No more politics. I welcome you, Patrick Maclean, to my court, and I wish you, Viscount Kingsley, happiness in your upcoming marriage. I look forward to meeting your wife."

She stood then, dismissing all of them, and they bowed and backed out of the room.

Kingsley stuttered with rage once the door closed behind them. "I will remember your words," he said, then strode away.

Jamie sighed. "You believe in making an impression."

"You and Rory were the ones who wanted me to be presented and take my place as laird of the Macleans," Patrick said.

"You made a favorable impression, I think. Despite her dismissal, she admires those who state their opinions."

"We will see," Patrick said. "I have never been one to back away from a fight."

"I noticed," Jamie said dryly.

Patrick looked around for Denny. He found him in the shadows, his face pale, his hands shaking, his brow beaded with sweat.

"Denny?"

Denny's eyes darted around, seemingly looking for someone.

The only person around, other than the queen's guards, had been Kingsley. "The Viscount Kingsley?" he asked.

Something flickered through Denny's eyes.

"You have seen him before?" Patrick said.

Denny looked confused, but his body was still stiff. The sight of Kingsley apparently stirred some reaction, but what?

"He is Viscount Kingsley," Patrick said. "The son of the Earl of Chadwick. The man Juliana was to marry."

"What do you remember, man?" Jamie prompted.

Patrick saw something flicker in Denny's eyes, then blankness again. And frustration. Denny bowed his head in defeat.

Whatever had been there was gone.

* * *

THE day was full of promise as Juliana rode with Kimbra and Audra. Bear ran aside them, and the guard stayed well behind. The chill in the air justified wearing her cloak with both the jewels and coins sewn into it.

Kimbra chatted as they rode, telling her about the Macleans and about her own family on the English border. "'Tis far prettier here," she said. "The loch is beautiful. Rory used to take Felicia here."

She pulled her mare to a halt at the edge of a lake that shimmered with sunlight. It was, as Kimbra said, breathtakingly blue against the heather-covered hills.

So different from the gray of the past days.

She looked around. No sign of another human. Had Diego been able to lose his own guard?

They dismounted and tied the reins of their mounts to bushes. The guard also dismounted and sat on a rock not far from them, but apart. Juliana helped spread out a blanket, then the food that had been prepared. There was roasted chicken, cheese, fresh bread and fruit. Wine for them and milk for Audra, who started chasing Bear.

"It is lovely here," Juliana said, sitting down on a stone.

"When it does not rain," Kimbra said ruefully.

"What is it like on the border?" she asked. The man she was to marry had estates not far from the border.

"Bogs and rocks and mountains. Not very good for growing things. Or cattle. So all the families turned to reiving."

"Reiving."

"Stealing," Kimbra said frankly. "Stealing cattle. Raiding homes. Robbing travelers."

Juliana did not know what to say then. Instead, she took a bite of chicken. She did not want it, but she knew it might be a long time before she had food again.

If Diego appeared. Had she had been a fool to trust him?

Perhaps he had not been able to wander away.

Audra ran back to them, Bear behind her. She sat down and took a leg. She looked loved and happy. Juliana's heart ached at the prospect of robbing that smile from her, even for a moment.

They ate then, soaking in the rays of the sun after so many days of rain. Audra dozed off, Bear beside her. Kimbra asked in a low voice about Juliana's home in Spain. "Audra and I sailed with Lachlan several times, and I hoped to go there, but we passed through one storm that was terrifying. I never wanted Audra to experience another one."

Juliana remembered the fierceness of the storm the *Sofia* had sailed through and understood. It had been bad enough for her, but she remembered the terror and fear in Carmita's eyes. How much worse to feel another's fear, especially one's own child.

She was facing the guard while Kimbra was staring out at the loch. Juliana caught sight of Diego as he quickly and silently approached the guard from behind. It was as if he appeared out of nowhere. He struck the guard, who slumped silently. Then Diego lowered him to the ground and bound the Maclean. Thank Mary in heaven he had not killed him.

Diego moved toward them and Kimbra turned around, as if she instinctively felt his presence.

Diego stood there, bowed as Kimbra sprung to her feet. Bear also rose, but he was familiar with Diego and made no threatening movement.

There were questions in Kimbra's face. Then the realization of what Juliana and Diego intended. She put her arms around Audra.

"I am afraid we will have to take your horses," Diego said in a low voice, "but I will leave them where you can find them."

"I am sorry," Juliana said. "You have been good to me, but I cannot stay. It can only bring grief to the Macleans, and I have my family to consider as well."

"Wait until Patrick returns," Kimbra urged.

"If I do, I will never leave," Juliana said softly.

Kimbra hugged Juliana. "Patrick loves you. It is clear. He will come after you."

"No," she said softly. "He will not. And you must convince him that I want to leave. This is a good marriage. I will make sure that no blame comes to anyone here."

"Juliana?" Diego's voice interrupted. "We must go."

She stepped away from Kimbra, and it was one of the hardest things she had ever done. She went over to the horses with Diego, and he helped her onto the mare she'd been riding. He mounted the guard's gelding, then gathered the reins of the other three horses. He handed off one set of reins to Juliana, and held the other two. It would be a long walk back for the guard, but it could not be helped. Someone would return for Kimbra and her daughter.

Without looking back, Juliana urged the mare forward at a trot.

Chapter 30

PATRICK had accomplished what he wanted. There was no reason to linger in Edinburgh.

He'd had his audience with the queen and established his place as the Maclean heir. He'd met Kingsley and confirmed to himself that the man was not fit for marriage to Juliana. Even the thought of her made him want to race back home.

Home. It was the first time he'd really considered Inverleith that since his return. But now it was home, and he was eager to return. Especially with Juliana there. His reaction to Kingsley had been bone-deep dislike. There was no way he would allow the marriage. To do so would doom Juliana to a miserable life with a miserable man. Nor did he want to live without her, he realized. He'd seen enough of Rory and Felicia, and Lachlan and Kimbra, to know he craved the same kind of love. God help them both, but he intended to ask her to wed. They would simply have to invent some plausible story to explain her presence.

Patrick said his farewell to Jamie. God's blood, but he found he really did like the man. Like a Campbell?

Denny touched his shoulder in question. They had been sitting in Patrick's room of the inn, each quiet, lost in thought.

"We will be leaving soon."

Relief flooded Denny's eyes. He had been restless since seeing Kingsley. Patrick understood that something had seemed familiar—and terrifying—to Denny, but he could not put it in words. Was there someone like Kingsley in Denny's past? Someone who appeared to be brutal and vicious? Then again, mayhap Denny did not even know why.

Patrick hoped that Kimbra and Juliana might unlock some of those answers. He picked up his saddlebags, eager now to leave. A loud knock came at the door, and it was pushed open before he reached it.

A travel-stained Rory and a grim-faced Jamie entered.

"She's gone," Rory said simply. "She and that bloody Spaniard."

It took a few seconds for Patrick to understand. "How?"

"They went for a picnic. Kimbra, Audra and Juliana. Damn my soul. I trusted her." Rory paused. "Even so, I sent a guard with them. Apparently the Spaniard went hunting with some of our men and slipped away from them. He surprised the guard with Juliana and took her and all the horses. By the time the guard ran back to Inverleith, Juliana and the Spaniard had disappeared."

A stunning emptiness settled in Patrick's chest. "They planned it?"

"Aye. They had to. I sent out men to search. We found the horses tied to bushes not far from the beach where there were several fishing boats. One with sails is missing." Rory paused. "The Spaniard is apparently quite canny in evading pursuit. They could have landed anywhere across the sound."

With the gold Patrick had given Diego as his share of the *Sofia*'s cargo, the Spaniard could easily purchase fresh horses for them. The emptiness turned to cold anger. Diego no doubt expected a fine reward from the Earl of Chadwick.

"I'm sorry, Brother. I should have been more careful but I thought Juliana was content at Inverleith. Kimbra is consumed with guilt but she always thinks the best of everyone despite what happened on the border. We thought . . ."

His voice trailed off without saying what they thought, but Patrick did not need him to finish. They had thought there was something between the two of them, Patrick and Juliana. He had, too.

Looby. He called himself every type of fool. *Hoddy peak! Cuckold.* He was aware his fingers tightened around the saddlebags.

"She left two letters," Rory continued, his expression contrite and full of a sympathy Patrick could not bear. "One was to me, apologizing and thanking the Macleans for our hospitality." His voice had turned ironic. He pulled out a piece of folded parchment from the purse hanging on his belt and handed it to Patrick.

He held it for a moment, then carefully unfolded the parchment and read.

Patrick,

I have decided to fulfill my marriage contract. I will tell them I was shipwrecked and Diego saved me. We were the only two survivors when the ship foundered near the English coast. That should forever put to rest the fate of the Sofia. *If anyone does come forth later, it can be explained away as someone taking advantage of a tragedy.*

This is best for all concerned. My mother. My family. The Macleans. You can live your life without fear for yourself or your family.

It is a fine marriage to a respected family. I can ask for no more.

Diego will provide escort as well as confirmation of the sinking of the Sofia.

I will always remember the Macleans and their hospitality.

Juliana

The coolness of the message struck him to the core as his stomach roiled. No mention of what had passed between them.

And leaving with Diego of all men. Images sprang to his mind of the two of them together. All unwelcome. She felt she could go to the Spaniard. She hadn't come to him. She trusted Diego. She had not trusted him.

He read it again. Each word of the letter was like a dagger into his heart. He feared for her. Nay, he was terrified for her. And he was furious. At both of them. Mayhap her intentions had been good. But to steal off like a thief in the night . . .

"I am going after them," Patrick said.

"We do not know where they are going," Jamie said.

"Middlesbrough," Patrick said. "That's the Chadwick seat."

"They could not be far ahead," Rory said. "They would have to cross Scotland, and I nearly killed two horses to get here."

"Diego is resourceful," Patrick replied, his throat thick. What if he had been wrong about Diego from the beginning? God's blood, he *had* been wrong. His hands ached to kill the man.

"Aye, I have noticed that," Rory agreed dryly.

"We need a map."

"Mine is gone," Rory admitted. "Juliana borrowed it."

The sinking feeling went deeper. How long had she planned this? Since she'd first arrived? Or since he bedded her? The sense of betrayal deepened.

Jamie broke in. "My guess is they would travel to Glasgow and down to Carlisle, then ride to the Middlesbrough."

"Edinburgh is the easier route," Rory interjected.

"They know you are in Edinburgh," Jamie protested.

Patrick swore under his breath. He tried to think as Diego would. The man must know he would come after him. "He will come through Edinburgh," he said with more certainty than he felt. " 'Tis the fastest way. He will hope you sent someone else and it would take the usual four or five days."

"One of us should ride ahead to the road from Carlisle just in case," Rory said.

"Us?" Patrick raised an eyebrow.

"I am at fault."

"Someone should be at Inverleith," Patrick said, "and you should not be involved with this."

"Aye, I am involved," Rory replied softly. "I cannot sit home again. Duncan and Archibald can take care of Inverleith now that the Campbells are no longer enemies."

Patrick hesitated, fought with himself. He did not want to entangle the Macleans further in his problems. But he'd learned in the past days the guilt that Lachlan carried about the death of their father, the guilt that Rory felt for not being at Flodden Field. They'd all needed healing.

Patrick finally nodded.

"Denny will go with us. He can fight like the devil, and he might remember something. I think he had a feeling about Kingsley, that he remembered something, but . . . it seemed to flicker away like the light of a candle."

"I am going as well," Jamie said. "I've been at the English court, negotiating on the behalf of the late king. I have acquaintances on both sides of the border."

Patrick had no illusions about the next few days. Despite the current negotiations between Scotland and England, they could all be seized as spies. And if his role in the *Sofia*'s disappearance was discovered, he would have a very short future. As would anyone with him.

He saw the determination in their eyes. His brother's. Jamie's. His old enemy. His throat suddenly felt thick.

"Lachlan may still be at the Charlton's tower," Rory

said, moving toward the door. "He is strangely fond of the old bandit. It is not far out of our way."

"Could she do it?" Rory asked suddenly. "Could she convince them the ship sank?"

Patrick shrugged. "She is not adept at hiding her feelings, and God knows what Diego will do or say."

"You know nothing about him?" Rory asked.

"Nay. He is wily in avoiding questions, but I did not think he would do this."

"Would he harm her?"

"If he does, he is dead."

Without more words and afraid his emotion might show, Patrick picked up his saddlebags and strode out, the other three behind him.

He was no longer alone.

DAYS passed in a blur. Juliana and Diego rode day and night, Diego frequently selling and buying new mounts. They rested only when they could not continue on. When rain came, Diego would find shelter, once in a small inn where he slept in the common room and she in a room with another woman. They posed as brother and sister traveling to see a dying relative, and she covered her face with a scarf when they encountered anyone. She was scarred by the pox, Diego said, and in every encounter the person quickly averted their eyes.

Privately, he treated her as an indifferent brother, looking to her most essential needs but sharing little else with her, particularly any information about himself.

Time was essential to the plan. The ship would already be almost two weeks late. How long would it have taken Diego and her to find their way to the Tees River and Handdon Castle after the ship was blown off course and foundered on rocks?

Though she'd often ridden in Spain, she'd never before been on a horse for hours upon hours, and every bone in her body ached. She could barely sit upright, yet Diego continued to push forward. She could not do less.

The exhaustion was numbing. Which was well. She could not bear to think about what she was leaving. She did not want to think that she would never see Patrick Maclean again. Never feel his warmth. The thrill of his touch. The comfort of his arms. The exquisite feelings he stirred in her.

They talked little, and she was grateful for that. Diego was more distant than she had ever seen him, his eyes cool and his manner stiff.

It had already grown dark when they approached a village. "According to your map," he said, "we should be on or over the English border."

They had been skirting the main road connecting the two countries for the past day. They had passed through Glasgow, then Carlisle before turning east toward Middlesbrough. The Earl of Chadwick's castle, Handdon, was just south of Middlesbrough.

He stopped his mount outside an inn. He took one look at her. "I will try to get rooms for the night."

She was too tired to protest.

Six days had slid by since they'd left Inverleith. She knew that only because of the nights.

He returned. "They have rooms. A private room for you. I will share space with others."

He offered her his hand and she slid down. He caught her and lowered her to her feet, steadying her. His gaze searched hers, then that odd smile returned. "I did not believe you would do so well, Juliana, or that any woman could."

Too weary to come back with a witty reply, she did not say anything. Instead, she covered her face with the scarf and hood of her cloak. The pox, Diego had explained.

He took the saddlebags he'd purchased and surrendered the horses to a stable lad along with a coin. "Take good care of them."

The boy had weighed it in his hand, then bobbed his head. "I will, your lordship."

Diego led the way upstairs, placed the saddlebags inside and closed the door. For the slightest moment, she stilled.

"The innkeeper said we are at Newcastle upon Tyne," he said. "Handdon Castle is another hard day's ride from here."

"They are all hard days' rides," she said.

A knock came at the door and a barmaid entered with two cups of wine and a large plate of food, including beef and bread and potatoes, and set it down on the table in the tiny room.

Diego nodded and handed her a coin, then sat down. They'd had nothing but bread today.

She could hardly keep her eyes open. She wished for a bath. For clean clothes, but that would not fit the picture they wished to present to her future husband and his family.

But then Kingsley may not want her at all after her tale. She would have traveled many miles with a man not her husband. She would appear in a dress that she would claim was begged. Diego was wearing the seaman's trousers and shirt he had taken from the cabin of one of the *Sofia*'s officers and had purchased leather bands to cover manacle scars on his wrists. She was quite certain he could lie his way through any questions.

"We can always return," Diego said, reading her thoughts.

"No."

"They would welcome you back."

"What about your reward?"

He shrugged. "One does not always win."

"Then why did you come with me?"

His dark eyes turned onyx. He did not answer.

"Diego?" she said. "Is that your real name?"

"No," he said, stretching back in a chair and taking a long swallow of ale.

"What is it then?" She had grown more and more curious about her enigmatic companion. He had fine manners when he chose to display them. Good speech. He spoke several languages well. Yet he could also lapse into the guise of a sailor or servant almost immediately.

"Diego does well enough for now."

"Do you have family?" she persisted, now that he had said more than usual. She suspected it was the same exhaustion that wracked her.

"No one that recognizes me," he said without emotion.

"But *they* exist?" she persisted.

"Curious thing, are you not?" he said with a trace of a smile.

"I like you," she said.

He flashed that sardonic smile at her. "Like?" he said as if tasting it. "Distressing word, that. I think I would prefer hate or despise or . . ."

"Why?"

" 'Like' is bland, senorita. Lifeless. I do not like being bland."

"You have naught to worry about," she said, surprised at how relaxed she was feeling, even if she was tired to the bone.

When he didn't reply, she persisted. "If you do not care about the money, why are you here?" she asked again.

He took another swallow of wine. "Perhaps because your Patrick is the only man I have ever admired. He and his brothers."

"Then why . . ."

"I agree with you, senorita. He will never be safe—none of us will—unless it is believed the *Sofia* went down during a storm. You offered the perfect solution. I knew he would not agree. He has too much honor." He said it almost as if it were a curse.

She swallowed hard. She was astonished at his statement, the admission that he cared about anything, but then she could not help but be irritated by the fact that he so easily agreed to offer her as a sacrifice, even if it had been her plan. Juliana realized all those emotions contradicted each other, but she was too weary to try to unravel them.

"Ah, you are distressed." The amusement was back in his voice.

"No," she denied.

"Or perhaps I have my own scheme," he tantalized.

Her curiosity won against her indignation. "I do not understand."

"Rest assured, I do not intend to throw you to the hounds. I have a grudge against men like the Earl of Chadwick as well as the Mendozas."

Another twist. Another riddle. Before she could reply, he stood. " 'Tis time for me to go and claim my place with fellow travelers. We leave at sunrise."

Before she could stop him, he left, closing the door softly behind him and leaving her to ponder his words.

Still dressed, she lay down on the dirty bed. Diego had surprised her once again tonight but she was too weary to solve his riddles. She would think about that tomorrow. Her thoughts turned to Patrick. The sharp edge of loss sliced through her heart. She recalled the first time she saw him on the ship, and the terror that had swept through her. He'd been the ultimate warrior then. He still was. But now that image was tempered by the gentleness of his touch, his instinct to protect.

That was the image that held steady. Pain twisted inside as she envisioned a future without him, without all those exquisite feelings he'd aroused. Without the feeling of belonging he brought to her.

Emotions tore at her as she closed her eyes.

She was doing the right thing. He would be safe after years of the worst kind of hell. She would make it so. That was all that mattered.

PATRICK, Rory and Denny reached Thomas Charlton's tower fortress at midmorning on the second day. Jamie and Denny had swung southwest to intercept the road from Carlisle. To Patrick's surprise, Denny reluctantly agreed to accompany Jamie. The border was too dangerous for lone riders.

They planned to meet at Hartlepool, a village near the River Tees. It was large enough, Rory said, to have several inns. He was familiar with the entire northern English coast where he'd engaged in smuggling French wines.

Patrick was now well versed on the first not-quite-cordial meeting between Rory and the Charlton. They had, in truth, almost killed one another. Relations healed, however, with the wedding of Kimbra, the Charlton's favorite healer, and Lachlan.

Charlton told them what he knew about the Earl of Chadwick and said Lachlan had traveled to London to learn more about him and his son, the Viscount Kingsley. He was obviously curious about the questions. Lachlan had apparently told him little.

"A business proposition," Rory said simply. "We want to know who we do business with."

"Smuggling?" the Charlton said with a sly grin. He had at times bought his own share of illegal goods from the Macleans. "Young Kingsley is not above it, but I would be wary of trusting him. He would betray ye in a second and take everything."

"So I have heard," Rory said. "And his father?"

"'Tis said the old earl is still mourning the loss of his oldest son. He is ill, and Kingsley has assumed much of his authority. I hear he is trying to establish himself with King Henry's court."

"And he is doing so," Rory said. "He has been in Edinburgh on behalf of Henry. He left about the same time we did."

"Devil ye say. He is at Handdon?"

"Or on his way."

"Be careful, Maclean."

The Charlton loaned them fresh horses and clothes. "Ye would not go far in England in those plaids," he said.

"Are there many inns between here and the River Tees?"

Charlton's gaze was even more curious but he refrained from asking questions. "There is one on the road from Carlisle. One about five leagues south, and then several in Newcastle."

"My thanks," Rory said. "I will see that the horses are returned."

"I will take your mounts in trade," the Charlton said, failing to keep a degree of eagerness from his voice.

"We will discuss that later," Rory said, and Patrick realized his brother had no intention of surrendering his beloved horses for the small, sturdy animals they were being offered.

They lingered to have a meal, then started out again. They should be well ahead of Diego and Juliana, but Patrick was not going to take chances. They would check every inn, and any other dwelling. If she had arrived, word would have started to travel. A bride rescued from the sea would be irresistible.

And if they hadn't, he planned to make sure they did not.

JULIANA and Diego left the inn at daybreak.

She had tried to comb her hair but in the damp air it refused to do as she wished. She braided it instead.

Their pace remained steady. She smelled the salt air as they neared the coast. In Spain, she delighted in it. Here, she resented it. It brought her closer to a marriage she feared and farther away from Patrick. Even if she was turned away by Kingsley, there could be no union with the Maclean. The past would always haunt them and be a threat.

They stayed mostly off the road, unless the terrain was too rough. At noon they stopped by a stream to water the horses and eat the bread and cheese Diego had purchased at the inn.

Her legs were stiff, her body sore. She gratefully found a dry piece of ground and sat down. And closed her eyes.

"AYE," said the innkeeper. "I think it could be them."

It had taken a gold coin before the innkeeper remembered. His was the third inn they had tried. They had almost passed it, having ridden past Newcastle. Neither thought there was any way a man and woman together could have ridden this distance in so short a time.

"Think?"

"You said the woman had golden hair. I did not see that or her face. A scarf was wrapped around it. Her brother said she'd had the pox." The innkeeper crossed himself. "But the man was as you described. Brother and sister they said they were," he continued. "Traveling to reach a dying mother. Stayed in different rooms they did, so I did not doubt their tale." He peered at Rory.

"You were right," Patrick said. "Their mother died. We were sent to meet them and tell them. How long ago did they leave?"

"Daybreak, my lad told me."

"My thanks," Patrick said, then hesitated. "I want to talk to the lad. Maybe he will remember something. We do not wish to miss them again."

The innkeeper hesitated.

Patrick produced another coin.

In minutes, they discovered that a man and woman had taken the toll road leading south.

How could they have traveled so far so quickly?

Patrick knew he would never underestimate either of them again. *The pox?* He cursed to himself and spurred his horse on. One more day and they would be at Handdon Castle.

Three hours later, they encountered a man coming from the other direction in a cart loaded with fish he was taking to an inland village. They asked about other riders. They were trying to catch up with friends who had left Newcastle before them.

He shook his head.

After he passed, Patrick paused. "They are not staying to the road."

"Would you?" Rory asked.

"Nay, though I cannot imagine they thought we might be so close behind them."

"They are probably still ahead," Rory said. "Let us look for any path that leads off the road."

The left side led to the sea and the landscape was mostly barren. "Water," Patrick said. "They will need water for their horses. So do we."

Thirty minutes later they went over a wooden bridge. They turned right along a path that followed the stream, then dismounted. Rory held the horses while Patrick moved quietly along the banks of the stream.

He saw the horses first. They were quietly grazing. Then he saw the sleeping form of a woman on the ground, a cloak covering her.

He moved forward toward her and suddenly Diego was at his side. "I wondered when the bloody hell you would get here."

Patrick didn't think. He just reacted. He hit Diego as hard as could, watched as he went down, and then he threw himself on him.

Chapter 31

PATRICK hit Diego again. He put all his anger and frustration and stark terror in the blow. Terror that Juliana had been in peril. Fear that he might lose her. Anger at what he considered betrayal by a man he'd brought to his home.

He hit again, then his arm was caught by Diego's fist, and they rolled over until Diego was over him. Patrick relaxed a moment, and it disarmed Diego. He loosened his hold slightly and Patrick jerked it back and struck him in the stomach.

Diego grunted and they changed places again, rolling on the ground.

He heard Juliana's voice.

"Stop it, Patrick! Diego!"

But he was not about to stop it. Diego had been with Juliana the last seven days or more. He had stolen her away, apparently with her consent. She had trusted him more than she had Patrick. He knew a fury stronger than any he'd felt in the galley.

He struck again and Diego countered, landing a blow into Patrick's chest, and he couldn't breathe for a moment. To his surprise, Diego did not take advantage but lay there, breathing hard.

Then Juliana was next to him. "Hit *me*," she said. "That is what you want to do."

Rory stood, watching.

Diego rose slowly, his breathing labored.

Patrick stayed on the ground, trying to breathe.

He glared at Diego, then turned his angry gaze on Juliana.

His heart skipped a beat, making breathing even more difficult. Her dress was embellished by leaves, and her hair fell in a braid almost to her waist. She looked so bloody appealing.

And her eyes. Despite the frown on her face, her eyes said something else. They devoured him.

He wanted to touch her. To assure himself that there was no injury. That Diego had not taken advantage. God's blood but he wanted to wrap his arms around her.

Instead he sat there as Diego leaned against a tree, his chest heaving.

Rory leaned down and offered Patrick a hand, pulling him to his feet.

Patrick felt as tongue-tied as a youth. He despised his weakness but his heart beat erratically, and it was not because of the blows. Then Diego's words came back to him.

I wondered when the bloody hell you would get here.

His gaze went to Juliana.

"You did not trust me," he said.

"You would have tried to stop me."

Aye, he would have. He wanted to tell her how foolish she'd been, but one look at her set expression made him realize that would not be the smartest thing he could do.

"Did hitting him help?" she asked.

She was no more the terrified maiden on the *Sofia.* Her eyes blazed with anger. And another kind of fire.

"Aye," he said.

"How did you find us?"

"Logic," he said righteously.

She narrowed her eyes. "You will not stop me."

"I can and I will. I will not have you sacrificing yourself for me."

"It is not just you," she said. "It is for Denny and Manuel and the others. And myself. I cannot hide the rest of my life. And . . . my mother . . . I would never be able to see her again."

"Aye. You could. We could steal her away as well."

"Then you will bring both Spain and England down on you." She turned to Rory. "I am sorry. I took advantage of your hospitality, but I sought only to help."

"You explained that in your letters," Rory said, "but I do not think it gave Patrick much satisfaction." His tone was cool, and even Patrick recognized the bite in it.

"Why Diego, Juliana? Why did you not talk to me?"

"You were gone." She lifted her head. "You left without giving me a choice about my life. You wanted me to sit and wait while you made decisions for me. I will not let that happen again. Ever. I will make my own choices, and my choice is Kingsley."

Rory used that moment to nod at Diego. "I think you and I should water our horses." He took the reins of his horse and handed those of Patrick's to Diego. "I prefer to stay," Diego said.

"Now *you* do not have a choice," Rory said, his voice hardening and his hand going to his dagger.

Diego shrugged. "I do not think I wish to fight Macleans again today." He started to lead Patrick's horse after giving it a disparaging look. "That is not much of a horse."

"It is a hobbler," Rory said, leading the way. "They raise them on the border. They are uncommonly sturdy. They can run all day."

Patrick heard Diego's complaints about the horses until their voices faded. Then his gaze went back to Juliana. "Do you care for him?" he asked.

"As a friend," she said. "He has been a good one." She gathered her cloak around her. "He has not touched me other than to help me on and off my horse."

He believed her about Diego, although he wasn't finished with the Spaniard. He wanted to know what game the man was playing. Or did he just amuse himself by pushing people around like chess pieces?

He stepped closer. She took a step as well, and the air became thick with strong, even violent emotions as she stood straight before him. Unyielding, yet there was something oddly poignant about her defiance.

He felt his soul bleed. The taste of betrayal had been riding with him these past few frantic days. Emotions stumbled around all over inside him. More emotions than he'd ever known or felt before. Emotions he had tamed as a boy and kept thoroughly contained during the past years, long before he went to France.

They were roiling around now, and he had no idea what to do with them, or how to harness them. They'd exploded moments ago with Diego, but those blows had done nothing to temper his emotions. He had convinced himself he would have no problems tamping down his desires. He'd been so wrong.

He wanted to take her in his arms. Touch her. Know she was safe. *Lie!* He wanted to do much more than that. He wanted to take her in his arms and keep her there forever.

But she had not trusted him. She *had* trusted Diego. That thought kept running through his head. It hurt far more than the whip that had so often lashed his back.

She must have seen his thoughts in his face because she took a step back, her gaze not leaving his face. No apology on it. No defense. Only steely determination.

"Why?" he asked.

"I wanted to right things," she said. "I knew you would not approve."

"And Diego?"

"I offered him a reward from my family." She hesitated. "But that is not why he came."

He waited.

"He is risking his own life," she said. "And not for gold."

His face must have shown his disbelief.

"In a moment of confession," she said, "he said you were the only man he'd ever admired. He knew this was the only way to put the *Sofia* to rest forever."

"With your life?"

"He said he had a plan to steal me away again."

"And you believed him?"

"*Si*. He is a complicated man. He has his own strange code of honor even as he claims it to be for fools only."

He disliked the affection he heard in her voice. It still rankled, nay, more than rankled, that Juliana had turned to him.

"Patrick?"

Her voice was soft, pleading.

For him? Or Diego?

"We must go on to Handdon."

"Nay."

She held out her hand. "Trust me."

The gesture nearly unmanned him. Her eyes were so steady. Honest. Pleading. There were no secrets hidden there. He could not do as she wished. He could not send her to a man like Kingsley. Nor was he convinced of Diego's motives. Or his ability to get her back without harm.

He reached out and took her hand. It was small and seemed so fragile. But he was learning she was anything but fragile. He felt humbled. So many wrong thoughts had run through his head, including wild jealousy. Regardless of what Diego thought, or wanted, it was clear to Patrick now that for the sake of his clan she had been willing to go to a man she feared. He, on the other hand, had done what he had done all his life. He'd escaped into himself and locked the doors when he'd found he was caring too much. *Risking too much.* He had left with little explanation and no promises, even after taking her virginity.

A small frown marred her brow. Still, her eyes softened when she looked at him, her eyes filling with a need that echoed his own. For a long while they stood without moving, without speaking, just drinking in the sight of each other. He felt the coldness inside drain away and in its place a sweet warmth began to grow. His breath quickening, he pulled her into his arms.

For a moment they did not move, simply allowing warmth to flow between them. She rested her head on his chest, and he felt a tenderness so strong it nearly paralyzed him. Sweet Jesu, but he wanted her.

She looked up. His lips touched hers, lightly at first, then with a fierceness that claimed her for his own. She trembled, and he felt her body speak to his of her own need. Exultation filled him as her lips responded. He'd feared he had lost her forever.

Her body strained against his and for the briefest second he hesitated. He needed to think, and she had a way of muddling that process. But the pulsing demand in his body became more insistent with every touch. His body burned, his mind fogged with need for her. Hunger racked him. 'Twas not only a physical hunger, but something deeper and far more perilous.

"Juliana," he whispered softly.

Juliana heard the rueful note of surrender in his voice as he tightened his arms around her. Heat pulsated in wild spurts, starting at her core and reaching out to claim every part of her body. She looked up at him. His gaze radiated fire, a fire that reached out and scorched her. Her heart pounded as he pressed her closer to him, and she held her breath as his hand lifted and his fingers touched her face.

Tremors of sensation ran down her spine, and the air sizzled between them. She knew she should move away. There was too much between them, too much distrust. Too many obstacles, but she could not make her body obey. She had yearned for this, the familiar smell and taste and feel of him, the warm yet explosive intimacy that made her feel both safe and imperiled.

He *was* dangerous. The way he made her feel was especially dangerous. She was bewitched by it, her body thrummed with it. His fingers feathered the back of her neck, and his lips caressed hers. For the moment, they were the only two people in the world. The distrust was gone, the tension fading as they reveled in each other.

Then he muttered something and stepped back. Dazed, she could only stare at him. Then she heard a cheerful whistling. She muttered as well and turned to see Rory and Diego coming back. Rory wore a satisfied smile on his face, and Diego—a pox on the man—looked smug despite his swollen cheek.

"NAY," Patrick said.

"Aye," Juliana mocked him as they discussed what should happen next. The air was growing distinctly colder, and she pulled her cloak tighter around her.

The three men argued as she listened. They could decide whatever they wanted to decide. But she knew what she was going to do. She was going to finish what she started, with or without their approval or assistance. At least now she would have today. He had come far for her, and his eyes said what he had not yet put into words.

She watched as he stood. He was wearing English clothes now. The white shirt but with a doublet and hose. The leather boots, though, were the same. "I will not have it," Patrick said flatly. "If I have to bind your hands and feet."

"It will work," Diego said calmly. "She is a fine actress. Kingsley would not touch her prior to the wedding, not with guests at the castle."

"Guests?"

"Your brother and I just talked. He said Kingsley made the announcement he was to be wed. Rory could take a gift from the queen. He would not be turned away, and he could look after her. Because of the bans, a marriage could not take place for weeks, and Juliana said Kingsley wanted it in London. I suspect they planned to bring her directly here because a Spanish ship manned by slaves would be suspect in London."

Juliana looked at Patrick. At least he was listening.

"It would be easy to help her escape in London," Diego said. "By then everyone will have accepted the tragic tale of the doomed *Sofia.* Lachlan, meanwhile, can fetch Juliana's mother."

Patrick stared at Diego. "You planned this from the beginning?"

"No. Not until Juliana convinced me that she was going to leave Inverleith one way or the other. I thought she would be safer with me, despite many opinions to the contrary."

"You could have told Rory," Patrick growled.

"He would not have permitted it. Nor would you have. He might have tried to keep her more confined, but Juliana was determined. She would have found a way."

"You meant for us to follow," Patrick said.

Diego just smiled.

"That's what you meant when you said it was bloody time for us to get here?"

Now Juliana glared at Diego. He had set an impossible pace, even as he suspected—even wanted—them to be followed.

He shrugged. "I wanted to know how determined you were. It was important. And I thought once the Macleans arrived, they would see the reason of the plan."

She wanted to hit him. Fortunately, his face was already well marked by Patrick. He deserved every bruise.

Rory chuckled. "It can work," he said to Patrick.

"Can is not good enough."

"I *will* protect her," Rory said. "Kingsley's standing with Henry depends on good will in Edinburgh. He will do nothing to jeopardize that.

"I will accompany Rory," Patrick said, and Juliana knew she had won.

"Jamie said you did not make a good impression on the young viscount," Rory objected.

"But I am your brother."

"He could not refuse you if he thinks you come from the queen," Diego agreed. "And I will be there until you arrive."

"No comfort there," Patrick muttered.

But it was obvious he had surrendered.

He looked at Diego. "I will kill you if anything happens to her."

"I expected no less," Diego said cheerfully.

Chapter 32

THE group rode to within a few miles of Hartlepool and separated.

Rory was to ride on to Newcastle and pick up a wedding gift before returning to the inn they had chosen in Hartlepool.

Diego was keeping low in the woods since they were too close to Handdon Castle to stay with them. He was, after all, supposed to return Juliana to her betrothed after a harrowing journey without funds. He would meet them in the morning to make the journey with Juliana to Handdon Castle.

But Patrick had no intention of allowing Juliana to stay with Diego. He would borrow the Spaniard's ruse.

The innkeeper sniffed as they entered and Patrick asked for a room. His eyes went to Juliana's masked face, then darted to the floor.

"My wife has been marked by the pox, but she carries no disease now," Patrick explained.

The innkeeper spit on the floor. "Scot?"

"Aye."

"Me brother died at Flodden last year."

"A lot of men died then."

The innkeeper hesitated, but greed won. He took Patrick's piece of gold in exchange for a private room.

"We would like some food sent up. My wife is . . . does not like going into public places." He tossed another gold coin up in the air and the innkeeper's thick arm shot out and caught it before it dropped to the bar. His scowl disappeared.

"Wine as well," Patrick said. "Not ale."

Once in the room, he paced. He still disliked the plan. Mayhap because, he was ashamed to admit, it came from Diego. It was hard for him to admit he had been wrong about the man. The easy relationship between Diego and Juliana plagued him.

He went to the window and studied the landscape outside. Juliana wearily rested in a chair with her face still covered until the food arrived. They could take no chances that someone might see the scar-free face of a bonny woman.

The inn overlooked a natural harbor and a number of fishing boats were returning. She rose and moved next to him. The sun was setting, and a golden glow spread over the calm water.

"You can always come back with me," he said. "The viscount is a dangerous man. And apparently not a fool since he has won the ear of the Queen Dowager."

"It is worth the risk." She moved closer and lowered the piece of cloth from her face.

He touched a smudge of dirt that only enhanced the smooth, lovely cheeks. "I almost lost you," he whispered.

"No," she said. "You will never lose me. I would have found some way back."

He leaned his forehead against hers and closed his eyes for a moment, remembering the deep fear and emptiness he felt when he read her note.

A knock came at the door then, and she quickly replaced the cloth and turned away from the door. Patrick opened it. A lad entered with a trencher of food and a pitcher of wine. Avoiding Juliana as much as possible, he placed it on the small table. He carried a candle and lit the oil lamp, then kneeled beside the fireplace until flames started to lick at the logs already in place.

Patrick pressed a coin in his hand. "We do not wish to be disturbed again this night. We have traveled far."

The lad nodded and left. Patrick shoved the table against the door that had no lock. He placed the trencher on the table and drew the two chairs up to it, both on the same side. He did not want even a table separating them.

The meal included bread and honey, fish, cheese and a pasty. The wine was poor, but far better than English ale. He watched her eat, enjoying the sight of her tongue licking her lips after a taste of bread and honey. She took a sip of wine, made a face, but then took another.

He took a sip himself. He was only too aware of the bed that dominated the room. When she had finished the fish, he took a piece of the pasty and tempted her mouth open with it, watching with amusement as crumbs sprinkled her lips. He leaned over and tasted them.

His lips danced on hers with a slow sensuality; he licked every vestige of crumbs, then tasted the wine on her lips and tongue as her mouth opened to his probing assault.

Her hands went up to his neck and stopped at the auburn locks that curled boyishly there. He tensed, trying desperately to keep control.

Juliana was not going to allow it. The wine, the warmth of the crackling fire, the rich smell of wood smoke mixed with the taste of each other came together in a wanton call she was not going to deny. Soon, she would belong to another man, but tonight she belonged with Patrick. She felt herself being lifted and she knew his resistance had been breached. Her head rested against his heart as strong, powerful arms held her tightly to him.

He set her on the bed, then hesitated as he stared down at her. Aching to erase the lingering doubts, she took his hand and pulled him down. When their lips touched again, she wondered at how tenderness and hunger could combine so sweetly and passionately.

She felt the ties of her gown being undone with deliciously agonizing deliberateness. His breath was warm and tasted of wine. Then the gown fell away and she felt gloriously free.

His lips found her breasts and nuzzled first one, then the other until her nipples seemed as hard and hot as the stones in the hearth. They tingled and ached. When she thought she could stand no more, his lips moved upward, kissing her throat, her mouth, the lobes of her ears until every nerve in her body was tingling and alive with wanting. She closed her eyes, drinking in all the new feelings, wondering how one body could feel so much pleasure, so much agony at once.

His hands ceased their movement with one last teasing stroke. He moved away from her, and she opened her eyes. He was releasing his own clothes while his eyes stayed on her. He so frequently seemed the observer, keeping his thoughts thoroughly locked inside. Now his gaze roiled with passion.

His clothing dropped to a puddle on the floor. The doublet, then his hose. Finally his linen shirt. He stood there before her, everything about him strong, but without the usual warrior confidence. Although his shoulders and chest were heavily muscled, his waist and stomach were still painfully lean.

She held out her hand, and he sank down on the bed next to her. His hand traced patterns on her skin, rekindling the flames that had roared so wildly before. She answered caress with caress, need with need, and hunger with hunger until they were both mad with wanting, their bodies arching and straining against each other.

He slid atop her, resting his strength on one arm. His maleness teased the sensitive part of her body until she whimpered for him. He entered, and she quivered with the first exquisite feelings.

There was no pain this time, only waves of sensation that grew with each of his carefully controlled movements until she felt part of a tidal surge moving toward some irresistible climax. Time seemed to stop as they reveled in this instinctive dance, first slow, then increasing the tempo together. Then there was one last thrust, and all the sensations she'd felt before were beggared by the new ones as sweet explosions rocked her very being.

Once they regained their breath, he rolled over, bringing her with him, and she rested her head against his heart. His hands moved gently over her body, loving it. The urgency was gone, but a honeyed sweetness remained.

She stayed like that until the room darkened and she closed her eyes, content for now in his arms.

PATRICK and Juliana rose before daybreak and left the inn. She did not bother with her hair. Looking the part would be an important aspect of Juliana's story. He saddled one horse and helped her up, then swung into the saddle behind her. She still wore the cloth around her face. She was wearing the same gown and worn cloak she had yesterday. Her hair was still in the long braid.

Yet she looked enchanting to Patrick.

He started down the empty street, his arms around her. Once out of the town he hurried the pace.

An hour later, they found Diego. He was sitting by a stream, washing his wrists. The ground around him was bloody.

Patrick dismounted, then helped Juliana down. He looked askance at Diego's wounds.

"I still have scars from the irons," Diego said. "So I needed a reason to bind my arms. 'I injured them trying to carry Senorita Mendoza over stones and rocks.' "

"Clever," Patrick muttered. "You become even more a hero."

"More of a reason to stay as well."

"They are too recent."

"I do not expect them to inspect the wound, but they will see dried blood. That should be sufficient."

They went over the story again and again as they rode toward Handdon Castle. The *Sofia* had encountered several storms in the crossing from Spain, which made the voyage late. A fierce storm blew the ship off course. It then lost its main mast and foundered. It started to list and take on water so fast the boats could not be lowered in time to be of use.

Her uncle had tried to rescue her. He pulled her from the cabin and insisted she hold the ship's rail with all her might. She did as she was told while all the sailors worked fiercely to save the ship. In the end, though, there was nothing to be done. Her uncle had been knocked off his feet and swept overboard. Other sailors had jumped ship as the *Sofia* started to sink, hoping to survive.

Juliana jumped, too, and managed to grab several boards, as had Diego, and they stayed together. He was one of the few sailors who could swim and he managed to drag her to shore. They did not see any other survivors.

Rory knew the coast and had chosen the perfect place for it to have happened. The water was deep enough that a wreck would not be evident, yet close enough to shore that it would be possible, though not likely, for someone to reach the cliffs. It was also along a barren area.

Patrick was reluctant to leave Juliana with Diego. He was even more reluctant to leave them at Handdon Castle. The only comforting fact was that the old earl was in residence, and he seemed to be respected.

He walked with them some distance, then faced Diego. "Take care of her."

"I will."

"Rory and I should arrive in two days. You can find one of us at the inn if you need us."

Diego nodded and handed him a pouch of gold coins from the saddlebags he had with him. "Take care of these for me. It would not do for a poor shipwrecked sailor to be carrying gold coins. Take the saddlebags as well."

"Aye." Patrick hesitated, then stuck out his hand. "I doubted you. For that I offer my apologies."

Diego took the hand and shrugged. "I doubt myself frequently."

Patrick turned to Juliana. He leaned down and kissed her hard. "When this is over, I hope you will be my wife."

She looked startled, then her face turned radiant.

Before he said anything more he would regret, he mounted again and turned his horse back toward Hartlepool. He did not look back again. He knew he would be tempted to lift her back on the horse and carry her away.

But he was slowly learning what his brothers already had learned about their wives. If you loved, you had to trust.

THE sun was beginning to fall when Juliana and Diego were offered a ride to the castle from a farmer taking produce there. Juliana's legs ached. She was hungry, thirsty and tired.

Once at the gates, guards questioned them as to their business. Their faces openly doubted the story they heard and they were about to tell them to leave when one hesitated. "'Tis strange enough to be true," he told the others. "I was told to expect a ship carrying the viscount's new bride."

"Is the viscount in residence?" Juliana asked.

"Nay, miss, though he is expected." He peered through the dust and grime at her, then made a decision. "Come wi' me," he said.

She limped to the door of the castle, Diego strolling alongside as if he had not walked several leagues. They were placed in a room opposite the great hall.

Minutes later she was ushered up circular stone stairs to

a richly furnished chamber. And old man sat in a chair overlooking the bay.

"The Earl of Chadwick," a tall, thin man announced. He then stopped, not knowing exactly how to introduce the two newcomers.

Juliana went over to the older man and curtsied to him, then knelt beside him. A blanket sat over his lap and his face was pale, his eyes watery. His beard did not look well kempt and his lips were turned down in a frown.

"I am Juliana Mendoza," she said. "I . . . our ship sank down the coast. My uncle and most of the hands died. I have been trying to make my way here for the past fortnight. No one . . . believed us or would offer assistance."

Blue eyes studied her coldly. "An unlikely tale. Do you have proof of what you've just said?"

"No. The storm came at night. I had put my jewelry in a box. I did not think about grabbing it when the mast came down and the ship started to roll." She hesitated, then plunged on. "My father is Luis Mendoza. My mother is Marianne Hartford. I believe she is a cousin of yours. She told me about coming here and playing with Garrett and Harry."

His gaze suddenly sharpened and he leaned forward. "Your mother? What does she look like?"

"Her hair is lighter than mine, her eyes strikingly blue. I always wanted mine to be that color."

"And the ship?"

"The *Sofia*."

"Who else, girl? Who else survived?"

"A sailor, Diego. I do not know of anyone else. He dragged me out of the water with some injury to himself and brought me here. I said I would try to see he was rewarded."

His eyes studied her for a moment, then he gestured to the servant who had brought her in. "Gibbs, there is a miniature portrait on my table. Bring it to me."

Gibbs quickly found it, and the earl studied it, then looked at her. "Jesu, you are Juliana." His gaze went over the torn and faded gown.

"My dress was ruined," she said. "Diego had a few coins in his pocket and bought this from a fisherman's wife.

"The dowry?"

"Gone with the ship. But my father certainly will reimburse you."

The earl frowned, then put a hand on her head. "Gibbs, you and Margaret must find some clothes and prepare a bath and food for this child." He turned back to her. "My son should be arriving any time now. He will be delighted at your deliverance."

Juliana wasn't sure of that, but at least she'd passed the first step.

"And bring that Spanish sailor to me. I would have words with him."

Gibbs left, leaving her alone with the earl. He gazed forlornly out his window toward the sea. She took the opportunity to look around his chamber. The bed was huge, and it dominated the room. His chair was pulled in front of the window and there was an elaborately carved table and chairs near the large stone fireplace. One large portrait dominated the wall across from his bed. It was of a beautiful woman with dark hair and solemn expression. She sat on a divan with two boys of twelve to fourteen years. One had a lean hawklike look with his mother's coloring. The other had brown hair, merry eyes and a broad smile. She felt a stir of recognition.

"Who is in the painting?" she asked.

"My sons. They were the only ones of six who survived. The dark one is Harry. The other is . . . was . . . Garrett, my oldest son. He died two years ago." His eyes clouded.

"Do you have any other portraits of them?"

"There is one of Garrett at twenty. It is in the hall. I fear I have delayed commissioning one with Harry." He bowed his head and she saw grief in the lines of his face.

"Thank you for welcoming me."

"I could do no less for Marianne's daughter," he said. "Gibbs will take you to your chamber. Margaret, my housekeeper, will take care of you. We will talk more later."

"Thank you," she said softly.

"It will be good to have a woman back in the castle," he said. "And children soon, I pray."

She followed Gibbs out, hoping that Diego was also receiving a fine welcome. She looked at the paintings in the hall and halted at one.

Stunned, she could not move for a second. Or three.

Gibbs had gone ahead of her. "Gibbs," she said. "Is this one of the earl's sons?"

"Aye, that is Garrett."

A chill raced up her spine as she stood looking at a portrait of Denny!

Chapter 33

AFTER taking a wonderfully scented bath, Juliana dressed for the evening meal. One maid washed her hair while others rushed in with gowns for her approval.

Had the situation not been so dire, she would have relished every moment. But as it was, she only wanted to see this finished. As Patrick had noted, she was not a practiced liar. She hated deception, and now everything was a lie.

She had not seen Diego since they arrived. She understood that he had been welcomed, given clothes and a bed with the earl's soldiers.

The earl was sitting in his place at the head of a long table filled with soldiers and their ladies when she arrived. He held out his hand for her to sit beside him. His eyes were warm, and his smile welcoming.

"You look lovely, my dear," he said in a tone that led her to believe he did not really think that had been a possibility.

"Is there any word from Viscount Kingsley?" she asked.

Please sweet mother in heaven let him dally several more days.

"Nay, but he should be here soon. I summoned him nearly a fortnight ago. I understand he had urgent business with the Queen Dowager."

She wanted to tell him that his son had said he was leaving days ago, the same time Patrick had left. He was not hurrying to her side.

Diego entered the great hall and sat at the end of the table. He was dressed now in new English clothes. Breeches, woolen shirt and doublet. He wore the same cocky grin.

She ate several bites, then asked innocently, "I know little of my husband to be."

The earl stiffened, then said, "King Henry thinks well of him. He has been successful in business."

A damning description with its omissions.

"And his brother? Garrett? My mother talked of him often. What happened?"

"He and Harry went to Castile for an audience with the king. We wanted to obtain rights to ports in Spain. I had written to the Mendoza family and they had suggested a marriage as well as a partnership. They could use our ports, and we theirs, but we needed approval from King Ferdinand.

"After the audience, they journeyed to La Coruna. Ferdinand had signaled his favor. Garrett was going to offer for marriage. On the way, they were attacked by bandits. Moors. Harry and his man were wounded but managed to escape. Garrett was killed, his body burned."

He paused, then added, "My wife died shortly after. I believe it was from grief. Garrett was everything you would want in a son. Honorable. Brave. Just."

"But you have Harry."

He nodded. "He has tried hard to live up to his brother. Now tell me about your mother. She had so much spirit and laughter."

She hurt inside even as she saw something in the earl's face. A sadness.

She could not tell the truth. Not yet.

"She is well," she said, refraining from saying her mother had been drained of that spirit and laughter.

And now all she wanted to do was see Diego and tell him about Garrett. The dead son. He probably had not seen the portrait.

She excused herself then. "I am very tired," she said. She reached out and placed her hand on his. "Thank you for making me welcome." She hesitated. "I have one request."

"It will be granted," he said.

"Diego. The sailor who saved me. He would like to return to Spain and he needs a mount to reach London and money for the voyage. Like me, he lost everything in the storm. I will see that you are repaid."

The wrinkled face creased into a smile. "An easy request. Tell him to come to my chamber later."

She left then, stopping first at the end of the table. "Sir," she said to Diego. "I would have a word with you."

Diego stepped away from the table and followed her out into the courtyard. She had no cloak with her, and she shivered.

"What is it?" he asked.

"There is a portrait of his dead son inside," she said. "It is Denny. I would swear to it, though he was much younger then."

For one of the few times since she had known him, he looked surprised.

"According to the earl, his name is Garrett. He was killed in Spain by bandits. Kingsley just barely escaped."

A smile spread over his face. "We shall bring him back to life. I always fancied being a deity."

"It should be before the viscount returns. I asked the earl to provide you with a mount."

"I will ride like the wind."

"The earl also wishes to reward you. He is expecting you in his chamber after the meal. You can see the portrait of his wife and two sons there. There is another portrait in the hall to the left."

"I am impressed, senorita."

"I will be impressed only when he arrives here," she said. "As soon as possible."

DIEGO rode as fast as he could without killing the mount the earl had given him as a reward. He went directly to the inn in Hartlepool.

Rory had arrived earlier with an elaborate silver bowl, and he sat in Patrick's room at the inn, drinking a cup of wine.

"I hope the bowl was not too costly," Diego said. "I do not think it will be used."

Patrick speared him with a look. "No more riddles, Diego. How is Juliana? Has Kingsley arrived yet?"

"Juliana is fine. Kingsley has not arrived. Yet." He paused. "You have not heard from Jamie or Denny yet?"

"Nay, but they should be here soon. They had a more difficult route."

Amusement played in Diego's eyes, and Patrick had to restrain himself. He wanted to know about Juliana's reception. Exactly what had happened.

"The Earl of Chadwick was enchanted with Juliana, as we all are," Diego said. "He told her all about his oldest son. The one that died. He showed her his portrait."

Patrick could barely restrain his impatience.

"He died in Spain," Diego continued. "He and his loving brother were attacked by bandits. Lucky Harry and his servant escaped."

Patrick was beginning to understand. "They killed Garrett?"

"Apparently they tried."

Diego was probably the most maddening person Patrick had ever met, but he was actually beginning to grasp what Diego was saying. "He is alive?"

Patrick shot a glance toward Rory, who was absolutely still.

"Juliana recognized the portrait," Patrick said.

"Si."

"She does not know that many people."

"No."

"Denny!" Patrick continued. It was a statement, no longer a question.

Patrick exchanged glances with Rory. "We mentioned Kingsley many times in front of Denny. He showed no reaction, though Juliana said he seemed to recognize something on the map."

"Maybe he does not wish to remember," Rory broke in. "When Lachlan lost his memory, he wanted to remember and even then it took months for it to come back."

"If his brother tried to kill him, then sentenced him to that hell . . ." Patrick said softly.

"We have to find him and get him to his father before Kingsley appears," Rory said.

Patrick shook his head. "Mayhap the earl will not want him now."

"I think he would," Diego said slowly. "Juliana said he talks about Garrett in a different way than he does Harry."

Rory grabbed his saddlebags. "I'm going to take the road to Carlisle. Mayhap we can find him."

Patrick wanted to do the same. God's blood but he should have brought Denny with them. But he'd watched Denny with Jamie and knew he'd come to trust the Campbell. He thought it best that Denny learn to trust others, and he did not want any of them riding alone. There were too many reivers and bandits along the border. If nothing else, Denny could fight.

"Take one of the hobblers," Patrick said. "They will last longer."

Rory nodded.

After he left, Patrick stared at Diego. "Can you go back?"

He nodded. "Aye. I seem to have the worst of luck. My ship sinks. My horse goes lame."

Patrick smiled. "You wear hard on people and animals."

"A talent."

* * *

PATRICK hated being left behind. He hated staying in the room at the inn, but he had built a very carefully crafted story. He told everyone his wife was still in the room but did not want to see anyone. No servant was allowed inside. After that first night, food was left outside the door.

There were no objections. The word pox incurred such fear and dread that no one wanted to be even near someone afflicted. But it also meant he could not leave.

He thought he would go mad worrying about Juliana. What if Kingsley arrived first? If he thought he was in danger, he would not spare anyone in his way. He had proved that in Spain.

It was early the next day when Denny, Jamie and Rory arrived. On seeing Patrick, Denny broke into the first smile the Maclean had ever seen on his face. Patrick glanced at them, and Rory shook his head. So they had not told him.

"Sit down, Denny," he said, indicating one of the two chairs. He sat down across from him.

"Does the word Kingsley mean anything to you?"

Denny concentrated but shook his head.

"You seemed to recognize something on the map. Do you know what?"

Again he shook his head.

"Chadwick? Handdon Castle? Garrett?"

A flash of recognition went through his face at the last.

"Spain?" he tried next.

Alarm flickered in Denny's eyes.

"You were riding with your brother, Harry," Patrick continued. "You were attacked."

A muscle fluttered in Denny's throat and he stood. Paced.

"Denny," Patrick said softly. "We think you are Garrett, the son of the Earl of Chadwick and the rightful Viscount Kingsley."

Denny stilled, his body radiating tension.

"He needs you, Denny. Your father needs you."

"My . . . father?" The two words sounded rusty.

Patrick and Rory looked at each other with startled surprise. "Aye," Patrick said softly. "The earl. Juliana has seen him. He is ill."

Patrick was not sure how much Denny understood. So many skills were natural to him. But memories of people, places?

"We need your help," Patrick said, then explained. "We want you to return to Handdon Castle with us. We want you where many people can see you, and your existence cannot be denied."

Denny was silent for a moment, then nodded.

"We will leave in the morning," Patrick said. "The four of us. Diego will go ahead tonight." He looked at Denny. "You are always welcome at Inverleith. If you are uncomfortable at Handdon Castle, or we are wrong, we will return home together."

JULIANA was in the courtyard watching a jousting match when four men rode up. Her heart fluttered as she saw the man in the lead.

The gates were open. Diego was somewhere, probably playing dice. He had returned yesterday, leading a limping horse. Apparently a rock was lodged under the mount's hoof. She'd wanted to run over and hug him. He was becoming dear to her but in an entirely different way from Patrick.

But now she watched as the newcomers approached. It was the fourth man, though, that captured every eye. She saw everyone in the courtyard come to a stop, one by one, and stand still, amazement and awe spreading over their faces.

Then someone's feet started working again, and the owner of the feet hurried inside.

The four men dismounted all in unison, and she thought she had never seen such a wonderful sight. Patrick. Rory. Jamie. Denny. The latter was gazing up at the castle, then around at the walls. She only wished Lachlan was here, but he was in London or on his way back.

Then the Earl of Chadwick emerged from the door, a cane in his hand. His eyes immediately went to the four men standing next to their horses. A look of such shock and joy crossed his face that she could barely hold back tears.

He limped over to Denny. "Garrett," he whispered. "Garrett."

He held out his hand. Denny hesitated, then took it, and the earl's arms clasped him.

She looked at Patrick and saw the smile playing around his lips. Had she seen him smile before? Certainly not like this. Her heart thumped so hard she thought everyone in the courtyard would hear.

Then the earl stood back. "What happened? Your brother said you were dead."

Denny's hand shook slightly.

"I think we should talk privately," Patrick said.

How easily he takes leadership, Juliana thought. He was the Maclean. It took nothing away from the other brothers, she knew. Each one had worked to see this happen.

They went inside, the earl staying at Denny's side, apparently unaffected by Denny's lack of speech. Once in his chamber, Denny stood in front of the painting. Tears fell silently from his eyes. "She . . . is dead?"

His father nodded. "I have to know what happened," he said after a moment.

"Thomas Charlton said you were a man of your word," Rory said.

The earl met his stare. Nodded.

"We brought him home to you. But we jeopardized others by doing so."

"I swear no harm will come to you."

"We think your son Harry tried to kill him," Patrick said. "But he lived. The wound robbed him of memory. I think he did not want to remember the betrayal."

The earl's eyes filled with pain. His hand went to Denny's arm. "I should have known. Mayhap I did know but could not admit it. I could not understand how you died and he did not. I know you would not have returned alive and left him dead."

He paused, then asked, "But where have you been all these months?"

Denny did not answer. The earl turned his gaze to Patrick.

Juliana watched Patrick make a decision. He did not trust easily. "He was a slave. On one of Mendoza's galley ships," he finally said.

The earl closed his eyes, then opened them. "Come with me," he told Patrick. They went outside and he called one of his servants. "I want two men to bring John Davie to me." He turned back to Patrick. "John was Garrett's servant. Now he is a captain in the guard. 'Twas Harry's request."

When the servant left, the earl turned to him with tears in his eyes. "Will he get better?"

"He already has. When he came aboard, I did not believe he understood anything. Now he understands everything, I think. He just chooses not to remember. When he saw that painting he remembered something."

"Thank you," the earl said.

Patrick hesitated. "What about Harry?"

"I want proof. I want to hear him myself. Then I will do what is necessary." He pierced Patrick with a stare. "Why did you do this?"

"He is my friend," Patrick said, "and I love Juliana Mendoza. I would not have her wed a murderer." He shocked himself with the words. It was the first time he had said it.

"I would have liked her for Garrett," the earl said. "I do not even know your name."

"Patrick Maclean. The others are Rory Maclean and Jamie Campbell."

"I have heard of you. There are legends about the

Macleans and the Charltons," he said. "I could not believe them. I do now. I am grateful for what you have done for my son." He paused. "Would you be there when I question John Davie?"

VISCOUNT Kingsley rode in two days later.

While they waited for him to appear, Patrick played court to Juliana. He realized he had never actually done that. He had no doubt that the earl would still be very pleased to have her as Garrett's bride, even without the Mendoza dowry.

Under some not-too-gentle persuasion, John Davie had confessed that Kingsley had conspired with Luis Mendoza to kill Garrett. Garrett, he said, had heard things he did not like about the Mendozas. He was going to oppose any business agreement between the two. He would not condone slavery.

Garrett had not been that easy to kill. He had been attacked near the Mendoza home in Coruna. Beaten. Stabbed. Then someone came and the paid assassins ran away. Later, Harry heard he had been cared for by a merchant and when he seemed to have lost his wits, Mendoza claimed him and sent him to the galleys. He had thought it a fine joke on someone who had humiliated him. A few months, and he would be dead.

Juliana had listened with horror. She'd never had illusions about her father, but murder . . .

"I will destroy him," the Earl of Chadwick said.

"Not my mother."

"No, never your mother. I will send for her. She has a home here."

"And at Inverleith," Patrick said, his arm around Juliana. She looked up at him with eyes that nearly unmanned him. She was so incredibly beautiful.

Harry returned that afternoon. He was immediately seized by two soldiers and taken to his father's chamber.

When he saw Patrick he started to protest, then his gaze went to the shadows where Garrett stood. His eyes widened. His mouth opened, but no sound came.

"Cain," his father said. "Your name is Cain. And like Cain I am casting you out. You will leave today with only what you have on your back. No horse. No funds."

"You cannot believe . . ."

"John Davie told us everything."

Hate filled Kingsley's face as he turned on his father. "You always preferred him. I did not exist for you. No matter what I did. It was always Garrett."

He grabbed a dagger and ran toward Garrett. Patrick stepped between them and the dagger caught his side. Still, his other hand grabbed the weapon and turned it back, stabbing the blade into Kingsley's heart before he lost consciousness.

PATRICK took Juliana to the cliffs that overlooked the sea and watched their last sunset on English soil.

He put his arms around her, thinking how much his life had changed in the past few months. How lucky he was. From ugliness had come such beauty. From hopelessness peace.

Because of Juliana.

He leaned down and touched her forehead with his lips. Because of his wound, they had not made love again, but he intended to fix that shortly.

And now they could go home. His wound was healing and they would leave the next day.

She had not left his side since the fight. His brothers had taken turns coming in as well. So had Diego and Jamie. Even Lachlan arrived, grumpy because he had not been involved in any of the action. He had discovered in London, though, that young Kingsley had been involved in several unsavory activities, including smuggling. He had been elated until he arrived and discovered all that had already happened.

Now he, too, was waiting for Patrick to improve enough to leave Handdon Castle. The Maclean brothers would ride home together. Jamie and Diego planned to travel with them to make sure, they said, they did not get into more trouble. "Wolves guarding the sheep," Patrick muttered to Juliana.

"I would not call Macleans sheep," she'd replied tartly.

But that was two days ago. And now they would leave on the morn.

He thought of Denny. His friend was getting better every day. Once he saw his brother, he'd remembered the attack and memories started flooding back. Not all. Maybe some would never come back, but he was speaking now. Slowly. Haltingly. It was clear now that he knew where he belonged. And the earl looked years younger. He would, Patrick knew, be patient.

Neither of them knew how long Diego would stay. He liked to say he was a wanderer, but they both had made it clear he was always welcome at Inverleith. . . .

The sea was churning, but the clear skies promised a fine day tomorrow.

"It is time to go home," he said. "To Inverleith."

She was silent and he realized that he had just assumed . . .

Fool him, but he had been that since he met her.

He turned her to him and put his arms around her. "Will you make it your home, too, yours and your mother's?" He paused and then said the words that he realized had been in his heart nearly from the first day he'd encountered her in the cabin of the *Sofia*. Words that had been so difficult to say.

He touched her cheek, and his lips brushed hers lightly. Then he said, "I love you, Juliana Mendoza. Will you wed me as soon as we return?"

"Aye," she said with a shy smile, and it made his heart

ache. She was never shy. She was strong and bold and gallant and he loved her with his life.

She reached up on tiptoes. "My lord warrior," she said, and then her lips met his. And not lightly. There was passion and love and an aching sweetness.

His heart swelled with a joy he'd never thought to have.

"No more, love," he said softly. "My warrior days are over."

He heard a deep chuckle and looked around.

Rory stood there. Behind him was Lachlan, a broad smile on his face.

"Go away," he ordered.

"Aye," Rory said, turning. But then he chuckled. "I think the Macleans have finally put the curse to rest."

PATRICK knew Diego was leaving. He had sensed it the night before as they had dined.

Diego had been unusually silent, thoughtful. It was most worrisome to Patrick that he was beginning to understand the way the Spaniard thought.

The Spaniard had stayed two months after their return to Inverleith. Juliana had begged Diego to stay for the wedding and he'd agreed. Patrick and Juliana had now been wed two days—two wonderful, glorious days in which the sun was brighter, the sky bluer and the stars brighter.

They had waited—impatiently—for Juliana's mother, who arrived, with Juliana's mare, Joya, a week ago. The Earl of Chadwick had brought her after presenting evidence to King Ferdinand about the attempted murder of his son and preferring charges against Mendoza.

The earl had insisted on going himself, finally convincing Patrick that he would be placing himself at peril again if he went. It was the earl who had the legal right—and position—to press charges against Mendoza and protect Juliana's mother. An English lord had been abducted, as had Scots. King Henry was demanding reparations from Spain. Where a lone Scot might have been hung for pirating a ship, an English lord was heralded for the act. Denny—nay, Garrett—was a hero. His memory was slowly returning, though physicians said there were probably events he would never remember.

Luis Mendoza was now himself in a Spanish prison and even being a relative of Ferdinand would not save him now.

The door to the stables opened, and the Spaniard slipped in. He started when he saw Patrick leaning against a post, his hands holding the reins of two horses.

"I thought I would ride with you," Patrick said.

Diego did not question as to how he knew he would be leaving. He just looked at the horse. "That is not mine."

"You did not have one," Patrick pointed out.

"I was going to steal a lesser one. That is one of your favorites."

"Aye, and he is yours."

"Why?"

Patrick shrugged. "Momentary madness." He swung up onto the saddle.

Diego did the same. "When it comes to good horseflesh, I do not argue." They left the stable just as the gates opened.

"I do not understand how you could leave the lovely Juliana," Diego said once they were outside the gate.

"I will be back soon enough."

Diego darted a quick look at him. "I am touched by your gift and your company," he said lightly and with that wry humor.

"Then why leave without saying farewell?"

"I never say farewell."

"Where are you going?"

"London, I think. To increase my newly obtained fortune."

"You can stay with us." The offer was out of his mouth

before he could stop it. Diego, if nothing else, was an unsettling presence. He had kept himself busy training with Macleans, but there was always that sense of watching.

Still, he owed Diego much.

"This is your home. Not mine," Diego said. "But I will remember the invitation." He urged the stallion into a trot. They rode without more words to the bluff above the natural harbor. Patrick drew up his horse then and Diego followed.

"I leave you here," Patrick said, thrusting out his hand. "My thanks."

Diego took it. Nodded.

"If you ever need anything, remember us. Any one of us will come to your assistance."

Diego looked startled for the first time since Patrick met him.

"I still do not understand why you risked your life in England," Patrick said.

"It amused me." But then any humor left Diego's eyes. "I have never had a friend before. Or a home. I never thought I wanted one. They never seemed real, much less true." He hesitated, then said, "You and your family showed me they can be true. It was instructive. I owed you for that."

Patrick had not really considered Diego a friend, and he was shamed by it now. But then he was new to this brotherly and husbandly business as well. Maybe he had learned something about friendship as well. "At least tell me your name."

"Diego will do," the Spaniard said as he had said months earlier. He said it this time with a grin. Then he turned his horse around back toward the road. He glanced back at Patrick. "You will be seeing me again, Patrick Maclean, you and your Juliana. I think it is destiny."

Then he put his heels to his mount and rode away.

In 1988, **Patricia Potter** won the Maggie Award and a Reviewers' Choice Award from *Romantic Times* for her first novel. She has been named Storyteller of the Year by *Romantic Times* and has received the magazine's Career Achievement Award for Western Historical Romance along with numerous Reviewers' Choice nominations and awards.

She has won three Maggie Awards, is a five-time RITA finalist, and has been on the *USA Today* bestseller list. Her books have been alternate choices for the Doubleday Book Club.

Prior to writing fiction, she was a newspaper reporter with the *Atlanta Journal* and president of a public relations firm in Atlanta. She has served as president of Georgia Romance Writers and board member of River City Romance Writers, and is past president of Romance Writers of America.

Enter the rich world of
historical romance
with Berkley Books.
Lynn Kurland
Patricia Potter
Betina Krahn
Jodi Thomas
Anne Gracie
Love is timeless.
penguin.com